Also by Laura Thalassa

THE
CURSE
THAT BINDS

LAURA THALASSA

Bloom books

Published by Bloom Books, an imprint of Sourcebooks
P.O. Box 4410, Naperville, Illinois 60567-4410
(630) 961-3900
sourcebooks.com

Cataloging-in-Publication data is on file with the Library of Congress.

The authorized representative in the EEA is Dorling Kindersley
Verlag GmbH. Arnulfstr. 124, 80636 Munich, Germany

Manufactured in the UK by Clays and distributed by
Dorling Kindersley Limited, London
002-351214-Jul/25
10 9 8 7 6 5 4 3 2

For Katie, who loves history even more than I do:
Ubi amici ibi opes.

Content Warning

The Curse that Binds contains some themes of depictions that might be sensitive to certain readers. Please check my website for a full list of content warnings.

Part I

CHAPTER 1
Roxilana, 7 years old

43 AD, Cantium, Britannia

The screams wake me.

For a moment, I am sure I dreamed them. These sorts of screams belong to nightmares and nightmares alone. But the agonized sounds continue, and I become confused, unsure of whether I even am awake.

Fear gnaws at my bones as I lie in my bed and listen to them. The sounds are high-pitched, terrified, *pained*. The longer I draw in short, shallow breaths, the surer I become that this is real.

On either side of me, my older sister and younger brother sleep soundly, blithely unaware of whatever is happening outside the walls of our house.

Across the room, one of my parents stirs, then sits up. I stare at them in the darkness, too afraid to call out or run to them but yearning to be close.

The screams get louder and more numerous, and

they're now accompanied by the roar and crackle of fire.

"Wake up, get up," my mother says. She must be the one awake. I can just make out her form leaning over my father. "Something's happening."

Outside, I hear the pound of footfalls and the heavy rustle of metal as people rush past our house. With every passing moment, the sounds grow louder, closer. There are shrieks and shouts and terrible, wet noises that scare me most of all. My siblings are stirring but then…then…

I hear the crackle and hiss of fire so much closer—first near our door and then, with a *whoosh*, upon our thatched roof.

A shout, then a scream—I think the sounds belong to my parents, but it's too dark. I cannot see, cannot tell. I'm shaking, and my teeth are chattering. Something is very, very wrong; that much I understand.

One of my parents rushes to my bedside and begins to shake me and my siblings. My mother, I realize. I can just make out the gleaming whites of her eyes.

"Wake up, wake up!" she whispers, her voice frantic, hoarse. Behind her, smoke is billowing, backlit by the unholy, orange glow of the growing flames. The bundles of herbs that hang from our rafters catch fire, and I can smell their clashing fragrances in the thickening smoke.

My brother and sister finally wake, and they begin to shout in confusion and fear, and someone's crying. Is it me? There's a lot of smoke. It stings my eyes. Maybe I *am* crying.

My mother tugs at me and my siblings, shouting commands at us, but fear has dulled my senses. My older sister gets up first, crossing the room toward our front door—or where it should be. But the smoke is so thick, her form seems to disappear right into it.

"Up, now!" my mother commands, giving my arm a swift yank.

I stumble forward just as part of our thatched roof collapses. I scream, backing away from it. I can't see my mother and brother, though I can hear them, and I still can't see the door. I turn in a circle, and now I know I am crying. Where is my family? Where should I go?

Somewhere in the distance, my father shouts, but it cuts off sharply. Where is he? Is he calling to me?

On instinct, I move toward the noise, trying to wave away the smoke clogging my lungs and burning my eyes. My heart feels like it's trying to escape my chest. I can hear the pounding of it, even over the roar of the flames.

Ba-bum-ba-bum-ba-bum.

More of the roof collapses, the burning thatch falling somewhere behind me. I scream, but it's quickly eclipsed by my mother's and brother's screams.

I turn back for an instant, and all I see is fire—hungry, hazy fire.

"Mother!" My hoarse cry ends in a hacking cough. How will she find her way out?

Babumbabumbabum.

More screams. *Their* screams. Are they stuck? Hurt?

Pieces of burning thatch fall on my shoulders, and in my panic, I flee in the opposite direction.

The door materializes through the smoke, and I rush through it. I've barely crossed the threshold and tasted the crisp air when I trip over something large.

I go sprawling, falling into warm, sticky mud. The

screams are louder out here, though they no longer belong to my family. Around me, people run through the streets while strangely dressed men dash around, swinging swords and slicing people down with them. Everything else is obscured by fire and smoke. Ash swirls in the darkness, and I'm sure this is the end of the world.

"*Mother! Father!*" My throat burns as I shout.

I'm about to scramble to my feet when my attention drops to the lump I tripped on. My gaze crawls up a bloody body and lands on my father's slack face, the flames dancing in his lifeless eyes.

I scream again, the sound mingling with all the other cries out here. I scream and scream and scream until I vomit, and then I scream some more.

Our house collapses fully then, the walls and the last of the roof caving in. I continue to scream, the sounds only interrupted by my frantic shouts for my mother and brother to escape and for my father to wake up.

It feels like something cracks wide-open inside of me, unleashing more than my terror and pain. I reach a hand to my chest, where a throbbing pain has started up, sure I've been struck, but I don't feel a wound there.

Someone grabs me with a roughened hand then, someone who wears leathers and armor that slaps and clangs as they move. There's a sword in their grip, and as they drag me off the ground and force me forward, they cut down a neighbor running by.

I'd scream again, but my throat hurts and there's that sharp ache in my chest. My father is dead. My mother and brother… I—I think I know their fates…but no, they cannot be gone too.

As for my sister, I do not know whether she's alive or

dead, only that she's not among the ashen-faced villagers these armor-clad men have taken captive alongside me.

Eventually the screams and the flames subside. The silence that sweeps in is somehow worse than the noise.

And when the sun rises, all that's left of my town are its smoking bones and a graveyard of unburied dead.

CHAPTER 2
Roxilana, 12 years old

48 AD, Rome, Roman Empire

I stare out the doorway of the apartment I live in, watching the early-morning goings-on of the lively courtyard of our insula.

Beneath me, many of the other occupants of this complex are already up, washing laundry or chatting as they get ready for the day. A few kids play knucklebones and street sellers set up baskets filled with produce and bread. A young mother soothes her crying toddler, holding the child close in her arms. At that brief show of love, a terrible yearning seizes me, and I have to tear my eyes away.

It's taken years for me to acclimate to this city—its language, its people, its customs, its sweltering stink. And as my gaze lands on two Roman soldiers passing through the complex's courtyard, I'm sure I *still* haven't fully acclimated. Not when my breath hitches at the sight of them and my skin grows clammy.

The childlike terror is an old, familiar sensation, but the rage that festers like a boil beneath my skin—that is new. These Roman soldiers might not be the same evil men who killed my family and burned down my home, but they could have easily destroyed someone's life, killed someone's family.

"Girl!"

I tense at the shrill sound of my adoptive mother's voice coming from inside our apartment.

"*Girl!*" Livia calls again. The irritation in her voice is unmistakable.

I wander back inside, bracing myself.

Livia stands by our kitchen table, which is littered with folded bits of cloth, some wound yarn, and a few stray loom weights.

She has a bit of gossamer-thin gauze fisted in her hand, her dark eyes flinty. "Why is the gold detailing on this veil not finished?"

My heart hammers as my gaze drops to the translucent yellow fabric in her hand.

Livia runs a thriving business tailoring clothes for the elite, and as her dependent, she expects me to assist her in all ways, including tailoring garments myself. But my hands are clumsy, and I work too slowly to make up for it. She knows this, but she also knows there are too many items and not enough time anyway.

However, mentioning all of this will only stoke her anger, especially when she caught me daydreaming, so I swallow my explanation before I can voice it.

This time, my silence angers her all the same.

"You useless, *worthless* thing," she spits out, shaking the veil in her hand and crinkling the delicate material, one of her deep brown curls loosening from her updo. "I saved you all those years ago, sheltered you, fed you—" Her chest is rising and falling faster and faster, and I'm trying not to cower or back up, which has only ever spurred her on. She takes a threatening step forward, and now my pulse races. "All for you to be a lazy, sullen girl. Now, answer me: Why isn't this finished?"

"I was about to—"

She closes the distance between us in two quick strides, then hits me, *hard*. The sudden force of it sends me careening into the wall, bits of plaster and pale-green paint flaking off from the impact.

"*Don't lie to me!*" The pitch of her voice has me cowering. It's the wrong reaction. It always is.

Livia hits me again, this time on my upper arm. I bite my lower lip to keep from crying out.

"I saw you standing there, daydreaming like you had all the time in the world."

Another hit, this one to the head.

I fold into myself, trying to become as small as possible. Tears well in my eyes, and more than the pain and terror, I hate *this* reaction.

"I'm sorry. I'm sorry," I plead over and over again. Anything to make it stop.

She kicks me once, twice, in the abdomen.

I choke on my breath, and it takes me a couple inhalations to regain my voice. "Please," I say hoarsely, "*Mother*—"

I don't mean to call out for my mother, to that warm, half-forgotten presence that hummed songs to lull me to sleep and brewed strange things in the pot that used to hang over our hearth. The woman who once must've held me as that mother in the courtyard held her child only moments ago.

Livia pauses, her foot pulled back. I can hear her heavy breaths and sense her acidic rage. I know she's fighting to keep herself from hitting me again. It scares me that she is so full of fury.

Finally, she lowers her foot back to the ground and drops the unfinished veil on top of my huddled form.

"You won't eat next until that's finished," she says, looming over me. "I don't care if it takes you all day and all night, you will get it done." To herself, she mutters, "Why I took you in is beyond me."

Her words are nothing I haven't already heard, but they still land like another blow to the head.

I know Livia once had a husband and daughter and that the two of them died in quick succession. She could've remarried and had more children; lots of Roman women do. Instead, she worked her business alone until she adopted me.

I cannot fathom why she made that fateful decision. Livia is hardly sentimental. Still, sometimes I catch her looking at me with a shine in her eyes, and I wonder if I remind her of the daughter she lost.

Whatever her reasons, every day feels like a held breath.

I rise slowly, my belly hurting where she kicked it. Sometimes even getting back up can anger her all over again.

Livia presses her lips together, her eyes flicking over me as she moves to the table. I can feel her anger and disgust thickening the air.

"Fix your hair," she says sharply, gathering up the yarn and the loom weights, "and put something more modest on. We're meeting with Septima Opimia later this morning, and she holds modesty above all else. She'll pass on our business if she sees you looking like a harlot..."

Livia's voice fades as pressure builds beneath my sternum. Strange, inexplicable pressure.

I place my hand over the source of it, taking in a shallow breath as the sensation crowds out all others, blunting even the throb of my flesh.

What is happening to me?

I've never felt anything like this…or have I?

Wasn't there a moment long ago…?

Flames and smoke and dull, glassy eyes fill my mind, scaring off whatever wisp of a memory I was about to touch.

And still, the pressure is mounting, mounting—

Livia's frown lines deepen, but for an instant, she looks concerned, like she might've taken things too far.

"What is wrong with you?" she demands.

I'm about to answer when, all at once, the pressure releases, like water breaching a dam, and something seals into place, right beneath my breastbone.

With it comes pain. I lock my knees to keep from falling as a sharp, throbbing sensation blooms in my left shoulder.

Est iwapagu sinavakap metum…[1]

I sway a little at the sound of a young, masculine voice speaking in a foreign language. It is like nothing I've heard before. And yet it's so close, almost as though it's coming from inside my own—

Logu suwwas iv'taburwa.[2]

My gaze sweeps over our apartment, taking in the table; Livia's agitated face; the chipped green walls; the long shelf that holds our pitchers, bowls, and cups; the massive loom leaning against a back wall; and, on either side of it, the baskets filled with fabric, yarn, beads, and tailored garments.

---

1 *Must stay on my horse…*
2 *Hurts so fucking bad.*

There are many things in this apartment, but a young man is not among them.

"Girl," Livia says, her voice a little more demanding, her face a little more annoyed, "pull yourself together."

I try to breathe around the strange sensations flowing through me—pain, alarm, determination.

"Just feeling faint…"

Iv'tassa e'waditvak singatasava. Lusavasa guxip ewwatavak metum…[3]

I place a hand to my head at the return of the young male's voice. It's definitely coming from inside me, but that only makes the situation more distressing.

Beneath the words themselves, there's desperation and exhilaration and *pain*—my shoulder continues to throb.

Pain that eclipses my own.

"Here." Livia moves to the shelf and grabs a pitcher and cup from it. She pours me a glass of watered-down wine. "Drink this and get yourself together," she insists, pressing the cup into my hands. Despite her abrasive tone, I think she's genuinely worried about me. At least, until she adds, "I don't want you to embarrass me in front of the senator's wife."

My hand shakes as I take a sip, trying to steady myself.

I'snut ivwagu ruvwavu bovotavak…[4]

The wine sours in my mouth, and I set the cup down on the table shakily. Whatever is happening, I'm not fine, and liquid won't help.

"I'll—I'll go fix my hair," I mumble.

Before Livia can respond, I stumble to my room. The space is small yet sparse, adorned with a stool, a shelf, a

3 *Ignore the pain. Have to keep fighting…*
4 *Running low on arrows…*

13

bed, and a couple of baskets holding my clothes and more garments to sew and mend.

Hastily, I place the veil I still clutch into one of them and then I collapse onto my thin mattress. Half of me expects Livia to follow me in and scold me again for laziness, but instead I hear her move about the living area, then leave our apartment.

I exhale—one less thing to worry about.

My shoulder still aches from that phantom pain, and my stomach churns from wine, and...and...

Si'nap sunwatud wi'va'ta dotzakummu etavaku inpuburpusa.[5]

I press my palms to my eye sockets.

Shut up, I tell the voice.

I know there are people who hear voices—is this what they deal with? This is awful.

Lasa otvas do si'n! Pesa govak pusanutapsa susazakunam wek i'nagatvup, vakosazakunam wek wovubga.[6]

Shut up! I say louder, beginning to panic.

What happens if the voice doesn't go away? What if this is my life now?

Unduwu, sak kikat vuratavaksa wusnubaga. Pesava mi'ratis zakunva'awugavusa sutvunut metum di'nvusagu.[7]

Damn you, get out of my head! I shout.

My mind seems to go very, very still, as though it's holding its breath. The brief silence draws my attention to the pain in my shoulder, my cheek, my stomach. I feel surprised, curious, and *hopeful*—so hopeful, though I cannot figure out why I'm feeling anything beyond simple confusion. And there's another sensation again, like water rushing, surging—

5 *Can't get the angle right with my arm shaking.*
6 *Damn this arm! The faster I kill my enemies, the quicker it can be over.*
7 *Of course the girl chooses now to speak. Right when I needed more distractions.*

You can hear me? This time, when the masculine voice speaks, it's in Latin. Rough-edged, accented Latin but Latin all the same.

My breath catches. Should I respond? It's probably a bad idea. No, it's *definitely* a bad idea.

Yes, I say anyway.

At my answer, I feel a wondrous thrill and breathless joy.

At last! he says, though I don't know if he's speaking to me or not.

What's that supposed to mean? I say, unnerved. I want the voice to go away, not for it to be eager to speak with me.

I will tell you more tonight, the voice says, *but I cannot talk at the moment. I'm trying not to get killed.*

Killed?

It takes a moment for the rest of his words to sink in. Wait, what's this about tonight? The voice is making plans? Oh, no, no, no.

We're not going to speak again, I insist. *Not tonight or any other time.*

We are, the voice says with horrible certainty.

He mentioned just now that he was trying not to get killed. I can't make sense of that. But I do know this: death is a permanent end. Probably even for wretched voices in my head.

Then I hope you die, so I never have to hear you again. It's a vile thing to confess, even to an abstract voice.

I don't regret it.

There's another pause, and I feel that rush of joy bleed away.

Just because you said that, I'm going to make sure *I live,* he says.

The voice retreats.

I wait a few moments, but I think he's gone.

I was wrong. The voice is not gone.

Whatever this entity is, he clearly survived the ordeal he was in the middle of because I hear him talk incessantly throughout the day, through the fitting appointment Livia scheduled with stern-faced Septima—who eyes my outfit and hair with begrudging approval and my swollen cheek with obvious disapproval—and as we meet with the family of a Praetorian Guard to fit them with lighter, brighter fabrics for spring and summer.

His voice is there while Livia lectures me on our way home, and it's there while Livia reads the notes on her wax tablet and I prepare dinner for her, my own stomach cramping from hunger. The voice has reverted into that other language. It's coarse and guttural and drags goose bumps from my skin.

And it won't shut up.

For the love of the gods, will you please stop talking? I beg after I nearly drop the pitcher of wine I'm pouring from.

I'm in a foul mood. My head throbs from the stress of having a second voice in my head, there's still that phantom pain in my shoulder, and I've been struck several more times today by Livia for being absent-minded. And that's all on top of my gnawing, swelling hunger. The cursed veil I'm supposed to detail remains unfinished, and I don't dare defy Livia's orders by eating.

I'm not talking. I'm thinking, the voice snaps back in Latin.

Well, it's distracting, I say, annoyed.

I've had to listen to your voice for years, and you could never hear me when I told you to shut up. I'm sure you can bear it for a day.

16

I don't breathe for a moment. *You've been able to hear me...for years?*

I hope I've misunderstood.

Unceasingly, the male voice responds.

My mind has been the one place in this entire world where I could find refuge. To know that somewhere out there, this voice, could hear my truest, deepest thoughts?

Just when I'd assumed the situation couldn't get any worse—I shudder.

Please leave me alone, I beg as I move on to slice cheese and pull apart a thick wedge of bread, ignoring the way my mouth waters.

The voice doesn't respond, and I think...I think he's trying to honor my wishes. Not that it stops me from hearing his voice in that other language intermittently throughout the rest of the evening. But I don't believe he intends to be speaking into my head. It's almost like my mind is listening in on a nearby conversation someone else is having.

It's still distracting as sin.

It's only later, when the moon is high in the sky and Livia has long gone to bed, that I finally return to the vexing issue of his voice.

I sit with my back to the wall of my bedroom, the unfinished veil in my lap and a needle in my hand. I sigh out a breath.

Are you there? I speak into my mind.

I wait for an answer. When none comes, I try again.

Hello? Can you hear me?

Nothing.

Of course the voice would be gone now when I actually want to speak to it—him.

Voice! I say, growing impatient. *Are you there?*

Gods, you don't need to yell. And my name isn't Voice. It's Memnon.

I have the worrisome urge to laugh—and laugh and laugh.

I have lost it. Truly, I have.

I see you didn't die, I say instead. I had been holding on to the slight hope that injury or blood loss might've taken him sometime between dinnertime and now.

Your disappointment gives me strength, Memnon says.

With his words, I feel a combination of annoyance and humor. The emotions are *his*, I realize. I'm not just hearing him speak—I'm *feeling* what he feels.

I push past my own discomfort at the thought. *Are you hurt?*

It's nothing I can't handle, he says gruffly.

So you are *hurt.* My pulse quickens. *Where?* I ask, even as my shoulder continues to throb.

I took an arrow to my back, he says hesitantly, *right beneath my shoulder blade.*

My breath catches. *I can feel it*, I admit.

I'm not entirely sure if the emotion rushing through me is mine or this voice's, but it feels like fingertips touching, like connection.

I swallow, then make another stitch in the veil, the lamp propped on the stool next to me flickering in the darkness.

A part of me is curious about *what* this voice is. Logic is telling me that my mind simply turned on itself, but I badly don't want to believe that.

What…are you? I say carefully.

What do you mean, "What am I?" Memnon asks, sounding affronted. *I'm a man.*

I'm not sure *man* is the right word to describe this

voice. He doesn't sound like a full-grown adult. More like a teenage boy.

So you're real and not just a part of my own mind?

I'm real, he says. He must sense my deep mistrust because he adds, *I'm staring up at the stars right now. I can see Orion the hunter.*

Orion the hunter. That's one of the few constellations I can easily recognize.

I cannot remember the last time I stopped and looked up at the stars, and right now, when my muscles feel leaden from a long day of work, I don't want to move.

But curiosity spurs me to my feet, so I set the veil aside and pad to the doorway of my room. Livia's bedroom is to my left, and I pause, listening to her soft snores before I decide to tiptoe across our apartment and slip out of the house. I have to shuffle down to the courtyard to get a good view of the sky. Tonight is cloudy, but I can make out several scattered stars. Among them are the three even dots of Orion's belt.

The sight of the constellation makes my stomach clench.

So Memnon's telling the truth.

Girl? he says as though I beckoned him. *Are you still there?*

Don't call me that, I say absently as I head back up the stairs and inside. I rub my arms against the chill.

What should *I call you?*

My throat tightens as I slip into my room and pick up the veil once more. I resettle myself on the ground next to my lamp and resume stitching, ignoring the painful ache in my belly.

Instead of answering him, I say, *So you can see the night sky. I'm sure all sorts of beings can see the sky. How do I know you're an actual person and not some vengeful spirit or a capricious god?*

I could ask you the same thing, he says.

I am thinking over that logic when he again asks, *What is your name?*

Do you truly not know? I ask, once more evading the question. *I thought you've been hearing my thoughts for years.*

You've spoken many names in your thoughts, he says, *names that are already foreign and difficult to remember, and I have not been able to figure out if any of them are yours.*

His admission sparks a curiosity in me. I know he's not Roman. The language he spoke is coarse yet rolling, the sounds guttural. But there are a lot of cultures with guttural-sounding languages, and I don't have a good enough ear to know which he might belong to.

Are you going to tell me your name? he prods.

I hesitate. People don't usually ask me for my name. Formally, it's Livia the Younger, my adoptive mother being Livia the Elder. Usually, if I'm being referred to as something other than *Girl*, it's Livia.

However, I don't want to give Memnon this blighted name I must answer to.

What would you like to call me? I say instead.

There's a moment of silence. *That seems like the sort of response a vengeful spirit would give*, Memnon says.

I press my lips together to keep from smiling. That's true enough.

I don't like my name, I admit.

Then give me a different one, he says, unfazed by my answer. *One that you do like.*

I pause my stitching and stare absently off into the darkness. My mind races, my heart beating frantically.

I already know the name I would like to give him, and that is the name my Northern parents gave me. But—and it's one of my deepest shames—I cannot remember what that name *is*. The only other person who might have once known it is Livia, though if she ever learned it, she must've discarded it as quickly as she came upon it.

I reach into my past, straining to recall *any* of the names of the people I loved—my sister, my mother, my extended family. Instead, all I see are the flames that burned my village. I can still taste the smoke on my tongue and feel the heat of that fire reaching out from the past, trying to swallow me up. I have spent so long running from the memory of those flames that the names I cherished burned up with it.

The only names I can think of are Roman ones. This is actually a bit distressing.

And that's bad because...?

I'm not Roman, I finish for him.

You aren't Roman? Memnon asks, sounding genuinely surprised.

You've been listening to my thoughts for years, yet you never figured this out?

"Listening" is such a generous term, he says. *More like "studiously ignoring."* After a moment, he adds, *Do you want me to help you with a name?*

Do I? The possibility sends a thrill through me.

Yes, I finally say. *I do think I want that.*

Okay, Memnon says.

He goes quiet for so long that I almost believe I am alone in my own head once more. The only thing that convinces me otherwise is the light, exhilarating sensation that I'm fairly certain belongs to him.

Roxilana, he finally says, his voice deepening with the roll of his voice.

The name brings goose bumps to my skin. It doesn't sound anything like the Roman names I'm used to. It sounds untamable, like something beyond the Empire's reach.

Do you like it? Memnon asks.

Yes, I say, a slow smile curving my lips. *I like it. A lot. I am…Roxilana.*

I swear I feel Memnon smile inside my head. The action causes my heart to gallop all over again.

Hello, Roxi, he replies.

I have to bite my lip to smother my smile. *I haven't even had my name for a full breath, and you're already shortening it?* I say.

Yes, well, you're less terrifying as Roxi, Memnon says. *Roxilana might cut my heart out of my chest, but Roxi…Roxi sounds like…a friend.*

I want to tell him that we are not friends, that we just met and I'm still not fully convinced he's even human, but… for my peace of mind, a friend sounds nice. Especially if he is going to be stuck in my head.

After a moment, I ask, *What does the name mean—Roxilana?*

If he tells me it means something like "donkey dung," I will mutiny.

Does it need to have a meaning? he asks.

Of course it must, I say. *I am a vengeful spirit and very easily displeased.*

If I spoke to anyone else like this, I would be reprimanded. But with this man that's not quite a man, I don't need to be an obedient Roman girl. I can be whomever I wish to be.

I can be Roxilana. The thought sends a surge of pleasure through me.

I don't know how I sense Memnon's smile, but I do. And in that moment, I think it might be the most wonderful thing in the world.

Roxilana means "blessed one" in my language, he says.

The last thing I am is blessed, but I keep that thought to myself—or at least, I assume I keep it to myself. I have no way of knowing if Memnon can hear every stray thought or just the words I want him to hear.

Are you really a human? I ask.

I really am, he says.

I make several stitches in the veil as I make sense of the fact that fate somehow connected me to an entire other person.

Where do you live? I finally ask.

That depends on the season, Memnon responds. *My tribe moves often, but generally we Sarmatians live near the Black Sea.*

Sarmatians. I roll the word around in my mind. I'm not sure I've ever heard of such a people. The Black Sea, on the other hand, I *have* heard of, though it's as remote to me as Egypt and Anatolia. As remote as Britannia, the island I came from.

I'm in Rome, I say.

I try to imagine that distance between us, but I simply cannot fathom it.

How can we hear each other if we live so far apart? I ask. It defies nature.

This is the work of gods and magic, Roxi.

A shiver runs down my spine.

Memnon seems much more accepting of this situation than I am. Then again, he's apparently had years to consider it.

I thread my needle through the edge of the veil, listening to the distant chatter of Romans still out on the streets.

If the gods are real, they have abandoned me entirely, I say softly.

No, est menulumguva amage,[8] Memnon says, *they were merely preparing you.*

I frown in the darkness. *Preparing me for what?*

Us.

8 My future queen

CHAPTER 3
Roxilana, 12 years old

48 AD, Rome, Roman Empire

It takes weeks to adjust to having another voice in my head.
Weeks of headaches and distractions and beatings from Livia
for being absent-minded. I feel like I am being unmade,
thought by thought. And all evidence suggests that, short of
death, there will be no end to this sharing of minds.

Eventually, I do get used to having Memnon's voice in
my head, thank the gods. It helps that his stray thoughts are
in a language I don't understand. And at night, after the
work of the day is done, we often chat.

What are you doing, little witch? he asks now, as I sweep
out the last crumbs and dust that collected in the living
room. Livia has only just blown out her lamp, and I can hear
her settling into her bed.

"Little witch"? I repeat, my attention snagging on the
endearment.

Do you like it? Memnon asks.

Despite its obvious oddness, I…do.

Why "witch"? I ask.

Because only a witch could reach across nations and speak directly into my mind, he says. *You must have more than a little magic in you.*

The thought makes me want to laugh, particularly when the hem of my stained stola is tied in a knot midway up my legs and sweaty wisps of my hair have escaped my bun.

I lean on the broom handle. *Yes, I'm very powerful.* The thought is more than a little appealing, especially when I feel so very powerless.

Memnon hesitates, as though he's about to tell me something important, but at the last moment, I sense him change his mind.

I was also considering "man-slaying sorceress," he says casually, *but you haven't ever killed a man, have you?*

Uh, no. I smile at the silly thought as I begin to sweep again.

Once you do, I might have to reconsider the nickname, Memnon says.

"Once I do"? I echo, raising my eyebrows even though he can't see the action. *I have no plans to kill anyone at the moment.*

You're a vengeful spirit; it'll eventually happen, he says with complete assurance.

I bite back a laugh. *Have you ever killed?* I ask. *I'm still convinced you're the one who's the vengeful spirit.*

Memnon grows quiet, and the levity bleeds away from the moment. *I have*, he confesses, his voice…strange.

You have what? I say, not immediately following. Half my mind is still on sweeping in near darkness, today's chore Livia is forcing me to complete before bed.

I have killed a man, Memnon admits. *Many, in fact. I killed my first in battle several years ago. I've killed dozens since, and I've hurt many others.* It all spills out of him, one confession begetting another and another.

At first, I cannot make sense of his words. We were just joking a moment ago. Surely he's not serious...

But he is. I can feel it in the twisting of my gut and the heavy silence sitting between us. My mind just doesn't want to accept what he's said.

Once it sinks in, bile rises up my throat, and I nearly drop my broom.

I should've known this confession was coming. The first time we spoke, he told me he was trying to not get killed. But I didn't ask questions. If I'm being honest, I didn't want to know.

Roxilana? Memnon says. *You've gone quiet.*

I set the broom aside and lean my back against the nearby wall, drawing in air through my nostrils.

Dozens? I echo hollowly.

Memnon pauses. *Why did your voice change?*

I can still taste that bile at the back of my throat. Memnon's not denying it. And my heart, my foolish heart, feels like Icarus, soaring too high only to falter and fall. And break.

My eyes drop to a lit lamp on the nearby kitchen table. It hisses softly, and the tiny flame reminds me of the other, larger ones that haunt my memory.

Immediately, I fall into the past. I hear the screams that end abruptly, then the wet, gurgling sounds. Death and more death. I can hardly remember the years before that fire, and I've entirely forgotten much of the time that followed, but that night...it will be forever burned in my mind.

That's...awful, I finally say, my stomach knotted and my heart aching.

I sense Memnon recoil from me, clearly put off by my words.

I am a warrior, he says. *Fighting is what I've trained my whole life to do.* After a moment's pause, he continues. *It is a great honor here, to kill an enemy.* His voice is some combination of offended and defensive. *Every person in my tribe must at least attempt to take a life. Not even our women can marry until they do so.*

Every Sarmatian must kill? Another wave of nausea rolls through me.

I think about the Roman legionnaires who massacred my family. I think about how I watched my house collapse in on my mother and brother, how I tripped over the lifeless body of my father. How I will never know what happened to my sister and that uncertainty will haunt me for the rest of my life. I think about the pain of surviving that night— the hunger, the beatings, the ugliness of being needed but unwanted.

Bitterness coats my tongue. *Congratulations to you, then, on your many murders.*

Mentally, I retreat from Memnon, trying to put as much distance as I can between his mind and my own.

Whatever fanciful daydream I made of Memnon, it's been toppled by harsh, disappointing reality.

The boy in my mind is just as bad as the rest of them.

———

I don't willingly speak to Memnon for many weeks. Even then, I'm bitter. Bitter at men who commit violence. Bitter that innocents pay for it with their blood.

During all that time, Memnon tries to talk to me. He explains himself, defends himself, pleads with me to listen.

I want to tell him that I cannot help *but* listen, unfortunately. And it *is* unfortunate because, while I do not understand that other language he speaks, a few stray thoughts of his come to me in Latin.

Wish she would talk to me...

Miss her...

And those stray thoughts chip away my resentment. Maybe that's why, when Memnon reaches out to me one evening as I'm folding finished garments for delivery tomorrow, I actually respond.

Or maybe it's simply his request:

Tell me about your family, the one you were born into.

I swallow, setting the stola aside. I might not remember my family's names, and I can only sometimes picture their faces, but I loved them.

There were five of us, I begin. *My mother, my father, my brother, and my sister...*

There's not much to my memories in the end, but what I can recall, I share—like the warmth and safety of sleeping next to my siblings, my father's graying beard and booming laugh, and the way I squirmed when my mother braided my hair. I talk about some festivals I don't have names for, the flowers my sister and I would weave into crowns, and the smell of our house after my mother made one of her strange concoctions in our cauldron.

A part of me is aware this must be boring, but Memnon listens, and he seems genuinely interested—and maybe a little relieved—when he comments here and there.

How did you lose them? he asks now.

My mood shifts, like clouds smothering the sun.

Roman soldiers attacked our village in the middle of the night, I confess, the words rushing out.

Memnon is quiet, but I can feel sadness and a bit of horror well up in him. *Did they kill your family?* He seems reluctant to ask.

I nod, but of course he can't see the action.

Yes, I force out.

That is why you hate battle, he says with sudden understanding.

I swallow but say nothing. I don't need to.

What is life like for you now? he asks.

I blow out a breath. I can hear Livia's voice in the court-yard below our apartment as she speaks with one of the neighbors and, beyond that, the bustling sounds of Rome filter in through the open windows. With it come the smells of the city—excrement and meat, smoke, and the faintest whiff of myrrh.

I take in the apartment—the loom, the piles of fabrics, the baskets of beads and yarn and thread. I look at the worn wooden table and the walls with their chipped green paint.

People live much worse lives, I admit. Ignoring the hunger pains in my stomach and the bruises on my arms.

I don't care about other people, little witch.

It's the first time Memnon's used the term since our fight, and despite the fallout from it, I find I actually do like it.

What is life like for you now? he repeats.

Before, I had everything, I admit. But then, I didn't actually have everything, did I? It simply felt that way. I clarify: *I was loved.*

And now? Memnon prods.

Reluctantly, my gaze drops to my bruises.

Now I'm not. And I think it is as simple as that.

It's quiet for a long stretch, and I listen to the sounds of the city.

Sometimes I hear…stray thoughts of yours, he admits. He's silent for another moment. *Roxi, is someone*—Another pause. *Is someone hurting you?*

I bow my head, my heart racing. Or maybe it's his heartbeat. It's hard to say. My answer lodges in my throat. I don't know why I want to lie, but I do. I can hear Livia's voice in my head. It sounds like my own: *I'm selfish, I'm stupid, I'm lazy*—

No, Memnon says, cutting through the acidic thoughts, *you're not. You're funny and kind and smart and a thousand other things, and if it was Livia who told you this, and if she hurt you*—His voice turns threatening, and I remember all over again how violent he is.

Memnon, stop, I plead.

He goes silent, though his emotions are angry, worried.

You have me, he eventually says, his tone gentling. *I care about you.*

I sit down heavily on one of the kitchen stools. My throat is thick with emotion, and I have to roll my lips together to stifle the sob that wants to come out.

Memnon's hurt people, and he's likely torn apart families just like mine. Yet every time we talk, he has been kind. It is more than I can say about anyone else who knows me.

You have me, he says again. *You always will, est menulumguva amage.*

A stray tear slips down my cheek, and I hastily wipe it away.

Okay, I say brokenly. I think this means I'm going to forgive him, and we're going to talk again.

I sense Memnon smile. Then, in Sarmatian, he adds something else, something I cannot hope to understand:

Vak busu dat dit kuppu sutvuvu evu di'nuvak, pesa suvup azakupusa. Pesa udugab vesamapusa.[9]

He switches back to Latin.

You can always talk to me, Roxi, even if you're mad at me. Even if you despise me. He pauses. *Will you do that? Will you speak to me, even in anger? Because I don't think I can take more of your silence.*

I sit there and think over his words, my fingers drawing shapes on the table.

Finally, I say, *I can.*

And I do.

---

9 *You will have everything once more, this I vow. I am yours forever.*

CHAPTER 4
Roxilana, 13 years old

49 AD, Rome, Roman Empire

I sit outside on a stone bench behind one of the villas Livia and I are visiting today, sweat gathering beneath my long tunic. The summer sun feels hot enough to cook meat, but I don't mind. Livia's inside the large house, gossiping with her client, while I've used the spare time to slip away and eat a wedge of bread and listen to the cicadas calling from the tall, dry grass.

As it so often does, my mind drifts to Memnon. I heard him only a short while ago, uttering some soft thought not meant for me.

I think about the beautiful, rolling notes of his native language and wish, not for the first time, that I understood them. I know Latin and a bit of Greek but not Sarmatian. For a long while, I was okay with that, but not anymore. I want to understand all his thoughts just as he understands all of mine.

Memnon? I reach out across our connection. *Can you teach me your language?*

Roxi?

That first touch of his awareness makes my breath catch. It's quickly followed by surprise and delight, the sensations flooding through me like snowmelt in spring. It's intoxicating—*he* is intoxicating.

I would love to, est menulumguva amage, he says, though I swear I also sense a spike of something else. Unease? Maybe I'm reading into things too much.

Can we start with that phrase? I say, taking a bite of my bread.

"Est menulumguva amage"? he echoes. If Memnon is busy with the demands of the day, he doesn't let on.

What does it mean? I press.

You'll find out soon enough, he says cryptically.

Soon enough? I scoff, even as a light, happy emotion works its way through me. *What sort of answer is that?*

I didn't promise I'd be a good teacher, he says, and I sense his smile. *Besides, I'm trying to leave a little mystery in our relationship.*

Oh, so now we have a relationship? I say. My blood thrums at the thought.

I feel his smile. *Oh yes, Roxi.*

Now I can't stop the grin that spreads across my face or the hopeful rush his words bring with them.

Vaksasavazaku pesa susagub mi'tasavakvu evupusa? he asks. *What do you think I look like?*

I realize this is his attempt to teach me Sarmatian: to think a sentence first in his language, then repeat it in Latin. Who knows, maybe it will work.

I don't know, I answer him.

Kezak di'napuvusagu do kusgu i'banud mi'tgasavakpa? Have you thought about it at least?

Of course I've thought about it, I say. My mind has wandered to this topic many, many times. Memnon's rich, arresting voice practically begs for a face to go with it.

I close my eyes, basking in the midday sunlight, and search my mind for the image I've cobbled together of him.

I imagine you with short, light brown hair and…smooth, oiled skin.

His laughter echoes down the bond we share.

Why are you laughing? I demand. If he thinks smooth, oiled skin is laughable…what must he look like, then?

No reason, little witch.

Do you look like a monster? I ask, somewhat surly, taking another bite of my bread.

Memnon laughs again, this time cocky. *Not a monster, Roxi.*

That makes my heart skip for some odd reason. I'm never going to see Memnon in the flesh, so what he looks like is irrelevant.

Sapu sanburvak? he says in Sarmatian. *What are you doing?*

I stare down at my bread. *Just eating lunch—and talking to you.*

I wish I were there with you, Memnon admits. He pauses, and this time, when he speaks again, it's in Sarmatian. *Botuvap iv'tabiwvusasa logu suwas wanubpusa.* He pauses, as though he's searching for the right words. *Pesa wetasavakvu wevugavusa sobivakvu kuvug sanupusa. Xu nudnutasavasa i'rugavusa sisa.*

Pusa vak danusa di'vak lib di'nvusa kuxivu xu vaksa ovaknud wotugavusa etvu kuvug sanupusa.[10]

I try to focus on the sounds that make up his language, determined to learn. It somewhat helps that I can pick out bits of his emotions, which feel giddy and ardent, much like the way I feel once wine hits my blood.

Vaksu i'k wanapsa i'tvuwavakgu est buvisu si'tsoxap vakos-guma, vak est vatnutapsa dukup mi'tavakgusdanad inavakasavak popmas,[11] he finishes.

After a pause, I ask, *What did you say?*

I feel his smile and more of his warm, heady emotions.

"Girl!" Livia's sharp voice cuts through my thoughts. The cicadas go quiet.

Shit.

I have to go, Memnon, I rush out.

I stand quickly and pop the last bit of bread in my mouth.

Is that Livia? he asks.

Yes...

Will you be all right? Memnon asks, alarmed. He now knows how she is.

"Girl!"

I have to go, I rush out. *I'll chat again tonight. And I'm serious, I want to learn Sarmatian.*

Botuvap ipis sinavakasa wanubpusa,[12] he says.

What did you say? I ask, rushing back to the villa.

His emotions seem conflicted, but I hear another smile in his voice when he says, *I can't wait to teach you.*

---

10 I wish it so strongly, my heart aches from it. I envy the sun that gets to touch your skin. And the bread that gets to kiss your lips. I envy the air that shares space with you and the ground that gets to hold you.

11 And my only fear when it comes to teaching you my language is that you might learn my secrets before I'm ready to share them.

12 I pray my heart will survive it.

CHAPTER 5
Roxilana, 16 years old

52 AD, Rome, Roman Empire

There's something mesmerizing about writing. The neat lines, the straight, sharp edges. The ability to look at rows and rows of lines arranged just so and draw from them *language*. To hear in your mind words that someone else spoke, someone else imagined and felt. To me, it's nearly as supernatural as having a literal voice in my head.

I watch as Livia writes instructions onto her wax tablet in the domus of the Juventia family. Longing grips me. I know what she's writing is largely mundane and that the task itself can be slow and tedious, but unlike tailoring clothes, I don't think I would mind the tedium, just as I never minded learning Sarmatian, though it took me nearly two years to really understand the language.

Livia, however, has chosen not to teach me how to write, and I doubt she ever will. Not when she has all the help from me she needs. Besides, educating me would raise my worth in ways that would make her decidedly uncomfortable.

"The tunic will need to have a Tyrian purple edging," says Quinta, our client, as she appraises her bored-looking son, Gaius. "I also would like a little gold detailing."

While Livia writes everything down, I take the young nobleman's measurements. He's probably only a few years my senior, yet he seems much older. Power has carved into him the way pain has carved into me.

Livia finishes writing out the instructions and tucks away her wax tablet and stylus.

"While you're here," Quinta says to Livia, "I was hoping to show you a few of my own garments I'd like embellished."

Livia glances at me briefly. It's taken years, but finally I can read Livia's looks and sense her moods. This time, I know she wants me to finish measuring Quinta's son, then assist her.

I give her a subtle nod as she follows her client out of the room.

Gaius stares after them as their voices grow distant. Once they're out of earshot, his attention moves to me.

I take a final measurement from his hips to the tops of his knees, then to his heels, knotting the bit of yarn I'm using to mark the length.

"You look pretty on your knees like that," Gaius comments.

I pause, not entirely sure the young noble is even speaking to me. Why, after all, would a senator's son bother to talk to a tailor's assistant? But when I glance up at Gaius's face, he's watching me with sharp eyes and an amused twist of his lips.

Gaius begins lifting the hem of his tunic up his legs, past

his knees, and heat floods my cheeks as I finally understand. He is talking to me, and the compliment—if it can even be called that—has claws.

Fear takes root. I've heard enough stories of privileged men having their way with whomever they pleased.

I lower the yarn. "I think that's all I need," I say quickly, trying to pretend the moment out of existence.

I rise from my knees, only for Gaius's hand to grasp my shoulder and push me back down.

"We're not done here," he says, and his eyes have a determined gleam in them.

Now my fear blooms into full-blown terror.

Roxi? Memnon reaches out to me, his voice full of concern. I have to ignore him just to focus on this moment.

I swallow. "There's nothing else I need," I insist. I feel like a fool, pretending his aggression away, but I don't know what else to do, and I can't think over my rising panic.

His grip on me relaxes, and I think he might let me go, but as soon as I stand, he steps into my space.

"But there's something *I* need," Gaius says. The amusement is back in his expression, but everything else about him feels menacing. He keeps stepping forward, forcing me to back up. My gaze darts to the doorway, but Gaius has positioned himself between me and it, and I'm not confident I could get past him if I tried.

"Please," I say, forcing my gaze to return to Gaius, though I don't want to look at him. "I need to get back to help your mother."

The nobleman doesn't seem to care about my plea or my reluctance. His hands move to my torso, roughly pawing at my body.

Roxi, what is going on? Memnon says, his tone growing sharp. *I can feel your fear...*

I hardly hear Memnon. My mind is racing. I think I'm in shock.

I place my hands on Gaius's chest, and I try to shove the man back.

"My mother can wait," he says. "Just relax." Gaius grabs my wrists and restrains them in one of his hands. "This is going to feel good, I swear it."

Once my wrists are in his grip, I panic and begin to struggle in earnest, trying to pry my arms free.

"Relax," Gaius growls out again as he shoves me against the wall. He uses his own body to pin me in place.

The young nobleman begins to feel me up again with his free hand, his fingers moving to my thigh, where he gathers the fabric of my stola.

No, no, no.

A scream is climbing up my throat, and it wants to claw its way out. I grind my teeth together to muffle it. This is a patrician household, the top of society. They can do what they want, when they want, with near immunity. No one will come to my rescue for this.

Gaius presses a clumsy, wet kiss against my cheek, and I squeeze my eyes shut, my jaw beginning to tremble, a tear leaking out.

Memnon—Memnon, Memnon, Memnon. I don't know why I chant his name. He cannot do anything more than I can.

Roxi, are you okay? Memnon asks, that edge still in his voice. *What is going on?*

Beneath my breastbone, pressure begins to build. It feels as though my mounting fear is pushing against my rib cage, determined to be set free.

40

Help, I plead brokenly, even though I know it's impossible. *I can't get him off me…*

Get him off…? Dimly, I sense Memnon's alarm, followed by his anguish and a rising ruthlessness.

Listen to me, he says, his voice like iron. *If you are being attacked, then by the gods, hurt that fucker.*

Hurt him? The thought comes like an epiphany, even as pressure continues to build in my chest, squeezing the air from my lungs and pushing its way up into my throat and down to my abdomen.

Memnon continues. *The eyes, the nose, the throat, the lower belly, and the groin are all weak points*, he says. *If you don't have a blade, use your nails, your knuckles, or your knees. Strike fast and hard.*

I go still as I listen, and Gaius mistakes it for compliance, releasing my wrists so that he can better lift his own garment.

Once you've landed a blow, Memnon says, *don't hesitate—run or attack again. Don't give him time to recover from his surprise.*

Land a blow, I repeat.

Okay, I—I think I can do that.

Only, the pressure inside me is becoming impossible to ignore. It's rapidly expanded to every corner of my body—arms, legs, fingers, and toes—heating my blood and pushing at the underside of my skin.

I move my hands back to Gaius's chest as he continues to fumble with our clothes, my thoughts churning.

Can't breathe through the pressure—don't know where to strike—need him to get off me—

My fingers dig into Gaius's chest and panic swallows up my reasoning. *Need to get him off me.* I latch on to that thought: *Need to get him off me.*

All of that dispersed pressure and heat *moves*, gathering

once more beneath my rib cage before flowing down my arms and into my palms. *Get off me, get off me—GET OFF ME.*

The pressure releases all at once.

Beneath my touch, Gaius is blown backward, his body enveloped in a cloud of pale orange smoke. He hits the ground hard, his head cracking against the marble floor.

For several seconds, all I can do is draw in ragged breaths. Gaius lies unconscious on the ground, that pale orange smoke filling the air between us.

Roxi, what just happened? Memnon asks. *I felt something through our connection. Are you all right?*

I turn my hands over, staring at my palms. I have to bite back a scream as more of that colored smoke seeps *out of my flesh*. It looks like burning incense. I curl my hands into fists, hoping to smother the smoke. Still, wisps of it slip out between the creases of my skin.

Gaius stirs on the ground, and I press my back into the wall, wishing it could swallow me up. Memnon told me I needed to react quickly at this point—either fight or flee—but I can't seem to do much more than gape.

The young nobleman sits up and groans, touching his head. His fingers come away red. It seems to take him a moment to see me and remember the situation.

"Did you…push me?" Gaius says softly, glancing around the room and the distance between us. It's his turn to be the disbelieving one.

I don't have an answer for him. All I know is that my fear is twisting my stomach in knots.

Are you all right? Memnon repeats.

I don't know, I say.

Are you hurt? he rephrases.

No. I'm shocked to say it because it feels like I should be, and maybe tomorrow there will be bruises, but... *No,* I repeat.

What is the state of your attacker?

I study Gaius, noticing the unsteady sway of his upper body and the blood dampening his hair. *He's injured.*

I sense Memnon's relief as well as something that feels like...pride.

Well done, Roxilana.

Of course a warrior like him would be pleased. My gut, however, still churns.

Are you safe? he asks.

Not...yet.

If he tries anything else, Memnon says grimly, *hurt him again.*

At the thought of doing so, more orange smoke spills from my hands and circles my body.

Across from me, Gaius pushes himself to his feet, his limbs trembling. He eyes me up and down like he's unsure what to do. Finally, he looks young. Young and uncertain and...*weak.* Once more, he takes in the distance between us, then backs away from me slowly. When he reaches the doorway, he spares me one final, wary glance, then dashes out. I can hear the slap of his leather sandals as he retreats.

As soon as he's gone, I place a hand over my mouth and slide down the wall, silent tears dripping down my cheeks.

Wisps of that light orange smoke still slip out of the palm pressed to my mouth. I'm breathing it in, and the sensation of it sliding into my lungs causes my flesh to pimple.

Roxilana? Memnon says softly. *I am still here with you.* He sounds like he's been there the whole time, sitting in the back of my mind, keeping me company the only way he can.

That makes me cry harder, my entire body shaking from the effort, and I have to use my hand to muffle my sobs. All I really want is to be held right now, even though my skin is still crawling from the last person who touched it.

He-he almost… I can't finish the thought.

What is his name? Memnon says, his tone so deceptively gentle.

I should be nervous about that gentleness. It doesn't match the swirling anger coming from him. I press my palms to my eyes. *Gaius*, I admit. Not that it matters.

Memnon cannot do much with the Roman name but curse it.

Something came out of my hands and pushed him away. It's still coming out of my hands. I don't mean to confess this, but I can't seem to screen my thoughts, not when my panic is building all over again.

What does it look like? Memnon asks, and he doesn't sound skeptical or unnerved.

I lower my trembling hands and study them, watching the thin wisps rise and curl from my palms. *It looks like smoke, but it's the color of sunset.*

There's a long pause.

You don't know what it is? Memnon eventually says.

Should I? I respond somewhat hysterically.

Again, there's that silence. It feels like there's so much behind it, but if there is, I don't hear any of it.

Roxi, he says softly, *it's magic. Your magic.*

Magic?

My body begins to tremble badly, and I am close to completely losing it. *What?*

I believe in magic—most Romans do—but only in the same vague way I believe in gods. It all exists in whispers

44

and prayers, in subtle turns of luck, portentous omens, and scribed spells one can buy for a coin.

I never assumed it would be blatant…not like this.

Memnon hesitates, then adds, *One of your parents likely had magic, and they passed it down to you.* After another pause, Memnon adds, *My father has power too. It looks similar—smoky. His is a deep green.*

My limbs still tremble, but I've gone very still.

You've seen this with your own eyes? I ask.

Yes, though few people besides us can see it. Only those who have magic themselves can view it in others.

I try to remember if I've ever seen anything like this smoky power before, but it's useless. My mind is too muddled with fear to think beyond this moment.

Do you…have magic? I can't believe I'm asking this.

Not yet, he says. Beneath his words, I sense wistfulness and a bit of longing. *But I think I will one day—it has to Awaken, like yours must've. The fact that we can speak in each other's minds is proof that we probably both have always had it.*

I press the heels of my palms back to my eyes. I would laugh at these assertions, except they make a certain sick sense, given everything that has happened to me up to this point.

I exhale a shaky breath and bow my head.

How do I make it go away?

It's your magic, Memnon says calmly. *It listens to you. Tell it to stop.*

I lick my dry lips.

Stop, I demand.

The line of orange smoke thins, then vanishes altogether, the final remnants of it floating up into the air and dissipating away.

It worked, I say, shocked.

Of course it worked. It obeys you, Memnon says. *Magic is your birthright, given to you by the gods. You can use it whenever you wish—to help you with tasks, to bring you wealth, to protect you.*

To protect me? I echo.

I feel his smile down our connection. *You don't have to worry about anyone hurting you ever again, little witch*, he says with conviction. *You are powerful.*

CHAPTER 6
Roxilana, 17 years old

53 AD, Rome, Roman Empire

I choke on a cry as a horrible pain startles me from sleep. It twists my gut, carving me open from the inside out.

I reach for my abdomen, certain my hands will come away bloody. Certain my insides are spilling out.

My hand closes over my dry linen tunic. No blood, no spilling guts, and yet—I groan from the pain, curling in on myself. My eyes search the darkness, looking for an intruder—or worse, *Livia*—my sleep-clogged mind unsure whether this agony is real or imagined.

It takes several ragged breaths for me to realize this pain is not my own.

Gods—

Memnon!

He doesn't respond.

Memnon!

Terror courses through me, the metallic tang of it coating the back of my throat.

New, lacerating pain blooms on my face, near my left eye. My hand moves from my stomach to cup the area above my cheekbone, and I put pressure on a wound that doesn't exist.

Not on me at least.

Please, please, Memnon, answer me, I beg.

Roxi? he says, his voice dazed and sluggish. *Wha—*

His voice morphs into a bellowed cry as the pain moves, dragging across his face, all the way to his ear. I feel the echo of it, so sharp that bile rises. It feels as though it's carving into the very bones of my face, and I bite my lower lip until it bleeds, just to keep from screaming or retching. It's all I can do to breathe through the pain—pain that must be a shadow of Memnon's.

What is going on? I force out the words.

Battle…struck down, he gasps out. *Dacian king above me trying to…my face…*

Memnon begins to scream again as the pain drags down his face to his jawline. All of this is in addition to that deep, gaping ache in his abdomen.

Over his pain, my own panic surges, stirring the magic in my veins.

Memnon! I am frantic, helpless.

I think that maybe my beloved friend is—is *dying*.

My breath comes faster and faster at the prospect of his life ending, of my mind being my own once more. No more sporadic commentary, no more chats, no more warmth and kindness from the only person in the world who I care about—and who cares about me.

Gods, but I cannot lose him.

I cannot.

I *won't*.

Since my magic Awoke, I've used it sparingly. I have a lot of fear of it and little control over it. But now, instinct guides me.

At my beckoning, my power thickens in my veins, burgeoning within me until it strains against my skin, eager to be unleashed.

You are the only thing that matters to me in this godsforsaken world. The confession burns coming out, but it doesn't matter. There is iron in my soul. *I won't let you die, Memnon. Not today.* I've never spoken like this—not to another living soul—but I can still hear his screams, and rational thought has fled my mind. Fear and determination crowd out everything else in me.

I gather my magic and lead it to that point beneath my sternum. If there were any place where Memnon's essence meets my own, it would be right here, so very close to where my heart lies trapped within the cage of my bones.

I focus on that point of connection and then I flood it with my power.

Use my magic, Memnon, I command, shoving it out to him the same way I do my thoughts. *It is yours.*

From the other end of my connection, I feel a dull tug on my magic that must be Memnon.

No sooner than he has drawn on it, however, than I hear Memnon's roar ringing in my mind. Light bursts behind my eyes, and then dimly, I sense another's magic mingling with my own.

Memnon's, I realize. Somehow, in his moment of need, his magic Awoke, just as mine had.

Roxilana, your power, he says wondrously, *it brought mine forth!*

I press the back of my hand to my mouth to smother my relieved sob. Tears begin to spill down my cheeks.

Through our bond, I sense Memnon's strength returning, even as I continue funneling my magic to him. The phantom pains in my abdomen fade away, though the throb in my face only dulls a little. He must…he must be healing it all.

I exhale, relieved he intuitively knows how to do such a thing.

The enemy king…is no more, he says.

My stomach twists at the admission, and I hear what Memnon doesn't say—that he was the one who killed him.

I stay as close to his mind as I can even after he mends himself, listening in on Memnon's stray thoughts as he gathers his newfound power and continues to fight.

The sky outside my window has just started to lighten when Memnon says, *little witch…it's over.* His voice is threaded with exhaustion. My face still aches ever so slightly; it's the only indication that Memnon is still injured there.

After a moment, he adds, *If it were not for your magic, I would be dead.*

I blink away the tears that want to slip free. I hadn't allowed myself to truly believe he was safe, not until now.

Thank you, for saving my life several times over, he says with quiet reverence.

I tuck a long lock of hair behind my ear.

So long as I am alive, you will never *die*, I vow. I won't lose Memnon like I did my family.

At my words, I feel something from him. It's stronger than warmth and deeper than fondness. There's a sweetness to it, like honey, and it comes on with an intensity that makes my breath catch.

Roxilana… Memnon says. His voice grows hoarse. *There are things on my mind that I have wanted to confess for a long time. Things—*

Abruptly, he stops speaking.

Memnon? I call out across our connection. *Is everything okay?*

It's quiet for a bit longer.

He curses to himself. *I'm sorry*, he says. *I cannot talk now. There is much to be done, and I—*Again, he stops himself, then seems to pick his words carefully. *Our enemies sought to obliterate my people. We have to gather and discuss a possible counterattack.*

Another battle? The thought makes my fear climb once more. I didn't think I had any energy left to be afraid, but apparently, when it comes to Memnon, I do.

Are you worried for me? he says, sensing my emotions. I swear there's a smile in his voice.

Of course I'm worried, I say. *I woke to you dying.*

That was before I had magic. Now, however…

Something trickles *into* me from the center of my chest.

I gasp. *Memnon's magic.* It feels like a summer storm rolling through me—simultaneously warm and refreshingly cool. My stomach dips at the sensation. Up until now, only Memnon's thoughts could enter me. Now, however, I experience his magic as though it were my own. I touch my sternum, marveling at it.

Little witch, your power Awoke mine, Memnon says wondrously, his words punctuated by the continued caress of his magic. *We both have magic—*Another interruption comes. Then, *I'm sorry*, he repeats. *I have to go.*

Wait! I call out, uneager to let him go.

Memnon pauses, waiting for me.

What color is your magic? I ask.

I feel his exhausted grin. *Blue.*

CHAPTER 7
Roxilana, 18 years old

54 AD, Rome, Roman Empire

The dynamic between Memnon and I has changed. It has been changing for a while, but at some point between when my magic Awoke and when Memnon's did, there's been this giddiness to our conversations, one that's left me breathless. It's like trapped laughter in my belly, so light and wonderful, I feel it could carry me away.

I haven't allowed myself to place a name on this emotion I feel when I speak to Memnon or think of him. I thought I was protecting my heart by doing so.

But I was wrong.

I didn't need to give the joy inside me a name for it to be crushed under the burden of reality.

Are you busy? I ask as I enter my bedroom, carrying a lit terracotta lamp in my trembling palm. With my free hand, I wipe away the tear tracks that stain my cheeks.

Never for you, Memnon says.

My stomach flutters at those words, loosening the knot in my belly. When did this man begin saying such devoted lines to me? Has he always done this? And if so, then when did I begin to take them seriously? Because I tuck away each sentiment like treasure.

I set the lamp down and, in the low light, unclasp the fibula at my shoulders, letting my stola slide down my torso. I step out of it, clad only in my tunic now.

What is it? Memnon asks.

I swallow as I remove the last of my garments and pull on a clean tunic. I run my hands through my hair, a little of my magic slipping out to loosen my updo. I can hear Livia moving around her room as she too readies herself for bed. She shouted herself ragged earlier and twice came at me, but I think the heat of her anger is banked for the night.

I still remember her shrill voice. *"You thought you'd live off me forever? You're a woman. It's your duty to marry! I've put it off long enough."*

I close my eyes and pinch the bridge of my nose. The truth is right there, but I don't know how to begin any of it, so I settle on: *I had a bad day, and I wanted to hear your voice.*

I sense devotion and another sweeter, deeper emotion from him, one I've also refused to name.

I wish I could give you more than my voice. Memnon hesitates, then continues. *I wish I could be there and hold you in my arms until all your pain and sadness were gone.*

I sit down on the edge of my bed, more tears stinging my eyes.

He continues, *I would whisper into your ear all the ways you are incredible. Because you are. You are the most incredible part of me, and honestly, if you need me to kill someone—*

Memnon! I bite back a laugh, though I know he can feel my amusement breaking through my sadness.

His tone grows serious. *And if you were still sad, I would tell you that you'll get through it, that I'm here to help carry the weight of hard days.* He hesitates again before pushing forward. *And then, if you'd let me, I would kiss you, Roxilana, and I would savor the sweetness of your lips.*

I don't think I'm breathing. Or—wait, I *am*, only there's not enough air for my lungs to take in.

Memnon, I finally say.

I don't know what he hears in my tone, but he laughs, the sound stroking me from the inside out.

Did you not like that? He doesn't sound the least bit dejected. *Fine, let's just be friends.*

My face crumples then, and I bury it in my hands. Why have we never openly talked about this? We most definitely should have.

My heart aches and aches and aches because of the unfairness of it all. Memnon is encased in the confines of my mind, closer to me than anyone else in existence, and yet he's still so far out of my reach. Too far.

And now that he's offered it, I *want* that kiss and everything else that his presence promises—but that's not my fate. All the yearning in the world won't save me from what's going to happen.

Roxilana? he says.

I'm still here, I say softly, drowning in my own misery.

He hesitates, maybe sensing my emotions.

You and I will always, always be friends, he finally says.

I nod to myself, pressing my lips together. *We will*, I agree. That is something, at least.

But if you could have more with me, he continues, *would you want that too?*

I lift my head from my hands, surprise masking my other

emotions. Magic leaks from my palms and my heart feels like it's in my throat. It's as though he pulled my own deepest wish out of the recesses of my soul.

Yes, I whisper down our bond.

It's utterly still between us for a moment. Then, Memnon's reaction floods me. I feel his exaltation and his relief.

Thank the gods, he says.

Despite my predicament, my heart races and my own joy rises now that we're finally, finally admitting this.

Would you *want that?* I ask.

I feel his giddy smile. *Would I want that?* Memnon repeats disbelievingly. *I have waited years to hear these words from you and to tell you how I truly feel.*

How do *you truly feel?* I ask timidly.

Like I could conquer the world just to lay it all at your feet. His voice turns serious. *Roxi, you are my first and last thought each day. I have longed for you more than I care to admit—not just as my friend and confidant but also as my lover and wife and* amage.

I can hardly catch my breath, and I feel so light I might float away. I'm shaking a little and smiling like a fool. When did it get like this? When did my own emotions become so intertwined with his?

The thrill of it draws out more pale orange magic from the palms of my hands, magic that only I and presumably other magic wielders can see.

You want me to be your lover? Your wife? I say softly. Memnon has kept the meaning of that last term—*amage*—from me, but it doesn't matter. I understand his intentions well enough.

I feel Memnon smile then, and the sensation does something funny to my stomach.

Yes, he says. *We were meant to be together. I am yours, Roxilana. Just say you will have me.*

I feel like a silly girl when I realize there's wetness on my cheeks—not from sadness this time but from *hope*. For a moment, I let myself fall wholly into the possibility of us.

Of course I will have you. Giving into my feelings for Memnon feels like magic itself—beautiful and impossible and wondrous. Nothing else in my life has ever come close to this all-consuming euphoria.

Until, that is, the reality of my life creeps back in.

As soon as I remember my earlier conversation with Livia, bile rises to the back of my throat.

"You selfish, little ingrate," Livia said. *"You will agree to marry whomever I choose, or I'll turn you out onto the streets, and we'll see how long you last there."*

A shudder works through me.

Livia hasn't yet made any significant wedding plans, but she mentioned a few names of potential spouses.

There's the lecherous jewelry maker with rotted teeth, Marcellus, who stares at my breasts every time we visit him for metal clothing adornments. But then there's another suitor, Titus, the textile merchant who smells like soured wine and unwashed body odor, who stands too close and spits when he talks.

Both men are old enough to be my father—possibly even my grandfather. But Livia doesn't mind, so long as my marriage means she'll get a familial discount on items she needs for her business and that, perhaps, she'd get to keep me on as her assistant.

A chill rolls through me as I try to imagine that life— married to a man whose touch I wouldn't want, working for a woman who has mistreated me for years. I knew I'd have to marry eventually, and I knew I likely wouldn't get a choice or even much like my options. But I hadn't expected to feel so desolate.

Roxi? Memnon says, calling me back.

I take a deep breath. *Yes?*

I feel another grin and the bright happiness that alights our connection.

I have been making plans, Roxi, Memnon says excitedly. If he's aware of the bleak turn in my thoughts, then he's trying to draw my joy back out. *I just needed to know you felt the same as I did before I acted on them,* he continues.

Plans? I echo.

Do you remember what I said to you the first time we spoke? Memnon asks.

You said many things to me, I respond slowly, not following.

I told you the gods were preparing you for us.

You did, I agree.

The preparations are over, he says.

I'm still not following.

Little witch, he continues. *I'm coming for you.*

I startle. *What?* I say with disbelief.

Just as Memnon and I have never openly talked about us, we've also never talked about meeting. I've always assumed it was because it would require traveling across the world, a nearly impossible endeavor.

At least, I assumed it was.

Memnon wants to come for me.

Hope—hope so vast I could fit oceans into it—rises in me.

Across our bond, Memnon grins again. *I do.*

My own lips curve up, and all my emotions are twisting and twisting.

Memnon, wait. I push the sentence out. *There's something you should know.*

I feel like my heart is cracking apart. If there is nothing better than true love, there is nothing worse than *doomed* love. I swallow and pick at my tunic.

Livia is arranging a wedding for me. I think I might sick myself, admitting this. I rush the rest of the truth out. *She's still deciding between grooms, so it won't be immediate, thank the gods, but it will surely happen before you could ever arrive.*

The connection between us grows ominously quiet. I can hear my own ragged breaths as I wait for Memnon's confusion or perhaps some sad and wounded response.

I should know better.

Some poisoned emotion spills down our bond. Not confusion, not sadness.

Jealousy. Vengeance.

No, little witch, he finally says. I hear his ominous laugh. *You won't be marrying* anyone *besides me.* His voice is confident and uncompromising. *I am coming for you. I will leave tomorrow at first light, and I* will *get there before a wedding takes place.*

And when I do, he continues, *I will make graves of these grooms and anyone else who comes between us.* Violent delight threads his words. *You're mine.*

CHAPTER 8
Roxilana, 18 years old

54 AD, Rome, Roman Empire

Memnon really is coming to Rome.

I don't fully believe it for the first several days, when he casually discusses the sights he's seeing. I'm still positive that the only people who actually travel such vast distances are semi-mythical figures, like Julius Caesar and Pompey. Like Alexander the Great and Augustus, Marc Antony and Cleopatra.

Then again, the boy who has haunted my mind for the last six years has become somewhat mythical to me.

Over the next several weeks, Memnon reaches out to me infrequently, but when he does, it's often to update me on his movements.

Roxi, I'm mounting my steed for the day. I won't leave it until the sun sets...

My men and I have entered Roman territory...

I am crossing the Danubius River...

Hope is a god, and it rules my every thought. I don't know what will happen once Memnon arrives—assuming he will, in fact, arrive—but the possibility is as exhilarating as it is terrifying. His threat to my future groom lingers at the forefront of my mind, especially as Livia presses forward with her plan to marry me off.

She's already picked out my husband, and it is a small blessing that it's neither of my two initial prospects. Instead, she has arranged to marry me to the textile merchant Titus's son, Quadratus, who is apparently taking over much of his father's business. I have seen my betrothed a time or two before. He seems pleasant enough, and I'm sure if Memnon did not exist, I might actually be giddy at the prospect of leaving Livia's home.

However, Memnon *does* exist, and he is coming for me, and that changes everything.

When Livia settles on the fabric for my wedding garment and then the veil, I'm unsure I'll ever wear either. And when the fabric is tailored to my body, I'm even more confident my Roman groom will never lay eyes on it, nor will his fingers graze the metal fibula that clasps it at my shoulders. I will never walk next to him in my orange wedding sandals, and he'll never smell the sweetness of the rose-and-clove perfume I would wear.

But the weeks slide into months, and my hope falters, held together only by the promises that Memnon whispers in my mind.

Little witch, I feel I'm growing near...

I've nearly found you. I sense it. I know you must sense it too...

Near as he is, I don't know that he's close enough. A date has been set for my wedding. The festivities have been planned and the guests invited.

Hope might be a god, but it is such a capricious, fickle one. It feels like it could gut me alive at any moment.

And then I'm sure it *will* gut me alive because, despite all of Memnon's assurances that he's closer than ever, my wedding day arrives.

CHAPTER 9
Roxilana, 18 years old

54 AD, Rome, Roman Empire

I lay in bed, listening to the sound of swallows chirping outside, dread souring my stomach. My wedding attire is waiting for me beyond the foot of my bed, but I cannot bring myself to look at it.

Are you awake? Memnon asks, jarring me from my thoughts.

I draw in a heavy breath. *Yes.*

Do you sense it, Roxilana? Our fateful meeting? Memnon's words feel like a caress. *I think today is the day. Passersby tell me I am close to the walls of your city.*

Memnon… I say softly. I cover my eyes with my hand. *My wedding—it's today.*

I'd been careful not to talk about the specifics of my betrothal to save us both the agony, but now that the ceremony is imminent, I cannot avoid discussing it any longer.

I sense his alarm. But rather than falling into hopelessness as I have, determination rises in him, paired with something like exhilaration.

We'll see about that.

The stola is the whitest I've ever worn, and the orange gossamer veil that goes on over it is as delicate as moth wings. I touch the fabric even as my gut twists with unease.

The gods must have a sense of humor.

I move to the window and stare out at the rooftops of Rome while, beyond my room, the faint sounds of singing float in from the distance. My muscles tense.

It's beginning.

I'm dressed and bejeweled, my cinnamon-colored hair braided and upswept and covered by my veil and a crown of flowers.

I'm supposed to be using this time to pray to Vesta about anointing this union. Instead, I send out a different, desperate wish to whatever god will listen—*please stop this wedding.*

Livia moves to the doorway of the room. "Are you ready?" It's not a question.

I nod anyway, my heart thundering as I turn more fully from the window to face her.

Livia's wearing a new stola for the occasion, and her hair has been elaborately coiffed, the long locks braided in the back with the end curls stacked at the crown of her head. The few pieces of jewelry she owns, she now wears.

She looks teary-eyed, and the sight is a shock to me. I have been so certain for so long that she was dying to get rid of me. That I was nothing but a nuisance. Seeing her emotional is a revelation.

She steps forward slowly, and in response, my magic sifts out of me, winding about my arms and torso, protecting me as it always does when she grows near. And like every other time this has happened, Livia does not notice the pale orange plumes of my power. To her—and seemingly everyone else in the city—my magic is invisible.

She takes my clammy hands and squeezes them in her own. "My sweet child, you are a vision."

I force out a tight smile as the singing outside grows louder.

"I know you have not wanted this. I have waited as long as I possibly could," she says fervently.

My brow furrows.

She notices the look and laughs. "You think I wanted to give you off? Of course not. I would've been happy to let things continue as they have." She swallows. "But this day had to come for you, as it must for all Roman women."

She's not wrong. Only a select few women ever escape being married off. And yet, I'd never applied that reasoning to my own situation.

"We have not always…gotten along," Livia continues. "I hope that can soon change."

"Gotten along?" I whisper, my voice hoarse. She makes it sound as though *I* was part of the problem. As though her rages were simply a matter of disagreement between equals and not a mother physically inflicting her own hurt and anger onto a child.

Livia looks ashamed for a moment before the growing commotion outside becomes unignorably loud.

"We haven't talked much about what will happen after today."

My gaze drops to my few belongings, which have been neatly placed in two woven baskets.

"There are some things, such as us working together, that will stay the same. But you will live under a different roof, and you will have new duties to your husband and his family…"

She shifts her weight, and my stomach twists.

"On your wedding night…" She clears her throat, her eyes dropping to the knotted rope that cinches my waist, then draws in a deep breath. "There are things that happen between married couples. Usually, it happens in the marital bed…" She still won't look me in the eye. "I'm sure you have at least heard of what I speak of—"

"Livia!" someone shouts into the room, saving me from this agonizing conversation. "They're here!"

She swallows. "Just be a good girl and listen to your husband. So long as you do as he says, you will be just fine." Her eyes are shiny with unshed tears when she gives my hands another squeeze, and I try not to wince at her affection, which feels grotesque, especially alongside her instructions.

"Come," she says, pulling me out of my bedroom.

Livia leads me into the main area of our house, where family and friends mill about. Once they see me, they begin to cheer, the sound blending with the singing happening out in the courtyard of the insula. Singing that's moving up the steps and toward our apartment.

My gaze makes it to the threshold of our house just as, from the open doorway, my groom steps into view.

Quadratus is stout, with curly, close-cropped hair, a wide smile, and a gap between his teeth. Most telling of all, he has kind eyes.

Strange that looking into them, what I feel most is panic

and dread. Like my future is a flip of a coin, on one side, I have the life of a tailor's assistant and a merchant's wife; on the other...Memnon and the vast unknown.

Quadratus crosses the room, his eyes fixed on me. Behind him enter his father, Titus, and the magistrate with his purple-edged toga. The rest of the groom's guests wait in the courtyard below, and Livia's guests leave our insula to join them until the ceremony is complete.

The magistrate scans the group of us. "Are both parties present?"

"We are," Livia answers for the room.

"All right." The magistrate unrolls a bit of papyrus and lays it out on the table.

The marriage contract. All it needs are our signatures for it to be complete. I stare at the papyrus, afraid I'm going to retch all over this pristine garment I'm wearing.

My groom moves over to me and reaches for my hand. My limb shakes as I take his.

I can't marry this man. I can't do it. I'm sure of it now that I'm touching him.

My gaze drifts to the doorway, and I fantasize about running straight out and not stopping until my legs gave out.

I could. It would ruin the reputations of everyone here, but I could do it.

Fear keeps my feet rooted in place.

Quadratus squeezes my hand, and when I glance at him, he gives me a reassuring smile, which makes this entire situation worse. Because I'm getting the impression that Quadratus is actually a good man. Maybe Livia deserves to have her reputation smeared, but I'm not sure my groom does.

The magistrate comes over to me and Quadratus. He nods to my groom, though he does not acknowledge me.

"I see you've found your bride," the Roman official says, his gaze dropping to our joined hands.

Livia titters with nervous laughter as she and Titus gather close.

The magistrate clears his throat. "Let's begin."

————————

Romans are big on omens. Good ones, bad ones—they dictate much of Roman life.

So when screams start up in the distance, I'm sure it's an ill omen for this marriage.

Not that I'd ever been hopeful about this particular wedding.

The magistrate, who has been droning about the legal obligations of this union, now pauses as the rest of the room shares uneasy looks. An omen like this might be reason enough to postpone the wedding. My heart soars at the possibility.

But neither Livia nor Titus indicate that they want the proceedings to stop.

So the magistrate resumes speaking, even as the screams continue.

I listen to them, the sound raising the hairs on my forearms. In Rome, when people scream, there's a good reason for it. Maybe an apartment tower has fallen, or a fire has broken out, or there's violence in the streets. And perhaps it's my imagination, but I swear the noise is getting closer.

"*Daughter*," Livia says sharply.

I blink, realizing she's been calling for me.

I clear my throat. "Yes…Mother?"

"Your vows," she says slowly.

My vows? We're already to that part?

Livia eyes me like she thinks I might run. And I feel

it in my blood again, that driving need to cast off all these garments and flee this house and never look back.

My groom gives my hand another squeeze, and when I glance at him, his face is reassuring.

"Where you are…" Quadratus prompts me.

There I am. That's how the vow goes. Short. Simple. All I need to do is utter those three words and the vows will be complete.

My skin pricks at the weight of everyone's stares.

I clear my throat, ignoring the way my magic is beginning to leak out of me again.

The screams draw closer. Beneath them, I hear something else, something that grows louder and louder.

Hoofbeats.

My heart begins to pound, and excitement replaces fear. Could it be…

Memnon?

The other individuals in the room are now glancing at the open doorway as the sounds of charging horses and screaming civilians become unignorable.

Little witch…I found you.

I press my free hand to my chest.

He's *here*. I don't think I fully believed he would be until this very moment.

A smile spreads across my face.

Yes, I say down our bond.

From my vantage point, I can see just a sliver of the courtyard below. Several guests from Quadratus's wedding procession begin to scatter, visibly terrified.

The magistrate leaves our side, striding to the doorway. "What in all the gods' names—" Whatever he sees steals the rest of his words from his tongue.

Livia glances nervously at me, then at my groom and future father-in-law. This is more than a bad omen; even she knows that.

All at once, the sound of stampeding horses halts, and the screams seem to die along with them.

Titus moves to the doorway, standing behind the magistrate. His knees visibly weaken, and he grips the doorframe tightly. When he glances back at his son and then me, I see the whites of his eyes.

"Father," my groom says, releasing my hand, "what is it?"

Before Titus has a chance to answer, the older man's attention returns to the courtyard. Then, rapidly, both he and the magistrate begin to back up.

"Get back!" the magistrate instructs us.

Livia whimpers as she moves to the far wall. The sound of her fear is so unusual that it nearly snags my attention.

But then I hear Memnon's voice—not in my head but outside, beyond the confines of the insula.

A shiver courses through me, drawing out goose bumps along my skin. In real life, his voice is fuller, deadlier, and more commanding.

"No one strikes another unless I give the order," he says in Sarmatian. The order is followed by the sound of metal clinking, leather straining, and boots scuffing on the stairs.

I can sense you within these walls, he says across our connection. *I am eager to meet you, my future wife.*

As though in a dream, I step forward, drawn by his words and this strange feeling I can only call fate.

"Memnon," I call out.

Quadratus recaptures my hand. "You need to stay back," he murmurs.

From Memnon, I feel a surge of excitement.

Your voice is lovelier than I could've imagined. I cannot wait to see you.

From the doorway, I notice strands of deep blue smoke—no, not smoke. *Magic.*

Memnon's magic.

My breath catches at the sight of it, and I stare, entranced, as it curls around the magistrate and Titus, forcing them to stumble back into my home.

Then, the biggest man I have ever seen fills the doorway, followed by four other bearded individuals at his back.

The smile that has begun to spread across my face wilts away. It's all I can do not to shrink back. There are five armor-clad barbarian warriors standing just outside the threshold.

My eyes, by their own accord, return to the first man, and I go still at the sight of him. He's the most foreign and ferocious person I've ever gazed upon. He's also the most *beautiful*—if something so obviously deadly could be called beautiful.

His skin looks like bronze—deeply tanned and oiled. His black hair hangs in waves down his back, held in place by a gold circlet, and more hair covers the lower part of his face.

The man's gaze immediately finds mine, and his smoky-amber eyes glitter like gems. It's impossible to notice them without also noticing the wicked scar that puckers the flesh to the side of one of them: the scar he got the day his magic Awoke.

My heart knows this man intimately, as does my magic. My very essence ends where his begins, and now that I've laid eyes on him, nothing—*nothing*—will ever compare.

"*Hello, my amage,*" he says in Sarmatian, the sound drawing out goose bumps. When he speaks to me, the roughness in his voice gentles. "*My eyes have waited years to see you.*" His gaze deepens. "*But it was worth the wait.*"

Memnon ducks his head as he steps inside, the other four men following him. Livia is screaming and Titus is shouting. The room collectively seems to shrink back as the men enter, and with good reason. All of them wear scale-mail armor and leather breeches. Scars and weapons adorn them like jewelry. These do not look like kind, placating men.

The magistrate, who's been lingering near the door, now edges around the five men and, casting them a final, frightened look, he slips out of the apartment, clearly not ready to lose his life over the brewing situation.

Memnon's gaze sweeps over the gathered group. "I am Memnon the Indomitable," he announces, "King of the Sarmatians."

King? I echo softly, a wave of vertigo washing over me. Memnon has never mentioned anything about being a king. But right now, he certainly looks it with the circlet on his head and the gold decorating his scale mail and weaponry. He carries more wealth on him than most people in this city see in a lifetime.

He continues. "My people are fierce, and my kingdom is vast. And today"—his gaze returns to me—"I've come to make this woman my queen."

My heart leaps at his words. For several inhalations, no one reacts.

Finally, I glance over at Livia. She cowers at the back of the room, her body visibly trembling, and again the sight of her frightened takes me aback. For so long, she was the looming menace. To think that she is terrified of Memnon, the one comfort in my life, is a strange twist of fate.

I face forward just as Memnon crosses the room to me.

He couldn't look less Roman if he tried. The long sleeves of his kurta have been pushed up, and his sun-darkened skin and several tattoos are exposed. That combined with his long hair and his strange battle attire have me mesmerized.

Quadratus moves in front of me, the effort as valiant as it is misguided.

Is this your intended? Memnon asks. I cannot see his expression, but for a moment, my heart trips and fear floods me.

I will make graves of these grooms, he had said.

Memnon's long, scarred fingers grip Quadratus's shoulder, and my magic begins leaking out of my palms. I don't know what will happen next, but now that I've seen Memnon in the flesh, I know with certainty that he is capable of ending lives. The violence written on his body is a testament to that.

But rather than accost my groom, the Sarmatian king pushes him aside as though the man were nothing more than a nuisance. Quadratus sucks in a sharp breath at the action, but he does nothing more. Whatever protection my intended was willing to give me, it stops here.

Pity for him, Memnon says, *he will leave this house brideless.*

He stands before me, massive, looming, and opulently attired in his armor, weaponry, and jewels. My mind could've never imagined a man as wildly beautiful as Memnon is.

Just as I drink him in, he takes me in as well, his eyes scorching in their intensity.

He cups my face, and gods, his touch! My knees go weak at the connection, and I cannot help but press my hand over his, just to keep that wonderful contact in place.

Memnon's surprisingly light eyes search mine as his thumb strokes the skin of my cheek. *Roxilana, the one who saved me from death, the one who Awoke my power.* His face breaks into a soft smile. *You are lovelier than I could've imagined.* He strokes my cheek again.

There's not enough air to breathe, and a deep part of me is sure my life only started now, at this very moment.

I remove my hand from his to lightly touch his face. My fingers trace the wicked-looking scar he received the day his magic Awoke. I follow the brutal trail of it across to his ear and down to his jaw. At the end of it, my fingers skim over the skin of his chin, then up to his full, curving lips. I soak it all in, entranced.

I cannot believe you're real, I say. I could spend a hundred years studying him and I'm sure it would not be enough.

My eyes rise to his, and for a moment, I fall into the depths of those intricate, brown irises, which are as dark as polished wood at their edges and light like amber at their centers.

My hand flattens against his cheek, and I lean forward, drawn in by—

"What is the meaning of this?" Titus demands, finally finding his voice.

Memnon, who had also been leaning in, now straightens, his gaze cutting to the man in question. Before he can respond, Livia steps forward, emboldened by Titus.

"G-Get your hands off my daughter, *barbarian*." Livia spits that last word out like an oath. Her eyes bounce from Memnon to the warriors that stand like sentinels near the door. "You offend the gods, coming in here on my daughter's wedding day."

"Ah, yes, her wedding day," Memnon says, his attention moving to my stola, then my flower crown and veil. Memnon says each word slowly, deliberately. "The only person Roxilana is marrying is *me*"—his gaze sweeps the room—"unless one of you would like to challenge me for her hand?"

It's quiet for several inhalations, likely while each person in the room measures up the Sarmatian.

"'Roxilana'?" Livia breaks the silence. "That is not my daughter's name. Whatever business you have with this Roxilana, you have come to the wrong house."

Memnon swings his gaze to her, and his eyes grow cold. "Have I, Livia?"

She blanches at the sound of her name on his lips. "How do you know who I am, barbarian?" she whispers.

He takes an ominous step forward. *How I have yearned to meet this woman, Roxi*, he says to me. *I have fantasized about the many ways I might punish her for making you suffer.*

To Livia, Memnon says, "I know *many* things about you, most of them unpleasant." He takes another step toward her. "Shall I list them? Or shall I save us both the hassle and simply cut you down where you stand?" As he speaks, his hand moves to touch the pommel of his sword.

A sense of calmness moves through me. My mind has agonized over this moment for the last two months, the moment I must act.

"No," I say, stepping between my adoptive mother and Memnon. "No blood will be spilled. Not when I chose you, Memnon." *Just as I have chosen you every day before this one*, I add down our bond.

Memnon's expression softens, longing replacing vengeance on his features.

Titus's voice cuts through the moment. "What sort of cruel trick is this, Livia?" the older man asks.

"Trick?" she says, her voice shrill. "*I* am the one who has

75

been tricked." Livia grabs me roughly by the upper arm. "I don't know what this is, girl," she whispers harshly, "or who you've gone and whored yourself to, but I will *not* have you ruining all my hard-made plans."

Memnon's eyes fall to where Livia's hand grips my forearm, her nails digging into my skin. The mood of the room shifts. He's still so close to her, and that banked vengeance rises once more as his magic pours out of him, magic that no one else in the room seems to notice.

Faster than I can follow, Memnon grabs Livia by the throat, forcing her to relinquish her grip on me, and in three quick steps he shoves her up against the back wall.

She gasps, pinned like a fish on a hook.

Memnon lowers his voice as he stares at her. "For years, I have fantasized about all the ways I could make you pay for hurting my mate."

Mate?

Livia chokes, her hands scratching at Memnon's. No one else in the room moves, all of us held in place by shock.

Ever since our minds first touched, Memnon has been my friend and confidante. But now, I'm having to face the reality of what he is: a king and a brutal warrior. One who moves and works with all the impunity a ruler has.

"It pains me to be merciful to scum such as yourself. But the woman you have repeatedly slighted I hold before all others, and since she has, unfortunately, asked me not to spill your bitter blood, I will stay my hand. But you *will* apologize to her." The command is punctuated by a ribbon of blue magic that encircles Livia's neck and settles into her skin.

With that, he releases my adoptive mother.

Livia crumples to the ground, her hand going to her throat as she gasps for air.

Behind me, I hear someone move forward.

Memnon reaches out a hand. "*Don't*," he cautions, never looking away from Livia.

When Livia glances up, she gazes fearfully at Memnon before turning to look at me. The eye contact is heavy; years unspool between the two of us—all that pain and companionship laid bare.

She opens her mouth, and I brace myself for her response, sure that whatever she has to say, it's not contrite. But the moment Livia's lips try to form words, her tongue seems to tie itself. She tries again, and the sounds come out as nothing more than a gargle. Her cheeks pinken with embarrassment and a touch of anger.

It takes me a moment to realize that whatever Livia was attempting to say, it was not an apology, hence why Memnon's magic stifled it. I stare, shocked that Memnon's magic can do this. That perhaps *my* magic can do this. I haven't used it in this manner before.

Livia presses her lips together then, giving up on saying anything. But now I sense rather than see that ribbon of Memnon's magic tightening around her neck. It begins to squeeze and squeeze like a phantom hand.

Livia's throat works, and she touches it, fear clouding her expression.

"I'm sorry." The words are ripped from her mouth. I see her swallow once, twice, three times, trying to shove something else down. The magic hasn't released its hold. "I'm sorry for hurting you and being...being a terrible mother," she finally says. Tears prick her eyes. I wish those tears were for me, but I doubt it.

There is a place within me where my pain and anger toward Livia fester. Where they might continue to fester long after today. But for the first time in my life, I can walk out of this house and leave her behind entirely. That is my sincerest wish—to never see her again, for her to become a memory and nothing more.

I move to her as though in a trance, crouching an arm span from where she lies.

"I'm leaving," I say. "And I'm never coming back."

Livia flinches.

Straightening, I cross over to Memnon, the gaping stares of my groom and his father pricking at my skin.

Memnon glances at his men, who have stoically watched this entire event unfold. "Ready the horses," he says in Sarmatian.

"This, this is outrageous," Titus says, but the words are spoken too softly to be a direct challenge.

Memnon's attention shifts to the man until he shrinks back. Then the Sarmatian's gaze flicks to the marriage document still resting on the table. He crosses over to it, the metal scales of his armor tinkling. His eyes rove over the text, and with a shock, I realize he can read.

He places his fingertips on the papyrus. A tiny blue plume of smoke is expelled from his hand, and as it curls against the document, fire sparks, then spreads.

"This wedding is called off," he says as we all watch the papyrus burn.

The Sarmatian king's eyes fall to mine, and they seem to smolder. "I have crossed rivers and kingdoms, I have fought armies and bandits to be here before you. For you are mine and I am yours, and those are my soul's deepest truths."

He reaches out, his palm extended in invitation. "Be mine before all the gods and live out your life as my queen and the ruler of my people," he beseeches.

I draw in a shaky breath. *This is the strangest proposal I have ever heard*, I tell him silently.

Memnon smiles a little.

After a moment, I take his hand in my own. "Yes," I say softly. "I will."

CHAPTER 10
Roxilana, 18 years old

54 AD, Rome, Roman Empire

I don't take a last look at the walls with their chipped green paint or meet the eyes of anyone else in that apartment. The only thing I concentrate on is the warmth of Memnon's hand and placing one foot in front of the other. We step out into sunlight so sharp, I have to close my eyes against the glare, and for a moment, enveloped in that heat and light, I am filled with absurd joy.

Once my eyesight clears, I take in the gathering below. Most of the wedding guests have scattered; those who remain cling to the edges of the courtyard, watching with wary eyes the group of fearsome Sarmatians astride their horses.

Memnon leads me down the stairs and over to his men. Among them is a riderless horse adorned with a bridle made of intricately carved wood and gold. I slow as I take the beast in. I have never sat on a horse, let alone ridden one. I don't know—

Memnon grabs me by the waist and hoists me up onto the creature. I yelp a little as my backside hits the saddle, and I nearly slide off it. Before I can, Memnon's magic is there, guiding me back into place. I marvel at the sight of it, at once both so similar to and so different from my own.

Memnon lifts himself into the saddle next, settling behind me.

I'm sitting sidesaddle when Memnon taps one of my thighs. "Little witch," he whispers against my ear. "This leg needs to be on the other side of my steed."

My face flushes. "Women don't ride like that."

"*Roman* women," he corrects. "But you are to be a *Sarmatian*, and our women sit astride their horses."

After a brief hesitation, I try swinging my leg over as Memnon suggested. Only, it snags on my long bridal tunic, the fabric pulling taut against my leg.

Gods, but this is embarrassing.

Worse, people are still watching—his people, plus the horrified crowd of onlookers gathered around us; I even manage to look up at the second-story windows of the insula and see some neighbors staring down at me with unbridled curiosity.

Before I can struggle too much, Memnon's hand runs lightly over my leg. Beneath it, I see his curling magic spread out, and the material caging in my leg splits up the side of my calf and midway up my thigh.

I inhale sharply, even as my leg slides into place. Now I'm sitting astride the horse, just as Memnon wanted, my tunic hiked up on one side and exposing me up to my thigh on the other.

Memnon pulls me against him, my backside cradled in his lap, my spine flush against his armor. This is by far the most intimate I've been with a man, and between this and my exposed leg, I feel positively indecent. The fact that this indecency centers around Memnon, the very person who has haunted my mind for so long, gives me a perverse thrill, Roman modesty be cursed.

Memnon whistles, and the group of Sarmatians, which consists of my husband and four other men, begins to move. My stomach tumbles as the steed beneath us lurches forward. I catch a final glimpse of the apartment I lived in for eleven long years. Livia stands in the doorway, weeping so hard her whole body bows from the effort. Perhaps I am wicked right down to my bones because the sight of her pain does absolutely nothing to me.

Memnon's horse exits the courtyard, and my apartment and the remaining wedding guests are swept from sight. Relief sweeps in, along with a lingering sense of disbelief.

I…escaped that life, that fate. Memnon rescued me from it.

I relax more deeply into the man himself as our mounted procession steers their horses down the cobbled streets of Rome, causing the locals to shout or dart out of the way.

Memnon's grip on me tightens a little. "It is a wonder, finally having you in my arms," he breathes against my ear. "Do you feel how perfect we fit against each other?" he says. "You were made to be here."

So many emotions course through me—giddiness, joy, fear, and a sense of rightness that goes far beyond fitting together well.

I glance down at his arm, studying the way tattoos wrap around it. My fingers begin to trace one of them, which is some sort of animal—maybe a ram. Beneath my touch, Memnon's skin pebbles and his fingers flex against me.

I cannot believe you are real, I finally say to him.

When I envisioned meeting Memnon, my mind never made it this far. I couldn't really imagine his face or his hair, his skin or the tattoos that decorate it. And I definitely couldn't picture his ferocious presence, no matter how many times he spoke of this part of himself.

Again, his grip tightens. *Neither can I,* he admits, his voice breathless even in my head.

Ahead of us, a cluster of Roman soldiers span the road, blocking our way.

Not just any Roman soldiers, I realize as we get closer, but the Praetorian Guard, the emperor's personal unit of soldiers. They wait for us, their armor gleaming in the sun, their shields and weapons at the ready.

At my back, Memnon stiffens, and a bit of his power leaks out, encircling us.

Roxi, you are safe, he promises.

Memnon releases my midsection for a moment to hold up his arm, making a closed-fist gesture. Behind us, the other horses slow, then come to a full stop.

For several inhalations, all is quiet as the two groups take each other in. The back of my neck prickles. It feels like we're on the brink of battle.

Slowly, the Praetorian Guard lowers their weapons. Only then do I let out a shaky exhale. The man I'm assuming is the group's prefect steps forward.

"On behalf of the emperor, your presence is required at the imperial palace," he announces.

The *emperor?* I cannot have heard him correctly.

Then again, at my back is a foreign *king.* Perhaps this is not an unusual situation for him.

I rode unimpeded into the heart of the empire, Memnon says to me. *I'm guessing your emperor is displeased about that.*

How did *you manage that?* I ask. No one gets into Rome without the emperor willing it.

Another wisp of Memnon's power unfurls from beneath his hand, twisting and curling into the air in front of us.

Magic.

"Did your emperor not get my missive?" Memnon says to the guard. "We had agreed that my men and I were to enter and exit Rome peacefully today."

I only know it's a lie because of what Memnon just silently told me. But between his formidable presence and the confidence in his voice, I wouldn't have guessed it.

The guard hesitates for the barest breath, then regains his composure. "I must insist we escort you to the palace."

For a long, tense moment, Memnon does nothing, and I can almost hear him weighing his options. Finally, he whistles, and one of his men moves up to his side.

"It seems our plans have changed," he says in Sarmatian. "Be ready for anything. These men are treacherous."

Memnon's gaze returns to the Roman guard once more, and in Latin he says, "Lead on."

CHAPTER 11
Roxilana, 18 years old

54 AD, Rome, Roman Empire

We're taken to the Domus Transitoria, Emperor Nero's palace, our group hemmed in by the many guards around us. I try not to gape as we enter the massive structure, but even among the opulence of Rome, this is unprecedented— marble floors, lavish frescos, gilded columns, statues of gods and rulers so masterfully crafted they could be the real people.

Our footfalls echo through the space as the Praetorian Guard take us deeper into the structure. Finally, we stop before a portiere, the curtains a rich Tyrian purple, and the prefect turns to us.

"Your men can come no farther," he tells Memnon.

Memnon nods. Without glancing at his men, he says in Sarmatian, "Wait here for me. Accept no offerings from these men; they are known for their deceit. Should any Roman move against you, strike them down. I will handle the rest."

I manage to keep my expression carefully blank, but inside I quake at his words.

Memnon's men move away from our backs. Only then does the prefect sweep aside the curtained doorway to let us through.

The receiving hall we step into is just as richly adorned as the rest of the palace, the floors marble, the walls painted with various myths of Rome. Low couches and side tables are scattered throughout the room for men to recline in and chat. Even with the gilded throne situated at the back, it hardly seems like an appropriate room to face off with an intruder such as Memnon.

The space is currently empty, save for the emperor's guardsmen that file in behind us, the prefect among them. I eye the men warily.

You are safe, my amage, Memnon insists again, his hand going to the small of my back and lingering there, his touch like a brand.

I glance up at him, and as soon as my eyes take in his profile, I cannot seem to look away, ensnared by his violent beauty.

Will you tell me now what that endearment means? I manage to ask.

Memnon glances down at me, the corner of his mouth curved up, like he might know I'm fawning over him. *Is it not obvious?* he asks. *It means* queen.

My eyes widen. I always assumed the term meant something like *dearest* or *beloved*. Some sweet sentiment that didn't have a proper Latin translation. Instead, he's been giving me a title I knew nothing of. And gods, he's been doing so for *years*.

I'm so caught up in the revelation, I don't notice the

86

older woman who strides through the far doorway, flanked by more guards. Not until she speaks.

"You'll need to disarm yourself before you speak with my son," she commands, her face pinched in displeasure. She's dressed in all the opulence of a ruler herself, adorned in reds and golds and dripping in jewelry.

So that must be Nero's mother, Agrippina. I've heard whispers about her—that her son might rule the empire, but *she* rules *him*.

Memnon looks vaguely amused at the order, but nonetheless, he removes his bow and the arrows strapped to his side, the weapons clattering as he drops them to the ground. Next, he removes his sword, then a dagger from his waist, tossing the blades away from him, the sound echoing loudly in the room.

He holds his now-empty arms out at his sides.

"Step away from your weapons, King," Agrippina demands.

Memnon steps forward, arms still stretched out at his sides. Without thinking, I move along with him, the action earning me a snicker from one of the many guards stationed along the edges of the room.

"Am I harmless enough now?" Memnon asks.

"There is no such thing as a harmless Sarmatian," Agrippina says. But she still nods to the prefect. He breaks away from the rest of the guards and heads to the back curtained doorway. When he returns, the emperor is with him.

"Emperor Nero Caesar Augustus," the prefect announces, "Head of Priests, Holder of the Tribunician Power, and Father of the Fatherland."

Nero is…not as I imagined him. Not as big, not as

heroic, not as noble—but then, perhaps I pictured the emperor to be the personification of Roman might, larger and grander than the rest of us mortals. But not even Nero's golden armor nor his rich purple toga and the cape he wears can offset his soft, boyish frame or the baby fat that still clings to his face.

Despite his innocuous appearance, the hairs along my arms rise. He may look young, but he does have a brutish set to his features that makes me want to avoid his attention.

He crosses the room while the prefect breaks away to take position nearby. It may not matter that Nero does not look like some hero of our empire because he wears his power like a mantle. It's there in his swagger and his loud, echoing footsteps, in the obstinate set of his jaw and the strange shine of his eyes.

When he gets to us, the emperor barely registers my existence, even as I dip my head. Instead, he openly stares at Memnon.

"A barbarian warlord," he says with awe. "I've heard stories of your kind."

"Nero," Agrippina cautions at his side, her expression a great deal more wary.

The emperor looks at his mother, who glances back at the gilded chair behind them. Nero scowls at her until Agrippina casts her eyes to the ground. Even then, he continues to stare at her, his expression growing colder.

"If you like the throne so badly, why don't you sit at it?" he says to her, his words biting, *challenging*.

My eyes dart between the two of them as the suddenly tense moment stretches on.

When Agrippina says nothing more, Nero returns his attention to Memnon. "My mother thinks you are a threat," he says. "And that it's unbecoming of an emperor to stand so close to a barbarian.

"But I know better. Only a fool would think of attacking me openly." Nero tilts his head. "Isn't that right?"

I sense Memnon studying the emperor, and it's all I can do to not look over at the Sarmatian king. *My* king. A thrill runs through me at the thought.

"Indeed," Memnon says.

Nero turns to his mother, who has only just lifted her head. "See?" he says, gesturing to Memnon. "The man is no fool. He even speaks the common tongue." Nero turns back to us. "Not many brutes do. No wonder you are king."

There's a mocking edge to Nero's words, though I cannot tell if the young ruler is aware of it himself.

His eyes trail up and down Memnon. "I hear you shoot from horseback. You'll have to give me a demonstration."

"Nero," Agrippina again cautions.

The emperor laughs, as though purposefully goading her. "Maybe we can make my mother the target. Then we'd see just how good of a shot you really are."

The earlier tension in the room ratchets up, and magic sifts out from my palms. Memnon is carefully scrutinizing both mother and son.

"I am not interested in starting a war," Memnon finally says.

"You would be ending one," Nero corrects, his casual tone chilling me. His mother's lack of reaction while her son openly discusses her murder is just as unsettling.

"But you surprise me," Nero continues. "You rode into Rome armed and dressed for battle, yet you don't want war? How *very* interesting."

Memnon says nothing to that, though to me he admits, *I wanted to impress you.*

My eyebrows rise, an action that shrewd Agrippina notices, her eyes narrowing and her lips pursing. But Nero is still captivated by Memnon and pays me no mind.

"What is your name?" Nero asks Memnon. The emperor's eyes keep dropping to his scale mail and perhaps the few scars and tattoos that peek out from beneath his clothing and armor.

"Memnon the Indomitable, ruler of the Sarmatians."

Memnon the Indomitable? I say across our bond, remembering that he mentioned this title earlier as well. I don't know if I'm teasing or curious.

Please tell me you're impressed, he says.

Oh, very. Normally, I'd have a wittier response, but right now, I feel like I'm in the jaws of some great predator, and managing a light tone at all is an effort.

"Well, *Memnon the Indomitable*," Nero says, cutting into the silent conversation happening between me and the Sarmatian, "I was told you entered my city uninvited and unannounced with a small contingent of men, then proceeded to enter the house of one of our citizens. Sometime later, you then left it with a woman," he says. "A woman who, I'm told, was to be married on this very day."

For the first time since he entered the room, the emperor finally turns and takes me in. His eyes have barely settled on me when Memnon's indigo magic begins circling around my body protectively.

Nero cocks his head as his eyes slide up and down my form. "Orange veil, flower crown, stark white tunic, a belted knot of Hercules, and—" Without preamble, he reaches out and lifts my skirts. Memnon's magic streams out of him then, and he takes an ominous step toward me and the emperor as Nero finishes, "Matching orange sandals. This looks to me like a fucking stolen bride."

Nero's eyes still have an unsettling gleam to them, but the levity he carried only moments before is gone when he drops my skirts and returns his attention to Memnon. If the emperor notices the Sarmatian king is now closer to him, he doesn't let on, though Agrippina looks positively alarmed.

"So," Nero continues, "I am perplexed when you say you are not interested in war. Because entering my city armed for battle and stealing away one of my citizens' wives is a call to war." The emperor's eyes briefly flick to me again before returning to Memnon. "Should I view it as such, Sarmatian?"

Memnon stares the emperor down, his brown eyes almost luminous. Whatever hopes of diplomacy either man had, they rapidly dwindle as Memnon's magic begins to pour out of him, gathering like storm clouds around us.

"No," Memnon says, "that was not an act of war." His magic shoots out of him, the arms of it reaching across the room in an instant, enveloping Agrippina and the guards posted along the edges of the room. *"This is."*

In unison, the eyes of Nero's mother and his guards roll back, and their legs fold.

Body after body hits the ground with a dull thump, and I choke on a scream at the sight of them lying motionless on the floor, my knees growing weak.

Are they...dead?

No, merely unconscious, Memnon says, overhearing my thought.

Nero glances around him, aghast. "W-What have you done?" he demands, his voice rising. "Guards!"

Memnon steps into Nero's space, and the young emperor stumbles back, then falls, hitting the marble floor hard.

Nero glares up at Memnon. "I shall have you whipped

in the streets for this and your whole army crucified," he declares, a panicked note to his voice.

Memnon bends down and threads his fingers through the emperor's curly hair. "Will you?" he says, amused as he tilts Nero's head back.

Then, to my horror, Memnon drags him upward, causing the young ruler to yelp and reach for his head, wriggling like a fish on a hook. "I would enjoy seeing your rotting corpse command my death," Memnon says.

Nero tries to lunge for the Sarmatian king, but it does no good. Between Memnon's magic and strength, it's painfully obvious the foreign ruler is entirely in control.

Memnon jerks Nero's head back again, baring his neck. "Look how vulnerable you are, mighty emperor. I could kill you—that might make a nice wedding gift for my *stolen* bride. I could make it slow, then force your men to fight one another so it looks like a rebellion from within your guardsmen."

I stare at Memnon as though he's a stranger. And that is the terrible truth. I never imagined him to be this cruel and calculated.

Nero is now visibly shaking, and for all his earlier confidence, he looks genuinely terrified. "What you're saying is impossible."

Memnon cocks his head, his hair stirring a little at the movement. "Is it?"

Over Nero's shoulder, two of the unconscious guards begin to rise, their bodies limp. I stagger back at the macabre sight. Memnon's magic churns around them, clearly propping them up. I've never considered using my power this way. I didn't know it was even possible.

The moving bodies catch Nero's attention, and I can see

the whites of his eyes as he stares at the upright men with limp limbs.

The emperor returns his gaze to Memnon. "H-how are you doing that?" he asks, his voice wavering.

"Do you still intend to stop me?" Memnon says. I swear his eyes begin to glow.

In Nero's own eyes, tears have formed. "Please…no. We can come to some sort of agreement."

Memnon raises his brows.

"You can have the woman," Nero adds.

"I want to believe you," Memnon says, "but you do not strike me as a man of your word. Shame." His power stirs up again.

Now I know I'm not mistaken—Memnon's eyes *are* glowing.

"Wait!" Nero pleads. "Wait—!"

But the light doesn't dim from the Sarmatian king's eyes. Strands of Memnon's hair lift into the air.

I stumble back as Nero cries out, *"What are you?"*

"The closest thing to a god you will ever lay eyes on." Memnon's voice has deepened, taking on an unnatural lilt. He releases his hold on Nero's hair, but only so he can grip the emperor by the temples. More magic pours out of him and strands of it slip into Nero's nose and mouth.

The young emperor's back arches and his eyes glaze over.

"Roxilana, the woman before you, *is mine.*" The hairs along my arms rise as I hear the power in his voice. "You will send in a marriage agreement, one that she and I will sign and you will oversee. You will personally sign off on our marriage because you believe in its validity."

A shiver runs down my spine at the order. Memnon is not merely asking the emperor to do his bidding; he is asking Nero to alter his very thoughts. Setting aside whether such a spell is even possible, wielding this sort of power is wrong. Unholy.

And I will be married to it.

"I have committed no wrongs," Memnon continues, power still threading through his words, "and you have come to remember that you *did* allow me entrance into the city. I and my people are honored guests, and my future wife and queen is to be treated with utmost reverence while we are here."

I edge away from the two men, my pulse racing.

Memnon pauses, and his head lifts. Those glowing eyes appear sightless, even as they look at me.

You're safe, little witch, he says softly down our bond.

I think that was supposed to be reassuring, but those illuminated eyes and his unyielding grip on the emperor are souring the effect.

Returning his attention to Nero, Memnon says, "You won't remember any of this." Magic tinges his words. "If anyone questions your decisions on this matter, you will make it clear that *you* are the emperor and everyone else must give you their unquestioning loyalty."

Memnon releases Nero, then backs up slowly. His hair lowers and the glow of his eyes begins to fade.

Memnon doesn't give a command to the individuals lying asleep on the ground, but they begin to stir, and then, one by one, they wordlessly rise to their feet.

I expect them to appear confused, but they stare blankly ahead. Not even outspoken Agrippina does much other than frown a little.

Another chill moves through me.

Nero blinks and his shoulders straighten. "Well," he says

a few moments later, clearing his throat. "This has been a thoroughly enlightening discussion."

I tense, a part of me sure this is where we get executed.

"Burrus," Nero calls out over his shoulder, his eyes still on us, "bring me a wedding document."

"A wedding document?" Agrippina murmurs as one of the guards exits the room.

Nero's eyes are on Memnon when he says, "The Sarmatian wishes to make a Roman woman his queen. We could do with an alliance between our nations."

Agrippina's frown deepens, but she still has that absent look to her eyes.

"And with an alliance," Nero says pointedly to Memnon, "perhaps we could discuss some business matters? Rome is always in need of mercenaries, and word is that you and your men are the best."

Memnon inclines his head. "I am always willing to do business with Rome," he says demurely, as though he didn't have this man by the hair only seconds ago.

Only you and I remember such events, Memnon says down our bond. *To him, we are honored guests.*

I glance at the Sarmatian king, astounded, even as his attention remains focused on Nero.

The emperor nods, scrutinizing Memnon, perhaps a touch suspiciously.

But whatever momentary suspicions come over him, they smooth away at the sound of quiet footfalls against the stone floor. Burrus, the prefect, reenters the room with a roll of papyrus, a reed pen, and an inkpot.

"Ah yes, the moment we bind you to your bride."

I shift my weight as Burrus comes up to Nero and hands him the pen. Two servants enter the room, carrying a small table between them. Crossing over to us, they set the piece of furniture down in front of Nero, then leave, quiet as mice.

The prefect sets the inkpot on the table, then unfurls the papyrus. My eyes devour the marriage document, noting the lines and lines of indecipherable text written on it. It looks a little different than the one I saw earlier today, but my heart still pounds at the sight of it.

Stepping forward, Nero dips the reed pen into the ink and writes his name at the bottom of the parchment. "Sarmatian," he says, still holding the wedding document in place, "do you write as well as speak Latin?"

In response, Memnon steps forward and takes the reed pen from the emperor. Turning the papyrus to face us, Memnon places a bracing hand on the document and writes his name in Latin.

Nero grunts after the king is finished. "Not bad for a barbarian."

Memnon turns to me and holds out the reed pen.

I stay rooted in place, even as my pulse gallops away. I traded one marriage for another. The fact that it is with a man I have loved for many moons does not matter to my nerves at the moment.

That, however, is only partly why I hesitate.

I don't know how to write, I admit.

Memnon's expression gentles, the shift causing my insides to tighten. *Then we'll do it together*, he says.

I swallow, then nod. *Okay.*

Tentatively, I take the pen from Memnon and turn to the papyrus before us, ignoring how my hand trembles. I sense Nero and Agrippina watching me, and my cheeks flush at their attention.

Moving behind me, Memnon reaches out and wraps his

hand around mine. I can feel his heat and the way his much larger body molds against mine. I'm so distracted by it that I nearly miss the moment he dips the pen in my hand into the inkwell.

"If the girl is illiterate, any marking will do," Nero says.

"I want all who read this to know my wife's name," Memnon says.

"Very well," Nero says, turning back to his mother and muttering something under his breath.

Slowly we'll do this, Memnon instructs. *R-O-X...* He goes letter by letter, naming each one as we write them. Though the letters look a little shaky, eventually my Sarmatian name appears on the paper.

Next to my ear, Memnon lets out a sharp exhale, and I can feel his shock down our connection as he stares at the parchment.

We're married, little witch.

"Well, there it is," Nero says. "You're..." His eyes unfocus, and my gut twists at his conflicted expression. He blinks. "I almost forgot—the *vows*." To Memnon, he says, "To complete the ceremony, you must say your vows. Sarmatian, they are quite simple. All you have to say is 'Where you are,' and your woman will finish the rest."

Memnon moves to my side and takes the reed pen, setting it on the table. Then he grasps my clammy hands, turning me to face him.

For the first time since I entered this room, I fully face him. I would be lying if I said Memnon no longer looks terrifying. Everything about him, starting with his wicked scar, seems to elicit fear. But his eyes are soft and oddly devoted as they look at me, and his thumb strokes the skin of my hand in a disarmingly comforting way, and I can feel his earnest intention.

Memnon doesn't wait for preamble. "Where you are," he begins.

Despite my nerves and the pounding of my heart, I give his hands a squeeze. *Cannot believe I'm doing this.* "There I am."

Now, we are married.

My heart still thunders, and my skin feels like lightning dances along it. Across from me, Memnon smiles so big, it seems to reach every corner of his face, and it transforms him from a menace into something else entirely. At the sight, my blood heats and my lower belly clenches.

He ducks his head after a moment, as though to hide his earnestness. That, somehow, only makes him more endearing.

"Congratulations," Nero says. "I give your union my personal blessing. May it be long and prosperous." After a moment, he glances at Agrippina. "Don't you agree, Mother?" he says, clearly goading her.

Agrippina couldn't appear to care less. Her eyes are still a little clouded and distant and her face is empty of expression.

Nero frowns, seemingly annoyed at even her tepidness. Facing us again, he says, "There are gladiatorial games later today. In honor of your nuptials, you will attend as my guests."

"That is very benevolent of you—" Memnon begins.

Nero smiles a little, looking pleased with himself, and Agrippina murmurs something agreeable.

"However," Memnon continues, "my men are eager to get back to our lands, and I…" Memnon's eyes drink me in, but he seems at a loss as to what to say. I can feel the heat of his emotions but nothing more.

"Nonsense," Nero interrupts. "You've traveled all this

way. You barbarians shall have a taste of Rome before you leave it, so you might know for certain that it is the best city in the entire world."

Memnon looks like he might protest, and his magic is beginning to spill out of him once more. But after a pause, the Sarmatian gives Nero a terse nod.

"Excellent!" Nero says. "My guards will lead you and your men to some rooms. Take a bath. Enjoy your wife. We will speak again this afternoon."

CHAPTER 12
Roxilana, 18 years old

54 AD, Rome, Roman Empire

Enjoy your wife.

My mind keeps snagging on Nero's parting words.

I've been so caught up in avoiding marriage to Quadratus that I hadn't really processed what being married to *Memnon* might mean or what that future would actually look like.

But I'm processing it now, as a palace servant escorts us and the rest of Memnon's men to the rooms we're to stay in here at Nero's palace. Gods, am I processing it.

The jubilance I should be feeling is marred by the reality of the last several hours. Memnon's violence, his foreboding magic, and the secrets he kept from me—secrets like the fact he is a literal *king*—all of it makes me feel like perhaps I was very, very naive to agree to any of this.

Perhaps I made a grave mistake.

The male servant shows us first the rooms where

Memnon's men will be staying, then he takes the group of us to…ours.

The servant stops in front of a wooden door and opens it. Deep within, I catch sight of rich red walls illuminated by flickering light.

"Your rooms, good king," the servant says.

Memnon inclines his head in thanks, and the servant dips his head and parts, leaving the group of us alone.

I eye the bedroom. I'm afraid to go in.

I don't know if he hears my thoughts or not, but Memnon places a gentle hand on my back. "Go ahead," he urges softly. "I need to speak with my men for a moment."

Haltingly, I enter the room, the tread of my sandals loud within the crimson walls of the chamber. Detailed frescos adorn them, most depictions of various myths, none of which end well for the woman.

I glance back to the doorway of our room, where Memnon speaks softly to one of his men, our marriage document tucked under one of his arms. I take a moment to stare at that broad back and the black hair that cascades down it, and I try to see the familiarity in it.

There is none. For as intimately as I've known Memnon's mind, physically, he's still a stranger to me.

Memnon clasps the warrior he speaks with on the shoulder, and with that, his men depart, the sounds of their footfalls and rustling armor growing fainter and fainter, until Memnon and I are painfully alone.

The Sarmatian king turns to me then, and I cannot help the bolt of terror that courses through my veins. Partly it's his physical presence, but I think it's more the memory of the way Memnon controlled an entire room against their will and the way none of them seemed to remember it afterward.

If Memnon could do that to an *emperor*, what might he do to me?

"Don't look at me like that," he says hoarsely in Sarmatian as he enters the room, placing the marriage document on a side table.

"Like what?" I respond in his mother tongue.

"Like you are afraid," he says, crossing over to me, the weapons that were returned to him now shifting with his movements.

I open my mouth to deny it, but the words don't come. "I *am* afraid," I finally whisper, edging away from him.

When he notices, he stops.

The two of us spend a moment staring at each other. He's painfully handsome, and there's an undeniable thrum between us. But I am unnerved by him. This isn't at all how I imagined our first meeting going.

"You bent an entire room to your will—you could've overthrown the emperor himself," I say.

Memnon watches me carefully. "I did," he agrees. "And yes, I could've."

I expected him to defend himself, and it throws me that he doesn't. "How is what you did even possible?" I finally ask.

He ducks his head, his jaw tightening. "I recently discovered that I have a certain…extra ability," he admits. "I can read people's minds with a touch and alter their memories through my will." Slowly, his gaze lifts from the ground to mine.

My breath catches. "So I cannot do what you just did?"

The corner of his mouth curves up. "No."

I take that in. "Will you ever alter *my* mind?" I ask, my voice hoarse.

The smile vanishes from his face, and for an instant, I see *woundedness* of all things. "Never."

"Never?" I repeat, skeptical. A power like that is far too tempting.

"I will swear an unbreakable oath on it, my queen," he says.

I don't know what an unbreakable oath even is, but I'm in no mood to be making pacts with this man. Besides, curiously enough, I believe him.

My gaze floats up to the golden circlet he wears. "I don't want your oath…*King*." I don't know how to say that word in Sarmatian.

It's xsaya, Memnon offers.

I tuck that bit of information away for later. I draw in a shaky breath, then blow it out. "How long have you been a ruler?"

"Four years," he eventually admits.

Four entire years.

"And you never thought to tell me?" I say softly, hurt at the omission.

Memnon has the grace to look apologetic. "I didn't want you to see me as anything but Memnon—*your* Memnon."

My Memnon. And now he really is mine.

His eyes search my own. "Do I unnerve you still?" he asks.

I hadn't realized he had noticed, but of course, through our connection, I cannot hide anything.

When I don't immediately answer, his eyes flicker. "It's my appearance, then."

I cannot deny that his large, battle-scarred body is partly to blame.

Memnon withdraws the gold-hilted dagger at his side. I stumble back at the sight of it, but I've no sooner moved away from him than Memnon gathers his unbound hair and brings the edge of the blade to his thick, dark locks.

His intentions register an instant before his arm moves. With one brutal stroke, he slices off his hair.

I let out a startled cry. "What are you doing?" I say, my eyes round.

Memnon drops the shorn locks to the ground, then grabs a clump of the remaining shoulder-length hair, cutting into it once more.

"S-stop!" I insist.

Reluctantly, he does so. But when he meets my eyes, I still see determination in them.

"Memn—"

He grasps his beard and begins to saw away at it too, taking out patches at a time. Somehow, it looks even worse than his shorn hair.

"Memnon, stop!" A bit of magic enters my voice, and my power reaches out, prying his hand and weapon away from his face.

But it's too late. The choppy sections of hair that remain look ridiculous, especially his beard.

I swallow as I take it in.

"You've ruined your hair," I say. All of it.

"It was frightening you." In his words, I hear the boy I grew up with—the vulnerable, sweet boy who whispered kind words to me late at night and confessed truths he told no one else.

My eyes sting. "Oh, Memnon," I say softly. I move to him. "You don't need to change yourself to please me." Tentatively, I reach out a hand. "Give me that blade."

Without a word, he flips the dagger in his hand, holding the hilt out to me. I take it from him, then move to his back. Unlike me, he doesn't tense or balk at the fact that I'm holding a weapon so close to him.

His hair is even worse than I first thought. I touch several bluntly shorn strands of it, trying not to react at the feel of it between my fingers or the fact that I can smell the perfumed oil he must've rubbed onto it. How many days I imagined touching this hair…

I don't think I ever imagined it would be in this context.

I'm not sure how much of his hair is even salvageable, and I am no hairdresser.

"You are better off sticking to violence," I murmur, continuing to run my fingers through the thick locks. I swear I see a shiver pass through him, but otherwise he holds still as I inspect the damage. "I'm going to try to fix your hair, but I'll need you to kneel."

I place a hand on Memnon's shoulder, and now I know I'm not imagining his reaction. Through our bond, I feel a burst of pleasure at my touch.

He lowers himself obediently, though after he does so, he glances over his shoulder. "Is this all just some elaborate ploy to get a king on his knees before you?"

"Memnon," I admonish.

He laughs, and my eyes are caught on that smile. "What?" he says innocently.

But now I'm grinning as I step in close. I bring Memnon's heavy dagger up to his locks, marveling at how big the blade is. Grabbing a longer section of hair, I begin to saw at the strands. Memnon's blade is wicked sharp, and it slices through the hair fairly easily.

I've never done this before, I admit down our connection.

I trust you.

My stomach twists at the admission, and I feel strange, unmoored. I trim another lock. *Your long hair must have meant something to you*, I say. All of Memnon's men had worn it similarly long.

He makes a noise in the back of his throat. *It's hair. It will grow back.*

Bit by bit, I shape his hair. Unfortunately, between the deep cuts he made to it and my own novice skill, I have to cut away most of it. The wavy locks that remain fall to the nape of his neck—or else they slip over his eyes.

Once I'm finished, I move around to his front and look at the uneven tufts of his beard. It really is worse than his hair. Parts of it have been cut all the way down to his skin.

I kneel before him and reach for his face, only pausing a finger span away. "Can I touch you?"

He makes an amused sound. "I rode for two months so that I might feel your embrace." His eyes dance like fire. "Of course you can touch me."

My breath hitches at his admission, and something as hot and bright as lightning courses between us. Lowering my gaze, I run my fingers through Memnon's beard, marveling at the bristly texture of it. As I do so, he closes his eyes, a smile touching his lips.

It's all going to have to go, I say.

He opens his eyes. "Do it."

I try to ignore that burning gaze as I bring the dagger's edge up to his jawline. If I knew little about cutting hair, I know even less about this. Luckily, I have a little magic to work with.

I use it now, calling on it to guide my movements as I draw the blade up his cheek, cutting away his facial hair.

Memnon stays still and lets me—for the most part. I notice that when I cup his face to get the angle of the cut just right, he leans into the touch. And just now, when my fingers graze his cheek, he turns and casually brushes his lips against them.

I narrow my eyes, even as I smother a smile. "You're a sneaky, wicked man," I say.

"I have no idea what you're talking about."

"Uh-huh."

I get to the section of his beard that obscures the bottom of his scar. Once I cut the hair away, I trace the thickened line of flesh, frowning. "This looks like it hurt."

At my touch, Memnon's eyes close again. "It did," he murmurs, "but I am grateful for it."

I move to his jaw and shave away the last bits of his facial hair.

"Why is that?" I ask, focusing on my work. I cannot imagine being grateful for something so heinous.

"Because it made you stroke my skin."

He opens his eyes and gazes down at where I kneel in front of him. That *look* again. I feel it in my very marrow, just as I have felt it before across our connection. My blood heats as I recognize it for what it is.

Longing.

I lower the blade, my gaze dropping to Memnon's lips. Want flares through me at the sight of them.

Those lips are *mine*.

The thought surprises me.

They are, Memnon agrees. *All of me is yours.*

I drag my gaze back to his eyes, and once more I see that yearning. I could swim in the depths of it, it's so vast. And it matches the ache within me, the one I thought I'd have to live with forever.

But I no longer have to simply yearn for Memnon; he's right here.

Of course you can touch me, he'd said moments ago. I hope he meant it.

I place a hand on his smooth cheek. There's no point in denying this pull I've felt to him. Without another thought, I lean in.

The moment our mouths meet, it's heat and flint and sparks. A shiver runs through me, and down our bond, I feel Memnon's elation.

His calloused hands cup my face so, so gently as his lips respond to mine, each sweep of them coaxing.

I drop his dagger, the weapon landing on the ground with a heavy clink. Then my hands are on him, skimming over his metal armor and the taut, warm flesh of his neck before I thread my fingers through his hair. I cling to him like I might fall away if I let go.

I can feel the full power of him then. Not just his physical muscle, but the magic he's steeped in. I swear I taste it—on his lips, his tongue. I'm breathing it in and bathing in it.

The longer we kiss, the more I notice this growing, spiraling need within me, one that I don't fully understand but that has me tugging at Memnon's armor.

Against my lips, he laughs softly.

I stiffen at the sound, and heat floods my cheeks at the mocking edge of it.

No, no, my queen, not mocking, never mocking, he insists.

I have dreamed of this moment for years, and still it surpasses my wildest imaginings. He runs the back of his index finger along my cheek.

His words banish my worry, and I'm simply happy. So unbelievably happy.

Memnon pulls away then, though he still holds my face in his hands. Around us, the air is obscured by our mixed magic—orange and blue, and where it's thoroughly mixed, a bruise-hued purple.

Memnon searches my features, his hands warm against my cheeks. "I cannot believe you are here in my arms." He smiles again, just as he did after we spoke our vows, and like then, it lights up his entire face, crinkling the skin around his eyes and softening that scar he wears. "I am sure I am the happiest man who's ever lived."

His eyes search mine and carefully, so carefully, he brushes back the strands of hair that have slipped free from my braided updo. "My *wife*. My Roxilana."

Wife. I can't help the grin that spreads across my face at the title.

My eyes move over his face then, taking in his features as he did mine. His sun-bronzed skin, his smoky-amber eyes, his subtly hooked nose and high cheekbones.

"My husband."

His eyes crinkle at their corners, and though my lips feel swollen, I have to fight the desire to pull him to me once more.

He runs a hand over his smooth jaw. "Do I now look like the pretty Roman boy you imagined me to be?" he asks, mirth in his tone.

With his shorn hair and his clean-shaven face, he could nearly pass for a Roman.

"I couldn't imagine anyone as breathtaking as you are," I admit.

I think it's finally settling in now that he is real, he is here, and he is *mine*.

Memnon takes my hand and clasps it between his. "Always yours."

CHAPTER 13
Roxilana, 18 years old

54 AD, Rome, Roman Empire

My face is flushed as we ride through the streets of Rome, following the escort Emperor Nero sent us. I sit astride Memnon's horse, riding it like a man does, my stola and tunic magically split to accommodate me. Whatever boldness and excitement I felt when I first made the decision, it's gone now.

Memnon keeps a possessive hand against my stomach, bracing me against his chest. His magic rings my torso and limbs, further binding me to him.

This is no normal ride; it's more of a procession, one that largely shows off Sarmatian might. Memnon must've used those peculiar abilities of his to allow us to ride so boldly— almost victoriously—through the streets of Rome, a place infamous for its Triumphs, processions that commemorate Rome's might and showcase the defeat of foreign kingdoms.

All eyes are on us. The people take me in, their eyes

drifting from my bridal crown and veil to the barbarian king at my back. I see them lean into one another and whisper, and I can't help the blood that rushes to my face. I may not have been born a Roman, but I was raised one.

You are shaking, Memnon notes.

I am...afraid, I admit.

Whatever for?

I've never had so much attention on me. And I don't think I like it.

It is they who fear us, he says. *They look at us and know my men and I could cut them down faster than they could scream. We are the stories they tell their children at night to make them behave.*

I scan the crowd, and sure enough, the people *do* look afraid—afraid and curious and perhaps a touch in awe. At least when they look at these Sarmatian warriors.

Maybe they are afraid of you, but they aren't afraid of me. When they look at me, it's just pity and derision.

"Oh, but they are afraid," Memnon insists, whispering the words in my ear. "They see you in my arms and they know that you are no Roman—not anymore. You are one of us."

As his horse canters forward, he continues, "Sarmatians are the fiercest in the world. They are trained from birth to ride horses and wield weapons. They must fight in at least one battle before they are allowed to marry. And you are to be their queen. You will wear the riches of my empire, and you will ride astride my horse as my people do, and you will show these people that you were *made* to rule my warriors."

I draw in a shallow breath, my trembling hand coming to rest over Memnon's where he holds me fast. I don't answer him—not even in my head—but I do thread my fingers between his and give him a squeeze.

I lift my chin, and I bear the stares a little better for the rest of the ride to the Circus Maximus.

Once we arrive, we dismount and stable the horses. Then we enter through the main arch, moving around the colonnaded walkway beneath the stadium seats, following the Praetorian Guard.

The Circus Maximus is enormous, so large it can fit thousands upon thousands of Romans. We see many of them loitering here, where the air smells vaguely like sweat and piss and sour wine. As we make our way to the imperial box, the stares become far more intense, largely because of how close our audience is to us.

"My king," one of the Sarmatians calls out from behind us, "I think you have some admirers. Without your beard, you're almost as pretty as your wife."

"I can protect you from them if you'd like," adds another of his men who walks ahead of me. I think I overheard Memnon call him Zosines.

Their reactions to Memnon's shorn hair are a lot better now than they were when they first saw him. Then, they wore varying looks of horror.

Apparently, cutting a Sarmatian's hair is not something they do, though I don't really understand why.

"The only admirers I'm noticing are you two fools," Memnon says.

"Three fools," another Sarmatian corrects.

"Four," the last of his men calls out.

Five, I add silently.

Memnon is behind me, so I cannot see his expression, but down our connection I hear him groan. *Not you too.*

"Sorry, Roxilana," one of his men says, "seems we're going to have to fight you for him."

"There's no need," I respond in Sarmatian. I glance over my shoulder at Memnon. "I'm willing to share."

That sends off a round of raucous laughter.

Don't encourage them, Memnon says, but I can hear the smile in his voice, and I sense that he's actually enjoying himself, despite the teasing.

"She really does speak Sarmatian," one of the men says in wonder.

The conversation dies away as we finally make it out of the colonnaded walkway and into the emperor's private section of the stands. The room we enter is roofed, and there a few senators and other high-ranking men meander, pausing to scrutinize us as we cross the space. On the far side of it are massive marble columns, and we pass through those, into the open air.

My breath stills when I catch a glimpse of the arena far beneath me. The sandy track is a long oval shape, bisected down the middle by a series of statues and obelisks. And right now, chariots race down that track, kicking up plumes of dust as they go.

We head down a set of marble stairs to a balcony below, where a line of upholstered chairs has been arranged to view the races. Among those chairs is a throne, upon which the emperor already sits, his guards nearby and a senator at his side.

When Nero sees our group, his eyes light—until he notices Memnon's trimmed hair. "Whatever happened to you?" he says as we approach. He sounds disappointed, like a child whose friends won't play along with him.

"I was inspired by Roman hairstyles," Memnon says smoothly.

"Is that right?" Nero's gaze slides to me, and realization

floods his features. Now he doesn't seem so brutish. In fact, he appears startlingly sharp, though his eyes have a lascivious gleam to them. "Yes, well, Romans *can* be quite inspiring, especially under the right circumstances."

I frown at him and distractedly press a hand to my sternum, a strange tightness gripping my chest.

Nero returns his attention to Memnon. "Well, I suppose you still have that barbarian look about you in other ways. Come, sit." He pats the empty chair next to him, then turns to the senator on his other side. "You're excused."

"If you don't mind," the senator protests, looking both intrigued and alarmed as he takes Memnon in, "I'd like—"

"*Begone.*"

The senator, who undoubtedly is very powerful and wealthy, reluctantly leaves his seat, his expression pinched.

Nero is oblivious, his focus already back on Memnon as my husband and I make our way to the open seats. Memnon's men stand to the side, while a couple of servants rush in and remove the excess seats from the balcony we're perched on.

Whatever is about to happen over the next few hours, I'm sorry for it, Memnon says.

One look at the overeager emperor has me biting the inside of my cheek. *Not as sorry as I am for you. Looks like you have a sixth admirer.*

Memnon's eyes flash with amusement just as Nero leans toward him. "Will you show me your tattoos?"

Thus begins the emperor's single-minded focus on Memnon, who looks less annoyed by the attention than I know he is, thanks to our bond.

While they chat, I watch race after race of chariots circling the arena.

"There is no better entertainment than the games," Nero

says to my right. "I doubt you have anything like it to the east, save what we Romans bring you."

"I have seen one arena local Romans have made in Panticapaeum, but it is nothing like this." Memnon gestures to the massive stadium we're seated in.

"But there is battle," Nero says, like that's some sort of consolation. "And there must be plenty of it. Otherwise, your kind wouldn't be known for your ferocity." None too smoothly, the emperor adds, "Rome could use a strong ally such as yourself."

I rub at my chest again, feeling a growing pressure bearing down on it. The sensation is accompanied by a restless tug beneath my skin.

Probably just nerves.

Memnon opens his mouth to respond when Nero leans forward, his eyes on the arena.

"Oh, oh, it's beginning, Sarmatian," he says, distractedly grasping Memnon's forearm.

What does he mean, *beginning*? The chariot races have continuously run throughout this entire…

The thought withers away when I return my attention to the arena. The chariots that streaked across the racecourse have disappeared, the clouds of dust they kicked up now resettling.

An announcer holding a metal cone shouts something too muddled for me to make out, but as the arena's repeaters shout it to their stadium sections, it causes the crowd to roar.

Moments later, men enter the arena and their names are announced, to various degrees of applause. None of it means much to me, but I watch it with a sick sort of fascination.

These must be gladiators.

"Some of these men are criminals, some are trained

116

fighters, and some are both," Nero explains. "We make wagers on who will win. I've got my eye on Darius right there." He points to a muscled Roman with a receding hairline and a broad, crooked nose who strides onto the field. "He is a beast in the arena," he tells Memnon excitedly. "Wicked as the worst of them but a gods-blessed killer."

I shiver as a round of applause goes up for him, and the man raises his arms, hands clenched in fists.

Roxilana.

I glance over at Memnon, only to find he's looking at me, even while Nero prattles on next to him. A soft smile tugs the corner of his lips as he studies my features. *This is not at all how I imagined our wedding day going,* he admits, *but it is still the single greatest day of my life.* He punctuates his words by laying out his arm, palm facing up in invitation.

Tentatively, I take his hand, threading my fingers through his.

How to explain his touch? Like a memory and a dream rolled into one. It's equal parts thrilling and comforting.

Before I can even fathom a response, a roar rises from the crowd.

With my free hand, I rub my sternum as several thick, wooden doors inset into the walls of the arena lift. From one of the darkened doorways, a cheetah slinks out. The large cat looks severely emaciated, and as it enters the arena, the gladiators scatter about, running to grab a few weapons someone must've set out while names were announced.

Nero makes a disappointed noise. "I forgot about the hunts today," he says.

Hunts? Memnon echoes down our bond.

From the other gates bound two snarling lionesses, both looking just as hungry and desperate as the cheetah.

The announcer is shouting something about the creatures as they pace across the arena, their eyes quickly fixing on the gladiators. I can see the bony protrusions of their ribs and hips and the ridges of their spines. The sight turns my stomach, and that pressure in my sternum deepens.

The crowd shouts as one of the lionesses slinks around a gladiator and gingerly swipes at the man, then roars again when the fighter jumps out of range. Nearby, the cheetah cowers at the noise from the stadium, its ears flicking as it glances around itself.

I hate this. I hate this so much.

The gladiator swings at the lioness and—

The creature yowls as the blade strikes its flank, and I suck in a breath.

I can feel Memnon's eyes on me, even as, on the other side of him, Nero chortles, then shouts some encouragement to the fighters.

Say the word, and we will leave.

One of the gladiators screams as the other lioness leaps onto him. He tries to get his blade between them as the lioness's mouth closes around his neck.

As the two tussle, the wooden gates rise once more, and a third lioness leaps out from one. But it's the other darkened doorway that draws my attention. From the deep shadows, a panther prowls out.

My heart slows as I stare at the creature.

I stand, every sense suddenly focused on the large cat.

Roxi?

That animal... I touch my chest absently again, my eyes fixed on the creature.

The panther is terribly emaciated, its spine and ribs prominent. It's so painfully hungry, I swear I can feel an echo of that ache in my own belly. It's also clear that the animal is too famished to be any real threat, even as its lips curl back and it flashes its teeth.

Without realizing it, I leave my seat and approach the edge of the balcony. Beyond the stone railing, the seating drops away to the arena below, where already the hunt has devolved into absolute chaos.

"Seems your wife likes a good hunt..." Nero's voice drifts in.

Memnon makes a noncommittal noise.

To me he says, *little witch, what is happening?*

Can he sense through me that something is off?

I lean against the stone railing, my gaze still pinned to the panther, who so far has managed to skirt around the fighting.

I...I don't know. My magic continues to beckon me toward the animal, and I am helpless under its compulsion.

I glance over my shoulder at Memnon. The Sarmatian king is standing up, his magic curling in waves around him. The emperor and the rest of the group around them seem unaware that anything is amiss, though I don't know if that's due to Memnon's influence.

Roxi, he cautions softly, like I am a skittish horse. His gaze drops to where my hands white-knuckle the railing, then to the bloody arena beyond. *If this is about marrying me, we can burn the document. I—I will leave you alone. Just please step away from the stadium's edge.*

I am deeply, deeply alarmed by Memnon's words, but at the moment, not even that is enough to deter me. Some magical instinct has taken root.

It is not that... I face the arena once more, where already one gladiator lies dead, a lioness feasting on his innards. I can sense Memnon approaching me when I catch sight of the panther once more.

Resolve settles over me, and with a burst of magic, I vault myself over the ledge and into the arena.

I hear Memnon's shout as, for an instant, I am weightless.

My feet hit the ground, my knees taking the brunt of the impact.

I catch myself on my hands while, around me, numerous gasps and shouts rise from the stadium.

Across our connection, I feel the sharp edge of Memnon's panic, followed by resolve. But even that I pay little mind to as I step forward onto the bloody field.

The smell of sweat and excrement is so much stronger down here, as are the sounds of battle. Fighters grunt and large cats snarl, and clouds of dust are kicked up from the skirmishes. A desperate hunger grips me, carving me up from the inside out, and that pressure in my sternum builds and builds, threatening to crack me wide-open.

My attention remains focused on the panther, who slinks around a bloody gladiator, even as another round of shouts rise from the stadium. From my peripheral, I notice the roll of indigo smoke rapidly spreading across the arena, wrapping around man and beast alike.

I'm about to look away from the panther when the creature's golden-green eyes swing from the gladiator to me—

Mine.

The thought echoes as, all at once, the pressure in my chest *erupts*, and my magic rushes out to the panther. The instant it grips the creature, a connection snaps into place, the force of it bringing me to my knees.

I bow my head, my breath coming out in a shaky exhale,

and I press a hand to my chest. Beneath it, I sense my bond to Memnon, but now, there is an additional connection there—one that binds me to...to the panther in front of me.

I only have a moment to wonder at this new bond when, as quickly as it's established, my awareness moves *down* it, until I'm looking *through* the panther's eyes.

I stagger—or rather, the animal staggers—as I stare out at the world, which looks sharper yet far less vibrant, the colors muted. But the smells are far more potent than anything I've ever experienced.

In particular, the iron tang of blood in the air has my gums aching with the need to bite down on something, that hollow pain in my stomach pushing out all sense of reason.

I turn my hungry gaze to the kneeling form across from me. Panic courses through me when I realize I'm looking at my own form, my head bowed and my veil obscuring parts of my face.

A sharp, frantic instinct to hunt pounds with my pulse, but as I stare at my own form, a far more dominant instinct overlies it.

Protect.

An instant later, I've snapped back into my own mind. I sway, thrown by the perspective shift as roaring comes at me from all sides. I glance up, realizing with alarm that while I've been preoccupied with this panther, we've been in the middle of an active Roman hunt.

I glance up at our surroundings, my power gathering within me. It's only then that I realize the arena and the stadiums beyond are largely obscured by thick, blue smoke.

Memnon's magic.

I push to my feet, slowly turning in a circle as I sense the panther approaching my side.

Behind me, Memnon stands amongst the magic that hides the other animals and fighters from sight.

His gaze moves from me to the panther next to me.

I have no idea what on Api's good, green earth is going on, he finally says, *but I am with you, my queen. I am always with you.*

My good sense is only now returning to me, lifting the strange fog that clouded my thoughts.

I place a hand on the panther's head. My awareness slips for a moment, and I'm in his mind once more. He's still starving, still weak, but now, above it all, I feel kinship as I stare out its eyes before returning to my own.

A single word sings between us as I return to my own head:

Mine.

I glance to Memnon as he tentatively approaches me, again treating me like a skittish horse. It reminds me of what he said earlier about burning our marriage document.

We are with you too, I finally say to Memnon, answering his earlier words. *Always.*

Memnon's brows pull together, his gaze bouncing between me and the panther even as a shadow of a smile curves his lips.

Thank the gods, he responds, relief edging his voice as he closes the last of the distance between us. *Because I wasn't certain I could willingly walk away from you.*

His expression sobers. *I have never known fear like the moment you jumped into the arena like that.* Beneath his words, I feel something else, some mixture of pride and desire. *That was one of the bravest, brashest acts I've yet seen.* He reaches out and lays a hand on my chest. *You may have been raised Roman, but your heart is all Sarmatian.*

I give him a shy smile, my words failing me.

The hushed silence around us has me finally lifting my gaze away from Memnon to the crowds above us. The stadium is eerily quiet, the spectators watching us with grim wonder. As Memnon's magic clears, I realize why.

The arena is a graveyard, the sandy earth coated in blood and bodies. Every last man and beast has been stabbed, sliced, bitten, or bludgeoned to death.

All except for us.

CHAPTER 14
Roxilana, 18 years old

54 AD, Rome, Roman Empire

The sun has set by the time our group returns to Nero's palace, this time with a panther in tow. Without a doubt, today has been the longest, strangest, most wondrous day of my life.

So when I cross the threshold into that red room, my feet barely hold me up. The panther is at my side, his stomach a little more filled out since we got him food and water.

It ended up being fairly easy to feed the big cat and bring him back here, all thanks to Memnon's ability to alter minds. I owe him an apology, for being quick to judge and condemn, but when I turn to do so, I find my husband lingering in the doorway of our room, murmuring with his men.

Facing forward again, I take in the bed, my breath catching when I remember Livia's few stilted words this morning about what married men and women do in beds. I still have only the most rudimentary idea of what *that* is, but the idea of doing anything with Memnon in a bed has me burning with nervous anticipation.

"Do Roman beds have teeth?" Memnon says at my back.

I blink, glancing over at him. "What?"

Memnon's men are gone, and my husband leans against the doorway, watching me with an amused expression.

"You're looking at the bed like it's going to devour you," he says, "so I wanted to know if it has teeth."

I laugh nervously. "No, it's just…" I take a deep breath, forcing the rest of the words out. "It's just that I don't know what you expect of me."

He raises his eyebrows, but his eyes gentle. "*Roxi,*" Memnon says, his voice lowering. He doesn't try to come any closer. "I don't have *any* expectations of you. Take the bed. I will sleep on the floor as I have done so for the past weeks. There is *nothing* I expect of you."

I swallow, even as warmth blooms in the pit of my stomach.

I give my head a shake. "I don't want that." Not at all. Taking a deep breath, I force my deepest truth out. "I want… you, Memnon. All of you, just as you promised in your vows today. And that includes whatever happens in beds." Maybe especially that.

I can feel Memnon's heavy, heated gaze on me and the deep thrill that runs through him at my words. It doesn't stop my own cheeks from heating at my admission.

Clearing my throat, I pull a blanket from the bed and arrange a makeshift pallet for the panther, studiously avoiding looking back at Memnon. Instead I distract myself by imagining Livia's scandalized horror at my using one of the emperor's finely woven blankets to warm a man-eating beast. I smile a little at the thought. A man-eating beast will sleep on the emperor's linens…while I sleep with a barbarian. She would choke on her own judgment.

The panther prowls onto the embroidered blanket, and he—and he's definitely a *he*—plops down on it.

I kneel in front of the great cat, admiring his beauty, and I reach out and stroke him. The panther closes his eyes, and I swear he smiles.

"I don't understand any of this," I whisper, "but I am glad we found each other."

I realize then that Memnon has still not fully entered our chamber. I glance over my shoulder and see him at the threshold of our room, staring out into the empty hallway.

Uncertainty grips me as he stands there.

Was that last conversation off-putting? Is he now second-guessing us? Maybe he's realizing after two months of journeying that this was a remarkably bad idea. Maybe—

Maybe I am simply protecting us, little witch, and I have absolutely no regrets at all. Memnon glances over his shoulder at me, a soft smile pulling at his lips as magic unspools from his hands. He turns back to the doorway and begins to murmur, and his billowing magic fills up the space.

"What are you doing?" I ask, fascinated.

"Warding the doorway," he says.

"What is…warring?" I've never heard of such a thing.

"Warding," Memnon corrects as his magic thins out, molding into a nearly translucent film. "It's a protective spell meant to guard against harm. I'm setting one up here in our doorway so that no can ambush us in the night."

Our doorway. A thrill runs through me at the reminder.

"Do you think that will happen?" I ask, concerned.

"Not with this, I don't."

I swallow at what he doesn't say: that in the world of kings and emperors, assassins lie in wait.

I watch as he finishes his work. In the low light, I can make out the glint of what looks like letters floating in the empty space there. But as soon as I tilt my head a little, they seem to vanish, little more than a trick of the light.

"I didn't know our magic could do such a thing," I say wondrously. What else might it do? The possibilities seem endless.

Memnon assesses his work, then turns and heads toward me. The day had many, many distractions, but now it's just us. His eyes fall to mine, the candlelight limning his features, and there is a storm in my bloodstream, one that calls to him.

He walks slowly, removing his bow and the gorytos full of arrows that he carries at his side, setting the weapons down next to the bed.

Memnon comes to *my* side then, his armor jostling as he kneels next to me.

"Have you thought of a name for him?" he asks, reaching out to run a hand along the panther's back. Surprisingly, the big cat seems to enjoy Memnon's touch, arching into it and chuffing out a happy noise.

I bite my lower lip, then release it. "I have no business naming anything," I admit, then sheepishly add, "but I have."

Memnon waits, his eyes studying my mouth.

"I was thinking…*Ferox*." *Ferocity*. "For his bravery in the face of hopeless odds."

The big cat leans toward me and rubs his face against one of the hands in my lap. I can't be sure, but I think maybe he likes the name.

"Ferox," he murmurs. "I like it. It's appropriately terrifying."

I smirk a little as I watch my *terrifying* new pet. He's flopped onto his side, his eyes closed happily.

"I thought so as well," I say. My smile melts into something more pensive. "I don't understand it, but I'm connected to the panther like I am connected to you."

"Through magic, you mean?" Memnon asks, peering at me.

I nod slowly. "I can...slip into his mind." I've accidentally done it several times since the first. "Have you ever heard of such a thing?"

Memnon's brows pull together and he shakes his head. "No, but it's clear the gods have blessed you, both with this animal and with this new ability to see through his eyes."

The Sarmatian rises to his feet then, unfastening the belt from his waist and removing it along with the weapons attached to it.

I watch him—I cannot *help* but watch him. As a seamstress's assistant, I have seen several men remove bits of their clothing; however, I've never seen *my* man do so, and I'm fascinated by it. He seems utterly oblivious to the strange, evocative way it's making me feel.

When his hands move to the straps of his armor, I push myself off the ground, leaving a content Ferox.

"So we're undressing now?" I say casually, crossing over to him.

There are not many fastenings holding the armor in place, but I reach for one he hasn't undone yet. Across our bond, I feel a spark of surprise at the touch.

"My armor is heavy, and my weapons were cumbersome. I simply wanted to get them off." He gives me a cautious look. "We do not need to get undressed, my queen."

A shiver rolls through me at the endearment. I think

128

Memnon still means to make me comfortable. It doesn't take much musing to know my own heart on this matter.

"Do Sarmatian spouses not undress in front of each other?" I ask softly, unfastening a leather strap.

I see Memnon swallow, and then the whites of his eyes when he turns his face to mine. "They do," he says.

"I am nervous and perhaps a little afraid," I say, referring back to our previous conversation. As I speak, I undo another leather cord holding his armor together. "But I meant my vows, and I meant my earlier words. I am yours... my king."

My gaze meets his. His own eyes look deep enough to dive into, firelight dancing in them. There are layers to Memnon's emotions—excitement, levity, joy, and something that feels warm and deep.

"And," I add, "I'm a Sarmatian now. It would be rude if I didn't follow your customs."

Memnon's mouth quirks, but he only says, "You're a queen. You can do whatever you want."

I smother my own smile. "That's a dangerous proposition," I whisper. I call on my magic to help me unfasten the last of Memnon's armor. "You don't know how greedy I can be."

The Sarmatian's eyes glint. "I've been in your head," he says. "I have an idea."

Memnon straightens and lifts the scale mail off, setting it aside. He groans and rolls his shoulders. "Gods, it feels good getting that off."

Now that the armor is gone, I can see just how built Memnon actually is. I only have a moment to admire him in his tunic before he removes this too.

I suck in a sharp breath as I take in his rippling, sun-bronzed torso and the beguiling tattoos that adorn his skin from arms to chest and chest to waist.

He looks like everything I'm supposed to fear, barbarian from head to foot, but gods, I only want to draw closer. His body is honed and muscular, likely from grueling hours spent fighting or something equally wretched—something I should probably mind.

I can't seem to make myself look away, even when it becomes apparent that I should.

A soft, knowing smile spreads across Memnon's face. He glances down at his stomach, where his abdominal muscles are prominently on display, before looking back up.

Do you still think I look like a monster? he asks, harkening back to one of our earlier conversations.

It's kind of him to assume I'm even capable of forming a coherent response.

Deliberately, he removes the circlet from his head, setting it on the side table next to our marriage document. He turns from it and steps up to me, and I don't have the sense to move away. Not when the lamplight is making light and shadows dance across those rolling, rippling muscles.

His attention dips to the cingulum holding my garment in place. He reaches out and lightly touches the rope, and I get a breathless thrill from the contact.

"Is this meant for husbands to untie?" he asks softly, a lock of his freshly shorn hair hanging in front of one of his eyes. Earlier, Nero had made mention of the knot of Hercules—the wedding knot; I hadn't thought Memnon would notice.

Apparently he had.

"It is," I say softly.

His fingers continue to trail along my cingulum. All

at once, his hand closes on the knot, and he undoes its bindings. The rope falls away, landing with a light thump on the marble floor.

The two of us stare at each other, and something is about to happen—

Memnon cups my face. His lips are a handspan from my own, but he pauses, giving me a moment to pull away should I not want this.

But I don't pull away.

"All that I am is yours," he whispers. He leans in and kisses me.

It's a soft kiss, gentle even. Not what I would expect from a warrior king, one who single-mindedly rode for months to find me.

Maybe that's why, almost shyly, my hands come up and grip his bare sides. His skin feels warm and forbidden, despite us being legally married. It *should* be forbidden—I'm drowning in sensation already, and we've only just touched.

Memnon slides his tongue along the seam of my mouth, and I part my lips in surprise. But as soon as I open my mouth, Memnon's tongue is there too, tentatively touching the tip of my own. I jolt, and reflexively, I push back against it.

He smiles at the pressure, his tongue and lips sliding along mine, and I realize as my grip tightens and my knees go weak that this, too, is part of the kiss.

I have heard so much talk of war and conquering—why are there not epics dedicated to this alone? There should be.

Memnon groans, his hands moving so he can gather me closer to him. My own hands skim up his warm flesh, and I'm still shy but far less unsure.

All at once, Memnon breaks off the kiss to press his forehead against mine.

"So beautiful," he murmurs, his gaze moving languidly over my face. "So godsdamned beautiful." He strokes my cheek. "It wouldn't have mattered what form you came in, as my heart has always been yours, but still, you are perfect."

His words flay me open. The precious few compliments I ever received on my appearance were always outweighed by Livia's frequent criticisms—that my eyes were cold and unnerving and my hair was too garish a hue. That I had a petulant set to my jaw and a displeasing look about me. That I dragged my feet often, lost focus easily (often to chat with Memnon), kept poor posture, and on and on.

The criticisms burn to ash under the adoring gaze of this man, who is looking at me like he might memorize my features.

I slide my palms up his back, a bit braver now, noting the dips and rises of muscles and scars. And there are a lot of them.

This is a man whose wings have never been clipped by Rome, a man who grows out his hair and wears trousers and decorates his skin with ink, and—my gaze settles on one of the many old injuries that mar his skin—a man who has known much violence.

I move my hand to the scar. "You've been hurt so many times." I hadn't realized just how much battle Memnon had seen. That itself shakes me—I assumed I knew the most intimate parts of his mind.

You do.

Memnon steps in closer. "My injuries are fine, though I wouldn't protest if you kissed my scars, just to make them feel better."

There's mischief in his eyes, and I push at him, laughing lightly. "I bet you would like that."

"I would," he agrees, a grin spreading across his face. "I promise I would kiss you back anywhere you asked."

"Oh, is that right?" I say jokingly. "Anywhere I'd like?"

His expression grows serious. Molten. *"Anywhere."*

I swallow. I am out of my depth with him, pulled out to sea by undercurrents I don't understand, but I sense his want in his words and through our bond.

My own desire runs up my spine and down my limbs, my nerves heightening it further. I'm terrified. Emboldened.

I back up, reaching for the metal fibula at my shoulder. I unclasp the fastening as I hold Memnon's gaze, and it drops away with the material it held in place, revealing a breast.

His eyes dip to my chest, and I hear his sharp intake of breath as I undo the other clasp. My wedding tunic falls to my waist, snagging on my undergarments there. I push it all down, my underwear and the tunica recta pooling at my feet.

I stand there, bared entirely before Memnon.

"You have my permission to kiss me anywhere you please…my king," I say softly.

For an instant, Memnon's eyes seem to glow like embers, and his magic unspools out of him, churning around his waist. I can hear it tugging at his trousers and boots, but it's not until the deep blue smoke clears and he steps forward that I realize he's entirely naked too.

"And you have mine," he says.

I can hear the pounding of my heart as I take all of him in. His skin is less tan from the waist down but just as muscular. Tattoos twist around his left thigh, and another adorns one of his calves. But it's not his legs or his tattoos that catch my attention.

There's nothing about him that I haven't already seen

from statues of the male form…and yet the size and shape of his phallus looks more like the fertility figures I've seen and less like the carved likenesses of gods. I don't understand why that would be.

He approaches me then and scoops me up.

I yelp, my hands going reflexively around his neck. "What are you doing?" I gasp. My mind cannot make sense of how incredible it is having so much of my skin pressed to his.

He glances down at me with fondness. "Is it not obvious? Carrying my wife to our bed."

At the mention of the bed, my magic begins to leak from my hands. I'm breathless with nerves.

He lays me out on our blankets, then follows me onto the mattress, draping his body along mine. "Do you still want this?" he asks, a crease forming between his brows.

As I stare up at him, a lock of hair falls in his eyes, over his forehead. Without thinking, I brush it back, my fingers trailing, then lingering over his skin.

"Yes."

He catches my hand, pressing a kiss to first my knuckles, then the base of my palm. "Okay."

"Do you?" I ask uncertainly.

He gives me a look. *"Little witch, the gods couldn't pry me away. Only you have that power."*

I smile at him, shy and eager and bashful all at once.

Almost reluctantly, Memnon gives me my hand back, but I simply wrap it around his neck and pull him to me, and then I'm kissing him again. Only now, an urgent drive edges my movements, and I'm searching for something more. Memnon kisses me back just as fiercely, his body rocking against mine.

He lodges one of his legs between my thighs. My cheeks heat when I realize I'm wet right there and that wetness is getting on his leg.

Mortification rolls through me. I swear I did not have an accident, and yet that is what it seems like.

I know you didn't, little witch. Memnon's voice cuts through my thoughts.

Gods! You heard that?

He laughs against my lips as he continues to kiss me, the sound warming me from the inside out.

Sully my leg all you want, Roxi. I like it. He moves the leg in question, rubbing it against the apex of my thighs, and I gasp as sensation rolls through me.

I break off the kiss to stare up at him in wonder. "What was that?" I ask softly.

Memnon arches a brow. "What, this?" He moves his leg again, and my eyes widen and my lips part.

"Yes."

He laughs again, the sound full of masculine pride.

"I'm not entirely sure," he says. "We'd better explore this further."

I have no idea whether he's teasing me or being earnest, but I nearly cry out in protest when he removes his now-damp thigh from between mine. Memnon shifts himself, moving slowly down my body, pressing reverent kisses to my skin as he goes. At the hollow of my throat, between my breasts, then beneath them…

"What are you doing?" I ask uncertainly.

His mouth skims over my stomach. *I could tell you, but I'd rather show you.* His lips slide past my belly button to the soft skin beneath it.

I tense as they move lower still, over my pubic bone, then—

I gasp when his mouth touches something that makes my body jolt in reaction. *"Memnon."*

Is this the place where my leg moved against you?

My cheeks burn with my embarrassment. That *is* that same place where his leg was. *You don't need to put your mouth there,* I say, flustered. Doing so seems…perverse.

I feel him pout against my skin. *I thought you said I could kiss you anywhere?*

I did, but…

But not here? He dips his head, and his lips stroke my inner folds.

I hiss out a breath. "Memnon." His name comes out as a whimper.

I can stop, he says, even as he slides his arms beneath my thighs.

I get up on my forearms to better see him. *Why do you sound so sneaky?* I ask.

His eyes meet mine down the expanse of my body, and desire burns within them. *Because I think I really, really want to continue kissing you here,* he confesses.

"Seriously?" I whisper.

His gaze is unwavering. "Seriously, Roxi."

I bite my lower lip. *Okay.* I can't bring myself to admit anything more.

A wolfish smile spreads across Memnon's face. *Okay,* he agrees.

With that, he spreads my legs apart, baring the most intimate parts of me.

Blood rushes to my cheeks, and I make a small noise.

This definitely seems perverse.

It's not *perverse,* Memnon insists, eavesdropping on my thoughts. *I'm just getting myself acquainted with all of you.*

With that, he leans back in and kisses the same part of my anatomy he did before. It's like touching fire, the sensation bright and blazing.

My fingers tangle in Memnon's hair, and my rational mind tries to convince the rest of me that I should push him away. But then he sucks on that section of flesh between my folds, and I cry out, my hips rocking against him and my legs falling farther open.

What in the gods' names is going on?

I don't know, little witch, but I do think we found the place you liked my leg touching.

Whatever he's doing with his tongue and his mouth, it far exceeds the earlier brush of his legs. Why have I never known my body could feel like this?

His mouth moves a little lower, and the next stroke of his lips causes my back to arch and my grip on his hair to tighten.

Do you like that? he asks, peering up from between my legs.

I nod breathlessly at the ceiling. *Yes.*

And this? He dips his head and traces some contour of my sex with his mouth.

I suck in air. *Yes.* How do I admit it's all making my toes curl?

But then his mouth moves back up to that small section of skin, and he laves it with his tongue.

A moan slips out. I feel my face flush, but I'm too distracted by this strange pleasure he's coaxing out of me.

He smiles against my skin. *And that feels best of all?*

"*Yes,*" I breathe.

Memnon begins sucking it in earnest, and it's overwhelming and wonderful all at once. I don't know why my hips keep rocking, and I cannot decide whether it's too much or not enough, but when I accidentally grind my pelvis against Memnon's mouth, the man groans.

Oh, I like that, little witch, he says. *Do it again.*

Memnon tightens his hold on me, like he's afraid I might try to escape his clutches. He sucks *hard* on that section of skin, and now I understand his bracing grip because I do try to get away. It's futile, but I do. However, there's nowhere to go. No escaping this intense sensation. And once I stop fighting it, gods forgive me, I *do* begin to grind against him again. And again, and again.

Memnon is making approving noises that should embarrass me, but I'm so far beyond embarrassed that all of it only fuels this restless, wonderful sensation gathering beneath his mouth.

I'm so focused on it that I don't realize he's removed one of his hands from my thigh. Not until he presses a finger *inside* me.

The action shatters something within me, and I cry out as suddenly, pleasure rushes through my body like a wave overtaking the earth.

Memnon groans as I shamelessly rock against him, his grip tightening on my thigh. *Fuck*, he curses down our bond, *I can feel you.*

He felt…*that?*

Yes, he says raggedly.

I force myself to release his hair. My breath is coming in shallow, heaving pants. "What…*was* that?" I ask dazedly.

Memnon looks smug as he lifts himself up from between my thighs. "That, beloved Wife, was an orgasm."

I raise my eyebrows. I've heard of orgasms, though I never knew women could have them.

138

Memnon presses a kiss to my inner thigh, then moves up my body. I can feel the heavy drag of his penis against my leg. My hips shift at the feel of it, and my legs are still spread.

Do you want more, he asks, *or would you like to stop here?*

More? I echo. I'm sated from whatever he did with his mouth, but the thought of there being more to explore heats my blood.

He searches my face, the firelight dancing in his eyes and casting his scar into stark relief. *You didn't think that was it, did you?*

"Maybe?" I say aloud, then bite my lip.

He touches my lower lip with his thumb, his brows furrowing. *Can I confess something to you?* he says.

I nod, fighting the urge to cover myself now that my body is cooling.

His fingers trail down from my lip to my neck, then fall away. *I know very little about intimacy beyond what I've heard,* he says.

This is the Memnon I am familiar with. Vulnerable, his heart laid bare.

But I want to know you *intimately,* he continues. *More than anything.*

I reach for him then, pulling him close, my lips finding his. He kisses me again, passion tempered by a sweetness I feel through our bond.

I want that too, I say.

He breaks off the kiss to see my expression. "Do you want it right now?" he asks, searching my gaze. "Because we don't have to do this tonight—"

"Yes, I want this with you right now." Whatever *this* even is.

Inexperienced or not, Memnon must have a better idea than I do because he pushes himself to his knees and spreads my legs once more, staring again at my core.

It's slightly less mortifying now that he's already placed his mouth on the area. I even find it a little…alluring.

Grabbing his concerningly large phallus, he rests the tip of it against that part of me he slipped his finger into earlier. Only, his penis is much larger than his finger.

I tense, certain that whatever orifice exists between my legs, it's not going to fit him. But to my utter shock, he *does* begin to sink into me. I whimper at the sharp bite of pain, and Memnon pulls out.

Are you okay? he asks, concern etched on his features.

I nod. *Is it supposed to hurt?* I ask.

I think it can for women, he says, *but…I'm not certain.*

It really hits me then that powerful, ferocious Memnon doesn't have the answer because he has never been with a woman. I want to pick apart why that is—

You know why, he interrupts, his eyes heavy on me. *There has only ever been you.*

Emotion lodges in my throat.

I still want to do this, I say.

Memnon looks a little torn. Finally, he takes a deep breath and presses a hand to my abdomen. Beneath his touch, I feel his magic sink into me.

What are you doing? I ask.

I don't want this to hurt you.

Once his magic takes root, he tries again, lining up his phallus with my opening. Then, for the second time, he presses into me.

There's no more pain, but there's a pressure and fullness that comes with the intrusion. Memnon shifts, leaning

140

forward and bracing himself over me as he continues to sink into me, deeper than before. Then deeper still.

I grip his back, my fingers digging into those rolling muscles as my body gives way for him, even when I'm sure there's no more room. Whatever that place is inside me, it stretches and accommodates until I feel Memnon's pelvis meet mine.

Above me, my new husband lets out a shaky breath, and our eyes meet.

"I'm...inside you," he says wondrously.

I let out a light, shaky laugh. He's always been inside me, his thoughts a companion to my own. But this is the first time his body has *moved* in mine.

I push back the lock of hair that wants to hang over his eye. "I can feel you there, in me. It's...," *Surreal. Incredible.* "Strange and wonderful."

Memnon's eyes shine.

Deep where we are joined, a throb starts up. There's some elusive movement I need...

Memnon must feel the same pull because he withdraws his hips, then sinks back into me.

I gasp at the wave of pleasure that comes with the action.

He curses, leaning his forehead against me.

I'm not going to last long, he admits.

Last long? I don't know what that means.

He gives me a pained laugh.

It means I need to get you to come before I do.

I run my hands over his arms. *Come?*

Orgasm, he explains.

Oh. I still don't think I have a great grasp of this urgency he's talking about, but if it involves another orgasm, I can be urgent.

I want you to orgasm while I'm inside you, he elaborates.

My eyebrows hike up. That sounds excitingly perverse too.

Memnon's magic slithers out from beneath his hands and down my body, toward the point where we are joined. I don't pay it much attention until I feel phantom fingertips stroking that place Memnon kissed earlier, the one that seemed to be the center of all pleasure. I make a small noise as his magic increases its movements.

From above me, Memnon smiles. *Does that feel good?*

I can only nod, my breath hitching.

Slowly, Memnon begins to move his hips again. There are no words that can convey the wonder and euphoria of it all. It was erotic enough that the man who's been inside my mind is now inside my body, but now there's the *feel* of this act. The pressure and thickness of him sliding in and out of me, combined with the persistent stroke of his power between my legs. It's filling me up and winding me tighter and tighter and tighter—

All at once, I break.

I cry out, my hands pressing Memnon as close as possible as another orgasm crashes through me.

Memnon groans. *I feel you around my cock and in my head...*

His thrusts drive deeper and faster. I feel more pressure, though I'm not sure the sensation is my own, and then—

"Roxilana." He says my name desperately as, across our bond, I feel him come.

I gasp at the echo of it and how it reignites the last remnants of my own orgasm.

I hold on to him as his motions continue on and on, no longer controlled. Eventually, his thrusts gentle.

He stares down at me, then laughs disbelievingly.

That was…earth-shattering. I'm not sure which one of us thinks it; it's as though for a moment, our minds themselves act in unison.

I reach up and touch Memnon's face near his scar and smile, shifting a little beneath him. I'm naked and sweaty and he's still inside me, even if the pressure is gone.

This is a perplexingly marvelous and very vulnerable moment.

"Hi, Husband," I say softly, shyly.

His eyes crinkle at the corners. "Hello, Wife." Memnon leans in and kisses me, even as he pulls out of my body. Between my legs, I feel a rush of wetness.

Urine? Blood?

Neither, little witch. Memnon reaches down between us and touches me right where we were joined a moment ago. A moment later, he holds his fingers before me, letting their glistening tips catch the light. They're not bloody, as I first feared, though there are slight streaks of red in the liquid. But for the most part, it's a whitish semiopaque color. Something our bodies must make, just for this.

I'm oddly aroused by the sight of that liquid and the sensation of it between my legs.

"When can we do that again?" I whisper.

Memnon gives a laugh that sounds like he's far too pleased for his own good. "Whenever you'd like, my queen, just so long as I get to hold you for a moment first," he says. "That's all I've wanted to do for years."

His words harken back to the nights we spent reaching for one another across the world, aching to embrace when we were sad or scared or hurt.

And now we can.

I know my expression softens; my entire body seems to

respond to those words. Memnon, my old friend and confidant, who cared for me when no one else did and whom I've loved for a very, very long time.

He draws me into his arms, and for the first time since the Romans burned my village, I feel safe. *Home.*

I lay my head on his arm, and Memnon and I stare at each other, small smiles dancing on our faces. I can see the glint of flame in his eyes.

We did it. Again, I don't know who thinks the thought, and I have to assume it belongs to both of us.

We did it.

The two of us bask in this moment.

"I cannot tell you how many moons I yearned for this," Memnon confesses in the dim light.

I place a hand on his cheek, marveling at the feel of his skin. I can't seem to stop myself from touching him.

"I remember those nights," I whisper. "I'd wish to the stars, the gods, the darkness itself that you could be with me like this." My thumb strokes over his skin. "I am glad those nights are over."

I roll on top of him then and begin kissing each of his scars—to make them feel better, of course. And then I show Memnon just how glad I am all over again.

CHAPTER 15
Roxilana, 18 years old

54 AD, Rome, Roman Empire

I wake to an empty bed.

The candles have long since burned out, and in this windowless room, the darkness is almost absolute. I cannot see the rumpled blankets next to me nor the divot left behind by a much larger body.

Memnon.

My own body seems to come alive at the thought of him, and I can't help the grin that spreads across my lips as I remember the night we just had. But as soon as my smile comes, it wilts away because even in the darkness, I'm sure the Sarmatian king is not in this room.

I reach down our connection.

Memnon?

My queen, you're awake, he says, surprised. He himself sounds highly alert, which makes me sit up, my blanket falling to my waist.

Where are you? I ask.

Coming for you.

I hear the scratch of unsheathed claws, and I remember that Ferox has been in the room this whole time. Embarrassment heats my cheeks, knowing what Memnon and I did while the big cat was in here with us.

Now I sense Ferox making his way to me. A moment later, the mattress dips as the panther hops onto the bed, moving to my side. He curls up next to me, and hesitantly, I pet his body, still getting used to his presence.

Across the room, the door opens, and I don't need to see the figure's face to recognize the staggering stature. My hands memorized him all through the night.

Memnon.

He murmurs something under his breath, and a burst of blue light ignites in his hand. He tosses the flare into the air, where it illuminates the room, casting Ferox and I in shades of blue.

"I leave for but a moment and already the panther has taken my place," Memnon says, striding in.

A smile curves my lips.

I rest a hand on Ferox's flank. "Don't leave and maybe you won't be replaced," I say tartly.

"Oh, believe me," he says, his eyes heated as he takes me in, "I have no intention of leaving your side ever." He rounds the bed so he can clasp my face and kiss me.

It's sweet but brief, over before it's barely begun. "This place, however, is a different matter."

I raise my eyebrows in question.

"We need to leave."

CHAPTER 16
Roxilana, 18 years old

54 AD, Rome, Roman Empire

Someone tried to enter our room.

I'm seated on Memnon's horse with my husband at my back, his men flanking us and the streets of Rome sweeping past us, when I learn of this. How someone with ill intentions tried to get to us and only Memnon's ward prevented them from doing so.

I shiver now, thinking about what could've happened had the magic not been in place.

I don't pretend to understand the treacherous ways of rulers, but it's clear that with power comes danger. Whether Memnon's magic wore off on the emperor is still a mystery, but the threat was real enough.

A horse-drawn cart rattles behind one of Memnon's men as his horse pulls it through the otherwise-quiet streets of Rome. I lean around Memnon's large frame to catch sight of the wagon. Resting inside it are supplies the men brought with them, along with a bored-looking Ferox, who idly watches the buildings go by as he's pulled along. A subtle blue sheen coats the panther. It's another of Memnon's wards, this one a spell meant to protect the panther from harm. There are more spells placed on all manner of items in Memnon's care, and I yearn to understand this aspect of our magic.

For all the years I've had my power, I've only ever used it for simple things—to stitch faster, to mend a broken pot or remove a stain from a tunic. And, of course, to heal wounds.

How do you know so much about magic? I ask.

Memnon shifts in the saddle, the hand not steering his horse resting on my thigh. *My father possesses power; he taught me about it long before I ever wielded it.*

At least one of my parents must have had magic as well, but their knowledge is lost to time.

Cautiously, Memnon asks, *Would you like me to teach you?*

There's no hesitation. *Yes.*

I both hear his husky laugh and feel the vibrations of it where his chest meets my back. It sends a pleasant shiver through me.

All right. While we travel, I'll teach you a little of what my father taught me, Memnon promises. *By the time we reach Sarmatia, you will certainly be better at it than I am.*

Up ahead, one of the arching gates of Rome comes into view. Unlike the rest of the city, there are people awake and about here, namely soldiers.

I tense when they see us.

Easy, little witch, Memnon says. *There is no reason for worry.*

As he speaks, plumes of his magic pour out of him and streak toward the waiting soldiers. They wrap around each man like a snake constricting its kill, until the magic envelops them entirely. When his power clears, the soldiers' movements appear unchanged.

I glance over my shoulder at Memnon. *What did you do to them?*

It's an enchantment, he says.

When he sees my quizzical expression, he elaborates. *An enchantment is like a ward, but rather than offering protection, it creates illusions.*

I watch the soldiers, trying to better understand the magic at play. I don't immediately notice it, not until one moment rolls into the next and the soldiers don't seem to see us. In fact, they seem to look everywhere *but* at our group. And when one of them does look in our direction, his eyes pass over us, as though we don't exist at all.

As we close in on the gate, Memnon's steed picks up speed. Faster and faster, he gallops. Behind me, I can hear the wooden wheels of the wagon clacking over the road. I glance over my shoulder and catch sight of Ferox sitting up, wearing what can only be described as an annoyed expression on his face.

I bite back my laugh and face forward, just in time to see those soldiers in vivid detail. Then we're racing past them. I'm under the looming archway for no longer than an inhalation, and then, I'm free.

Free like the swallows soaring above us and the bees that move about the wild grass beyond us. I'm drunk on the air whistling past me, and on a whim, I stretch out my arms just to bask in it. I'm certain that if we rode any faster, I might just get swept up and carried off by one of the Four Winds.

I think I'm laughing, but then—no, there's wetness on my cheeks.

Memnon says nothing, though his hand moves from my thigh, wiping my cheeks.

I thought I'd never leave that city. I've never been so happy to be wrong.

"I've never been so happy either," Memnon whispers against my ear, raising goose bumps along my arms.

I lower my arms and lean into him, downright giddy as Memnon and his men steer the steeds east, toward where the sun rises. Somewhere far off in the distance, at the very edge of the known world, lies my new home.

Sarmatia.

"We will begin small," Memnon says that evening as we stand among the wild grass we've staked out for our camp. Apparently, we will be doing this every night. It's gritty and nowhere near what I would've envisioned for a king, but I'm thrilled at the novelty of it.

Memnon's men and Ferox have all wandered into the wilderness around us to hunt game, leaving me and Memnon to set up camp. And Memnon has used this as an opportunity to teach me about magic.

"You seem far too excited about this," I say, the breeze tugging on the dusty wedding attire I still wear. "It's making me nervous."

"Roxi, have I ever let you down before?"

I can't directly look at him, I've realized. When I do so, I start to blush or else I simply stare. Somewhere between yesterday and today, I decided that he's absurdly gorgeous, and now I cannot act normal.

"Your teaching skills in the past have left something to be desired," I say, toeing the ground with a sandaled foot.

"Yet you still learned to speak Sarmatian beautifully," he fires back.

I pout a little at the compliment. I'm pretty sure it's cheating to say nice things to someone when you're supposed to be bickering with them.

Out of the corner of my eye, I notice Memnon grin a little. At the sight, my stomach flutters and my throat catches. Memnon is no longer wearing his armor or his crown, and without them, he seems less intimidating, more laid bare.

He draws close to me, then catches me by the chin, turning my face to his. "You really do speak our language beautifully," he says softly, his expression sincere. Heat rises to my cheeks as I dip my eyes, even as he searches my features. "Now, why won't you look at me?"

Ugh, he's going to make me say it. "Can't you just read my thoughts?"

His eyebrows rise. "Can't you just tell me?" he fires back.

Gods. *Fine*.

"You're pretty," I rush out. "Really, really pretty. And I cannot seem to—"

"I'm *pretty*?" Memnon's eyes are wide with disbelief and the corner of his mouth is twitching.

"Yes," I say. "Is that truly so—"

Memnon's lips crash into mine, and all thoughts *vanish*. I fall into the kiss the way I fell into each one last night. The memory of Memnon's skin against mine heats my blood, and I want him now as I had him then.

Memnon groans against me, breaking off the kiss to lean his head against my own. "Gods, it was bad enough being in my own head all day, Roxi. But now hearing your thoughts really isn't helping."

They don't have to be just thoughts, I say across our bond.

He curses. Then shakes his head. *I want to make an actual bed for you to lay on before I'm inside you again.*

Memnon pulls himself away from me and clears his throat. "Do you know how to build a fire?" he asks.

I give him an arch look. I cannot believe we're actually going to do this when we could be resuming last night's activities.

"No," I say grumpily, "I'm completely inept at this one very necessary life skill. Yes, of course I know how to build a fire."

Memnon narrows his eyes. "But can you build one without ever touching a log?"

Now I hesitate, and my sexual frustration dissipates.

As Memnon stares at me, he reaches out a hand to his side and says, "*From broken boughs and dried-out logs, I call forth wood of this wilderness to gather before me.*"

My skin tingles, and I feel the brush of his power as it passes by me.

"That was an incantation—words spoken with magical intent," he explains. "Incantations can help amplify your power." As though on cue, the shrubs around us rustle, then part as branches of varying sizes barrel into our makeshift camp, clattering to the ground between us.

"All right, little witch, use your magic to build us a fire."

I reach out a hand, just as Memnon did, biting back a grumble. I assumed Memnon was going to teach me about wards tonight, not ask me to play with sticks. I focus on my power anyway and try my best to move it down my arm and out my hand. A small burst of pale orange smoke releases from my palm, and I give it a single command: *stack the firewood.*

It doesn't surprise me when the branches do just that,

arranging themselves exactly how I pictured they would in my mind.

"Good job, Roxi," Memnon says. "Now, light the fire. And this time—incant the spell."

"Gods, I forgot what a bossy teacher you can be," I mutter.

Memnon steps in close. "Would you like me to supplicate myself before you later? Would that make you feel better about my demands of you now? Because for you, Roxi, and you alone, I would. I might even enjoy it…" His breath tickles my skin, and my eyes lift to meet his.

I can feel the heat between us rising up, up, up—

Memnon's gaze drops to my feet, and he curses, kneeling before me. I glance down in time to see the hem of my tunic has caught fire.

The Sarmatian king grabs the fabric and, using his bare hands, stifles the fire until it's extinguished. He holds the ruined linen and begins to laugh. "You were supposed to light the wood on fire, little witch, not yourself."

"But I did get you supplicating yourself before me." The words are out of my mouth before I can stop them.

A surprised laugh slips out of Memnon, and I feel his delight at my remarks. "That you did."

Before I know what's happening, he wraps his arms around the backs of my thighs and rises, picking me up with him. I yelp, grabbing for his shoulders as he spins us around.

"Beautiful, beautiful Roxi, if I'm a terrible teacher, then you're a terrible student."

"That sounds like something only a terrible teacher would say," I insist.

He laughs again, and I'm suddenly greedy for that laugh. I want to capture it, bottle it up so I can listen to it at whim.

Since I can do no such thing, I think I'll have to settle for giving him a reason to laugh every day.

"Maybe," he agrees. His eyes drop to my lips, and he turns serious.

"Why are you staring at my lips like that?" I say softly.

"Can you not hear my screaming thoughts?" Memnon says. "I very much want to kiss you."

I run a hand over his cheek, which is still smooth despite the fact that his facial hair has had a whole day to begin to grow back. I think he might intentionally be keeping it short for me.

"We still haven't made camp," I say.

"Fuck camp," Memnon murmurs.

"That also sounds like something a terrible teacher would say."

Memnon smiles, but then his expression turns serious once more. Slowly, he lets my body slide through his arms until the two of us are face-to-face.

An ache grows in me as the moment drags on, and my face heats again. He really is beautiful.

Memnon leans in, and at last, his lips meet mine. A shiver races through me at the contact, and I can feel my magic sifting out of my palms as my mouth moves against his.

He lowers me to the ground, and the kiss goes on and on and on. I cannot get enough of the way his body seems to wrap around mine.

"Ehy!" one of Memnon's men calls out as he stomps back into camp. "You two lovers going to make out until the sun rises, or are you going to help us finish setting up the damn camp?"

I grin as I break off the kiss. "Naughty teacher," I say breathlessly, "kissing your pupil."

Memnon's eyes are heated as he stares at me, and for once, there's no quippy response. He flicks a hand, and the fire lights itself and piles of wooden poles and folded felt lain out a little ways off now build themselves into tents.

"You happy now?" Memnon calls out to his man.

"Show-off," his comrade mutters.

Memnon steps away from me and holds out his hand. "There are two final spells I do want to show you."

He leads me around the newly erected tents, toward the edge of our campsite. We only stop once we've passed the tents and draw near an olive tree.

Memnon turns his attention to the land around us. "You wanted to learn about wards."

A thrill runs through me. *This* is the knowledge I've yearned for. But as my eyes sweep over our campsite again, I grow skeptical. "You're going to ward this whole place?" That seems far too vast an expanse of space for either of our powers to cover.

But even as I think it, Memnon raises his hands and begins to speak—no, *incant*—in Sarmatian. "*A roof to cover us and a wall to encircle us.*" Memnon's magic pours out of him, swarming between our tents. "*Form an impenetrable barrier that our enemies may not pass through.*"

The indigo smoke rushes around camp, filling the space, then thinning out until it shapes itself into a semitransparent dome as delicate as insect wings. The deep blue color drains away from the phantom structure, leaving behind lines and lines of what look to be text that float in midair.

I walk up to this…ward, studying the way the strange writing glints in the waning light. Reaching out, I touch one such letter. It shivers a little under my touch, and I can sense the warmth and brightness of Memnon through it.

Is this real writing? I ask.

If it is, I cannot read it, Memnon says. *It's simply the signature my magic leaves behind.*

I'm still touching the ward, and now I push my hand through it, then my arm. Finally, I step across it entirely, curious what it feels like. But like Memnon's ward in Rome, this one doesn't *have* a feel to it beyond that very subtle warmth.

"So if I were an enemy," I say, turning around to get another look at the ward, "I would not be able to cross this?"

Memnon shakes his head. "No. Tomorrow, I will have you help me create the ward—"

"Really?" I can't help the eager smile that spreads across my lips.

Memnon looks enraptured by my expression. "If making wards together means you'll look at me this way again, then gods, yes, my queen, we can make all the wards in the world."

I press my lips together, feeling giddy and pleased and *excited*. "Perhaps you're not so bad a teacher after all," I say. "Just don't let it get to your head."

"Oh, little witch, it is far too late for that."

CHAPTER 17
Roxilana, 18 years old

54 AD, Somewhere in Illyricum, Southern Europe

Traveling through foreign lands with five grown men and a panther is a lot less uncomfortable than I imagined it to be—partly due to magic and partly because I'm now the wife of a king. Not that my elevated status affords me much. Sarmatians are far more egalitarian than Romans, which means that every member of our party is equally responsible for providing for the group's needs.

We all cook; we all set up camp and break it down. We all hunt—even me, though to no one's surprise, I'm atrocious at it. Especially when it comes to handling a bow and arrow.

What I lack in basic survival skills, I make up for in magic, especially now that Memnon is giving me spell-casting lessons. And unlike my hunting skills, I'm *good* at this. My wards and enchantments are strong and long-lasting, and my magical signature looks like threads on a loom, the weave complicated and ornate. Beyond that, my magic allows me a growing number of luxuries: cleaning my body and my clothes when water is scarce, illuminating the darkness when the sun goes down, and… soundproofing the tent when Memnon and I are alone.

By the end of the first week, I've learned the names of Memnon's men and a bit of their personalities. There is Itaxes, who has rich brown hair that falls nearly to his waist, a big booming laugh, and eyes that crinkle often at their corners. Sattion speaks infrequently, but when he does, everyone listens. Rakas is the burliest of Memnon's men, with a gap between his front teeth and a penchant for telling bawdy stories over the campfire.

And then there's Zosines, Memnon's cousin and child-hood best friend, the man Memnon has, through an elaborate Sarmatian ritual, made his blood brother—who also wears rings on every finger and metal adornments in his deep brown hair, and whose sharp eyes linger, more often than not, on me.

The days quickly fall into a lulling sort of pattern. We wake, we ride, we pause for a meal at midday, we ride some more, we make camp, we hunt and practice magic, and we eat and chat over an open fire. Then we go to bed, and Memnon and I explore what it means to be young and in love.

And I'll never make it to Sarmatia—I won't, not when I'm certain I'll die of happiness first. Not a single version of marriage I ever heard of made it seem like this—like whimsy and hope and happiness and, most of all, *love*. Love like fire that burns and consumes.

And maybe young girls who are sold off like grain to lecherous old men or careless young men or philandering rich men don't feel like this. I certainly felt trapped and powerless when Livia forced me into marriage.

Once I've gotten a feel for riding, the men pick up a fifth horse for me to travel on, to relieve some of the burden poor Memnon's steed shouldered, carrying two adults on his back.

The group of us sticks to winding streams, avoiding the main roads whenever we can. I don't understand why, but I don't question it. Nor do I mind. I'm coming to enjoy the scent of wet earth after a rain and wild grass under the heat of the midday sun. Even the smells of wild oregano and sage perfume the air. To think I got used to the casual squalor of Rome when I could have been enjoying this.

But today is one of the rare times where we've made our way back onto a paved road, one that is bordered by overgrown flowering bushes of mustard and spiny broom, hypericum and wild carrot. Memnon reaches over and plucks a flower from one such bush. He then lets his horse fall back until the two of us are abreast.

I raise my eyebrows at him. "Making a flower chain, are we?" I ask.

"I have become a little obsessed with the thought of you adorned in flowers. I did so like the crown of them you wore when we married."

My heart leaps at the memory.

Memnon's eyes twinkle as he rolls the wildflower stalk between his fingers. After a moment, he blows it from his hand, a little of his magic exiting his lips. The flower floats across the space between us and the thin stalk of it slips behind my ear, nestling into hair.

"Beautiful soul mate," he murmurs.

Soul mate? I echo the term, warmth blooming low in my belly. He called me something similar the day he found me.

According to what my father knows of gods and magic, we are

159

a bonded pair, our essences entwined through our power. We have been since birth, and we will be until death.

I don't know when I started smiling, but my cheeks hurt from the intensity of it. It's everything I already knew about our situation, yet hearing Memnon state it like this makes it beautiful, poetic. As though our love was scribed in the stars.

I guess you're stuck with me forever, I say.

Forever, Memnon echoes, though it sounds more like a vow than anything else as he stares at me.

The longer he looks, the more my cheeks heat. I still can't seem to hold his gaze without getting flustered.

Memnon's gaze dips to my cheeks, and his own expression turns playful. Unfortunately for me, he now knows I get flustered too.

"Ehy!" Zosines calls from ahead of us, cutting through the moment. "Trouble up ahead."

A Roman centuria lingers to the side of the road, likely to rest and eat a meal, the roughly hundred or so men milling about near a large oak tree.

Considering how expansive and militant Rome is, I shouldn't be surprised to see the empire's soldiers during our travels, but their presence here is still an unpleasant shock.

The soldiers' eyes rove over us as we pass them. Memnon and his men aren't wearing their armor, but their long, oiled hair and beards, their tattoos, their bows and arrows, even the shapes and detailing of their clothes and their distinctive horse gear all speak to their culture.

"Fucking barbarians," one Roman soldier says, spitting to the side. "What are you doing this far west?"

Stay close, Memnon tells me, ignoring the Romans entirely.

"This one is pretty," one of the men says, nodding to

160

Memnon. His eyes drop to the gold hilt of my *soul mate's* dagger. "And he's a fancy bastard. Tell me, what godless tribe are you cunts from?"

I'm not sure who in our group, besides me and Memnon, knows Latin, but no one responds to the question, though I feel the thrum of Memnon's ire across our bond.

"Does it matter?" another soldier calls. "They all look the same…except for *that* sweet thing," he says, nodding as his eyes land on me. His attention snags on my tunic and my exposed leg. "She might not look Roman, but she dresses like one, and look at those sandals. She's a bride!"

"Most immodest bride I've ever seen," says one of the other soldiers.

Memnon's horse slows, his body tensing. I can see a bit of his magic curling from beneath his palms.

It's fine, I say down our bond.

It's not, Memnon insists.

"Are we killing Romans today?" Zosines growls in Sarmatian. "I wouldn't mind making jewelry of their armor—and their teeth."

Memnon doesn't respond. He's taut as a bowstring, even as more eyes land on me. I feel those eyes on my bare calves, where the long skirt of my wedding tunic has hiked up, and I sense them noticing how I'm straddling my mare, rather than riding sidesaddle.

"Wonder if she rides a man as well as she rides that horse."

Another pats his thigh. "I'll give her a free ride."

"Aye, fancy bastard!" one of the Romans shouts to Memnon. "How much to stick my cock in your whore?"

Faster than my eyes follow, Memnon grabs the bow slung over his shoulder and fits an arrow into it. I only have a moment to register that he's brandishing a weapon at all before he shoots the projectile.

The arrow lodges itself into the eye socket of the Roman soldier who insulted me. A line of blood slips down the man's cheek and he teeters for a moment, then crumples to the ground.

Around me there's shouting and movement, and Memnon's deep blue magic swarms the area, but my gaze is still fixed on that fallen Roman soldier.

Memnon killed him for insulting me.

I finally manage to tear my gaze away when Memnon angles his steed to the head of our group, another arrow already fitted into his bow.

"You flirt with your fucking death when you speak ill of my *wife*." Memnon's voice has deepened with his anger. Wood creaks as he pulls the bowstring taut. "Now, *who's next?*"

Sattion, Zosines, Itaxes, and Rakas have all grabbed their weapons as well. The air is thick with the promise of violence.

"Hold your places!" a hard, masculine voice shouts. "Hold your godsdamned places and stay those hands." A centurion steps forward, his pockmarked face stern. He takes in Memnon, then the rest of us.

"Lower your weapons," the centurion commands our group.

"Our king does not take orders from *anyone*," Zosines bites out in thickly accented Latin, his bow still drawn and ready.

"King?" the centurion says, reassessing our group before his eyes settle on Memnon. "If you're a king, where's your army? Your retinue? Your *crown?*"

"He doesn't answer foreigners' questions either," Zosines adds.

The Roman commander glances over his shoulder at the dead man and the rest of his tense, shifting soldiers before returning to look at us. His gaze pauses on me for a moment.

"This is the woman you killed my soldier over?" His eyes skim me up and down with dispassionate calculation.

Memnon doesn't answer, just tracks him with his bow.

"I'm sure you care about her honor," the centurion continues, "but you, great king, are alone out here on the road threatening the might of Rome, so I will say this one more time: put down the godsdamned weapons or else my men will overpower you, and I will let my men make an honest whore of your bride."

They are ugly, grotesque words, and I feel terror creep into my bones at the sound of them.

Ahead of me, wind stirs Memnon's hair.

Zosines curses under his breath. "Roxilana, comrades," he barks out, "*retreat—*"

Memnon's power erupts out of him, the force of it throwing the commander and the closest of his soldiers back before it swallows them up. Within the blue smoke, I hear a scream. Then another.

Behind me, Itaxes, Rakas, and Sattion are rapidly securing their weapons and turning their steeds around. Ferox hunkers low in the wooden cart, his ears flattened back.

Zosines maneuvers his horse to my side and grabs my reins from me. Without a word, he steers our horses back down the path we came.

"What are you doing?" I shout to be heard over the growing number of screams as we retreat down the path.

"Getting us away from Memnon before we die!" he shouts.

"Die?" I echo.

Behind me, Memnon thunders to the Romans, "You think me a barbarian?" He laughs, the haunting sound carrying on the wind. *I will give you barbarous.*

I glance over my shoulder in time to see a second wave of power explode from my husband, and in the thick soup of it, the screams multiply.

"There are many things you don't yet know about our king. His power is one of them."

But I do know his power.

I think.

I glance over my shoulder again, where I should be able to see his lone figure. Instead, all I see are waves of Memnon's magic swirling around like a vortex. Lightning streaks through the plumes of it. As I watch, a section of the swirling mass expands in our direction.

It should seem ominous, but it's not fear I feel.

Memnon…

You are safe, my queen, he says. Even down our bond, his voice sounds different, *off.*

I face forward as Zosines drives us down the path.

"Release my horse's reins," I command.

Zosines sets his jaw, ignoring me.

"Zosines—"

"No, my queen, I won't. It's too dangerous."

I glance back over my shoulder. Across our bond, all I feel is his wrathful power.

There's no time to argue with the warrior.

My magic funnels down my arm and into my palm. With a thought alone, I release it. The orange ropes of my magic jerk the reins from Zosines's hand and into my own.

I'm still terrible at riding horses, but I have more than enough resolve to make up for it. I pull on the reins and turn the beast back around toward the cyclone of magic.

From behind me, Zosines curses. "Roxilana... fuck—*wait*!"

No. I've already waited eighteen long years for Memnon. I'm not going to abandon him now to Roman forces and the whims of his power. My magic rushes out of me, forming a wall at my back and blocking Zosines's path.

"Roxilana!" Zosines shouts.

I press my legs into my mare's flanks. "Come on, girl," I whisper, threading magic into my words. "Run as fast as you can."

We charge back down the path. Behind me, I hear Zosines curse again, though his voice is soon lost in the cacophony of screams.

Even with my own spell ushering my mare on, I sense an increasing tension in her that slows her movements the closer we get to Memnon. I don't blame the creature; the shrieks are horrifying.

Ahead of us, the storm cloud of Memnon's magic rolls and flashes. The outstretched arm of it snakes down the path, reaching for me as I approach it.

From the corner of my eye, I catch a furred flash of shadow bounding up alongside me.

Ferox.

I'd assumed my panther was still safely sitting in the cart.

My heart hammers in my chest. "You don't have to come with me," I tell him.

I have no idea whether he can understand my words, so

I slip down our bond to try to convey the sentiment. I hold the feeling within my awareness, but it's absolutely pointless because, once I'm inside the panther's head, I feel his own steadfast conviction that he will remain by my side even in danger. That we are a unit.

I slide back into my own head, a lump of tenderness lodging in my throat. I press one hand to my horse, and the other I outstretch for Ferox. I don't know if Memnon's magic will affect either of these animals, but I will not let them race into that magical vortex without my protection.

"*Neither blade nor magic shall injure you.*" I push my power out, and the soft orange plumes of my power wrap around the beasts, thinning out until I can only see the slight sheen of it against their bodies.

Mere moments later, Memnon's magic is upon us, and we're swept into that magical maelstrom.

Flickering blue smoke surrounds us on all sides. In here, the screams are more muffled, but I swear I can taste the edge of their agony. Or perhaps that's simply Memnon's magic I'm tasting.

That volatile power caresses my skin and invades my mouth and nostrils, slipping down my throat with each breath I take. I have seen it knock out grown men and make others dance like puppets, but Memnon's magic is entirely different with me. Supple and soft, it flows over me, running itself through my hair and down my skin like fingers.

It's a battle, steering my horse onward. She jerks her head back as her steps slow, fighting the magical compulsion that spurs her on. I assume she cannot see Memnon's power as I can, but on some deep, instinctual level, she must sense it. Gradually, however, I draw her toward the section of the magical storm that seems to flicker the brightest and most frequent.

That's how we find Memnon.

First, I see the rump of his horse, then my husband's back. His hair blows in the breeze of his magic, lifted off his shoulders as though it could float away. My husband sits rigidly still in his saddle.

"Memnon?" I call to him.

His body doesn't so much as flinch. Now my mare rears up, her front hooves pawing at the air, and I nearly slide off my saddle. As soon as her front legs hit the ground, I swing a leg over the saddle and dismount.

I have no sooner landed than my horse turns and gallops back down the path, the flashing blue magic swallowing up her form.

Only Ferox remains, the panther moving in close to my side as we cautiously approach Memnon and his horse.

Memnon?

My queen, Memnon's voice whispers in my head.

He still sounds different. Alarmingly so. And neither he nor his horse are moving, both rooted in place by some sort of bewitchment he's cast on them both. I step up to the horse, the golden bits of his bridle gleaming under the brief bursts of light.

Through the thick soup of Memnon's magic, I can still hear the roar of screams. I quake at what might be happening to those soldiers, what's so awful even Memnon's own men fled from it.

I approach the side of Memnon's saddle, and before I can talk myself out of it, I hoist myself onto the seat, facing backward, toward my husband. Only then do I glimpse Memnon's full face.

His eyes *glow*, as though they are lit from behind, looking like amber and flame. And yet for all their illumination, they don't seem to see anything at all. His jaw is clenched, his face like stone.

What has happened to my husband?

As though he heard the thought, those eyes drop to mine. The being staring out through them is unrecognizable.

I hesitate for a moment, unsure of who this version of Memnon is and how familiar I can be with him.

Around us, the screams begin to die off, fading away like wisps of smoke. Not much time left for those souls.

With featherlight fingertips, I touch Memnon's cheek. *Memnon, whatever is happening, please, fight it.*

Memnon continues to stare blankly at me.

Please, I beg.

You're safe, he insists, misunderstanding my motives.

I trace his scar. *But nobody else is.*

The silence between us is loud.

I rack my mind, trying to think of a way to stop him, when my gaze drops to Memnon's mouth.

If he cannot be persuaded, maybe he can at least be distracted.

I swallow, unsure if this will work. But the screams are weakening, and time is running out. Making a hasty decision, I lean forward and press a kiss to Memnon's mouth.

For several breaths, his lips are unyielding against mine.

Then his hands move to my arms, and he squeezes them softly, a shudder working its way through him. Finally, his mouth moves against mine, tentative and perhaps a little perplexed.

The pained shrieks die off, and with a sigh, Memnon ends the kiss.

His eyes are closed, and for several inhalations, he remains that way, his hands still gripping my upper arms. When he finally opens them, they're back to their normal hue.

Memnon reaches a hand out, his knuckles stroking my cheek while his brows pinch together.

I stare at him warily. He looks like my Memnon once more, but I…I don't know.

His eyes lift over my shoulder as his magic clears, and my skin prickles at the deep silence. I turn in the saddle, following his gaze.

I wish I hadn't.

Where once there was a mighty army, now all that's left are bloody, mangled bodies. Blood oozes from their eyes, their ears, their noses and mouths. Their bellies are split open, their innards bursting forth like overripe fruit.

Memnon killed them all.

———————

"I…am not like you."

Memnon admits this quietly over the last remaining embers of our dying campfire.

His men have all retired for the night, their meals largely uneaten. I would've assumed vanquishing a foe would be cause for celebration, but like me, Memnon's men seem largely unnerved by the Romans' grisly deaths. Perhaps because that was no ordinary battle—it was a massacre.

I sit cross-legged next to him, Ferox's head in my lap, stroking his dark fur. Like me, my panther was unharmed by Memnon's magic.

"I was planning on telling you." I see his throat work. He stares at the fire. "My magic is not like yours—not entirely."

My hand stills on Ferox. I already know Memnon can alter minds, and I remember seeing his glowing eyes once before. Even what I saw today wasn't unprecedented. The

169

Roman arena had been a bloodbath as well. It doesn't make what I witnessed earlier any less frightening.

"You are a witch," he says. "You have magic, and you can use words and writing and ingredients to heighten the power you were born with. But me…" He pauses to grab the wooden canteen of wine we've passed around all evening and takes a swig of it, like he needs a little extra courage for what he's about to say. "My kind—my father's kind—we are called sorcerers," Memnon says, setting the wine aside.

Sorcerers. I've heard that term used before. I assumed it was another word for *witch*, though there has always been a certain darkness to the former term.

"If I use too much of my power," Memnon continues, "it can take over, like it did today, and…my magic is bloodthirsty." A charred log pops in the silence, and my flesh puckers.

He searches the dying flames. "My men were right earlier. I gave them the order to stay away," he says, harkening back to a previous conversation this evening.

"Why did none of you follow her?" Memnon demands.

"My king," Itaxes beseeches, "you ordered us to retreat anytime you use your magic. You swore that lingering would mean certain death."

"Then die a warrior!" Memnon roars. "Better that than a coward, to let my bride chase after me."

Now Memnon says, "Had they tried to get you, they would have died the same way the Romans did. It has happened before."

"What happened today has happened before?" I echo, aghast. How could I have been so close to Memnon all these years yet still know so little about him?

"Because I didn't want you to know," he confesses. He

170

won't look at me. This whole conversation has been pried from his mouth. "I've killed my own men before. I cannot explain it or atone for it. My power takes on a life of its own, and through me, it has done godless things." He swallows, his eyes finally rising to mine. "And you...you ran right into it." Memnon's voice breaks, and his eyes shine too bright. "I am sorry, Roxi," he says, his voice hoarse, "so sorry."

I nod, searching his face. "Your magic didn't hurt me." Or Ferox, for that matter.

He gives me a sad smile. "It is incapable of doing such a thing. Every bit of me loves you. Even the wretched parts."

It's quiet between us, with only the fire's final crackles filling the air.

"So which is it?" I finally murmur. "Are you kind and gentle or ferocious and violent?"

Memnon searches my face. "I'm all of it," he admits sorrowfully. The weight of that confession looks heavy. "And I am sorry for it." He bows his head. "But all of me—all my power, all that you love and fear about me—I lay it at your feet. It is yours."

CHAPTER 18
Roxilana, 18 years old

54 AD, Sarmatia

It's a hot, cloudy day when we pass an innocuous stone set to the side of the road. It's not as massive as some of the Roman markers that dot these roads, nor is it carved or inscribed with precise Latin letters that speak of things I cannot read. The only detail that sets this large rock apart from any other is the red, familiar-looking dragon painted onto it.

My husband rides up to the stone and, after pressing a kiss to his fingers, slaps its surface. One by one, the others do this as well, until only I remain.

Tentatively, I steer my horse to the large rock and, reaching out, trail my fingers over the brilliant-red body of the dragon. I realize then why the image looks so familiar. Memnon has an identical one tattooed onto his chest; I traced it with my finger just last night.

My eyes rise to Memnon.

"Welcome home, my queen," my husband murmurs, his eyes heated.

We've officially entered Sarmatia.

———

Memnon's kingdom is not what I imagined it to be.

There are few paved roads here and fewer buildings still. The world around us is a flat expanse of grassland as far as the eye can see, and it has been that way in the days since we entered Sarmatian territory.

It seems unlikely that the great Sarmatian civilization that haunts Roman nightmares could amass in such a desolate place, and yet—

"There it is!" Rakas shouts, cutting through our late-afternoon silence.

I close my fist, snuffing out the magic I was playing with, and glance around while the men stir in their saddles. Their eyes sharpen as they gaze into the distance, and they seem to fully come alive then.

Itaxes whistles. Zosines lets out a whoop. Even Sattion flashes a rare smile. And Memnon, beloved Memnon, is bursting with excitement. It feels warm, like undiluted wine in my veins, obscuring my own churning emotions.

It takes me several moments to see the squat, peaked structures marring the sharp line of the horizon. Once I do, I know what it must mean, even before Memnon's words brush my mind.

We've made it, Roxi. We finally made it home.

I touch my cheek self-consciously. I've used magic daily to clean my body of sweat and grime, to braid and upsweep my unruly hair, to mend and whiten my travel-worn wedding dress and polish my sandals. Still, no amount of magic can fully hide the fact that my tunic has thinned and my sandals are scuffed and my body hasn't been immersed in water in many, many weeks.

Beyond my physical appearance, there are deeper issues I've ignored until now. Namely, that I am nothing more than a tailor's assistant. That I neither read nor write. I'm a poor shot with an arrow, and I can only passably ride a horse. I have never been placed in a position of power and would not know the first thing about ruling.

I am unfit to be the wife of the Sarmatian king, and soon all his people will know.

What terrible thoughts poison your mind, Memnon says. *Many outsiders marry Sarmatian nobility. This has always been our way. No one balks at this, just as no one will balk at* you, he reassures me. *But I also do not think you see yourself as my people will see you—radiantly beautiful, the kind of beauty that makes men's knees weak. And ferocious, with your tamed panther. And then there is your magic and the wild, wonderful things they will see you do with it. No, Roxilana, I am certain my people will be just as enamored with you as I am.*

I don't know what to say to such an overwhelming compliment. But I clutch at his faith in me.

Memnon whistles then, the sound bringing the group to a stop.

"Men," he calls out, "get your armor on and whatever else you wish to wear before our people." Memnon turns to me. "Forgive me, little witch."

I look at him quizzically as he hops off his steed and reaches into a saddlebag. "Forgive you for what?" I say.

I swear, if he tells me something awful, like that he is actually already married, I will throw myself off this horse as dramatically as possible.

He turns, and in his hand, something glints. "I had wedding presents for you," he explains, coming over to my horse.

Wedding presents? I stare down at him, still braced for bad news when he takes my hand and slides a ring onto it.

"I meant to give you this back in Rome," he says as I stare down at the golden band fitted with a polished carnelian stone. "But I got a little distracted, and once I remembered, the timing never seemed right."

Emotion clogs my throat. Finally, I laugh, though it sounds more like a sob. My relief is great, but even it is being eclipsed by this unexpected sweetness.

My hand trembles as he takes it, then tries the ring on each finger, not stopping until he finds it fits perfectly on my middle one. "I have heard that the Romans spouses wear these."

I nod. "They do," I say, finding my voice. My eyes meet his. "It is too lovely."

He shakes his head. "Not too lovely. Not when you are the one wearing it." He grins. "And thank the gods you like it because I have a whole matching set."

He returns to his saddlebag and pulls out the rest of the jewelry as I stare at the carnelian ring, my heart beating fast.

It hadn't fully felt real—eloping, leaving. But wearing this ring and preparing myself to meet Memnon's people feels real.

I hop off my horse as Memnon brings forth a necklace and earrings and a bracelet. All of them are gold and embellished with carnelian stones. The necklace alone must have thirty of them, each one hanging like a teardrop. I have rarely seen such wealth, and now I will be the one wearing it.

If I had felt like an imposter before, it is nothing compared to now.

"Hush those thoughts," Memnon admonishes, reaching around me to fasten the necklace around my neck. "You are a queen—*my* queen—and this jewelry honors that fact."

Once it's around my neck, my fingers brush against the metal and stones while Memnon, with a little help from his magic, fits the earrings through my lobes.

"When did you get all of this?" I ask.

"I have had these for many, many moons," Memnon says.

I swallow as he takes my hand and places the gold-and-carnelian cuff onto my wrist.

"I always intended to come for you," he says, meeting my eyes.

I rise to my tiptoes, then and kiss him. *I love you.*

And I love you, he says, stroking my cheek, the back of his hand rubbing against one of my earrings.

When he breaks away, he backs up, his eyes heating as he takes me in. "I like seeing you in my jewels," he admits. His eyes flick to my head. "Would you like your veil?"

Because I am to ride into his city as his bride. Just like the Romans and their triumphs, this is a victorious parade. It would only be appropriate if I played the part of his foreign betrothed.

I smile at him. "Yes."

Memnon smiles back at me, his eyes full of banked fire, while his magic pulls the stowed-away veil from the wagon Ferox currently lounges in.

It is wrinkled and a bit travelworn, but as it floats through the air, then settles on my head, Memnon's magic mends and smooths it out.

He's staring at me still.

"What?" I say.

"I'm going to try something, but you might hate it."

Before I can form a response, Memnon's magic lifts dozens of wildflowers from the grass around us.

A laugh escapes me as they come together and form a flower crown, then settle atop my head. I touch it, my heart feeling light as air and bright as the moon. "You couldn't make me hate it if you tried," I say.

He lifts his brows. "Oh, I seriously doubt that." But he's grinning; we both are. Memnon steps forward, his eyes nearly glowing.

Do you feel like an imposter now?

Yes, I answer without hesitation.

Surly thing, he says fondly, his gaze dropping to my lips again. *Ride at my side so that I might proudly show you off to them all.*

I'm nodding, even though the prospect is terrifying. I don't think I'm capable of denying Memnon anything at this point.

Less than an hour later, the group of us is mounted once more, the men wearing their gleaming armor, Memnon his crown, and I my jewels, my orange veil blowing at my back.

Memnon looks like a god, his armor-clad body swaying in the saddle with every step his horse takes, the gold pieces of it flashing in the late-afternoon sunlight.

Some time ago, Memnon's people caught sight of us, and now they've lined the road into the city.

Once they catch sight of their king, they begin to cheer wildly, the sound drowning out everything but my own panicked thoughts. I can feel myself trembling, my muscles tightening with nerves, when Memnon's indigo magic reaches me. It slips into my mouth and down my throat. For a moment, it tingles my flesh, and then I exhale, my nerves leaving me with my breath.

All will be well, little witch, he says, adoration tinging his words. *I am right here with you. Always with you.*

A wave of tenderness for this man comes over me as we ride on, and I think Sarmatia is blessed to have such a man as king.

Now that my own thoughts are unclouded, I slip into Ferox's head, concerned for my panther. Like me, he is on edge as he stares at the gathered crowd of people from his seat in the creaky wagon. They point at us—at him—their eyes wide.

Ferox does not have the best association with large groups of people, not after what he endured. So when I return to my own head, I send my magic back to him, casting a wordless spell meant to soothe his nerves the way Memnon's power soothed mine.

Several children dash out to us, a couple shouting to Sattion and Itaxes, the rest encircling Memnon's horse.

My husband laughs, leaning over to tousle their hair. "Thank you for the warm welcome," he murmurs.

The children glance shyly at me before moving on to greet the other soldiers.

"These are all your people?" I ask, staring at them.

"This is but a fraction of our people, my queen. We rule over a confederation of tribes that stretch from the Danubius River to the Tanais."

Once we enter the city proper, I see that it is not truly a city, not like I am familiar with, but rather an enormous settlement. Everywhere I look, there is an endless sea of covered wagons and tents made of felt and hide. Most of the structures appear as light as the wings of a bird, and I suppose that's the point. Nothing is permanent when you're a nomad.

I stick close to Memnon's side as we make our way to the center of the massive encampment. Behind the swell of the crowds, I can see tents, pens with animals such as sheep and goats, and stalls where produce, textiles, jewelry, and weapons are for sale. It may not be as permanent a city as Rome, but it functions just as Rome does.

At the center of the settlement is an open, grassy area that must be the communal section of this temporary city. Standing at the far side of it is a line of warriors in scale mail as well as several individuals in tunics and trousers in vivid reds and blues, embroidered with fantastical creatures and detailed with gold appliques. In the middle of this line is a single empty chair before them.

A throne for Memnon.

He and I ride up to the line of people, and when I start to fall behind him, his magic comes out, an arm of it wrapping around my mare and ushering her back next to his, ensuring that we ride in as equals, leaders.

Once we're directly in front of this line of what must be the city's most important individuals, Memnon halts his horse, his power stopping my own.

The crowd has closed in on us, their cheers ongoing, but the people standing before us are silent, waiting.

Memnon dismounts, his armor tinkling as his boots hit the ground. He approaches an older woman wearing a pointed headdress and a long kurta with elaborate gold stitching. Her chin is lifted, and her expression is flat.

When he is directly in front of her, Memnon gets down on both knees and takes her hand, pressing her knuckles against his bowed forehead and the circlet that adorns it.

"Irreverent Son, you choose now to follow royal protocol?"

Son?

From this angle, I cannot see Memnon's expression, but I feel his amusement down our bond.

His mother continues, "I suppose this is the least you could do after disappearing for a season and leaving me to rule these wildlings in your stead. Up, up, let me see you."

Memnon stands but only so that he can lift his mother into his arms and swing her around. I'm guessing that whatever royal protocol he was following, he's now broken it. But the other individuals watching seem neither shocked nor scandalized. In fact, one even whistles, and a few others clap until whoops and cheers ring out across the crowd.

Eventually, my husband sets his mother down, and she clasps his face, searching his features.

After a moment, she pats him on the cheek. "Your hair is all gone, shorn like a sheep." She shakes her head, though I swear I catch a flash of amusement on her face. "And look at that softness," she says, touching the corner of one of his eyes. "Let me meet the woman who has coaxed it out of my battle-hardened son."

Her eyes move to me then, and I sit there on my mare, caught like a fly in a web as I gaze back at Memnon's *mother*. I know little about her, other than a few stories Memnon has told me over the years, but this woman, this *true* queen with her shrewd, assessing stare, intimidates me.

Memnon comes over to my horse and reaches out a hand for me.

All will be well, Roxilana, he reminds me.

This is a wonderful moment for him, I realize as I grasp his palm. It's hard to grasp because, despite his earlier spell, my own heart is leaping and my breath is shallow and my limbs are screaming at me to run and run and run.

But the expression he wears is so full of love and reassurance that I take strength from it. I swing my leg across the saddle, ignoring the fact that his family is seeing far more of my exposed thigh and calf than anyone else here is revealing.

I drop into his arms.

"Steady, little witch," Memnon whispers, our foreheads nearly touching. "Remember, I am always with you." He gives my arms a light squeeze, then leads me forward.

I'm aware then of what everyone else must see: My long wedding tunic lightly dragging along the ground, held together by the metal fibula. My orange veil and flowers, the opulent jewelry I'm dripping with. The panther prowling at my side.

Perhaps I do not look like an imposter. Perhaps I do look like someone worthy of their king. I cling to that possibility as Memnon leads me across the flattened grass to his mother and the rest of the waiting nobles.

When several shocked murmurs break out, I assume the worst. But a moment later, Ferox comes to my side, his head slipping under my hand, and I realize the disruption came because of him. Briefly, I dig my hand into his fur and draw in a steadying breath.

As quickly as the noise comes, it quiets again, and now a hush falls over the gathered crowd.

We stop in front of Memnon's mother. I don't know what the custom is here, but I dip my head in reverence.

"Mother, this is my wife and my gods' fated mate, Uvagukis Roxilana, Queen of Sarmatians."

My head is still dipped, but I can feel the weight of Memnon's mother's gaze on me. My cheeks heat under her inspection.

"Roxilana, this is my mother, Uvagukis Tamara, Warlord of the Two Rivers, Queen of Sarmatians."

"Daughter," she says gently, "lift your head."

Daughter. The word sends a happy thrill through me, and my throat tightens and my eyes prick.

I glance up, forcing myself to meet Tamara's eyes. Just like in her voice, Memnon's mother wears power in her features. It's as moving as it is terrifying.

"Well, aren't you just lovelier than sunrise?" she says.

I smile uncertainly, unused to compliments from anyone besides Memnon. "Thank you," I say, dipping my head again. "It is an honor to finally meet you."

She sucks in a pleased breath. "You speak our tongue beautifully. I almost forgot that while my son was learning your language, you must have been learning ours."

She knows about our connection? I raise my head a little higher, peering at her.

But it's not Memnon who answers my question.

Tamara gives me an arch look, pressing her curving lips together. "Oh, don't look so shocked, Daughter. I knew about you before *you* knew about Memnon."

There's that term again. *Daughter.* I force back the emotion that wells in me—the childlike hope for something I lost long ago, something I searched for but never found in Livia.

She gives my hands a squeeze, her own palms and fingers speckled with nicks and scars.

"My son has spoken about you for years," she says softly. "From what I have heard, you have saved his life once before. For that, you have my endless thanks."

I'm certain this woman is going to make me cry.

"You have been my daughter for years," she continues,

182

unaware of my own churning mood, "but finally I get to properly embrace you." With that, Tamara wraps me in her arms.

A moment of déjà vu comes over me. The mother who birthed me, I believe…I believe she hugged me like this. Wholly and with great affection.

My arms come around Tamara, then tighten. I hold on to her like I might be swept away if I let go. Before I am fully aware of it, tears slip down my cheeks.

When Tamara pulls away, she clucks her tongue. "We cannot have you crying. Not for this." She tenderly wipes away my tears with the pads of her battle-scarred hands. "It's all right," she soothes. Her hands move to my own once more. "I know this is all new," she says, nodding to emphasize her words, "but it's going to be wonderful. *You* are going to be wonderful." She squeezes my hands again. "I can just sense it."

She lowers her voice and adds, "Tonight, we are going to have a great feast. As the king of our people, Memnon must be there. You, however, will not. You will be introduced properly tomorrow."

I give Tamara a perplexed look, but rather than elaborating, she passes me to the young woman next to her, whom Memnon has been quietly murmuring with while his mother and I spoke.

"Roxilana, this is Katiari, your sister-in-law," she says, nodding to the woman who bears a striking resemblance to her, with her green eyes and curving mouth. "She will help get you settled. Rest. Tomorrow is a big day."

I don't have time to ask what she means nor say goodbye to Memnon before Katiari takes me by the hand and pulls me out of the clearing and into the gathered audience beyond, Ferox at my heels.

At my back, I hear Tamara's voice boom out to the crowd. "Your king has returned, and he's brought with him our future queen. Tomorrow, there shall be a wedding, and a week of celebrations shall follow. Rejoice, for the great line of the dragon shall continue!"

The last thing I hear are the roars of the people.

The late-afternoon air stirs the loose wisps of my hair as I follow Katiari away from the gathered crowd.

She steers us toward a tent with a leather jug sitting outside it. Snatching up the vessel, she unstoppers it and takes a large swallow.

"So I was thinking," Katiari says, handing me the jug, "while the rest of camp is distracted by Memnon's return, I might show you around the settlement before I take you to our tent."

Though my bones are weary from riding and my nerves are frayed from arriving at my new home, I would sooner fall on a blade than turn down an offer by Memnon's sister.

"That sounds wonderful." I lift the jug she gave me to my lips. Without thinking, I take a swig of it, expecting water or wine.

Instead, I nearly choke on the flavor of sour dairy.

"What in all the gods'—"

"It's kumiss," Katiari says as I force the drink down, the corners of her mouth wavering, like she's trying not to laugh. "Fermented mare's milk." She takes in my expression. "Apparently it takes some getting used to, but it's a beloved drink amongst us Sarmatians." She leans in close. "More importantly, it lights up the body the same as wine." Her gaze flicks over me. "And I mean this in the kindest way possible, Sister, but you look like you could use a little something to…relax."

I lift my brows. "Is it that obvious?"

Katiari gives me a soft smile. "Only up close."

She lightly touches the metal fibula at my shoulder, and as she does so, I notice her knuckles are tattooed. I hadn't realized Sarmatian women also inked themselves.

Her eyes linger on the fastening at my shoulder, and for a moment I think perhaps she's pondering about my ways and customs before her eyes lift to our surroundings.

"I'm sure it's a lot to take in," she says. "Hence, the kumiss."

I glance at the jug, then cautiously bring it to my lips again. The flavor is still a shock to my taste buds, but this time I'm braced for it. And once I feel the warmth of the drink coat my throat and spread through my stomach, I'm reconsidering my initial thoughts on kumiss.

I hand the drinking vessel back to Katiari. "So you and Memnon are siblings?" I decide to open with.

She nods. "Yep. I'm his younger, prettier sibling." She doesn't say how much younger exactly, but as I take in her profile, I would guess she's no more than a couple years younger than me.

I try to fathom the thought of growing up with a sibling, but all I feel is a deep yearning for the bond Memnon and Katiari must have, a bond that I might've had, had my world not shattered all those years ago.

"Will I meet your father?" I ask without thinking.

"My father's dead—fell in battle nearly ten years ago."

I feel myself pale with horror. "Gods, that was thoughtless of me," I say. "I'm so sorry."

She waves my apology off. "He died valiantly while

185

protecting our people, and speaking of his sacrifice only honors him, so it's all right." Her boots and my sandals crunch against the earthen pathway. "Memnon's dad, however, is still alive. Eventually you'll meet him, though on his own terms I suppose—he's not from around here."

I hadn't realized Memnon and Katiari didn't share fathers.

Hiding my surprise, I say, "Memnon's father isn't Sarmatian?"

"Nope," Katiari says distractedly. She points to our left, to an area beyond the final line of tents. "There are the corrals where we keep our oxen. Our horses are on the other side of camp.

"The most important parts of camp are at its center," she continues. "The great tent and the main clearing, where we met, are the two main assembly areas, though there are others as well. Tanneries, forges, butcher shops, and the like are located on the edges of camp with most dwellings somewhere in between. Smaller shops and stalls are interspersed between houses."

I nod as I take it all in. In truth, Katiari's explanation of this settlement is hard to gasp when I cannot yet distinguish one pathway from another.

She tilts her head toward me. "As for Memnon's father, he visits as often as he sees fit—but he comes from a long way off, so I assume the trip is challenging."

"How did your mom and Memnon's dad initially meet?" I ask, my curiosity growing.

"Memnon didn't tell you?" she asks, steering us down yet another pathway. People lingering outside their homes watch us with interest.

I shake my head.

Katiari eyes me, then stops altogether. I pause, watching

as she blows out a breath. "Of course he'd put me in this position," she mutters to herself.

Katiari glances to the heavens, then back at me. "Okay," she finally says, coming to some sort of decision. "Memnon should be the one to tell you, but I can try to explain."

My brow furrows. "I *do* want to know." It would help me feel a touch less lost when it comes to my husband's family.

"So, you know Memnon has…" Katiari lifts a hand and wiggles her fingers.

I press my lips together to keep them from twitching. "Power?" I say.

"*Yes.*" She sounds relieved that I know this. "Well"— she begins walking again, and I trail after her—"his father, Ilyapa, is the one he inherited it from."

"Okay…" I say, not sure I understand where she's going with this.

"Ilyapa is the King of the Moche Empire, some great and distant nation," she says, "one too far away for ordinary people to visit. However, like I mentioned, Ilyapa is *not* ordinary. Long ago, he used his magic to come here, and once here, he searched out my mother. From what I understand, he'd heard of a place where female warriors fought alongside men and got curious.

"At that time," Katiari continues, "Tamara was the queen of our people and one of Sarmatia's fiercest warriors."

"So they met," I say.

"Yes. Apparently she nearly cut him down and only his magic spared him some gruesome fate."

My eyebrows rise. "And from that they…fell in love?" I say skeptically.

Katiari throws back her head and laughs. "Love? No, I don't think it was ever love. But power is drawn to power, and they both had plenty of it. As my mother tells it, Ilyapa wasn't here for long, but he was here long enough." She gives me a knowing look.

"And that," Katiari finishes, "is how my dear brother came to be." She punctuates the thought by having another drink of the kumiss before passing it to me.

Distractedly, I take a sip, hardly noticing the sour flavor as I grapple with the story of Memnon's origins.

I hand the kumiss back to Katiari, and the two of us continue in silence as the last dying rays of light settle over the tented city. Several Sarmatians are lighting torches staked into the ground along our pathway.

"My mother and Memnon's father *do* like each other," Katiari finally says, "and perhaps their lives would've looked different if they weren't both rulers, but that is not the world we live in."

"No, it isn't," I quietly agree. The world we live in exalts power and punishes love as weakness. Perhaps the only reason Memnon and I have what we do is because my husband is willing to use his immense power to get what he wants.

"We should probably get back," Katiari says. "I'm sure you're tired, and tomorrow will be an eventful day."

A bolt of nerves courses through me at the thought of getting married—again—tomorrow and, this time, publicly.

Katiari smiles and bumps her shoulder against mine. "Hey, it'll be all right, I promise," she says, reading my facial features. "Besides, I can always slip you more kumiss if you need it. Just ask."

I give her a grateful look. "Thank you, Katiari," I say sincerely. "For the tour and the kumiss, but most of all, thank you for making me feel welcome."

Her eyes soften. She takes my hand and squeezes it. "Hey, we're sisters. That's what we do for each other."

My heart swells because, as I stare at her, I think she means it.

I nod, flashing her a shy smile. "Sisters," I agree, testing the word out.

"Exactly." She threads her arm through mine then, and together we walk back to my new home.

CHAPTER 19
Roxilana, 18 years old

54 AD, Northern Sarmatia, near the Borysthenes River

I wake in an unfamiliar place, full of unfamiliar smells, to the soft murmuring of distant voices. I reach out, my fingers trailing over the dark wooden wall next to my bed.

There's a heavy weight on me, and when I look to it, I realize it's Memnon, his face buried in the crook of my arm, his body half on me, half off. He smells like wine and campfire, and he's snoring softly.

Lying on the other side of him is the ever-opportunistic Ferox.

I smile at the sight of these two crammed into a bed that was meant for me alone.

I run my fingers through Memnon's hair. "You're not supposed to be here," I whisper. That's what I was told last night, when Katiari settled me in this space.

"Mmmm," he groans, his arm tightening around me, his face nuzzling against my side. *Little witch, you are my wife. This is* exactly *where I'm supposed to be.*

I bite my lower lip, liking the possessive way he declared that. "Your family wanted us to stay in separate tents before the wedding," I whisper, glancing at the cloth door that separates this wagoned bedroom from the rest of Tamara's tented house. At least, I *think* this is her tent. Maybe it's my sister-in-law's. I was told and shown so much after we arrived, and I'm still disoriented by most of it.

Yes, well, my family has wanted me to do lots of things over the years, many of which I ignore, so this is nothing new, Memnon says.

He lifts his head and smiles at me, his hair sleep tousled. "Good morning, my queen."

I run my fingers along his cheek. "Good morning, *my king*."

Memnon's eyes positively heat at the endearment. He leans in, taking my mouth with his. The kiss has barely begun when he cuts it off with another groan, pinching his eyes shut.

"Are you okay?" I ask, pushing myself up a little.

He nods, still wincing and still lying like a stone on top of me. "Just a little hungover. There were a lot of toasts last night."

At the feast I missed. A mixture of envy and relief rolls through me.

Now I press a hand to Memnon's forehead, letting my magic seep from my palm and sink into his skin. The wordless healing spell is thick like honey, and I vaguely sense it take hold through our bond.

My hand slips from Memnon's face as his expression sharpens from pain to something hungry and yearning. He kisses me once more, but this time, his body rolls against mine, the movement limned with lust.

I can still hear voices murmuring somewhere close by, and the conversation gets alarmingly louder and louder—

The curtained doorway is pulled aside. It takes one inhalation for Tamara to see me, and one exhalation for her to notice her son *on top of me*.

Gods take me now.

"Memnon." Tamara's voice is full of disappointment. Not shock, however. "What are you doing here?" she demands, a harsh note to her voice.

Heat rushes to my face. This is her second impression of me, entangled with her son in possibly her own bed. And not even a day after she said all those nice things about me too.

"She's my wife," Memnon says, flashing me a smile *and still not getting off me*. "I'm doing exactly what husbands are supposed to do with their wives."

"I would prefer my grandchildren were made *after* the wedding," Tamara snaps.

"Oh, it's definitely too late for that," Memnon says.

Gods above and below. I close my eyes. *Memnon, you are making this situation so much worse.*

He grins down at me, unrepentant.

Tamara sighs. "I can trust you about as much as I can a wolf among sheep."

Leaning forward, she tugs the blanket off us and swats Memnon's backside. "Out, out. Your men are surely looking for you."

Memnon leans in and gives me one more quick kiss before standing. "My wife is no sheep," he corrects his mother.

Tamara makes an assenting noise. "If she's willing to sleep alongside dragons and panthers, I suppose she can't be."

I grimace, my face still hot with embarrassment when Memnon backs away from the bed.

He presses a kiss to his mother's cheek, and then he's gone.

She and I stare at each other.

I open my mouth to say something, but words fail me.

Tamara raises an eyebrow. "Are you planning on catching flies?" she says.

My brows come together in confusion.

"No?" she answers for me. "Then close your mouth and get up, Daughter. You have a wedding to get ready for, and we need to turn you into a bride."

The morning is a blur of mostly unfamiliar feminine faces—with the exception of Tamara and Katiari. Most are female relatives in Memnon's extended family or friends so close they are considered family. Some names are murmured to me amid the bustle, along with their relationship to the husband I'm remarrying today. There's Mada, Zosines's heavily pregnant wife, who has rich brown hair plaited down her back, and there are Alde and Opoea, Memnon's twin cousins. There is Achaxe, Tamara's aunt, who is nothing more than a wisp of a human. There are others, with names and faces that all bleed together.

I'm far too overwrought with nerves to retain any of it.

Despite my weak protests, I'm summarily disrobed and ushered into a small tub. Then, hands belonging to those unfamiliar faces scrub my hair and body and buff my nails. So many eyes see my nude form that my alarm must draw in my panther because Ferox stays close to me, never much more than an arm's reach from my side. It initially adds to the tension in the room, but once the women realize Ferox won't harm them, they mostly ignore the big cat.

Most Sarmatian women seem to wear their hair in braids, but once I'm pulled from the tub, the women insist on letting my long locks cascade freely down my back, save for a few thin, delicate braids at my temples that they weave together at the back of my head.

I'm helped into what must be a traditional Sarmatian wedding garment. First, I pull on the pale, embroidered breeches, then a matching tunic, the fabric detailed with swirling, golden designs. Lastly, the women slide my arms into a long, crimson kurta with a high collar and draping sleeves. Edged in gold, the deep-red garment falls nearly to my ankles and fastens together just beneath my breasts. Dozens of hammered gold plaques in the shapes of deer have been stitched onto the kurta.

I glance down at my outfit, smoothing a hand along my stomach. It's drastically different than the Roman wedding tunic I wore for months. In fact, it's unlike anything I've ever worn. Strange and opulent, heavy and fitted, and every time I move, those gold pieces seem to shiver. In the heat of summer, I can already tell it will be sweltering, but none of that seems to matter because *I am getting married*. And well, okay, this isn't the first time, but in Rome, it was a hasty set of signatures. Brief. Transactional. Today, however, it will be a celebrated event. This feels like a true beginning.

Katiari comes to me and takes my hands, giving them a soft squeeze. "Each of us sewed a part of this outfit, putting our love and hope into your marriage," she says as the tent quiets around us. Tamara and the rest of the women gather around the two of us as she finishes, "We wish you a prosperous marriage and welcome you into our family."

My throat tightens with emotion. "Thank you…*Sister*."

The word is rusty and unsure on my tongue, but Katiari smiles and gives my hands another squeeze, nodding, and the two of us share a moment. Hopefully the first of many. I lost a sister long ago, but now I'm blessed with another.

Tamara steps in and places a hand on my shoulder, and I realize then that the three of us are a familial unit.

"You may have woken up a Roman woman," my mother-in-law says, "but tonight, you will go to bed a Sarmatian one."

"If she goes to bed at all," Mada throws in. Some of the women titter at that.

Someone calls from outside the tent, "Is the bride ready?"

Tamara looks at me, her eyebrows raised in question.

I nod. "I am."

CHAPTER 20
Roxilana, 18 years old

54 AD, Northern Sarmatia, near the Borysthenes River

No one has told me how, exactly, the ceremony is to unfold, and up until now, I haven't thought to ask. But as the women lead me through camp and onlookers gather to toss flowers along the pathway, I wonder if perhaps I should have.

Magic sifts from my palms, the pale orange plumes of it wrapping around my wrists and twisting around Ferox, who prowls at my side.

To my left, Tamara holds my arm lightly as she guides me. "I can feel you shaking," she says. "There is no need for nerves. This is how many Sarmatian brides come to us—alone."

I take a steadying breath and nod as we walk through the camp, a few of the women who helped dress me following in my wake; the rest of them, including Katiari and Mada, slipped away before us.

I see them again soon enough, for at the edge of camp,

they wait in a semicircle. Between them stands a horse with a gilded bridle and a tooled leather saddle, one Katiari holds the reins to.

My steps slow as I take in the horse, then our location. "Are we traveling somewhere?" I ask uncertainly.

"You are," Tamara corrects, leading me over to the animal.

My pulse quickens. "Why?"

Haven't I traveled far enough to get here?

Tamara sees my face and rubs a small circle on my back. Leaning in closely, she says, "This is part of the wedding festivities."

Before I can ask her what she means, I hear the distant sound of howls—human ones. It raises the hairs on my arms, and my eyes grow wide.

Unlike me, however, the other women giggle and titter.

"Hurry," Katiari says, "hide her."

Tamara quickly turns me and steers me back down the path, while some of the other women look to the gathering crowd and shoo them away.

"What is happening?" There's a note of panic in my voice as the group of us—including Ferox and my horse—is ushered into an empty tent nearby.

No one has told you what's happening? Memnon says, clearly eavesdropping.

No, will you?

I feel his smile down our connection. With me, Memnon is often sweet and earnest, but right now, I sense another emotion commanding him, one that is neither sweet nor earnest. Whatever it is, it's hungry. Excited.

I'd rather find you first, he says. The tone of his words raises gooseflesh on my skin.

Katiari puts a finger to her lips, and the rest of the group goes deathly silent.

The outside noise grows louder, and as it gets closer, I can make out individual howls and shouts from men, along with the pounding of many, many hoofbeats.

I look from face to jovial face, confused about what exactly is happening. The hoofbeats grow thunderous, and suddenly, it's as though a stampede of them is upon us. Outside the tent, dozens of mounted riders gallop by on the open steppe beyond the tent, howling and whooping.

Little witch, where are you? Memnon calls. *Come out, come out.*

He's more than a little convincing, but when I take a step toward the curtained doorway, Katiari snags the back of my kurta.

"Not yet," she whispers.

The thunderous sound of the mounted riders seems endless, but eventually it does taper off, their cries growing fainter until they vanish altogether.

In the silence, I finally whisper, "What in the gods' names was that?"

"That was your husband and his men, looking for you," Tamara says curtly.

Katiari says, "Hurry, we need to get the horse out and Roxilana on it."

With that, I'm bustled back out of the tent, where the onlookers linger, their faces growing ever more excited when they see us.

Katiari brings the horse to my side.

"Up, up," Tamara orders me.

I don't stop to ask her about the urgency in her voice. I hoist myself up and into the saddle, swinging into the seat easily. Unlike my Roman garments, the tunic and breeches I wear were made for riding.

"This is what will happen next," Tamara explains. "You will ride as far and fast as you can. It is my son's job to capture you and your horse."

"*Capture?*" I repeat incredulously.

"To prove he will follow you wherever you may wander," Katiari explains. "It's a wedding thing."

"Once he's caught you," Tamara continues, "he will bring you back here, where the wedding rites will be held."

The howls, which had faded away entirely, now start up again.

"They're heading through camp!" one of the onlookers shouts.

"Better get going," Tamara warns as Katiari hands me the reins. "Oh, and, Roxilana?"

I glance down at Memnon's mother.

"The longer a bride can hold off being captured, the stronger a match they're said to be."

I've barely had a chance to process that when Katiari slaps the horse's rump and the creature takes off, running out of camp and into the wild grass beyond. The golden ornaments on my kurta tinkle and my unbound hair whips behind me, and I have the wild urge to laugh.

From my periphery, there's a flash of black, and I glance over to see Ferox bounding alongside me. He looks exhilarated, like this is all great fun to him.

I reach a hand out behind me. "*Hide us from sight,*" I incant. Orange smoke unfurls from my palm, stretching out over the three of us. I'm not sure the hasty enchantment will do much to hinder Memnon, not when he was the one who taught me this trick, but I figure it's worth trying as we charge forward onto the steppe.

Better ride faster, little witch.

I glance behind me. Far in the distance, I make out a group of mounted riders. They're no longer galloping around the settlement. Instead, they wait on the edge of camp, near where I exited, their attention cast roughly in my direction. I don't see Memnon among them.

In fact, he's nowhere to be seen at all among the vast, flat expanse of summer grass that stretches as far as the eye can see.

But then I notice a faint blue line of magic no thicker than a cord extending away from me. I follow it with my eyes until it seems to vanish into thin air.

He's tracking me!

I am. I can hear the laughter in Memnon's words.

And you've hidden yourself, I add.

Should I not have?

Before I can answer him, his form comes into hazy focus—first, his gleaming armor and crown, which glint in the sunlight, then the rest of his body and the steed he rides on, a steed that is alarmingly near to me.

Are you not going to reveal yourself to me? he asks.

Rather than answer, I face forward and urge my horse onward. A moment later, Memnon's deep blue power slithers up alongside me, then thickens, encircling me and my steed as though there is no enchantment hiding our forms. It sinks into my horse's fur, and the beast begins to slow.

Memnon is closing in quickly, and though I know he cannot see me, it doesn't seem to matter, not when that blue line of magic stretches between us. It takes nothing but a twist of my wrist and a slight tug on my power to cut through the weave of my enchantment.

As soon as it comes down, Memnon's gaze sharpens, then heats.

You look radiant, my bride, he says, and through our connection, I feel the thrill of his excitement. *Sarmatian clothing suits you.*

You look good too, I say. *Good enough for me to consider giving up right now...*

You should, he replies. *I promise I will make your surrender memorable.* He slows his horse as he approaches.

Going to snatch her from her saddle... Memnon's idle thought passes through my mind like it's my own.

He's no more than three arm spans from me when, out loud, he says, "It was a good effort—"

I swing my leg over my horse and hop off, dashing into the knee-high grass, Ferox bounding to my side.

I can feel Memnon's amusement behind me.

You're still thinking of running from me?

Not just running.

I whisper an incantation beneath my breath and send my power out between us. I rotate around in time to see my orange magic spread and thin into a wall that encircles me.

Memnon hops off his horse, his armor clinking together as he moves.

He strides up to the magical wall, and I can't help the way my breath catches at the sight of him. He's dressed almost identically to what he wore yesterday and the first day we met. In the full light of summer, with his dagger strapped to his side and that scar edging his face, his shortened hair shifting in the breeze, he looks beautiful and deadly.

When he gets to my ward, he stops, staring at me

through the orange-tinted surface of it, the darker threads of my spell's signature still visible.

As I back away from the magical wall, it leaches of color.

"You think this will keep me out?" Memnon says.

I *had*, but the confidence in his voice has me questioning my assumptions.

Memnon places a hand against the ward. Beneath his touch, my magic thickens and shifts, moving toward his palm.

"There is no keeping me out, little witch." My magic crawls up his fingertips, then the back of his hand and wrist. As it does, the rest of the wall melts away, the power dissipating until the two of us are staring at each other with nothing in between.

Memnon drops his hand. "Every part of us longs for the other—even our magic."

My heart constricts, and my eyes rise to his face. "What happens now?" I ask softly.

"You could run some more—I'm always happy to chase you—or you could come back with me so I can officially make you my queen."

I hesitate. "It didn't take very long for you to catch me…" I had hoped to linger out here for a while.

He huffs out a laugh and steps up to me. "Ah, I see. Someone told you that strong couples stay out here for a long time?"

I nod.

"And you're afraid our people will think we're a weak match if we don't?" He squints as he asks it.

Now I hesitate, not wanting to admit that they'd likely see us as weak because *I* am weak, and the haste of this wedding ritual would only validate that truth.

Memnon's voice lowers. "Our people could never think such a thing of you. Not when you bring their king to his knees." As he speaks, he drops down to one knee, then both. His fingers move to the laces of my pants, and he begins to undo them.

"Memnon," I gasp, my hand covering his as I glance over his shoulder to the settlement in the distance. "What are you doing?"

Memnon smiles. "Making your capture take longer." Then he tugs down my pants.

The feel of his roughened palms on my bare thighs feels unreasonably good. It always does. There's magic in his touch, magic that has nothing to do with our supernatural abilities.

I glance uncertainly at the distant camp again, still nervous, until deep blue plumes of Memnon's magic shroud them from sight and a phantom hand tilts my head back down to him.

"They cannot see you," he reassures me. He runs a thumb along the seam of my sex, eliciting a hiss from me. "Now," Memnon continues, "would you prefer I taste you while you're standing or while you're reclining?"

"Taste?" I suck in a breath at the thought, even as that languid warmth begins to pool between my thighs.

"Reclining it is," Memnon announces.

His magic does the rest, dragging my torso back until I gently hit the ground. My legs are trapped together at the ankles by my lowered pants and my soft leather boots, and Memnon uses this to his advantage, lifting my bound feet up and spreading my legs wide enough for him to slip beneath them and settle my thighs on either of his shoulders.

Any lingering resistance I might still have is banished

by the first brush of Memnon's lips against my slit. Without meaning to, I shift my hips, my legs falling farther open.

Memnon huffs out a laugh at my body's response, his hands lovingly sliding up my thighs.

He presses kisses up and down my outer lips, gently nipping at them as he goes. I let out a moan and reach for his head, eager to thread my fingers through that rich, dark hair of his. His magic, however, presses my arms back, pinning them together above my head.

"What are you doing?" I ask, wriggling. I feel like meat on a spit.

Memnon pauses his work to look up, and I can't help but notice the obvious desire in his eyes and the soft smirk on his lips. "Keeping you at my mercy."

I'm reminded then that this ritual is about capture and surrender.

I will make your surrender memorable, he said.

Memnon's arms pull my thighs apart as much as possible, and then he leans in.

No longer is he interested in teasing me. His tongue dips into my opening, and then his mouth finds that point right above it, the one that makes my muscles tense and pleasure coil in my belly.

He sucks on that fold, his teeth lightly scraping over it every so often. I writhe and shift beneath him, my hips tilting uselessly, my arms tugging at their magical bindings.

I want to feel him—my hands in his hair, his heavy body against mine, my heels dragging down his back. I want his warmth and the friction of his form, and the absence of it makes me feel caged within my own skin. The conflicting sensations seem to only wind me tighter and tighter, until I'm taut and poised like the string of a bow.

I think Memnon knows it too and is eager to watch me come undone because, amidst all of it, I feel a phantom finger stroke along the edge of my entrance.

That's all it takes.

If I was a bowstring before, then my orgasm is the arrow, shooting through my body. I come with a cry, my release swallowing me up.

Between my legs, Memnon groans, his hold tightening as he must feel an echo of my release down our bond. When he looks up at me, his mouth glistens with my slick, and his eyes have the barest edge of a glow to them. Idly, he strokes a hand up and down my skin, his gaze finding mine. "Love watching you come—and feeling it too."

Gently, Memnon lifts my thighs from his shoulders and disentangles himself. But the moment his skin is gone, his magic is there, tugging my pants back up my body and releasing my arms.

I sit up, my gaze finding the far-off settlement.

"I think we've been gone appropriately long," Memnon says, leaning over me and pulling out a long blade of grass from my hair.

I stare at that blade and bite my lower lip. "They're all going to know what we've been doing out here."

Memnon laughs. "And absolutely no one will argue that we are not a strong match. But," he says, picking off another strand of dead foliage from my hair, "if you prefer, I could use my magic and clean you off."

I stand up and dust my hands. "I don't prefer it," I decide. I think I *like* the idea that they can see him all over me.

I glance down. "Come, Husband." I reach out a hand for him. "You've thoroughly captured me, and I'm at your whim. Now let's go get married."

We stand before the settlement's sacred fire, the flames dancing high into the sky. An Anarya priest stands before us, their masculine form clothed in a long, feminine kurta, a tall headdress resting on their brow. Around us, the camp's inhabitants have gathered, Memnon's closest kin and friends standing nearest us. Ferox sits at my side like a sentinel.

"Today we bear witness to the binding of these two souls," the priest announces, their age-roughened voice carrying across the small clearing. They incline their head to Memnon, indicating for him to speak.

My husband's eyes shine more than usual as he takes me in. "From the gods that made me to the gods that take me," Memnon recites, "from this first breath to my last, I am yours."

As I stare into Memnon's smoky-amber eyes, the sensation that flows over me is something out of a dream. Too strange and joyous to be real.

He gives my hand a squeeze. *It's your turn to say the vows.*

My heart beats fast as I haltingly repeat what Memnon said. "From the gods that made me to the..."

Gods that take me, Memnon fills in for me.

"—gods that take me." I smile at him, my hands trembling in his. "From this first breath to my last, I am yours."

Memnon grins wide, the expression reaching all the way up to the corners of his eyes, while the people around us cheer.

"And now, the bloodletting," the priest says.

Bloodletting?

Memnon unsheathes his gold-hilted dagger and Zosines approaches us, holding a drinking horn that's partially filled with wine. I stare, alarmed, as Memnon pushes up the shirtsleeve of his arm, then brings the edge of his dagger to the light brown skin there.

Memnon, what's going on?

There's iron in his voice: *Making you mine.*

Zosines angles the drinking horn roughly under Memnon's arm right before my husband drags the blade across his skin, parting the flesh.

A dizzying amount of blood wells up, then spills from the wound, dripping down Memnon's arm before Zosines catches it in the drinking horn, where it mixes with the wine. I sway a little on my feet at the sight of the wound.

You didn't tell me about this part of the ceremony.

Memnon's gaze meets mine, and I can see both guilt and resolve in it. *I'm sorry.*

Zosines turns his attention to me, that bloody drinking horn still clasped in his hand. I can sense other gazes now turning to me.

Oh.

My eyes drop from Memnon's weeping wound to the bloody blade held loosely in his grip, my stomach churning.

I'm supposed to do it too, aren't I? I ask, dragging my gaze up to Memnon.

A muscle in his jaw jumps, like maybe he hadn't thought through this part—or perhaps he regrets it. *Yes.*

I'm unnerved and perhaps a touch frightened, but I can feel our audience's curious eyes on me, and with every moment that passes, the tension grows tauter. This is not a place where weakness thrives.

I extend my hand for the blade. If Memnon or anyone else notices how I shake when it is placed in my grip, they don't say.

My fingers wrap around the warm gold hilt. The blade is

still bloody, and I have to draw in a fortifying breath to calm my rising nerves.

Pushing my sleeve up, I gingerly place the edge of dagger to my inner forearm, ignoring how Memnon's blood smears onto my skin.

Zosines readies the drinking horn beneath my limb, and if I hesitate for much longer, the crowd will notice. I choose to look into Memnon's eyes, drawing courage from him. He gives me a small, proud nod, and before I can reconsider, I force the blade down my arm, holding Memnon's luminous gaze as I cut open my flesh.

The pain comes an inhalation later, and it's a shock, an incredible shock. I gasp, dropping Memnon's blade, as warm, rich blood spills from the wound and into the waiting drinking horn Zosines holds in place.

You did well, little witch, Memnon praises me, an odd mixture of concern and pride warring in his features. *The pain will be over soon. The ceremony is nearly complete.*

He steps into my space and clasps my hand in his, our bloody forearms pressed together. Zosines gives my husband the horn of bloodied wine, and Memnon holds it up between us as though in offering.

"I drink of your essence and of mine," he says, his gaze unwavering. "Just as our blood is now one, so too are we." Bringing the horn to his lips, he takes several long, deep swallows of the drink before handing it to me.

I glance uneasily at the liquid in my grip. I've had spiced wine many, many times, but never was it seasoned quite like this. I can feel Memnon's and my blood mingling; aside from sex, this is the closest we'll ever be.

"I drink of your essence and of mine," I say softly. "Just as our blood is now one, so too are we." I tilt the horn back and swallow down the liquid, the wine largely masking our blood's metallic taste.

Once I'm finished, I lower the drinking horn, my eyes meeting Memnon's luminous ones.

The final line we say together, Memnon tells me. He whispers it across our bond.

He gives my hand a squeeze, and we speak as one: "For good, for ill, and for always, my life is bound with yours."

His magic and mine ignite where we grip each other, the flames from it scorching our palms and burning up our arms, sealing our wounds and binding us together in the process. Our power sinks into our skin and I sense it traveling through my veins before settling beneath my sternum.

I stare at the remaining magic smoking off our arms. *Was that...supposed to happen?*

But Memnon's not looking at our clasped hands. He's been staring at me, his expression fervent. *Yes,* he breathes into my mind. *Finally.* He sounds both relieved and delighted. *Our flesh and our souls are fully joined to one another. Where one goes, the other must follow.*

I don't follow the nuance he sees in this moment, but it doesn't matter. His ardent words and intense expression are enough to make my breath hitch and giddy warmth to spread through my veins.

Mischief sparks in those irises of his. *Now, little witch, there was something I meant to do the first time I married you,* he says.

What was that? I say, searching his gaze.

Kiss you. He pulls me in and presses his lips to mine.

In my shock, I drop the horn, letting the last of the bloody wine spill across the ground as Memnon's lips sweep over mine.

Around us, the cheers turn to whistles and howls. My skin pricks at the noise, but I'm too consumed by the taste and feel of Memnon to pay it much mind.

When he pulls away, his lips glisten. He grins then, the flash of his canines making his smile a little wolfish. I smile right back, drunk on this moment.

The priest steps forward, holding a golden diadem in their hands. It is fringed with dangling gold beads and inset with smooth, round rubies.

I realize as the priest raises it above me that this is *my* crown, that right in this moment, I'm not just marrying Memnon but also getting coronated.

My eyes widen as the priest places the diadem on my head, fitting it so it rests over my forehead just as Memnon's circlet rests along his.

"I crown Uvagukis Roxilana *queen*." More cries from the audience. "I present to you all your newly married king and queen! Let no man break what the gods have joined."

———

Bonfires roar around the central clearing, and undiluted wine and kumiss are passed around by the jugful. A musician has struck up a lute, the plucked notes of it quick and jaunty, and the massive clearing is now filled with dancing and singing, drinking and laughing.

Set before the open space are two gilded chairs—our thrones—and on them Memnon and I sit. The only one missing is Ferox, who skipped the evening's festivities to prowl the grasslands beyond camp.

Sarmatians approach me and Memnon to pay their respects and deliver gifts. Already there are piles of exquisitely wrought weaponry and jewelry, intricately woven textiles and perfume encased in blown-glass bottles. It's more wealth than I could possibly imagine, and there is still an unending line of guests waiting to introduce themselves.

My gaze strays to the twisting bodies, and yearning heats my blood.

Will we get to dance? I ask. My eyes linger on Katiari, who laughs as she twirls among the dancers, her partner another young woman.

Would you like to? Memnon asks, glancing over at me.

Yes. The word rides on a wave of longing.

Memnon reaches out, ignoring the line of waiting guests and his mother's arch look from where she stands nearby.

Are you sure it's okay to leave? I ask, glancing back.

They have your entire reign to meet you, but we only have until dawn to enjoy this wedding night.

With that, Memnon leads me from my seat and into the sea of dancing guests. Once they notice us, they clap and cheer, reaching out, fingers brushing against our hair and clothes and skin. It should be invasive and uncomfortable, but I have already drunk a horn and a half of undiluted wine, and it's chased away whatever misgivings I might've had.

Memnon pulls and spins me about, causing the golden adornments on my outfit to shiver as the two of us move.

Sarmatians dance differently than Romans, but my limbs feel fluid, and there's a rising wildness in me that might be my magic or inebriation. It causes me to arch my head back and laugh with abandon at the dark sky.

When I lower my gaze, Memnon's fire-bright eyes are on mine, along with the grazing touch of his hands. He's looking at me like he could live in this moment forever; I know I could.

I wind my arms around his neck and pull him close,

threading my fingers through his hair. *The gods must hold us dear,* I say down our bond, *because I am sure no woman has ever felt the way I do about you.*

This love is the thing of dreams and wishes. Too sweet for the real world.

Memnon touches my lower lip. *And no man has ever felt the way I do about you, Roxi, though I'm sure some have killed for even a shadow of it. You are my everything.*

I can't stop the smile that comes then. I wonder if people have died like this—intoxicated on their own happiness. It would not be half so bad an ending. Much better than Cleopatra's exit, an asp bite to her breast, her heart already broken. Much better to die at the peak of love.

What makes you think this is the peak? Memnon interrupts. There's a secretive glimmer in his eyes, like he already knows more about what's to come than I do.

Who knows, maybe he does.

We dance as one song blends into another and the stars tilt in the sky. We stay until sweat wets my hair and drips between my cleavage and too many people press in on us.

Are you ready to leave? Memnon asks.

I glance around at the revelry, which seems livelier than ever.

Can we?

You are a queen. You don't need someone else's permission, Memnon says, a smile curving his lips. *But you'll be pleased to know us leaving early is part of the tradition.*

He whistles between his teeth and, holding my hand tightly in his, weaves us in and out of the dancing guests.

Someone must hear Memnon's whistle because a man to the side of the clearing brings Memnon's horse to us, the creature now adorned with garlands of wildflowers.

Already, guests are drawn over by the activity. Before more of them can stroke my skin and clothes, Memnon lifts me onto his steed, then follows me onto the saddle.

Amongst the gathering crowd, Tamara comes over and shouts above the rest, "The royal bride and groom are riding out for the night. Let's give them a final toast—to the king and our new queen!"

The revelers cheer, horns and cups rising into the air as the fires around us crackle and pop.

With that, Memnon clicks his tongue and off his horse lunges, the guests parting as we pass through them. Hands touch our clothes and legs as we ride by. Then we're through the main crowd and charging down the trampled paths, the tents flying by us. Every so often, we pass a stumbling guest or indiscreet lovers.

Is that typical? I ask when my eyes fall on yet another couple tangled off to the side of the path, the man driving himself into the woman from behind.

I can feel Memnon's rising humor. *Yes.* After a moment, he adds, *We're a city made of tents. There are few secrets here even with the aid of walls, and many don't care about those.*

We reach the edge of the settlement, and the land opens up before us, the ground and the sky two different shades of black.

"Where are we going?" I ask as Memnon steers us into the darkness. Somewhere out here Ferox prowls.

"Away," he whispers against my ear.

We ride until the settlement is nothing more than a few pricks of light on the horizon. Eventually, even that disappears.

We ride for some time longer before Memnon's steed slows, then stops.

"This is it," he announces, swinging off his horse.

I stare into the darkness. Even in the weak light of night, I can still tell there is nothing here. No buildings, no tents—there aren't even fences or ruins. Just vast grassland.

Memnon holds out a hand for me to dismount, and I swing off his horse and into his waiting arms.

Our heads are close, our mouths even closer, and my heart patters like rain. We have spent weeks upon weeks being intimate, yet here I am, *nervous*.

"You don't need to be nervous," Memnon says softly. "It is just me."

Just him and little else.

I glance around us. Stars dapple the sky, and among them hangs a thin crescent moon. The balmy, late-summer air has a chilled edge to it, and I feel as though I am swimming through water. The only noise here is the soft hush of the wind through grass.

"What is this place?" I ask softly. "Why have you brought me here?"

"It's tradition for the newly married couple to ride out and spend their first night alone on the steppe. Something about getting back to the basics of life—so long as you have the earth beneath you, the sky above you, and your woman at your side, you have an enviable existence."

After a pause, I say, "So we're camping again."

Memnon's laughter breaks through the darkness. "I hate to confess this to you, my queen, but we will spend more time than not...*camping*."

Do I tell him that I could fall in love with this way of existing? If it means more of his laughter and closeness, I would happily endure it.

Memnon releases me so he can hold his hand before him.

In his palm, his magic swirls as it forms an orb. Gradually, it begins to glow, the bluish light of it pulsating brighter and brighter until Memnon flicks his wrist, and it lifts into the sky. It floats only a short distance above us.

Beneath the orb, Memnon smiles, the glow casting his face into unearthly blue hues. His eyes shine like pools.

He raises a finger. "Give me a moment."

"Okay…"

Memnon gives me a long look, like he can still tell I'm jittery, and I swear he almost says something before he returns to his horse, pulling two items from the saddlebag strapped to the beast's sides.

When he returns, he shakes the first item out, unraveling a blanket he then spreads over the grass. The second item, he presses into my hand. I realize a moment later it's a canteen. When I unstopper it and take a sip, I taste wine spiced with cinnamon and clove. It's not diluted the way it would've been back in Rome, but it's spiced the way I like best.

I choke on a laugh, my eyes watering for some odd reason. "You got me spiced wine?" I say. The Sarmatians don't usually season theirs—bloody wedding rites aside.

Under the light of his magic, Memnon's gaze grows soft. "I will get you whatever your heart desires so long as you draw breath—maybe even after that as well," he says with a wry twist of his lips.

I laugh again, then take another deep pull from the skein. "You're just trying to get me drunk, aren't you?"

He presses a hand to his heart like I've wounded him. "You've figured out my master plan."

I pass the wine to Memnon, who also takes a long drink of it.

"I really do like this," he says, pulling the canteen from

his lips and appraising it. He restoppers it and tosses it onto the blanket he set out. "Now come here," Memnon says, his magic reaching out for him. "I'm cold, and your body heat might be the only thing that will keep me warm tonight."

Another peal of laughter escapes me. It's high summer. "So dramatic," I say, even as I all but trip over to him.

"How dare you suggest such a thing," he says *dramatically*. He leads me over to the blanket, where the two of us sit, our eyes on the heavens. Only then does he grab the canteen and pass it back to me. "I swear the stars look different since you've been by my side," Memnon says.

"Different how?" I ask, bumping his shoulder playfully.

He bumps me back. "Less lonely. And far more beautiful."

"Is that right?" I say.

He turns to me. "Everything is more beautiful since I found you—the sky, the grass, horseshit, all of it."

"Ah yes, lovely horseshit, how can we forget that?"

The two of us laugh, leaning together like coconspirators. Somewhere in there, I hiccup, which causes us to laugh harder.

On a whim, he turns and presses a kiss to my shoulder. I don't even think it's meant to be amorous, but my body reacts, and I tilt my head to his, finding those lips with my own.

He tastes like spiced wine and wonderful, wicked thoughts. I cannot get enough, taste enough. I get to my knees, pulling him closer. I *need* him closer—much, much closer.

His hands find my face, then my shoulders. The tingling sensation of magic slips up my arms, under my tunic and kurta, down between my breasts—

I inhale sharply. It feels like a caress. An intimate one.

Memnon smiles against me. "Do you like that?" he whispers.

"Are you doing that?" I ask.

He smiles. "What do you think, little witch?"

I think that if he is going to tease me with his magic, it's only fair I do the same.

Tentatively, I send my own power out, imagining it like phantom limbs. I will my warmth into the touch as my magic moves over his body.

Memnon inhales sharply when it reaches his cock. He bows his head and groans. "You're going to torment me?"

"Just a little."

Then, things happen in a rush. Armor and weapons, clothes and boots—we strip away all that glittering, intimidating opulence until there is nothing between us.

Memnon lays himself over me, his face so close. "I love you, my queen," he says, searching my face, his expression serious, fervent.

"And I love you, my king."

Memnon smiles then, and not even the darkness around us can dim the light of it. He shifts his hips, the head of his cock right at my entrance.

Memnon kisses me fiercely as he sinks into me. There's only me, him, the endless grasslands around us, and the heavens above us.

"I am yours forever," he breathes against my lips. He pulls away to search my gaze, his features bathed in the soft orange glow from my magic. "Forever."

CHAPTER 21
Roxilana, 18 years old

54 AD, Northern Sarmatia, near the Borysthenes River

The days of celebration run into one another. Singing and dancing begin midmorning, and kumiss and wine flow from sunrise to well after sunset. People pass out in the streets of the settlement and wake only to begin celebrating again the next day.

But then, on the fourth day of festivities, something changes.

A distant commotion beyond the walls of the tented dining hall drags my gaze from the line of guests waiting to meet me and Memnon. Moments later, Tamara enters the large space and briskly approaches us, the adornments on her large headdress tinkling.

She steps in front of the young couple greeting us and leans in close. "Memnon, your father is here."

I glance sharply at Tamara, but my mother-in-law's expression gives nothing else away—no joy, no anger, nothing at all to indicate how she might feel about Memnon's father joining us. I myself am reeling from this revelation. I remember the stories of Ilyapa, King of the Moche, and his ability to travel here. Even knowing this, I hadn't expected to meet him so soon after arriving.

Memnon rises, his eyes fixed to the entrance of the tent as a group of armed Sarmatian warriors enter, two civilians in their midst. They approach our throne, scattering the line of waiting guests in the process.

Once they stop and the warriors move aside, I finally lay eyes on Ilyapa, the man who gave Memnon his magic. He's tall and willowy, and beneath his hammered gold crown, his straight hair falls to his shoulders, the dark strands threaded through with silver. His skin is pale brown in color, but it lacks the sun-deepened hue that Memnon's carries, as though this man spends most of his time inside. And though he must be older, his skin shows only the first signs of wrinkles.

Memnon steps forward and eagerly embraces him.

"My son, my wonderful son," Ilyapa murmurs. He speaks in fluent Sarmatian, but there's some haze to the words that makes me think magic is at play.

Ilyapa eventually steps back to hold Memnon at arm's length. Though Memnon's father might be tall, his son is taller still.

"I swear you have gotten bigger since I saw you last," Ilyapa says.

"It *has* been several seasons," Memnon says.

His father smiles at him and pats him on the cheek. "Too long," he says with fondness. He brings Memnon in close then, and kisses him on one cheek, then the other.

I can feel my husband's pleasure and the pride brimming from him.

Memnon steps back from his father and turns to his left. "Eislyn." He dips his head. "As ever, it is a pleasure to see you."

Only then do I realize there's a *woman* at Ilyapa's side—Eislyn, Memnon called her. Once I fix my gaze on her, I cannot look away.

She is unlike anyone I've ever seen. Her hair is pale and bright, so bright, like spun sunlight, and from between the shimmering locks, I can make out the odd, pointed tips of her ears. And though her eyes are blue like mine and her skin is similarly pale, there is some element to her that I lack, like comparing glass to clay. Eislyn is delicate and lustrous, and…I am not. Not like her anyway.

She doesn't see me. In fact, she doesn't seem to see *anyone* save for my husband. Him, she openly stares at even once he returns his attention to his father. The look has my heart racing and my stomach twisting.

I don't like it, I realize. It's not simply a covetous look—I've seen a few of those since I arrived here—it's the certainty in Eislyn's eyes that she could capture Memnon's interest if she wanted to and that she just might.

"Memnon, I heard fortuitous news," his father says, following his gaze. "Tell me the spirits whisper the truth."

Again, Memnon's pride brims over. "Father," he says, turning back to Ilyapa. "I'd like you to meet my wife and queen." He steps aside, gesturing to me. "This is Roxilana."

Memnon's father assesses me with dark, inquisitive eyes. "So you are the woman the gods have bound to my son," he says. His voice raises the hairs on my arm. I cannot say why.

Hesitantly, I rise from my seat. "I am."

He steps forward, past Memnon, studying my features. "I hear you have magic."

Next to him, Eislyn's attention has finally shifted to me. Her expression is placid, but her eyes are as sharp as her strange beauty.

"I do," I say softly, coming to Memnon's side.

"Mmm," Ilyapa murmurs, still taking me in. "Very good, very good."

He glances around at the warriors and the gathering crowd, his eyes lingering longer than necessary on Tamara, who stands off to the side, her features neutral. "For now, however, I would like to give you both your wedding gift— should you be brave enough to accept it."

"Brave enough?" I echo, perplexed.

I glance at Memnon, who appears neither surprised nor confused but rather…grim. What gift could possibly make a battle-scarred king look so apprehensive?

"Yes, Daughter, *brave* enough," Ilyapa says, recapturing my attention. He leans in close. "For you see, you will have to travel to my kingdom to enjoy it."

You father is joking, right? I ask Memnon as he, myself, Ilyapa, and Eislyn head through camp, toward the entrance of the settlement.

Memnon's expression is still unnervingly somber, his mouth turned down slightly at the corners. *I do not think so.*

I stare at Memnon, thrown by his answer. *What does that mean?*

"Let me speak to my new daughter," Ilyapa interrupts. "Eislyn, lead Memnon to the ley line."

Ley line?

Eislyn is only too happy to step in close to my husband and draw him away from my side.

Meanwhile, Memnon's father moves in and tucks my hand into his. "How are you taking to married life?"

"It is wonderful."

I can feel his eyes on me. "And my son? Does he treat you well?"

I turn to look at Ilyapa and say earnestly, "He's the best thing that ever happened to me."

A smile touches Ilyapa's lips, though it quickly dims. "And his magic—you are okay with it?"

My brow furrows. "Why wouldn't I be?" Even as I say it, I see the slaughtered Romans and the dead gladiators. I see Nero with his panicked eyes and his pleading face. It's like a cloud covering the sun, this remembering.

Ilyapa tilts his head, his gold disc earrings catching the light as he assesses me again. "I cannot tell whether you are lying or simply do not know."

"Do not know what?"

Ilyapa studies me a bit longer. "Memnon comes from a blighted lineage, dear Daughter."

"He has told me he's a sorcerer," I say. "I've seen what his power can do."

Ilyapa nods. "Has he told you about what it costs him?"

My brows draw together in confusion.

"Ah, he hasn't." Ilyapa leans in conspiratorially. "The way he looks at you, I am not surprised. I wouldn't have either, had I found my soul mate. I would've waited until she was inescapably mine."

A chill runs down my spine at the possession in his words, and I think I am fortunate to be bound to a man like Memnon and not his father.

"But you should know: In our lineage, a sorcerer's power comes at a price. The more we use it, the more it eats away at our conscience until there is nothing left of it."

That chill amplifies, spreading through me. "What?" I

222

say softly. *This* must be the joke, one I do not fully understand. Memnon has never mentioned this, and after all the other revelations we've had, he would've, right?

"Memnon will…lose his conscience?" Because the man will not stop using his magic. That would be an impossible request for either of us.

Ilyapa studies me. "I didn't mean to frighten you."

That's essentially a yes. I study Memnon's back, trying to not let his father's words burrow under my skin. "Has this happened to you?" I ask, turning to look at Ilyapa again. "Have you lost your conscience?"

"Nearly all of it, dear Daughter."

I raise my eyebrows, my heart beginning to race. "But the way you embraced Memnon…" I protest. Surely that cannot be faked?

"I am proud of my son and committed to my legacy," he says, "but I kiss cheeks and embrace family and feel only a spark of fondness where once fires raged. I long to get back what time and power have taken from me," he admits, "but it is beyond even my reach." He stares after his son. "Perhaps I am wrong about Memnon's fate," he continues. "You and he are bound by forces larger than any of us, and the gods love to be unpredictable."

I taste bile as I gaze at my husband's back. I had not anticipated losing the best parts of him piece by piece over the ensuing years. A conscienceless Memnon would be terrifying.

My attention drifts from him to Eislyn. The woman now lays her hand on my husband's arm and leans into him in a way that is far too familiar, even if he sidesteps the touch a moment later. My unease spills over from future maladies to more immediate ones.

"Who is she?" I ask, gut churning.

"Eislyn?" Ilyapa says as we exit the settlement and head onto the open steppe land. "She's interesting, is she not?"

"Mmm." I nod. It's the best response I can muster.

"She comes from a realm beyond land and sky," Ilyapa says conversationally. "She is older than even the trees. She refers to herself as a fairy and her kind, the fae."

She sounds disturbingly like a goddess.

Ilyapa notices the shrewd way I watch her. "You're smart to keep an eye on her. She is clever and very beguiling."

"Has she beguiled *you*?"

He laughs. "Oh yes. Me and the rest of my line," he says, his gaze flicking back to Memnon.

That bit of news is a blade to my heart, one I can barely breathe around.

"Your husband has kept her at arm's length," he adds. "His half brothers, however …"

I raise my eyes. "Memnon has brothers?" I assumed Katiari was his only sibling.

"*Three*," Ilyapa clarifies. "And they would do well to not meet your husband. Some of my sons have more power and less heart than others."

I peer at Ilyapa, questions bubbling to the surface.

My attention drifts back to the woman at Memnon's side, and I scrutinize her. "If Eislyn is from another realm, what is she doing here in ours?" I ask.

"She was banished from her own."

We reach a large mound then, one that rises like a boil from the earth around it. I have seen a few of these during my travels with Memnon, and he told me they were called kurgans, Sarmatian burial mounds.

What business we have visiting one right now is beyond

my understanding, but Memnon must know, for he and Eislyn walk up the earthen hill.

I give Ilyapa a quizzical look. "I am very confused about this gift of yours," I admit.

The wizened king laughs lightly and pats my hand again. "Help me to the top of this hill, then I will explain."

The four of us climb the kurgan. The top of it is flat and barren, though the view of the land around us is amazing.

"Roxilana, have you ever traveled by ley line?" Ilyapa asks as Memnon moves to my side.

My brows come together. "Ley line?" There's that term again.

They are magical roads that certain beings can use to travel great distances in a short amount of time, Memnon explains, grasping my hand.

I glance down at where our fingers intertwine, my heart hurting a little as I remember Ilyapa's earlier words.

In our lineage, a sorcerer's power comes at a price. The more we use it, the more it eats away at our conscience…

Memnon's brow furrows as he senses my conflicted mood. *Roxi, are you all right?*

I give my head a shake, then nod, my emotions in knots. *It doesn't matter,* I tell him. Now is no time to discuss this.

I refocus my attention on Ilyapa and clear my throat. "I've never heard of such a thing."

"Then this will truly be an experience," Ilyapa says.

"Memnon, take my hand," Eislyn says, her voice lilting.

My husband's eyes are still on me, his brows creased as he absently grips her hand. Eislyn grasps Ilyapa with her other hand.

Her gaze is unwavering on my husband when she says, "Follow me and don't let go." She takes a step backward, then vanishes into thin air.

I don't have time to cry out in alarm. Not before Memnon and Ilyapa move along with her. To my horror, their bodies are swallowed up by the air itself too. Or at least most of their bodies—I can still see Memnon's disembodied hand tightly gripping my own.

A scream is building in my throat.

It's all right, my queen, Memnon says, a touch of humor easing the previous concern in his voice. *This is the doorway to the ley line. All you have to do is step forward.*

If anyone else suggested such a thing, I would mutiny. But with Memnon, conscience or not, I'd follow him to the edges of the world. So I take those few fateful steps forward.

When I inhale, I am in Sarmatia. When I exhale, I am somewhere else entirely.

I stare wide-eyed at my surroundings, struggling to make sense of them. It appears as though I'm in a tunnel of sorts, one made of smears of light and color. It stretches on either side of me seemingly forever.

I've barely had a moment to process the sight when Eislyn begins leading us down the tunnel.

Around me, the color shifts and changes, the sight of it making my head pound.

What are you thinking? Memnon asks.

I glance at him only to catch him staring fondly at me, though that crease is still there between his eyebrows.

With my free hand, I reach out and smooth it, making the decision to leave the hurt and ire back in Sarmatia. We will speak of it later. For now, I will simply enjoy the moment.

I'm thinking this is the most unbelievable experience I've yet had, I admit.

More unbelievable than having a voice inside your head? he asks, the corner of his mouth curving up.

I fight back a grin. *It's not a competition, Husband.*

For an instant, his eyes seem to glow. *I want you to call me that again, tonight, when I am inside you.*

Memnon. My eyes widen.

I can feel his humor down our bond. *They cannot hear us, little witch. We can talk about anything at all, and Eislyn and my father would not know. Like how I enjoy the way you try to escape when I am eating you out, and the sounds you make when you are getting close to orgasming—*

"We're here," Eislyn announces over her shoulder, her gaze briefly touching on the two of us. If she notices my flushed cheeks or quickened breath, she says nothing.

She turns and steps *into* the wall of the tunnel itself. Again, I have to swallow a shout at the sight of her body disappearing from view.

The rest of us follow her, leaving the ley line and stepping out into a muddy, shaded forest.

The longer I look, the more I realize that this is no forest like I've ever seen. The trees are tightly packed together, and their leaves are waxy and shockingly green.

The air seems to lie on our bodies like a blanket, heavy and mildly warm, and it practically vibrates with noise from whatever fantastical creatures lurk within the dense foliage. The land is alive in a way I have never experienced.

"Ah, we are here," Ilyapa says, stepping forward.

I glance past him, trying to understand where *here* is, but I cannot see anything beyond the dense vegetation.

He pulls aside a curtain of vines and places his hand on an enchantment hanging in midair, one I didn't notice. A deep green color flushes it for an instant before it dissolves away.

I gasp.

The vegetation in front of me dissipates like steam from a pot, revealing a palace made entirely of glittering, white marble. I take a halting step toward it, mesmerized by the sight. It looks like something the gods themselves designed. There's a columned entrance and colonnaded walkway as well as three domed roofs, the grandest set beyond the main entrance. The longer I stare, the more unbelievable it seems.

"*This* is your wedding present," Ilyapa says proudly.

I stagger back. Even Memnon halts, his face wiped clean of expression. "What?" he says, turning to look at his father.

Ilyapa looks immeasurably pleased. "I didn't mumble, Memnon. This is yours."

Memnon glances from him to the palace. I follow his gaze, my breath hitching in my throat.

It's been hard enough to accept the copious wedding gifts we've received from my new people and harder still to wear the diadem that rests on my head. But a palace?

Not even Memnon, king that he is, has such a thing.

"Come, let me show it to you both," Ilyapa says. Already Eislyn wanders ahead of us, her fingertips trailing over the flowering plants she passes.

There are columns of marble carved into the shapes of trees, gold vines wrapping around them. The leaves are made of gilded marble, and the flowers that bloom along these stone trees and vines appear to be made of blown glass, their centers golden. I touch the tree trunk, the bark of it as rough as the real thing, and then my finger runs over the slightly serrated edge of a marble leaf. I marvel. No mortal craftsman could've made this. This must be the work of gods or magic, though I know not which.

The stone trees bend into an archway of sorts, and beyond them lies a set of massive, bronze doors. Ilyapa steps up to them and pushes them open with ease, a little of his pine-green magic leaking out with the action.

Our soft footsteps echo inside.

"This is the Khuno River Palace. No one besides Eislyn and myself know about this place—and now you."

I don't know what to make of that—any of this, really—but Memnon seems to. He strides forward and embraces his father. "Thank you. You honor us."

"No, no, my son," Ilyapa says, pulling away and lightly gripping Memnon by the back of his neck. "It is *you* who honor *me*."

I remember Ilyapa's earlier comments about how blunted his emotions are, and I wonder what it is, exactly, that he feels right now, giving his son an entire palace. I wonder if his heart is truly as cold as he says it is.

"Come," Ilyapa says to Memnon, patting him on the shoulder. "There is more yet I want to show you."

I watch the two of them enter the palace, though this time, I don't follow. Blunted emotions or not, Memnon is having a bonding moment with his father, and I sense he doesn't get this much.

"They are quite a pair, are they not?" Eislyn says, coming to my side.

I startle a little. I've been so consumed with this place that I forgot she was here with us.

She continues, leaning in conspiratorially. "Ilyapa says he doesn't have a favorite child, but, well, you have eyes and ears."

I nod absently, my skin prickling with awareness now that this woman is at my side. I still cannot decide whether she is a goddess or something else, but when I turn to her, I'm just as ensnared by her features as I was the first time I laid eyes on her.

Finally, however, she meets my gaze.

"Congratulations," she says, nodding to my diadem, "on both your marriage and your crown."

"Thank you." I dip my head, proud when my diadem does not topple off.

"What did you do before Memnon found you?" she asks, her gaze wandering over me as though her eyes might uncover my secrets.

"I was a seamstress."

Eislyn raises her eyebrows. "From seamstress to queen. What an immense leap."

I cannot tell whether the words are meant to be sweet or unkind. Eislyn's face gives nothing away.

"Come," she says, her hand moving softly to my upper back. "This calls for a toast." She leads me into the palace, steering me to the left, the opposite direction that Memnon and his father went.

We pass through what looks like a sitting chamber with reclining couches made of jewel-toned fabric, our footsteps echoing around us.

"The palace has no servants, so any needs you have require magic to accomplish." As she speaks, we enter a dining hall. A single table made of polished wood occupies the space, running the long length of the room and decorated down its center with green glass leaves and flowers and candles.

"However, we have some clever spells in place." She lifts her hand and snaps her fingers. Fire bursts to life along the row of candles. "*Wine*," Eislyn commands, folding a bit of power into her voice.

Delicate blown-glass cups shaped like flowers slide off the boughs of a nearby marble tree, where they had discreetly hung, and they float down to a side table next to a beaked glass jug.

"There is an underground chamber where we keep wines and beer," Eislyn says as the jug lifts into the air, "but there is almost always something to drink here in the kitchens and dining hall."

The glass jug pours its contents into first one flower glass, then the other, before it resettles on the table. The glasses, however, continue on, rising from the side table and drifting along the air until one lands in my waiting palm.

I'm trying not to gape—at the cups, the magic, the room itself—though I am overwhelmed.

Eislyn raises her glass to me. "A toast: from lowly seamstress to lofty queen. May all such ambition be duly rewarded."

Her words cause an uncomfortable lump to form in my belly. I lower my glass.

"I did not marry Memnon to be queen," I say softly.

"Oh?" Eislyn arches a pale eyebrow. "Then I overestimated your ambition. Shame, I do appreciate a determined woman."

I frown into my glass. That definitely seemed like an insult.

Eislyn clucks her tongue. "Stop acting like your wine is poisoned and *drink*. You deserve it. In fact, I think we should have another toast since I botched the first one." Once again, she lifts her glass. Guarded, I follow.

There's a glimmer in her clear blue eyes. "To being a beloved first wife," she says, giving me a closed-lip smile. "Enjoy the exalted position."

My eyes widen at her words and my glass trembles a little as I lower it once more.

Eislyn's expression turns distressed. "Have I made a mess of this toast too?"

I give my head a shake if only to knock away the thoughts now cluttering it. "What do you mean, 'first wife'?" I ask hoarsely.

Her distress turns to surprise. "Warriors are allowed multiple spouses," she says. "Most do it—especially kings. It is nearly expected of them." She tilts her head, that pale-blond hair spilling over her shoulder. "Did you not know?"

I shake my head again, stunned into silence. In the distance, I can hear Memnon and his father talking, their voices drawing closer.

I move to the long table and set my glass down, its delicate base clattering against the polished surface.

Memnon and Ilyapa enter then, Ilyapa looking jovial. Memnon, however, seeks me out with his eyes, his expression somber.

Roxi, is everything all right? he asks. *I can sense your distress.*

Another shake of my head. *No, I don't think I'm all right.*

"Memnon, you made me look bad," Eislyn accuses.

Without meaning to, one hand goes to my stomach, the other to the table.

It will be all right, I tell myself. *It all has a reasonable explanation.*

What has a reasonable explanation? Memnon asks, crossing the room. He cups my face, his eyes searching mine. He dips his head, trying to better peer at me. "Have I done something?"

"No." But I can feel my lower lip trembling. Gods, I do not want to lose my composure.

"She had to learn from me that you will undoubtedly take more wives," Eislyn says.

Across from me, Memnon goes rigid. "What?" he growls, slowly looking over at her.

I can feel the flame of his anger and a surge of his power. Blue wisps of his magic curl around my face.

"Why, in all the gods' names, would you think of bringing such a subject up? To my new bride, no less?"

His attention returns to me. *Roxilana, I will not be taking more wives*, he says fervently. *Not ever.*

I nod, but I'm not looking at him.

Memnon moves away from me, toward Eislyn, his power spilling out of him. "Eislyn, *you had no right.*"

She lifts her hands placatingly. "I did not mean to startle her. I was merely making a toast to her new position. I thought she *knew.*"

I look up to see Memnon's hair lifting and his eyes beginning to glow. If I was distraught before, now I am alarmed. In three quick steps, I cross to Memnon, placing a hand on his forearm. "It was a misunderstanding," I say, even as I eye Eislyn apprehensively. I'm fairly certain it was no such thing, but I am not ready to see the woman get disemboweled over it, and that may very well happen if I don't stop Memnon. "It was just a shock."

"You had *no* right," Memnon repeats to Eislyn, his power deepening his voice.

"I didn't know. Truly." Eislyn glances at Ilyapa, perhaps for aid, but Memnon's father doesn't seem keen to jump to her defense.

Memnon stares at her like he doesn't care what the fuck she knew or didn't; he's ready to cut her down for her sheer audacity.

"Eislyn, apologize for being naughty," Ilyapa finally says, watching the situation with a detached sort of curiosity.

"Memnon, a thousand apologies." She dips her head. "I have offended you and wounded your new wife, and for that, I am sorry."

Memnon's hair is still rippling, and his eyes are glowing. I move around to his front and place a hand on his cheek.

Memnon, I say, turning his face to mine. *It's okay.*

Rising onto my tiptoes, I press a kiss to his lips. At first, he's unresponsive, but then he draws in a sharp breath, like maybe he is returning to life. He kisses me back, his hands finding me. Slowly, slowly, his power recedes into him.

He shudders against me, and when I look at his eyes next, they have dimmed back to the beautiful smoky-amber color they usually are.

"Well, before we cause any more marital strife, I think we should see ourselves out," Ilyapa says. He retreats to the archway out of the dining hall, then pauses.

"Oh, I almost forgot," he says, rotating back around. "Memnon, there is a second part of your gift, one Eislyn is willing to share with you."

My husband casts a wary glance at the woman, his power right there, barely banked. Eislyn crosses the room to him, ignoring the hostility still pouring off him.

"Part of your father's wedding gift—our gift—to you is that you may learn how to travel these ley lines." She touches her temple with two fingers. "I give you my permission to use your magic and take the knowledge from my mind."

A muscle in Memnon's jaw clenches. Down our bond, I can sense his complicated emotions. His desire for such a skill is battling his simmering annoyance.

Finally, he grimaces and dips his head. "Thank you for this gift," he says.

He takes a deep breath, then another, like he's readying

himself. Then, stepping into Eislyn's space, he grasps her head, his fingers flexing as his power twists out of his hands.

It happens quickly, the blue lines of power slithering into her mouth and nostrils. Her eyelids flutter, and she grasps his forearms as his magic takes hold.

I have seen Memnon do this to the unwilling. It is strange seeing his power at work when his subject *is* willing.

All at once, Memnon releases Eislyn, backing away to my side.

His father looks between the two. "Did it work?" he finally asks.

"Mmm," Memnon says, giving a subtle nod, his eyes a little hazy.

Eislyn is slower to retreat, her attention still fixed on my husband.

"Then we should leave," Ilyapa says.

He approaches us and embraces Memnon once more. "Congratulations, my son. There aren't many things truly worth living for in this life, but a good woman is one of them." He pulls away, patting him on the cheek. "Enjoy newly married life. And make me some grandchildren I can spoil next time we meet."

Ilyapa releases Memnon, then comes over to me. "Dear Daughter," he says, taking my hand. He gives me a gentle smile, his gaze searching my own. "You have knowledgeable eyes, but they are not shrewd, not the way a queen's must be. I lament that the next time I see you, they will look shrewd." His smile tightens, turning bleak. "Power always exacts a cost. Always."

With that unsettling line, he lets go of my hand and hugs me.

Conscienceless or not, Ilyapa gives me the sort of hug

that Tamara does, one that makes me feel like I belong. Like I am family.

Giving my back a final pat, he releases me.

"Come, Eislyn," he says, backing away. "It is time we left. Who knows what machinations await us back at our palace?"

Eislyn comes up to me, stepping in close. "I hope we can be friends," she says. "I have counseled your husband's family for many generations. It is my wish to see the mother of his future children well and happy."

I nod and try for a smile, but the truth is, I don't like her, and my intuition is telling me to watch her closely, that she is a slippery thing.

She turns from me and hugs Memnon, holding him for a touch too long. "You can ask anything of me," she says softly, "anything at all, and I will give it to you. You understand?"

"I want nothing," Memnon says, extricating himself.

"Nothing more, you mean," she responds, touching her temple. "I guess we'll see, won't we?" She backs up, nodding to both of us. "Felicitations on your marriage."

With that, she and Ilyapa leave, their footsteps retreating, the large double doors groaning first to open, then to close.

Once they're gone, I feel the tension leave my body. Suddenly, I'm tired.

Tired and a little dejected.

"Is it true?" I ask. "That Sarmatian kings take many wives?"

I think of how Eislyn fawned over him. There are many more women back at our settlement who would do the same thing if given the chance.

Memnon's nostrils flare and he grimaces, but after a moment, he reluctantly nods. "It's true."

"*Have* you ever considered multiple—"

He laughs—*laughs!*—before I can even complete the thought.

"Why are you laughing?" I demand, my hurt rising.

"Because it is *preposterous*."

"It doesn't sound like it is," I say. "It sounds entirely"—unbearably—"normal."

"Yes," Memnon agrees, nodding, mirth still in his eyes. "Sarmatians are allowed multiple spouses, and many previous kings have done so. Those kings, however, *wanted* other wives. I do not. I never touched another woman before you, and I do not intend to—*ever*."

For the first time since Eislyn spoke the words, I feel I can breathe again. Still, Memnon hasn't been completely forthright with me. "Would you still feel the same if you lost your conscience?"

He rears back like I've hit him, but his eyes, his eyes look guilty. "What?" he says softly.

My earlier hurt rises, despite my best efforts to leave it back in Sarmatia. "Your father told me about the cost of your power."

Memnon's face falls, and he looks boyish and young. "I'm sorry," he breathes, casting his eyes downward. "I meant to tell you, but I was afraid."

"Afraid of what?" I say, searching what I can see of his features.

"I was afraid it would scare you off," he admits, glancing back up at me.

"I deserved to know," I say adamantly. "And I shouldn't have learned it from your father."

He nods, and I see his throat bob as he swallows. "I should've said something."

"Yes," I agree. "You should've." I step in close, placing my hand against his cheek, his ropey scar pressed to my palm. "I've seen you *kill*," I say softly. "This knowledge was never going to be what scared me off." I take a deep breath and drop my hand, taking a step back. "Just please promise me you'll protect your conscience—I happen to be very fond on it," I say wryly.

Memnon gazes at me deeply, then lifts his chin. "Command it of me—along with forbidding me to take other wives."

I open my mouth to protest, taken aback.

"You are a queen," Memnon elaborates. "You command me, and I command you."

"I don't want to be commanded," I say. "Nor do I want to command you."

Memnon smiles slowly. "But I *will* command you, and you *will* inevitably command me back because we are both headstrong and stubborn in our own ways. And we will clash, but then we will fuck and make up because I love you and you love me."

I search his face.

"So I will begin," he continues. "You are not to touch another man…or woman. You are mine and mine alone."

I guffaw, thrown by his demand. "That would *never* happen."

"Would it not? And how do I know?" he says. "Where is my reassurance?"

"There were no others before you either," I say testily.

"But there almost was." Memnon steps in close. "Would you have married that man had I not stopped the wedding?"

I search his gaze. The truth is, I don't know. Women are

supposed to be meek and agreeable. Livia beat that notion into me.

"Would you have let him touch you?"

"*Memnon*. I will never let another touch me," I vow. "And *you* are not to touch another man or woman. Nor are you allowed to overuse your magic and lose your conscience.

"Oh," I say as another thought comes to me, "and I want Eislyn to keep her hands to herself when it comes to you."

"Or else what?" Memnon challenges, lifting his chin.

My power begins leaking out of me. "Or else *I will make her do so.*"

My king's eyes smolder, and he looks pleased. Quite pleased. "There's my queen." He leans forward. "I *do* like the sight of you jealous."

I give his shoulder a playful push, and he laughs again, then scoops me up.

I yelp, wrapping my arms around his neck as he strides out of the dining hall, heading deeper into the palace.

"I agree to your many commands," he says, gazing at me fondly.

"As you should," I say tartly.

I glance over his shoulder as he makes his way down a long hall with more marble and gold accents. "Where are you taking me?"

"Have you forgotten?" he says. "I'm still determined to get you to call me *husband* while my cock is buried in you."

"*Memnon*."

He grins. "Your mock outrage is *such* a turn-on, little witch."

"You know," I say conversationally, "you don't have to say everything you think."

"Lucky you, you'd still hear it anyway."
And with that, he carries me away.

CHAPTER 22
Roxilana, 18 years old

54 AD, Northern Sarmatia, near the Borysthenes River

On the final day of wedding celebrations, I'm startled from sleep by a sharp slap on the ass.

"Wake up, Daughter, we have ritual business to attend to."

I blink awake, trying to sort myself out. I'm in Memnon's tent—*our* tent—the space large and brimming with wedding gifts. Somewhere in sleep, I kicked off the blankets. I grab for them now, intent to burrow beneath them and return to my dim dreams.

Only, the linens are snatched from my grip.

"Roxilana, get up." Tamara's stern voice cuts through the sleepy haze of my mind, and I startle.

I sit up before my mind has a chance to second-guess it. Absently, my hand reaches for Memnon, but the warm body splayed out at my side is Ferox's, and my husband is nowhere in sight.

"He's been called away on kingly business. He will be back later. Now, *up*."

As Tamara speaks, Katiari enters the tent, moving over to one of the chests in the room rather than greeting me.

I frown as I push myself out of bed. Near me, Ferox stretches, then curls back up on the blankets, uninterested in what's happening around him.

Both Tamara and Katiari are already dressed in short kurtas and trousers, though judging by the dimness of the room, the sun hasn't fully risen yet.

"What's going on?" I say, my gaze moving from mother to daughter.

Katiari pulls a pair of trousers and a lightweight kurta out of the chest and tosses them to me.

"Get dressed," Tamara commands, backing away, as imperious as ever. "The kurta is optional."

"I brought wine," Katiari adds helpfully. She holds up a jug I didn't notice before.

My gaze moves from her to Tamara. "What do you mean, 'the kurta is optional'?" I say, lifting the garment from the bed. "What sort of ritual business is this?"

"You'll find out soon enough," Tamara says ominously.

I eye her as I begin to dress, only a little self-conscious that they're seeing my body. They already got an eyeful on my wedding day.

Once I finish dressing and move to pull on my boots, Katiari crosses over to me and extends the jug of wine. "You really should drink."

I give her a perplexed look, even as I take the jug.

What sort of ritual might I need wine for?

I unstopper it and hesitate for the barest of moments

before I tip a little into my mouth. When I taste the heady, undiluted wine, I wince.

Tamara grabs my diadem from where it rests on a nearby side table, fitting the thing on top of my mess of hair.

"There," she says, her fingers trailing lovingly down my cheeks. "Now you are ready." She backs away. "Come, dear Daughters," she says, making her way to the tent's entrance. "The day is getting started without us."

I lean over to Ferox and place a ward on him so he can safely wander through camp and the wilds beyond. And then, following Tamara and Katiari, I slip from the tent.

Outside, dawn is just beginning to blush, yet already, the air holds a promise of heat as we begin to walk.

I lean into Katiari. "From sister to sister, will you tell me what is going on?"

Her gaze darts around me to her mother. "She would have my head," Katiari whispers. She steps in a little closer and takes my hand, squeezing it lightly. "But all will be well. That, I can swear on." She takes the jug from me and swallows a mouthful before passing it back. "Drink up, Roxi. Today is the final day of celebrations."

I drink my share of wine as we wind our way through camp, the alcohol sitting like a fist in my stomach as we pass by the smoking remains of last night's fires and the occasional passed-out reveler.

At last, we arrive at a large, indiscriminate tent. Tamara pulls the flap of it aside, and the first thing I notice is the smell. Thick, cloying incense fills the space with its pungent aroma.

A moment later, I notice the many women congregated inside. Nearly every age is represented, from young girls to withered crones, and unlike the sleeping revelers outside this tent, they are quite alert. When they see us, they dip their heads.

I swallow. I'm still unused to the casual reverence I'm given, especially when I don't have Memnon at my side to ease the shock of it.

At the center of the tent, a few pillows have been tossed onto the carpeted floor. Next to them are several bone needles, a cosmetic bottle, and the incense burner. A woman with curly, dark brown hair and a smattering of freckles across her nose kneels near these, and Tamara and Katiari lead me to her.

The woman clasps my hand. "Lovely to see you, my queen. Come, sit. The women of your new clan have been eager for this moment." She leads me from my mother- and sister-in-law and down to the pillows, where I stiffly sit.

Around me, someone begins a chant, and the other women in the tent join in, the sound filling the air just as much as the burning incense is.

Tamara turns and addresses the room. "Today, we honor my new daughter, our queen."

The chant grows louder, and I sway a little where I'm seated, the smell of the incense making me lightheaded.

Tamara continues. "She will bear the clan mark of the royal family to acknowledge her status and lineage."

Bear the mark?

"A dragon to symbolize her marriage to our king, Memnon the Indomitable, leader of the dragon clan," she says.

My gaze drops to the bone needles and the cosmetic jar in front of me and understanding washes through me.

Oh gods. I'm getting tattooed.

This was the secret kept from me until now, when I'm

surrounded by kinswomen. I glare up at where Tamara stands because I can do nothing else. I know very little about being queen, but even I can figure out that protesting now would earn me only ire from the women who are to be my family.

It's an impossible position she's put me in, and she must know it too.

"Please lie back," says my tattooist, as she settles herself in front of me and preps the bone needles.

I do so, though I'm beginning to tremble. I feel exposed, lying before a room of women who will watch as someone pierces my skin again and again. And the only person who feels truly safe to me has been called away on kingly duties.

Tamara settles herself behind me, Katiari at her side.

My mother-in-law leans forward and squeezes my shoulder. "It is a sign of strength to make no sound," she breathes as the tattooist begins to heat a bone needle over the flame of the incense burner.

"Damn you," I say softly to her.

She smiles and gives my arm a squeeze. "That's my daughter. Already the fire of my clan heats your blood."

The room is still chanting, the notes of it pricking at my skin.

The tattooist leans over and opens the wrapped collar of my top, exposing a breast and the smooth skin above it. I lock my jaw to keep from gasping. Embarrassment burns my cheeks as the room stares on.

The tattooist grabs a bone needle whose tip is coated with charcoal and moves it over my heart.

At the first prick, I suck in a sharp breath. The needle digs into my skin, depositing the pigment into my flesh. I grind my teeth together, tears welling in my eyes as it's wiggled about. It hurts far more than a small needle has any right to. At least it doesn't hurt as much as a lashing.

When the needle is removed, blood wells from the wound, but Tamara is there with a small cloth, curtly wiping it away. The bone needle reenters my skin a moment later, and *gods* but that hurts.

In and out, the needle works, moving over my skin. The pain is sometimes sharp and sometimes throbbing but always constant. Now I understand the alcohol.

"Katiari, do you still have the wine?" I ask.

Rather than answering, my sister-in-law scoots closer to me and presses the jug to my lips. I drink greedily, eager to numb the pain as much as I can.

Perhaps it works, or perhaps it's that pungent incense that clouds my mind, but I swear the longer I lie there, enduring the tattooist's needle, the more the pain drifts away—and half my mind along with it. It's a good thing too because the time stretches on forever, an eternity of dulled pain and bloodletting.

And as it goes, the women of my clan continue to chant songs of gods and battles, and though none of them—not even Tamara—have magic, I cannot deny that their voices stir up something my own power reacts to. I begin to hum with them, my magic lazily weaving through the tent until the pain itself becomes its own sort of background hum—

"*What is the meaning of this?*" Memnon's voice thunders through the tent.

I jerk against the bone needle piercing my skin. The tattooist hastily removes it, and the singing stops.

Through the haze of the burning incense, I see Memnon's murky form stride forward. I push myself up to my forearms, the rest of my top spreading open.

His eyes first land on my face before they drop to my chest. At first, I think he might be staring at my exposed breasts, until I feel a line of blood slip down my skin. His eyes begin to glow as he kneels next to me.

With those unnerving eyes, he peers down again at my skin. Then, pressing a gentle hand to it, I feel his magic flow out of him and sink into my flesh. My tattoo itches for several seconds before the pain fades away entirely.

"I'm sorry, my queen," Memnon says, his eyes dimming back to their normal hue. "I didn't know. I swear it to you."

I touch his face. "I know," I say hoarsely.

His finger traces over the nearly completed tattoo. Through the haze of alcohol and that peculiar incense, I note that the design is…beautiful.

Gently, Memnon takes my kurta and covers me back up. Then his gaze lifts over my shoulder to his mother, and his eyes begin to glow again.

"You had no right," he accuses, his magic deepening his voice.

His mother stares at him for several moments.

"Everyone, out," Tamara finally commands.

Women and girls hurry out, their eyes wide and their heads bowed.

I'm sorry, Memnon says again down our bond, his voice still that unnatural timbre.

I do not resent what your mother did, I tell him. *Merely how she did it.*

Once the tent is empty of all but me, Memnon, and his immediate family, Tamara rises from the ground, lifting her chin imperiously. "I had every right to do what I did. Your wife is one of us now. You know as well as I do, she must bear our markings, just as all other high-ranking family members do."

Memnon's nostrils flare, but slowly his magic ebbs away. Once he seems to have it under control, he turns to his sister, who still sits behind me.

"Katiari, go to my tent, find the most exquisite Roman garments you can, and bring one back here."

"Memnon—" his mother protests, while his sister silently retreats from the tent.

"I am your king," he bites out, his eyes blazing. "Mother or not, you will address me as such."

Tamara looks taken aback but only for a moment. Then I see a spark of admiration in her. Power acknowledging power.

"*My king*," Tamara begins again, "the entire point of today was to make your wife one of us. If she wears Roman garments, you will undo all my efforts."

"Yes," he agrees. "*Your* efforts. Not Roxi's. Not mine. Katiari will bring the outfit here, and our queen will choose what she wants to wear. Just as, from this moment forward, she will choose whether she wants to bear the ink of our people."

"And if she doesn't?" Tamara says hotly.

"Then she won't."

Tamara scoffs. "You will be challenged for this," she says, drawing me into this.

Despite the alcohol and the incense, this conversation is sobering me quickly. "If my critics are foolish, then yes, I will be," I say.

Again, that look of speculative appreciation comes over his mother. Eventually, she dips her head. "Very well. I have spoken my bit. I will take my leave." She dips her head and strides out of the tent. Only she pauses, right at the tent flap. Tamara glances over her shoulder, her gaze meeting mine. "Congratulations, Daughter. You now wear the mark of our family. Welcome to the clan of the dragon."

CHAPTER 23
Roxilana, 18 years old

54 AD, Northern Sarmatia, near the Borysthenes River

"I have a surprise for you." **Memnon walks backward in his** training leathers as he speaks, leading us down one of the many paths that cut through the tented settlement.

"Oh really?" I say, trailing after him, Ferox at my side "Should I be worried?"

Sarmatian surprises, I'm learning, can go either way.

He laughs, his eyes alight with excitement.

"You should always be worried with me, little witch."

I give Memnon a look, though I cannot help the smile that spreads across my face. Being around him is like soaking in the sun, and lately I've had so little of it.

Since the end of the wedding celebrations, life has returned to normal—or what must be normal for Sarmatians. For Memnon, that means dealing with kingly duties while Tamara trains me on the ins and outs of my new roles here.

"What exactly is this surprise?" I ask.

He glances over his shoulder. "You'll see," he says secretively. "We're nearly there."

Sure enough, we walk only a little farther when Memnon tugs me toward a small, innocuous tent with a blue fabric doorway.

Pulling the cloth aside, he gestures for me and Ferox to enter. Inside, the space is cozy and sumptuous, the ground covered in a large circular rug, a wooden table and cushioned bench at its center. On the table is a wax tablet, a stylus, and a small stack of scrolls.

My eyes lock onto the scrolls. Without thinking, I reach for one of them, my curiosity getting the better of me. A leather thong holds the roll of it together. When I glance at Memnon, a question in my eyes, he nods encouragingly.

"Go ahead," he says. "Take a look at it."

My gaze drops to the scroll once more. It feels like stealing sweets, untying the leather cord and opening the rolled papyrus. Written on it are lines and lines of Latin. I've seen the shapes of these letters for years, and though none of it means anything to me, understanding feels so close I can taste it.

My thumb runs over one of the letters as Ferox comes to my side, leaning against my leg. "What is the surprise?" I ask again, still beguiled by the writing.

"You cannot read," Memnon states.

I pet Ferox absently. "You already know that."

"But you want to," he adds, his eyes fervent on me.

"*Yes.*" My voice is hushed. Reverent.

A grin breaks out across his face, tugging at his facial scar. "Then I will teach you to read and write, right here in this little tent, which has been enchanted to quiet the outside noise and warded so that only you and I can enter—"

"Truly?" I interrupt with a whisper, lowering the scroll. I stare at him, disbelieving. "You will teach me how to read?"

Though I have received jewels and weapons, crowns and palaces since coming here, this is by far the most precious wedding gift of them all.

"I will," he says. "Unless, of course, you still think me too terrible a teacher," he adds.

I begin to tear up. "You're a great teacher," I say, unable to go along with the joke.

Memnon's face grows serious, though his eyes still twinkle. "Then, the better question is: which language would you prefer to learn first? Latin, or Greek, or—"

I don't let him finish.

I fling myself into his arms, holding him close. "*All of them*," I whisper.

Memnon's arms come around me, his grip tightening as he breathes against my ear. "Then you will learn all of them, my queen."

"When can we start?" I ask.

Slowly, Memnon releases me, regret etched on his face. "Not today, unfortunately. In fact, we probably should get going. We have official matters to attend to."

"*We* do?" Up until now, it was Memnon and Memnon alone who had the official matters.

He gives me a smile that is only a little pinched at the corners. "Now, my queen, we're going to preside over our people."

CHAPTER 24
Roxilana, 18 years old

54 AD, Northern Sarmatia, near the Borysthenes River

I'm terrified. Terrified out of my wits.

I sit on my claw-footed throne, Ferox at my feet and Memnon at my side, trying not to tremble like a leaf.

I squeeze the armrests tightly as I stare out at the crowd gathered in the great tent. None of Tamara's preparation has diminished my nerves. I regret wearing the stola I donned earlier. At the time, I didn't know I would be presiding over these people; I simply wanted to wear a garment that felt familiar. Now, however, seated in this chair and staring out at a sea of Sarmatian faces, the stola only seems to illuminate the fact that I am *not* one of them and do not belong on their throne, ready to cast judgment.

A makeshift aisle has formed down the center of the tent, and it is here that people wishing to speak to Memnon—and me—line up.

A light summer rain patters against the tent's roof as the

first people approach us. A barrel-chested man with a frizzy, brown beard walks up alongside a lanky boy. Both walk with their chins held high, and there is a visible level of pride in the man's eyes.

When they are only six paces or so from us, the man stops and bows, his son following suit.

"Your majesties," the man says, straightening, "I'd like to request my son join in the next battle."

I startle at his words, my eyes moving to the boy. The youth might be thirteen, though certainly no older than fourteen. He still has peach fuzz on his upper lip.

Memnon leans forward in his seat, his leathers groaning with the action. He nods to the man, then turns his attention to the son. "What is your name?" he asks, leaning a forearm on his knee.

"Kasais, my king," the boy says, his eyes flicking to Memnon, then darting quickly away.

"Kasais," Memnon repeats. "A strong name." He continues to study the boy. "And how are you with a spear, Kasais?"

"Decent," the boy answers, "though I am much better with a bow."

"The finest shot for his age," his father interjects.

"The finest?" Memnon says, peering at the man and raising his brows. "That is high praise, but then"—his scrutiny returns to his son—"that comes from your father, who clearly adores you. How would *you* say your mounted shot is?"

"Good," Kasais replies. "Though I'm better at firing a forward-mounted shot than a Parthian one."

Memnon nods. "Yes, well, shooting backward on horseback is a difficult skill to acquire, which is why few besides our people can do it at all."

My husband settles back into his throne and watches Kasais. "Are you ready for battle?"

"Aye," the boy says, nodding.

"You have prepared your mind and body for the act of killing—and potentially dying yourself?"

Kasais lifts his chin and clenches his jaw. "Aye."

Memnon smiles. "Good. Very good." He nods. "Then I give you my blessing. You will ride with your father and all the rest of my warriors in the next battle. May the gods bless you and protect you."

Kasais grins broadly, and his father's eyes water. Both bow, then leave the tent.

After they leave, I exhale. I have seen many boy soldiers—Rome is full of them—but this was still hard to bear witness to. And I know it's Memnon's people's way, but all I can remember right now were those times I felt Memnon's pain down our bond. He'd been young as well. *Too* young, in my opinion.

But though I am queen, I am a foreign woman and a stranger to these people. I doubt my protests would mean anything at this point. So I swallow down my unease and watch as a pregnant woman with long, braided hair walks up to our thrones.

She stops and bows, and when she straightens, her eyes move to me, her other hand going to her stomach. "I humbly request that my queen says a prayer to the gods that I might deliver my child safely."

My hands tighten on the throne; I hadn't expected to be directly addressed so soon.

After a moment, I clear my throat. "Of course," I say. "I would be happy to pray for the safe delivery of your child."

She bows again, then leaves.

And so it goes. There are some disputes between neighbors, a few more blessings and prayers, and then, there's Zosines.

When he first enters the tent, I assume it's as a guard coming to flank Memnon. But then I notice the woman walking behind him. She's lithe, her deep brown hair worn loose at her back, her skin a rich honey color.

"Permission to marry Leimeie, Phandarazous's widow," Zosines says.

I cannot smother my sharp inhalation, the sound drawing the eyes of many in the room.

Zosines already *has* a wife, Mada, one who is set to give birth any day now. By all accounts, Zosines adores her, and after meeting Mada on my wedding day, I understand his praise; she is a lovely human.

So why is she not enough?

Memnon arches an eyebrow. "Another wife, my brother? Are you, who spoke so fondly of Mada during our travels, already so eager to turn your affection toward another?" he says, echoing my thoughts.

"Mada brings me much joy still," Zosines says, his words overly stilted and formal. "This is no reflection on her worth as a wife. She is good to me in all ways."

"And yet you request another," Memnon says. Some of the other men in the room shift a little, as though uncomfortable with the direction of the conversation.

"I am a warrior," Zosines says, taking a step forward. "It is within my right to take more than one wife."

Outside, the rain pelts harder against the tent, as though even it has thoughts on the matter.

"But it is not just any woman you are asking for, is it?" Memnon raises his brows, his face stern and his voice hard. "Phandarazous has not been dead for a season. Hardly enough time to grieve his loss."

"This is what he would've wanted," Zosines insists.

"Is it?" Memnon ponders. "And I wonder if you would make such a request of *my* wife, should *I* die."

The room quiets, the sound of rain particularly loud as tension fills the space. Zosines is careful to look only at Memnon when he answers, "I imagine you and our queen would enter the afterlife together."

I glance sharply at Memnon, uncertain what Zosines means by that. But Memnon's attention is wholly focused on his blood brother.

"Mmm." Memnon makes an assenting noise. His eyes slide to Leimeie. "What are your thoughts on this?"

She dips her head. "Zosines is a great warrior and a good man. Phandarazous's last wish was for one of his friends to care for me."

Quieter, Memnon says, "And is that what *you* wish?"

Zosines's jaw tightens, and his eyes grow flinty while Leimeie glances up at Memnon. Her gaze touches his for a moment before she dips her head again and nods. "It is."

Memnon's expression turns thoughtful, and he looks at Zosines again. "Then, my friend, it is my great honor to approve of and bless this union."

I startle at Memnon's words as Zosines's anger melts from his face. He shakes his head, then outright laughs, embracing his wife-to-be, his smile large.

"You had me worried there for a moment, Brother," he says to Memnon over his betrothed's shoulder. *"Thank you."*

My heart is thundering in my chest.

Zosines's eyes briefly touch mine, and I swear they darken with some hidden emotion. It barely registers.

This isn't right, I protest.

Roxi, if you are a warrior, you can claim however many spouses as you can hold on to, he says.

I remember that; of course I remember that. But I hate it as much as I hated seeing that boy walk in here asking to fight.

I do not like it. And I know I cannot immediately change these things, even with my position.

I know. But there are reasons for this practice.

I glance at Memnon, curious to know what those reasons could possibly be, when a hulking man wearing damp battle leathers, a sheathed axe, and a dagger stalks down the aisle, past the waiting line, right up to us.

The warriors that flank me and Memnon tense, several of them reaching for the hilts of their blades, but Memnon lifts a hand, halting them.

In front of us, rain drips from the warrior's hair and skin, but he doesn't seem to notice. His bloodshot eyes are focused solely on Memnon. He doesn't bow before he begins to speak. "You dare to sit there and pretend to rule—you, who let your aging mother rule in your stead while you spent months away. You who have come back emasculated, your hair and beard cut like a prepubescent boy.

"It's bad enough that you bring back a Roman bitch, but then you take her to wife and demand the rest of us call her queen."

The man spits at me then, the glob of it landing less than an arm span from Ferox, whose tail flicks in response.

At my side, Memnon settles deeper into his throne, his posture almost irreverent. His eyes, however, are sharp as daggers as they narrow on the man. Down our bond, Memnon's anger is rapidly expanding. I can feel it like an inferno in my chest.

"I won't stand for it," the warrior says.

"Is that a challenge?" Memnon asks, sounding bored. It's an act. I can practically taste his rising bloodlust.

In response, the warrior withdraws his axe.

Memnon rises, then saunters forward as the warrior shifts his weight and adjusts his grip on his weapon. His power vibrates between us, barely leashed.

"You know, there's a reason they call me Memnon the Indomitable," he says softly. As he speaks, his magic reaches out and plucks the warrior's axe from his hand, casting it aside as though he were swatting away a fly.

I forget to breathe, me and the rest of the room spellbound by this faceoff.

"The last people to speak ill of my wife were Roman soldiers and their centurion," Memnon says, his voice far too calm. "All that's left of them now are bones. Do you still wish to challenge me?"

I can feel how tightly wound his power is, how intensely he's restraining it.

The warrior snarls, reaching for another sheathed blade and lunging for my husband.

I swallow a yelp as, rather than retreating from the attack, Memnon steps *into* it. Faster than I can follow, he draws his own dagger and, in one smooth stroke, shoves it through the warrior's belly as the latter falls upon him.

The man slumps against Memnon, his breath coming out in choked rasps. Using whatever last reserves he has, he stabs Memnon in the side.

Now I do cry out, rising to my feet as fear floods my veins and power pours out of me. Through our bond, I can feel the throb of this wound, and I nearly clasp my side at the sensation. Memnon, however, appears unbothered.

My soul mate's voice is clear and commanding when he says, "Disrespect me, and I will punish you. Disrespect *your queen*, and I will kill you." He drags his dagger up the warrior's belly, splitting him open. The man's ruined intestines spill out with his blood.

Memnon shoves his opponent away, the man's body hitting the ground with a wet thump. Then, almost as an afterthought, he pulls the blade from his side, tossing the weapon aside.

To the nearby warriors, Memnon says, "Drag his body to the fields and leave him unburied."

I rush over to him then, nearly tripping over Ferox in my haste, while around us, people stare, stupefied.

I drop to my knees before Memnon and press my palm to his wound, my nausea rising as his blood seeps between my fingers. Immediately, heavy ropes of my magic sink into him.

"*Heal the flesh, mend the wound,*" I incant.

Beneath my hand, Memnon's skin tugs together as it heals from the inside out.

Memnon places his own hand over mine. *You're trembling, little witch.*

You were stabbed. There's a note of hysteria to my words.

It happens from time to time, Memnon says lightly. Though his body still holds some of his earlier tension, he's looking at me with soft eyes. *I like you tending to me.* Then, the mirth leaves his face. *Angry warriors think with their pride, and they are quick to act. You and I must be quicker still.* He dips his head to peer into my eyes. *Do you understand me?*

I do. He wants me to fight—and to be the aggressor if the situation calls for it.

I glance back down at his wound, wordlessly commanding

my magic to clean away the blood on his skin and clothes. Pressing my lips together, I reluctantly nod.

Okay, I say down our bond, though it's hard to even fathom the violence he's suggesting. *If it happens again, I will...try.* The thought makes bile rise up my throat.

When, *my queen*, Memnon says grimly. When *it happens again*.

CHAPTER 25
Roxilana, 18 years old

54 AD, Northern Sarmatia, near the Borysthenes River

"My king! My queen!"

I jolt awake; the transition happens so rapidly that my mind is still halfway immersed in my dream when I sit up and blink out at the darkness. Like me, Memnon sits up quickly.

Muttering a spell, light blooms in his hand, the bluish orb of it floating up to the top of the tent like a seed on the wind.

Itaxes rushes into our tent, breathing hard. "Attacked!" he calls out. "We are being attacked!"

Memnon hastily throws the covers off, rising from the bed. I'm quick to follow, my heart hammering against my rib cage.

"From what direction?" Memnon asks as he heads to our chests to retrieve clothes, armor, and weapons. I'm his shadow, echoing his movements as I open my own chest.

"Northeast," answers the man, his form ghostly under Memnon's bluish light. "They're heading for our main entrance. But they could have easily sent some fighters to the back to drive us out."

I glance to the darkened wagon, looking for Ferox, but the room appears empty. Panic claws up my throat. Swiftly, I slip down our connection until I'm staring out my panther's eyes. I crouch in the wild grass outside the settlement, staring back at the city.

Thank the gods, he's safe. For now.

Stay here, I order Ferox.

I withdraw from him, my awareness returning to the tent.

"Rouse everyone you can, starting with the warriors," Memnon commands Itaxes as he quickly dresses. "Send someone to wake my mother and sister as well; they will handle logistics within the settlement. And tell any able-bodied adult to grab what weapons they can and fight."

Itaxes nods, then dashes from our tent.

My eyes meet Memnon's. Before either of us can speak, the whoosh of fire roars in the distance, and screams start up.

The breath in my lungs stills. The past is a terrible song that sometimes sings to me of old horrors. I hear it now.

Memnon shakes his head. "Tonight will not be like the last attack you lived through," he swears to me, speaking with all the authority of a king and a commander.

I nod, swallowing.

He nods along with me, and then his gaze moves to the clothes still clutched in my hands. He jerks his chin in their direction. "Get dressed, my queen," he commands.

I nod again, then do so with fumbling fingers while he moves to another chest that holds his weapons.

When Memnon turns back to me, it's with a bow and gorytos. He uses his magic to secure them to my body.

"Now grab your boots," he says.

If this were any other time, any other situation, I might think his commands were silly, even overbearing. But right now, when fear and adrenaline cloud my mind, I'm grateful for them. I stumble over to where I set my boots last night and pull them on.

Outside, the shrill screams and crackling fire are growing sharper, *closer*.

When I rise, Memnon's there, his weapons and armor strapped to him, looking wrathfully beautiful, his eyes eerily illuminated by that blue orb of light. His gaze sweeps over me, and through our bond, I feel his thick, rich approval.

Memnon drags me to him and crushes his lips to mine. But it lasts only for a moment.

He pulls away, still cupping my face. "Look at you," he says, his eyes appraising my outfit and the weapons strapped to it. I can see the pride in his eyes. "You look like the vengeful goddess I feared you were."

I certainly don't feel that way. Not when the sour tang of my own terror sits at the back of my throat.

His expression turns serious, and my barely banked fear is rising again, threatening to swallow me whole.

"I am going to ride out with my warriors, and together we'll drive back as many enemy fighters as we can, drawing them out of our city, then battling them on the plains."

I'm nodding—or maybe I'm shaking my head. I'm a child with childish worries and thoughts and I cannot, cannot—

Memnon grips the side of my face. "You *can*," Memnon

says, giving me a firm shake and disrupting my chaotic thoughts.

He tucks a lock of my hair behind my ear. "The children and the elderly will be led to the main tent behind the clearing," he says. "There they will be vulnerable. Protect them."

Again, my eyes well, and I'm afraid. So afraid.

"You don't need to be afraid. You are not that child anymore. But now there are others, and they are counting on *you*."

My stomach drops at that.

He pulls me in and kisses me fiercely, his lips devouring mine. But the contact is over before it's begun, all that fire and passion and desperation touching my lips for mere moments.

"I need to go," he says, backing away.

"Memnon!" I call out after him, fear rising like a leviathan.

"The vulnerable, my queen," he reminds me. "Please, help them."

The fire is roaring louder, both in my head and outside it, and the screams are mounting.

"Don't die!" I plead. My voice breaks as I say it. I cannot endure that loss.

At the doorway, Memnon glances over his shoulder. "I wouldn't *dare*."

Then he slips through the tent flaps, and he's gone.

I stumble out of the tent, my bow and gorytos slapping against me uselessly. People are screaming and running, entire neighborhoods engulfed in flame.

The taste of smoke and ash clings to my tongue, and my eyes water from the sting of it all.

Gods above and below, this is my past relived.

Through the melee, I catch sight of the raiders. The enemy is on horseback, weapons in hand, shouting hair-raising war cries.

I see one such fighter nock an arrow wrapped in oiled linen. He steers his horse toward a nearby tent, clearly intending to light his arrow on fire.

Since the moment I woke, I've been drowning in fear, but now, it is utterly eclipsed by a dormant, vengeful part of me. The same part of me that watched my mother die, my brother die, and my father die. The part of me that watched my sister disappear into smoke and darkness.

The part of me that was taken captive long ago.

All the pain and rage I've locked away like a prisoner flood down my arms, coiling as I set my sights on the enemy warrior.

I release it in a wordless burst, aiming across the way at him. I don't know what I expect when it hits the mounted archer, but certainly not for it to cleanly cleave his head from his body.

For several seconds I stand there, horrified, as his head topples off and his torso slumps over, blood spraying out of the neck. I gag as I process what just happened, what I just *did*.

But there are more mounted fighters rushing by, ones who hold more weapons and are using them to cut down civilians like myself. So when one such warrior gallops toward me, blade brandished, I wipe my mouth and straighten, my magic rising once more.

I'm still angry, still full of pain, and not even my horror

can smother this burning violence inside me. When I was a child, I could not fight back. I could not protect my family or anyone else.

Now I can.

A cry rips from my throat and my magic lashes out, slicing through the oncoming rider. His horse rears up, fire glinting in its spooked eyes as half the man's body tumbles off the saddle, his blood and innards spilling across the ground.

My nausea rises swiftly this time—too swiftly—and I turn and retch.

Killed them. I killed them.

Powerful queen, Memnon says down our bond. *Protecting our people. I could not be prouder.*

A sob slips from me, even as his words hold me together. *Don't you dare die on me,* I tell him again. I've now seen just how easy it is to lose one's life in battle.

Wouldn't dream of it, Roxilana. But that threat goes both ways. Stay safe.

I nod. *I will,* I vow, despite having no business making promises on such things.

I take a deep breath, pulling myself together, then sprint down the winding paths that lead to the settlement's main tent.

Around me, the city is a sea of flames, the heat so intense I begin to sweat from it.

I reach out a hand. *"Douse the fire!"* I incant.

My magic leaps from my hand, looking like another plume of fire-fueled smoke as it moves to the actual flames. Within moments, it smothers them.

I don't have time to see more than that.

The clearing and the large tent beyond it are up ahead. People are streaming to it, and I can hear wails and whimpers coming from inside. Worse, a couple of enemy riders have discovered it and are circling around the structure.

Twenty paces ahead of me, one such fighter strikes down a mother and the small child she carries in her arms.

My shriek sounds unholy, and my power reacts without conscious intention, streaming out of me and splitting the warrior in two.

I dash to the woman and child, placing my hands on their bloody bodies. I don't know how badly either of them are hurt.

"*Heal their wounds, seal the skin,*" I incant.

One of the other riders shouts, then points in our direction.

Must get to the tent.

Grabbing mother and child, I drag them with me toward the structure.

An arrow whizzes by, so close I hear it hiss near my ear.

"*Give me strength and speed,*" I incant under my breath. Immediately, the weight of the two becomes more bearable and my legs move faster.

I'm nearly to the tent's entrance when—

THWUMP.

I cry out, falling into the tent, mother and child spilling from my arms, as an arrow embeds itself in the flesh between my neck and shoulder.

Several people inside the tent rush to my side.

"Help them, help them!" I say, pointing to the two individuals I carried in here.

Blood streams from my shoulder wound, and it hurts like the gods' wrath, but I pay it no mind as I turn back to the doorway.

Pressing a hand to the felt wall of it, I incant. "*Make this structure impervious to fire."* I've no sooner spoken that spell than I begin another: *"Let no enemy come within."*

"Roxi!" Tamara calls out behind me, concern in her voice.

I don't bother turning to look at my mother-in-law. *"Make the walls of this tent strong as stone."*

Layer upon layer of my orange magic fans out, spreading over the vast space. I can see the web of wards crisscross over the fabric, looking like glittering lace.

"Allow no smoke to enter this space." Vaguely, I'm aware of the drain these wards must be having on my power, but adrenaline and determination mask it.

"Roxilana." Tamara gently grabs me by the shoulders. "You are hurt."

"I know," I say distractedly.

Was that enough wards? Should I make another?

"Can you heal yourself as Memnon can?" Tamara asks, demanding my attention.

I hesitate for a moment, forcing myself to focus on her and her words. Then, I nod.

"Good." She grasps the arrowhead in my shoulder and yanks it out with violent force.

A surprised shriek rips itself from my throat, the agony darkening my vision. But as soon as I register the pain, the worst of it is over.

Tamara places my hand on the wound. "Heal yourself." Like Memnon, she has that commanding tone, one I cannot ignore.

Though my mind is on other people and things, I force out a silent healing spell, and thick ropes of my magic move to the wound.

Once I feel the last twinge of pain disappear, I drop my hand from the injury.

Tamara slowly releases me, peering at my shoulder. I hear her sharp inhalation.

"You really can do what my son can."

I guess she hadn't fully realized it until now.

I nod, my gaze drifting to the rest of the room, which is filled to the brim, mostly with the young and the old, though there are a few men and women roughly my age or a little older. Despite the crowd, I know this is only a small portion of the people who live here. The rest of them must be fighting for their lives.

"Look at me," Tamara orders, calling my attention back to her.

Dazedly I do so.

She gives my cheek a gentle slap. "*Look* at me."

My gaze sharpens.

"There you are," she says. She braces my face with her bloody hands. "Listen carefully to me, Daughter: you cannot help others if you yourself aren't okay. You understand me?"

I nod, and she shakes her head. "Say it."

"I understand."

Now she smiles softly, then pats my cheek. "Good. Then go and make use of your magic."

I waste no time doing so, leaving her side to hunt down the mother and child. When I find them, I finally see that it was the mother and not the baby who sustained the injury—a small blessing. Though based on the blood drenching her side, the wound is in desperate condition.

I drop to the ground next to her, vaguely aware of the other people who've gathered around, helpless. No one stops me when I place my hands on the woman's side, though she screams, the sound causing her baby, tucked against her other side, to begin to wail too.

Swiftly, I incant, *"Heal the wound."*

Beneath my touch, I sense muscle and sinew reforming and stitching itself back together. Again, I'm distantly aware of the toll I'm placing on my magic, but right now I cannot be bothered to care.

When the last of the wound seals up and my magic tapers off, I lean back on my haunches, breathing heavily.

Around me, someone gasps. "She healed her!"

I rise, retreating from the woman as more people exclaim. Now isn't the time to explain my magic, not when hooves still pound outside and arrows ping uselessly against the walls of the tent.

Screams fill the air beyond the structure, accompanied by the telltale whoosh of more flames. The sound drags me back to the walls of my childhood home again. Smoke fills the air. The whole village is burning, *dying*.

No.

These people might be safe, but everyone outside this tent is not.

I'm going to have to break my promise to Memnon.

I move to the wall of the tent and place my hand against its surface to reinforce the wards already in place.

"No enemy shall enter, no weapon shall pierce, no flame shall alight. I offer you my protection. My magic will defend you. My blood will spill before yours does. This I vow." My magic spreads out along the material, the shimmering threads of each layered ward weaving together. The spells will not hold forever, but hopefully they will be strong enough to last the night.

I place a hand over my heart then, bowing my head. *"Guard my body against harm."* Another burst of power, this one running over my skin like a stream, coating me in magical armor.

This, I also hope is enough.

I move to the tent's entrance, bracing myself for whatever lies beyond it.

"Roxilana, where are you going?" Tamara calls out from behind me.

I don't pause. "To protect my people."

Outside the main tent, enemy fighters battle armed Sarmatians. Metal clangs as blade meets blade.

I pull my bow off my shoulder, sighting a mounted warrior who holds the severed head of a woman by her braids.

I nock an arrow; my earlier nerves have settled. "*Find your mark and land true*," I spell-cast, releasing the arrow.

My shot goes wide, my aim still dismal; however, as the arrow arcs across the sky, it curves back on track, closing in on my target.

The fighter sees the incoming projectile and tries to duck, but it slams into his neck all the same, entering and exiting his throat with such force, it knocks him off his steed.

I stride forward, my rage still simmering, and this time the nausea doesn't rise. I'll deal with the consequences of my actions later.

The enemy's horse, now riderless, trots forward, its movements a little spooked. Still, it's easy enough to catch its reins and stroke its neck, tendrils of my magic reaching out and soothing the beast. Beneath my touch, it calms, and after slinging my bow across my chest, I hoist myself onto its back.

I may not be Sarmatian and I may have no natural inclination toward horse riding, but sitting here in the enemy's saddle, my power at my fingertips, feels right in some deep, inexplicable way.

I urge the horse forward into a gallop, leaving the clearing behind and heading for the outer reaches of the settlement. My goals are somewhat complicated—I don't simply want to protect my people. I also have a driving need to find Memnon and Ferox. Though they are technically fine for now—I checked on both via my bonds—the attack still rages.

And then there's the matter of my own unexpected rage, which I've kept bottled for a decade and now wants *out*.

Gods save me, I let myself have a taste of my own inner darkness.

"*Die*," I incant anytime I pass an enemy rider.

Die. Die. Die.

This spell is efficient, slicing my victim's necks right at their jugulars. Their hands go to the wounds, their eyes wide with surprise. I neither pause to watch them crumple in their saddles nor do I think about the deeper moral consequences of these acts. I will later, but for now—

A lancing pain cuts through my bond with Memnon, so sharp I choke on my own breath.

Memnon?

His thoughts are muddled and faint, but the pain, that is bright and loud.

No. Gods, *no*.

This is my worst fear come to life. Memnon, injured, maybe even…dying.

My hold nearly slips from the reins as terror washes through me. But as soon as it comes, it's eclipsed by a far more powerful drive to find my mate and heal him. In the past, when I felt Memnon's injuries, I was hopelessly far from him. I'm not anymore.

Hold on, I say down our bond. *I'm coming for you.*

No, Roxi, Memnon begs. *Stay with our people.*

You *are my people.*

Without him, there is nothing else.

I urge my stolen horse on, faster and faster still. Memnon tracked me across the vast Roman Empire with his magic alone. I can do the same.

I call on my magic once more, my arms tingling as it moves down them, weaker than before. No matter. I don't need much.

"Lead me to my soul mate."

My power snakes out of me, the orange line of it weaving through the tented city. I follow it as best I can, taking detours when my magic cuts through tents untouched by fire.

A projectile hits me, throwing me forward with a grunt. I gnash my teeth against the throb of impact, even though the arrow clatters uselessly to the ground, the ward I placed on myself holding strong.

Straightening, I place another protective ward on myself, taking Tamara's earlier words to heart: I cannot help Memnon if I get myself killed.

The line of my magic leads me out of the burning city to the steppe beyond. In the distance, I make out writhing shadows, their forms cast in bluish hues beneath the light of the moon and a large blue orb of light that Memnon must've cast.

My throat constricts, and hope takes root. He must be close if his magic lingers nearby.

I urge my horse on when, out of the corner of my eye, an enemy moves.

I raise my hand, magic weakly gathering in my palm as I ready my attack—

"Ferox?" I nearly weep at the sight of the panther slinking toward me.

To think I almost attacked him.

I stop my horse long enough to lean far over the saddle and reach for Ferox's head. "Thank the gods you're okay."

He nuzzles my palm with his nose. I pet his snout and head, and as I do so, I speak: "*Protect this body against harm.*" Power spills over Ferox, coating him from head to toe. I nearly shudder with relief, knowing my panther is safe.

I cannot say the same thing about my husband.

I right myself in my saddle, staring down at Ferox solemnly. "I'm heading into that battle," I tell the big cat, jutting my chin in the direction of the fighting. "You will stay out here where it's safe, and I'll find you after the fight."

His tail twitches with what seems to be annoyance, but he watches me as I nudge my horse into action. We've only made it a short distance, however, when I realize Ferox is shadowing us.

"Ferox."

He doesn't look at me and doesn't slow.

There's not enough time to force him to stay away from the battle. Memnon's pain still throbs across our bond, though it's feeling worrisomely faint.

I huff out a breath. "You will put your safety before my own," I say to Ferox. "And rip out the throats of any who threaten you."

With that, we rush straight for the melee, following the orange line of my magic.

As soon as we enter the battlefield proper, it's clear that the biggest issue is distinguishing friend from foe. Back in the settlement, mounted men lighting arrows or attacking civilians made their loyalties obvious, but out here, it feels like everyone is an enemy. Swords clang, and men bellow and rage as they battle, their breaths heavy and puffing.

Mud squelches beneath my steed's hooves, and it's only as I begin to see the bodies and hear the low moans that I realize the ground is wet with blood, not water, and it's no longer safe to ride without crushing people.

I swing myself off the horse, Ferox moving to my side. Then I'm stumbling, running after that thread of my magic until, suddenly, it dips down to the ground.

And there he is.

A guttural cry leaves my lips, and I fall to my knees.

Memnon's not moving, his eyes closed. My gods, my gods, my gods—

The panic is back, its mouth gaping wide, ready to swallow me up.

I draw in a deep breath. Memnon had been so steady with me earlier; that's how he needs me to be right now.

So I pull myself together and scan his body in the near darkness, looking for injuries.

Memnon's arm appears to be partially severed, but that does not seem to be what mortally wounded him. Lower down, his blood-spattered scale mail has been punctured right through his abdomen, though the weapon that did so is long gone.

My lower lip trembles. Gods, it's bad. I know it's bad, and I haven't even gotten a good look at the injury itself.

Gingerly, I move aside his armor as best I can and lift his tunic beneath. His stomach is smeared with blood, and more oozes from that abdominal wound.

I slip my hand between his clothing and his skin, pressing my palm to where his injury still weeps blood. "*Heal the wound. Mend that which is broken,*" I murmur.

My magic slips out beneath my palm, coming out more slowly than it should. I draw on more of it. More and more.

I just need him to survive. Then it can all give out.

Beneath my touch, I feel my power sink into his skin. Memnon's flesh shifts beneath my palm as it reforms and begins to seal back up.

I gather more power still, even as my muscles throb and my temples pound.

Ferox crouches on Memnon's other side, his form tense. I hear a low growl come from him a moment before he lunges.

I drag my gaze from Memnon in time to see my panther leap over my shoulders, right at a looming fighter brandishing a sword—one I hadn't heard or seen in my desperation to heal Memnon. I stare in horror as Ferox collides with our attacker, knocking them both to the ground.

There's a scream, then a spray of blood as Ferox rips out his throat. I stare at my panther, tears welling in my eyes as I realize he just protected me and Memnon when we were defenseless.

Ferox continues to pin the man down for several inhalations, until he's sure the man no longer draws breath, and then he returns to my side, licking his lips.

I press my head to my panther's temple. "Thank you," I whisper, my voice wavering. Ferox butts me with his nose, rubbing his blood-soaked snout against me before he turns back around and scans the battlefield, his body held rigid.

Guarding us, I realize.

Another pang of warmth ripples through me. When this is all over, I'm going to get Ferox the biggest hunk of meat I can.

Memnon shifts beneath my hands, and my attention snaps to him.

He's alive.

Gods, he's *alive*.

A sob shudders out of me as I kneel there, blood and mud soaking into my pants. I press a kiss to his forehead and gather him onto my lap as best I can, my head bowed over him. I don't realize I'm crying until I feel a tear slip off the bridge of my nose and fall onto Memnon's face.

Beneath my palm, Memnon's skin fully seals up, and my magic tapers off. I slip my hand from his abdomen then and move it to his other injury. Already, my power has healed most of his arm, the limb now fully reattached. The wound, however, still gapes open.

Gently, I lay my hand on it and force out more of my power, hating how little is left. What remains is thin and wispy, and it burrows into his skin sluggishly. Still, little by little, the injured flesh of Memnon's arm mends itself.

Beneath me, my husband shifts, and I glance down just as his eyelids flutter open. At first, I'm sure it's a trick of the light. I don't dare hope for more. But then he reaches out and brushes his bloody knuckles against my cheek.

"So fucking beautiful," he whispers to himself. He says it so intimately, like we're tangled with each other in bed and not out here on this bleak battlefield.

Those words undo me.

Keeping a hand on his arm, I lean in and press a fierce kiss to Memnon's lips. And now I'm crying against him, my whole body shaking with my sobs.

His arms come around me slowly.

I break off the kiss and lean my forehead against him. *I was terrified you were going to die on me*, I admit.

"I would never leave for the afterlife without you," he murmurs hoarsely, stroking the back of my hair. "I don't know if you remember, but I made you a promise long ago that I wouldn't die in battle."

I *do* remember.

I hope you die, I said, so I never have to hear you again.

Just because you said that, Memnon responded, I'm going to make sure *I live.*

I pinch my eyes shut, pressing my lips together.

"Ssshhh," he says softly. "It's okay. I've got you."

I nearly laugh at the ridiculous statement. "I'm supposed to be the one reassuring you." The sob caught in my throat distorts the words a little.

"Tomorrow," he says, tucking a strand of my hair behind my ear, "when I'm moving inside you, you can reassure me *all* you like. I do so love praise."

My brows pull together, and then I begin to laugh in disbelief. He's half dead and weak from blood loss, and he's making sex jokes.

Once I start laughing, I can't seem to stop. I laugh until it becomes sobs, and the tears I tried to fight back slip down my cheeks.

"I'll do whatever you want," I say, even as I sense the final dregs of my magic seeping from my palm into Memnon's skin. Black dots smudge my vision.

"Whatever I want?" Memnon voice sounds far too thrilled at the prospect.

Beneath my hand, the last of Memnon's arm wound seals itself up, thank the gods.

I lean in close to him, darkness swarming my sight. "So long as you live to see the end of battle, *whatever you want*."

The words are no sooner out of my mouth than my eyes roll back and I collapse onto my husband.

I wake briefly, my body cradled against a firm, familiar chest, a wet snout pressed against my hand.

"She will be fine, Ferox. Our queen has simply overspent herself."

My eyes fall closed, my lids so, so heavy.

When I rouse again, I hear, "…a few confessions from the prisoners so far."

"What have they said?" Memnon's voice rumbles against me, and I realize I must still be in his arms.

"They were Dacians. Word came from Rome that you took a wife, and their king, Zoutoula, wanted to weaken us while we were distracted with festivities. They said was to avenge the death of their previous king—the one you killed." A long, heavy silence follows. I try to open my eyes, but they feel leaden, as do my limbs.

"Where's the leader of this raiding party?" Memnon asks.

"Dead, just over there," the warrior responds, adding. "We think it's Bastiza, the king's eldest son."

Gently, Memnon lays me out on the grass. "I'll be gone just a moment," he whispers against my skin, though I'm fairly certain he doesn't know I can hear him. "Ferox," he says, "I know you don't take orders from me, but attack anyone besides me that thinks of getting close to her."

I can't see Ferox's reaction, but his warm fur brushes against me as he lies down at my side.

A warm, calloused palm presses itself against my head. "*Gods protect my mate from harm.*" Memnon whispers the ward beneath his breath.

I can sense the subtle touch of his magic as it drapes over me like a cloak. And then he's gone, his boots squelching against the bloody ground.

I cannot say how long it takes me to pry my eyelids open, but by the time I manage to do so, the first rays of morning paint the sky pink and orange.

I'm still outside the walls of the tented city. From what little I can see and sense, blood dampens my clothes, skin, and hair. My entire body trembles, though I don't really feel those tremors, just the heavy, throbbing weight of my limbs. If I weren't so damn exhausted, I might be alarmed.

With effort, I get my arms under me and push myself up into a sitting position, my body swaying until Ferox sits up as well, leaning against my side, his body helping to keep mine upright. I lean my tired head against him in thanks.

All around us, Sarmatian warriors prowl the battle-field, some checking on what must be the wounded, others clustering around a line of kneeling men with their hands bound behind their backs.

I stare at the line of captives, my anger rising. Even now, I can smell blood and raw flesh on the wind. These men are responsible for this carnage. They were the ones who set upon us while we *slept*. They lit our homes on fire and cut down our people. They sought to hurt us, *annihilate* us.

I glance over at Memnon, whose battered armor glints in the sunlight. He's coated in blood; it soaks his torso, it's smeared across his face, and it drips from his hair. He looks monstrous, so it makes no sense that pride swells in me at the sight of him bathed in gore.

Like the rest of his men, he strides through the grass, weaving between the dead. When he gets to one of the corpses, however, he pauses, studying it with a grimace. After a moment, he withdraws a dagger from his side and crouches next to the body. Bringing his blade to it, he begins to saw through flesh. I hear the distant squelch of blood, and it makes my stomach churn.

When he's done, he wipes his blade on the body's clothes, then picks up something. It takes me a moment to realize what he's gripping is a *head*. I have to force down my rising sickness as I stare at the thing's hideous visage. Memnon stalks over to the group of captives.

"Is this what you wished for?" he asks, holding the slack-jawed head up. "Your leader's death?" The silence that falls across the field is absolute. Not even the bugs or birds break it.

"Look at him!" Memnon commands, shaking the head. "Tell me it was worth it!"

The captives remain grimly silent.

"No one crosses our people and lives!" Memnon bellows. The Sarmatians gathering around him whoop and howl, adding to the macabre moment, and some of the captured soldiers shrink in on themselves.

"And you"—his gaze sweeps over the prisoners—"you unfortunate few—you won't simply die," Memnon says, shaking his head.

The first tendrils of unease coil in my belly.

He paces down the line of them. "I trust you have heard of my power?"

A chill works through me at the malevolence in his tone. I've never heard him like this.

"In case you haven't," Memnon continues, "let me tell you now: I can bend your mind to do *anything*."

That chill deepens as my unease grows. I remember back in Rome how not even Nero, the emperor himself, could escape Memnon's power.

"You will leave this place and return to your people,"

Memnon orders. "And there will be one thought and one thought alone in your mind: *slaughter*. You shall do to those you love what you have tried to do to *my* loved ones. And then you will die, either by your brethren's hands or, if they won't kill you, then your own."

Someone from the line wails, and I feel that cry. I have seen—and committed—a lot of atrocities over the last night. But none of them come close to this.

"From this moment on," Memnon says, "consider yourselves *cursed*."

Memnon drops the severed head, the appendage hitting the ground wetly. He moves to the line of captives, who are now writhing in their bindings, trying to escape the Sarmatian king. Their feet must be tied as well because they get no farther than a few arm spans by the time Memnon reaches them.

One by one, my husband grasps their heads, his darkened magic entering their noses and mouths. Many of them thrash against him, but as soon as his power takes hold, their forms go preternaturally still and their eyes unfocus.

I'm shaking again, shaking from renewed horror. They may be the enemy, and gods how I hate them, but what Memnon is making them do...

Please, Memnon, I plead. *Stop this cruelty.*

Right in the middle of his work, Memnon bows his head. *You're awake.*

I don't think he expected that, and for a moment, I am sure he is ashamed.

Please, I beg again.

This is war, my queen, he says. *I am sorry you must see it.*

But he is not sorry he must *inflict* it. That is clear enough. He hesitates only an inhalation longer, then raises his head and resumes his malevolent work. Once he's finished, he straightens. The men at his feet are subdued, their eyes glassy, distant.

Memnon nods to Sattion, who stands nearby. "Cut the prisoners loose and let them each take a horse."

There are no more whoops from the group. There is no glee or triumph, just somber silence broken only by the sounds of men moving through the grass, a few low moans from the injured, and the sound of rope being sawed through.

Sarmatians gather the needed horses, many of which are speckled with blood. It's unnervingly civil, how the beasts are handed off to the now-freed prisoners, who patiently wait for their steeds.

I watch, horrorstruck, as these former captives hoist themselves into the saddles and ride off. My mind is filling in their futures—how they will return to their people and open fire on them with their bows or skewer them with their swords.

Perhaps there is justice in this retribution, but still, it sickens me.

My skin pricks as Memnon pivots his attention to me. Scarred and bloody, muscled and armored, he looks every bit the barbarian Romans told terrible tales of.

His men are still talking to him, but he ignores their words, striding across the battlefield toward where I sit.

Fear rises in me, and I try to scoot away, but my limbs are still far too heavy and hurting to move.

Please don't run from me, Roxi, he beseeches.

It's not like fleeing is a viable option for me in this state. Unfortunately.

When Memnon reaches me, he kneels and scoops me up as though I weigh nothing.

Put me down, I say.

My husband's grip tightens, and I feel a flash of hurt across our bond. *You're still too weak to walk*, he states.

Then have one of your warriors help me.

I will not ask someone else to take care of my wife in my stead. You can hate me, but you will do so in my arms.

If I had the energy for it, I would scream.

Memnon carries me to a warhorse and swings us both into the saddle, using his magic to assist him. He maneuvers my legs so that they're on either side of the steed and presses my back against his chest.

You overused your magic, he explains as he does so, his voice so gentle. *The leaden sensation will go away, but it takes a while. Until then, I've got you.*

My lower lip quivers. I hate that I can still see those cursed Dacians far in the distance and already Memnon is back to being the caring, supportive husband he always is. I hate that it makes my horror and fear of him seem petty.

He glances over to Zosines, who stalks around the battlefield, checking on the wounded.

"Bring me Bastiza's head."

I'm trembling as Zosines retrieves the severed appendage and brings it over to us, handing the grotesque thing to Memnon.

If I had the strength, I would physically recoil from my husband. As it is, I lean away from the hand that holds the head, right into Memnon's bracing arm.

"Warriors," he calls out. "Mount your steeds and ride with me. It's time to announce the attack is over."

Now the shouts return, the men rallying around their victory.

Memnon urges his horse forward, and together we ride

around the battlefield, circling the corpses until all his fighters have hoisted themselves onto their steeds. Then, with Memnon at the front, we gallop back to the smoking husk that is our city.

Many of the structures have burned, and the survivors sit outside what remains, their eyes hollow, haunted. Scattered among them are the wounded and the dead. As their gazes lift to Memnon, however, their expressions brighten. A cheer rises, then catches, following us through the settlement to the center of camp.

The main clearing is a mess of bloodstains, gore, and lines of bodies. The main tent beyond it sits silent, but as the cheers rise, the doorway parts and people creep out.

Memnon steers us around the clearing's perimeter once, twice, holding up the severed head for all to see as Sarmatians rapidly gather.

Once the area is full of onlookers, he tosses the head into the center of the space, dirt and grime collecting on it as it rolls.

"That is what remains of Bastiza, son of Zoutoula, King of the Dacians. He is the man who led our enemy here, into our city, to kill us while we slept.

"He sought to smoke you from your homes and pierce your bodies with his weapons. He sought to take you captive so that he might bargain your lives for our land. But one does not fight with Sarmatians and win!"

Shouts go up as the crowd grows.

"And we cannot be killed."

Another shout goes up.

"And we will have our vengeance!"

The battered, weary people around us are roaring now, their weapons raised in the air.

286

"We shall use his skull as a chalice and drink to his defeat," Memnon declares.

Drink from *what* now?

More cheers. People spit at the head, or else they kick more dirt at it.

"And the next time we see the Dacians in battle, they will tremble before us. We will not stop fighting them until we have razed their kingdom to the ground!"

CHAPTER 26
Roxilana, 18 years old

54 AD, Northern Sarmatia, near the Borysthenes River

Since the surprise attack, the mood around camp has been grim. Many, many homes have burned to the ground, leaving people with only the clothes on their backs. The people themselves are in rough shape. Many are wounded, and those who aren't have the unenviable job of bathing and burying the dead—our dead, at least.

The enemy's dead are treated with the utmost disrespect, their bodies left out for the scavengers or else placed on pikes outside the settlement, macabre warnings to anyone else thinking of ambushing us.

It takes three days for my magic to return in full, in part because as soon as I'm able to use it, I do, despite Memnon's protests. Like him, I move about camp and heal as many of the injured as I can. It's grueling, fatiguing work, made all the harder by the lingering ache in my bones, an ache that not even Memnon's spells can soothe for long.

But I want to help. There's something about this work that soothes the grief I feel over killing people. Grief I largely must keep to myself because no one but Memnon understands my complicated feelings toward war and death. So I tuck it away and do what I can to rebuild the settlement.

Nearly a week after the ambush, I'm woken by the slap of leathers on my body.

I jolt, sitting up quickly as Ferox snarls at my side, clearly annoyed. Besides the big cat, the space next to me is empty, as it tends to be in the mornings.

Memnon's already off to work. My throat tightens at the thought of him. I've been a little jittery around my husband, much to his dismay, since he cursed those Dacians.

Instead of Memnon, a mother-in-law-shaped shadow looms over me.

"Whatever it is, *no*." I turn over, resettling myself into my bed.

The blankets I'm snuggled under are ripped away, and the leathers are picked up, then dropped on me once more.

Tamara gazes imperiously down at me. "Today, you will train."

"You do realize there are other ways to do this?" I say. "You don't have to always wake me up to get what you…" Her words catch up to me, and my gaze moves to the leathers she dropped on me. "Wait, *train*?" I echo.

"Yes, *train*, dear girl. I hear you have little experience with a blade or a bow. Shame, considering I also hear you hate Romans more than I do."

I clear my throat. "I have a *little* experience with a bow." Specifically what Memnon, Zosines, Rakas, Itaxes, and Sattion taught me when we traveled here from Rome.

"A little will not save you in every battle. Nor will your magic, wondrous though it is."

I rub my eyes.

"Well?" Tamara says, looking at me pointedly. "Up, up—"

Biting back some grumbling, I rise. "Did Memnon put you up to this?" I ask, my voice hitching a little. Next to me, Ferox stretches out, unsheathing his claws and ripping a little of our blanket.

Tamara scoffs, moving to our weapons chest and removing my bow and gorytos from it. "That besotted fool is too in love to ask this of you."

"And I'm guessing you're not," I say as she returns to me and hands the items over.

Tamara catches my chin, tilting my face so I get a good look at her soft, green eyes. "It is *because* I love you, dear Daughter, that I insist you become a dangerous thing. Otherwise, how can you protect yourself or your king? Or your people? Because you will certainly need to."

At her words, my mind flashes back to bloodied, dying Memnon. I suppress a shudder.

"All right," I concede. "I'll train."

She leans forward and gives my cheek a soft peck, then releases me. "Put the leathers on," she commands like the queen she was a short time ago. Backing away, she adds, "Bring the panther if you wish for him to join."

She heads for the doorway of our tent.

"I'm going to make a fool of myself," I call after her.

"Good," she says over her shoulder. "A little humility never hurt anyone."

The sun is bright and the day is hot by the time I'm mounted on horseback, Tamara to one side of me, Ferox to my other. The only respite is the cool breeze that stirs the tall grass.

Puffy, white clouds roll across the heavens above us, and I stare in awe at them as the two of us head out into the steppe. Ahead of us, mounted men and woman ride across the plains with bows and arrows, aiming their projectiles at makeshift targets.

My own weaponry hangs heavy on my body, and I taste bile at the back of my throat as I watch those arrows arc across the sky. It was easy enough to shoot an arrow when I was simply hunting for game. But now, after seeing arrows kill humans—after killing humans myself with arrows—the thought of using these weapons again makes my stomach turn.

I killed so many people.

At the time, I felt like I had no choice. Now, however, I do. I can turn around right now and return to camp. I don't have to be a warrior queen. My hands tighten on my reins.

In the distance, a familiar figure moves into my line of sight, distracting me from my thoughts. There's no leaking magic and no regalia to indicate who he is, but Memnon never needs those tells. His long torso and broad back are enough—as is his shorn hair and the tattoos that run along his form.

My husband's tunic is gone, and his sweat-slicked body gleams in the sun. He sits on his steed, one hand lazily holding his bow, his other holding the reins. He rides like he and his steed are a single, fluid being. Even far away he's hypnotizing to watch.

You shall do to those you love what you have tried to do to my loved ones. And then you will die... I shiver at the memory as I stare at him.

Memnon must feel eyes on him because he turns his horse, then stills when he catches sight of me and his mother.

My queen? he says down our bond. *Is that you?* Hope and joy surge across our bond.

If I had known you would be bare chested like this, I respond, my levity a little forced, *I would've come out here much, much sooner.*

I feel his smile, and then he's charging forward on his steed, riding as swiftly as his horse will carry him.

"Well, that didn't take him long," Tamara says, smirking a little. She turns her horse around and begins to head back the way we came. Ferox, the traitor, begins to slink away alongside her.

"Wait, you're not staying?" I call out. My desire to follow both her and my panther rises again.

She laughs. "You don't need me to learn how to fight. Everyone out on this field is more than capable of teaching you—starting with your husband."

I stare after her and Ferox, my stomach knotting, even as Memnon closes in on us.

"Oh, one last thing," Tamara says, pausing. She glances over at me in such a casual, measured way that I know this moment was premeditated just as many others have been. "If anyone asks, this was *your* idea, and you will train like this every day from this moment on," she commands me. "That is *my* order to *you*."

I feel myself pale.

"Make yourself strong, dear Daughter, so that no one can hurt you. Because you may not yet realize this, but every single life here depends on you. Not your husband, *you*."

I don't exactly understand the deeper meaning beneath

her words, only that the responsibility she's placing on me is terrifying. Now I better grasp why Memnon never spoke of being king. Because even when he's not fighting or strategizing, leading or listening to his people's complaints, there is the constant, relentless pressure to be everything for everyone. And whether Tamara is aware of my own conflicted feelings, she's forcing me to consider my role.

She nudges her horse and trots away from me, Ferox trailing behind her, just as Memnon closes in.

"What are you doing out here?" Memnon asks when he reaches me.

"I…" I can still get out of this. An excuse forms on the tip of my tongue. I swallow it down. "I wanted to train with you." I force out the next bit. "Every day, if possible."

Memnon's face breaks out into a smile. "Truly?"

No.

"Yes." I stop myself from looking over my shoulder at his mother's retreating form. "Absolutely."

"All right. Then grab your bow and let's begin."

———

It's like we're traveling together all over again. The weapon, the practice, the instructor. Memnon has me standing stationary, bow in hand, an arrow nocked.

"Widen your legs," he instructs, tapping his booted foot against my inner leg. "And I want your upper body more upright."

He leans over me and points in the distance to a lifesized straw dummy. "We're going to aim for that."

He steps in closer, moving to my back, and I can feel the warm press of his chest against me. He smells of sweat, leather, and horsehair. It shouldn't be nearly as appealing to me as it is. So much so that my hand slips on the bow and the arrow flies, veering wildly off course.

Memnon gives my backside a slap. "Don't distract yourself."

"Then stop rubbing your sweaty chest all over me."

He pulls me against him. "Straighten your form," he says again.

Now you're definitely just doing this to mess with me, I complain.

"You're going to have a lot worse distractions on the battlefield," he says, annoyingly unruffled. "Now, grab another arrow and let's try this again."

Grumbling under my breath, I pull another one out and nock it.

"Good," Memnon says, and I hate how, despite how spooked I still am by him, I preen under his praise. "Now sight your target and aim for the chest. That will be the easiest mark to hit."

I do as he asks, pulling back on the bow string.

"Once you're ready, shoot."

I take a deep breath and focus on the target. My power sifts out of me, coiling along the arrow's shaft.

"Wait," Memnon says, pressing a hand to my bow and forcing the weapon down. He shakes his head. "No magic for this," he says.

I glance at him questioningly. During our travels, he hadn't minded that I used it when I trained.

Memnon must hear my unspoken question because he explains, "In battle, you cannot solely rely on magic to save you. As you saw days ago, it can run dry." He steps in behind me once more, his body heat warm against my own. "This, my queen, you must learn from practice and repetition alone."

So it's going to be like reading, he means. I try not to get dispirited by that because I know this means it will take a long time to master.

"Know your weapon," Memnon continues. "Like your horse, it is another limb. Find your target, and this time, when you release your arrow, let your heart go with it."

I close my eyes for a moment. When I open them, I focus on nothing but the tautness of my bowstring, my grip on the fletching, and the target.

I release the arrow and watch it fly across the field, then sink into the stuffed dummy's low belly.

"Good, my queen. Very good," Memnon says, and again, his praise feels like a stroke across my skin. "Like sex, the point where arrow meets flesh is another sort of intimacy," he says. "If your essence is in that arrow, then when it finds its mark, a part of you is there, with your victim, as they die. It's a holy moment."

He speaks of the act with such reverence that, for a breath, I almost believe him. But then, I have my own opinion of that moment, one that's been tormenting me since the night of the attack.

"It's murder," I state softly. I've seen my share of it in callous Rome, and now I have done it myself. There is nothing holy about the act of taking a life. Memnon should know this even better than me, considering how he so recently invoked a curse to kill his enemies.

"It *is* death," Memnon agrees. "An end point and a beginning, a crossing over from this land to another. It deserves respect."

I stare at the straw dummy, my arrow still sticking out of it.

Memnon clasps my shoulder. "Let's do this again, only this time, we'll try it on horseback."

———

We train for hours: on the ground, on an idle horse, and then on a moving one. I'm terrible at it all, but especially on the moving horse. I'd have better luck hitting my target blindfolded than actually aiming at this rate.

Unfortunately, I've also gained an audience, one that has laughed intermittently throughout my training today. Unlike me, most of them have practiced their fighting skills since they were children. Watching their queen fumble at what they can so easily do is apparently quite amusing.

After retrieving the latest round of spent arrows, Memnon rides up to me. Without preamble, he reaches out, wraps an arm around my midsection, and drags me off my horse and onto his. I yelp as I'm weightless for a moment, before my backside hits Memnon's thighs.

I look quizzically up at him as I sit sidesaddle on the beast, but my warlord husband is busy directing his horse into a tight turn.

"The queen's training is over," he calls over his shoulder to the lingering onlookers.

Thank the gods. The day was starting to feel endless.

"Where are we going?" I ask.

"You made me a vow back on the battlefield."

My brows rise at his unexpected response even as my stomach twists at the reminder of that night. It takes me a moment to recall this vow.

I'll do whatever you want, I had promised him.

And now he's collecting on that promise.

Despite my exhaustion, a thrill runs through me. My own

pounding desire for Memnon began today when I first caught sight of him on horseback. It's only been building since, and not even my recent skittishness around him can quell it.

Behind us, the other warriors whoop and whistle, like Memnon is racing away with some war prize, rather than his wife.

I thought a warrior wasn't supposed to give into distractions. Or whatever horseshit line he fed me earlier.

Yes, he agrees, *warriors shouldn't give into distractions. Kings and queens, however...they can do whatever the fuck they please.*

My mate doesn't bother returning his steed to the corral. Instead, once we reenter camp, he steers the horse toward the tent we use for my reading and writing lessons. We've barely reached it when Memnon swings himself off the horse and wraps the reins around a nearby post.

Before I can finish dismounting, Memnon pulls me from the saddle, turning me in his arms and wrapping my legs around his waist as he carries me into the tent, heedless of the looks we're getting.

I raise my eyebrows as I twine my arms around his neck but say nothing.

Inside the structure, the wax tablet and scrolls from our last lesson still sit out on the table. Memnon sweeps the items aside, letting them clatter to the ground so he can lay me out on the wooden table.

So what is it you want me to do? I ask. That, after all, was the big promise.

He places a hand on my chest, pinning me to the hard wooden surface. *Many, many things.*

Beneath his palm, his magic spreads, dragging my tunic off. His power moves down, tugging at the pants and boots I wear and shucking them off too.

No sooner have they left my body than Memnon steps between my legs. His arms come under my hips, and the table groans as he lifts my entire pelvis up, dipping his head to—

I cry out as his lips meet my folds, then try to snatch the sound back. We didn't place a spell on the tent to muffle our sounds; anyone could hear us.

Memnon places one of my legs, then the other, over his shoulders, then dips his head back down. I bite my lower lip hard to stifle another cry.

Louder, Memnon commands. *I want everyone to hear you, my queen.*

There's no magical compulsion in the order, but…

Whatever you want, I told him. I meant it too.

So when he sucks that extra-sensitive fold of skin into his mouth, I don't muffle my cry.

My hands grapple for purchase, but there's nothing but the edges of the table to hold on to.

Memnon's mouth stays right on that spot, swirling, teasing, even nipping. I whimper at the flood of sensation as it builds and builds and—

His mouth moves away from it, and I gasp out a wordless protest. I'm close to climaxing.

Please, Memnon, I beg.

Say it out loud, he commands, his grip tightening.

"Please, Memnon," I pant. My fingers move to his hair, twisting in his short locks as I try to maneuver his mouth back to where it left me most breathless, but still, he resists.

Louder, so our people can hear you.

This insufferable king!

"Gods take me, Memnon! Give me my orgasm!"

He grins. *I love it when you get commanding.* His mouth

returns to that place just above my opening, and lazily he sucks on that small fold of skin. It's so much sensation yet not quite enough.

I suppose I can give you an orgasm, he says down our bond, *but only if you promise to be loud.*

My face heats at the prospect. I know everybody in this city hears everyone else, but I'm still unused to this.

Whatever you want. I throw my earlier words back at him.

He smiles wolfishly at me, unrepentant, before returning to his ministrations. Memnon redoubles his efforts, his magic slipping into my pussy like phantom fingers. That's all it takes.

With a scream—a fucking loud one too—I shatter against his face.

Now that he got exactly what he wanted, Memnon is *merciless,* teasing that sensitive point above my core, wringing out every last bit of my orgasm.

The last echoes of it have only just abated when he lowers my hips to his own. I don't know when he loosened his own trousers, but now I feel the press of his cock against my opening.

"Did you think we were done, little witch?" Memnon says, amused. "We're only beginning."

He drives his cock forward then, seating himself in a single surging thrust. I gasp at the sudden intrusion, the pressure and fullness somehow erotic when it should simply be uncomfortable.

My body barely has time to adjust to him before he pulls out and slams back in, hard enough to make the wood groan.

He begins to fuck me in earnest then, his hips pumping in and out in a dizzying rhythm, the table creaking and shaking as it bears the load, that slick sound of sweat and fluids filling the tent beneath our louder gasps and groans.

My breasts bounce with each thrust, and the friction of our bodies meeting at that single point has me consumed. I'm about to sit up when Memnon's hand wraps around my throat, pinning me in place.

He shakes his head as he continues to thrust. "You're going to lie there and continue to obey me."

I raise my eyebrows. *Am I?*

Yes. And when you come, and you will come again, you are going to be louder than you were during your last orgasm.

If it didn't feel so good and if I hadn't made that cursed promise, I might argue with him. As it is, I get a perverse thrill at Memnon's commands.

Memnon's magic comes out again, teasing my nipples before moving down to that sensitive knot of flesh. I feel the soft brush of power against it, and even that light touch is nearly too much after Memnon's earlier attentions.

"*Memnon.*" There's a pleading note to my voice.

He adjusts the hand on my neck. There's a wicked gleam in his feverish eyes.

I did not become a king because I was merciful, he says down our bond, and I cannot help but recall his recent, terrifying cruelty toward the Dacians. *So take it.*

And with that, his power moves over every sensitive point I'm aware I have. It's an unnatural amount of sensation, and I'm helpless to fight against it.

I moan, giving myself up to the numerous touches.

Memnon squeezes my neck lightly.

Say my name again, he orders.

I can do better than his name.

"My king," I whisper. "My king, my king, my king…"

Memnon slows, looking at me like I've used my own magic on him. When he composes himself once more, he rebuilds his pace.

He squeezes my neck again, this time a little harder, then bites his lower lip when he feels me tighten around him.

That's not my name, he says, but the accusation has no fire behind it, not when I can feel his pleasure at my words.

The next time he drives into me, I lock eyes with him. "Memnon," I breathe.

Louder. He punctuates the command by deepening his strokes.

My orgasm builds rapidly, so rapidly—

"*Memnon!*" I cry out his name *revoltingly* loud as I come.

That seems to do it for the warlord. His hand reflexively tightens on my throat, heightening my release as he pounds into me harder, deeper. Then he's coming, an echo of his climax passing across our bond.

He collapses against me, his chest sweaty and heaving as his hand falls away from my neck. Outside, I hear someone whistle lasciviously, but I don't care. I don't care because what in the gods' names was that?

We've had sex, we've made love, but until now, we've never done anything so…feral.

Memnon moves a lock of hair out of my eyes. *But did you like it?* he asks.

I…did, I say, surprising myself. I give him a look. *But you must know that.* Surely he felt all my reactions to his words and touches. To his magic.

He grins, then presses a kiss to my shoulder. "I did too."

"Then it's settled: every time you cheat death, I'll ply you with perverse sexual acts."

"Better be careful offering such things, little witch," he

301

admonishes. "Your definition and my definition of *perverse* are two different things."

My feet touch the ground, and still naked, I step in close. "Then you better not die, so you can teach me the difference."

Because, as it turns out, Memnon's not a half-bad teacher after all.

CHAPTER 27
Roxilana, 18 years old

54 AD, Somewhere within Sarmatia

The Sarmatian kingdom is a vast expanse of land stretching from the Danubius River in the west to the Tanais River in the east, and from the Borysthenes River in the north all the way down to the Black Sea.

Or so I'm told. The names geographically mean very little to me; all of this land is too far east for my Roman frame of reference.

But I think that it's going to mean something more to me soon because the settlement is moving.

Tents are broken down and folded or rolled up. Chests are loaded onto many, many ox-drawn carts, and wooden wagons now become families' homes while we travel from one grazing area to another.

Within a few short days, the expansive city is packed up and carried off, our caravan stretching as far as the eye can see in both directions.

It is as we move across the endless expanse of grasslands that I learn the complicated truth about being a Sarmatian. According to Rome, these are Roman lands. It's obvious enough—every so often, we pass some Roman marker declaring such—but it is just as clear by the reverence we're given in the towns we pass through that Memnon is considered king here.

We travel south and west, following ancient roads Memnon tells me about. Only this time when we travel, I am ill-suited to it.

I hunch over on the outskirts of camp, retching up my breakfast into the grass, just as I did yesterday, and the day before that, and the day before that.

I draw in a deep breath, grimacing as hunger gnaws at me, so sharp it seems to cramp my belly.

Roxi?

Memnon's voice is full of concern, but I'm grateful that his kingly duties have drawn him away from my side. He's been increasingly worried about my travel sickness, and I don't have the energy to both manage my symptoms and soothe away his concern.

I straighten my tunic and, after placing a spell on myself to ease my nausea, return to my wagon. An apology is on the tip of my tongue for Katiari, who has taken to sharing breakfast with me. She's seen my recurring nausea several times, yet somehow it never gets less embarrassing.

Only this morning, as I step into my creaking wagon, it's not just Katiari who waits for me. Memnon's mother is there as well in all her finery, her brow wrinkled.

"Morning, Tamara," I say, startled.

"Valiant Daughter," she begins.

Oh no. No casual conversation ever begins this way with her.

I glance at Katiari, who mouths *sorry* to me.

"You asked her to come here?" I say accusingly.

"As she should," Tamara answers for her. "And as my son should've as well."

The former queen comes up to me and takes my hands, the bracelets along her arms shivering as she gives my palms a squeeze. "How long have you been sick?"

"I don't know…" I say. "A fortnight?"

Tamara's concern doesn't diminish. "Any other unusual symptoms?"

Again, I'm confused. "Food tastes a little off." I mean, that is a normal issue that comes with sickness.

She presses a hand to my breast, and I suck in a sharp breath at the unexpected touch.

Memnon, your mother is cupping one of my breasts.

What? he says, alarmed. *Gods*, he thinks, probably more to himself than to me. *I'm coming.*

"Does that hurt?" she asks, drawing my attention back to her.

Beneath the shock of her touch, I realize that yes, in fact, my breasts are tender. Actually, really tender, now that I think about it.

I nod.

Memnon, you don't need to come. I can handle your mother.

Tamara removes her hand. "When was the last time you bled?" she asks casually.

"Bled?" I echo.

I suck in another breath when I finally put together her probing questions. Could I…?

My pulse races at the possibility.

"It's been a long time." I don't know how long. Longer than it probably should've been. "Do you think…?"

Tamara smiles softly at me. "You won't know for sure for a while yet, but yes, it is likely." She pulls me into a hug. "Congratulations, my daughter. This is wonderful news. So, so wonderful."

"What is wonderful news?"

I startle at the sound of Memnon's voice.

He stands at the threshold of the wagon, his eyes moving from me to his mother, then his sister. "And what is this about you groping my wife?"

I'm still too shocked to groan.

"My son," Tamara begins.

I cut her off. "I'm pregnant."

His eyes widen, and I think it's his surprise I now sense coursing through me.

The beginnings of a smile pull at his lips, and his eyes take on a sheen. "Truly?" he breathes. He glances down at my stomach.

"I mean, I think so, yes." I nod, my smile growing.

A surprised laugh bubbles out of him. "You're serious?"

I bite the inside of my cheek.

"Your mother believes that's why I've been sick. And why she was fondling me."

Tamara lets out a huff, though I see her pressing her lips together against her own smile as she watches her son.

Memnon laughs again, and in three long strides he crosses over to me. He sweeps me into his arms, and then he kisses my lips, my cheeks, my neck. "It's not travel sickness?" he says, pulling away.

I shake my head. "Just pregnancy, apparently."

I feel his relief, though it's quickly overtaken by a joy that seems to have wings.

"Gods, Roxi, we're going to have a baby?" The hope in his eyes makes them shine brightly.

Again I nod, flashing him a shy smile. This isn't something we talked about, nor have I spent much of my life dwelling on parenthood, but seeing his reaction, excitement starts to well up from within me. This...this might actually be wonderful.

Memnon grins back at me, the action stretching to every corner of his face.

"I love you, I love you," he says, cupping my face. He kneels and presses a kiss to the soft skin of my stomach. And then he whispers a final line meant for another being entirely. "I love you."

CHAPTER 28
Roxilana, 18 years old

54 AD, Southwestern Sarmatia, North of Odesa

Despite Sarmatians' penchant for war and their ongoing dispute with the Dacians, I don't expect battle to happen.

Not until it does.

We have only resided at our new settlement—a grassland bordered by a creek, rolling hills, and many, many burial mounds—for a week or so when preparations for it begin.

Revenge has been on every warrior's lips since the Dacians ambushed us, but up until now, it was spoken more as a wish.

Now, it's a sobering reality.

Every time I think of it, my pulse quickens and I remember Memnon's bloody, broken body lying in the tall grass.

I'm still wrestling with my own horror over the blood I've spilled and Memnon's unholy cruelty to our enemies, but I also don't think I can endure another skirmish hidden away in the safety of camp while he battles it out.

So when the day of battle comes and Memnon suits up for it, I follow him over to the chests and grab my own weapons—daggers for close combat, a bow and arrows for long-range fighting. My gut twists as I touch each one, and I tell myself they're precautionary.

"Little witch, what are you doing?"

When I glance up, Memnon is watching me, his expression unreadable. Across our bond, however, I can feel pride and protectiveness warring for dominance within him.

"I'm coming with you," I say with as much authority as I can, forcing my voice not to quake. I strap on my gorytos, then secure my sheathed blades to my waist.

Memnon moves to me, placing his hands over mine to quell my movements. "I know the last battle still haunts you, the *killing* still haunts you," he says gently. "You don't have to do this."

My gaze meets his. "I cannot let you go out there unprotected," I admit hoarsely. Again, the image of Memnon bleeding out flashes behind my eyes.

His expression softens. "What happened last time is not normally how these battles go," he reassures me.

I give my head a shake. "For good, for ill, and for always, my life is bound with yours," I remind him, reciting our wedding vows. "I'm coming with you. You'll have to curse me to stop me."

He stares at me a bit longer. Then, seeming to make up his mind, a slow, wicked smile spreads across his face. He clasps me by the back of my neck and pulls me in close. "You will not die. Swear this to me."

I nod quickly, foolishly, like fate is something I can outmaneuver. "I swear I will not die."

His hand slides from my neck and settles low on my belly. "And you will protect our child as well."

I swallow, the weight of that responsibility settling on my shoulders. "I swear that too."

"You will wear my wards," he says, his voice commanding.

I raise my eyebrows. "Only if you wear mine."

His eyes shine in the low light of the tent, and he inclines his head ever so slightly. "Always, little witch."

"Okay," I agree, nodding back to him.

"Then it's settled," Memnon says. "You'll wear my wards, and I'll wear yours. And side by side, we shall fight."

I only start trembling once our camp is a dark smear at our backs. Fog clings to the ground, stirring as our horde's horses pass through it, making the land look ghostly, like the dead have come to watch.

I ride at the front of the amassed warriors, Memnon at one side, Ferox at the other. Despite my best attempts to keep my panther safe back at the settlement, the stubborn creature refused to stay behind. So here we are, the pair of us heading back out to battle.

Next to me, Memnon's body no longer wears the languid ease it did during training, though I don't sense much tension coming from him. Certainly not the corrosive fear that's flowing through my veins.

"You can still turn back, my queen," Memnon says.

I draw in a deep breath, trying to steady myself. It'll be okay. All I have to do is keep an eye on Memnon. And not die. That should be easy enough.

"I'm not leaving you," I insist.

He glances over at me, his eyes full of that once-unnamable emotion I now recognize as love.

I give him a tight smile, hardening my spirit.

Somewhat comforting is the knowledge that Katiari rides with the group. If she can be brave enough to face down enemies without the use of magic, surely I can do this with my power.

Memnon halts, and the rest of us follow suit.

I strain my eyes, searching for what caused us to pause. Eventually, I see them.

Dacians. They look like specters out in the mist. And what I can see of them…there are many. Far, far too many. More by far than there are Sarmatians.

One of the Dacians breaks off from the group, his horse cantering forward, fog swirling at the creature's ankles. The hairs on my arms rise at the sight of him.

Come, Memnon says, *ride with me.*

Getting closer is the last thing I want to do, but when Memnon urges his steed forward, I can't help but coax my own horse to follow, Ferox silently joining us.

The mounted figure pauses in the middle of the field, and I can feel his eyes on me. My crown, my face, the Roman tunic I defiantly wear, and the Sarmatian armor resting over it.

It's only as we near the man, however, that I make out his features. He's older than Memnon, with a graying braid running down his back and a thick beard obscuring the lower half of his face. Like Memnon, he wears a circlet under his peaked helmet.

He must be Zoutoula, the Dacian king himself. He looks old enough to have ruled his people for decades, but Memnon killed the previous Dacian king a year ago when his power Awoke.

Since the attack, he must've learned his son had fallen in battle, and then—then he must've witnessed his own warriors cutting down their loved ones. He likely had to order their deaths just to stop the carnage.

The Dacian looks at my husband with abject hatred, his eyes red-rimmed.

"Wretched beast," Zoutoula opens, "the days I have fantasized about your death." He takes in Memnon's face, grimacing.

"You gave me a wedding gift," Memnon says, unruffled, "and I sent you my many thanks for it."

Zoutoula snarls. "For the honor of my father, Dacia's former king, and my son," His voice hitches, "who should have been Dacia's future king, I will make your death slow, and then I will have my warriors defile your body in every imaginable way."

At his words, my magic rises, coiling around Memnon and instinctively shielding him.

Is my wife being protective of me? my husband says, his tone light.

He will sooner die than touch you, I vow.

Zoutoula must notice me bristling because his gaze swings to me. His features shift, just a little. There's still plenty of hatred there, but there's also a calculated gleam in his eye as his gaze touches on my diadem, then my face, and I know he's plotting some grisly death for me. That knowledge tastes like iron on my tongue, and I'm absurdly grateful for the numerous wards Memnon placed on me before we left camp.

Zoutoula says, "It was a mistake to bring your pretty wife to battle. If she lives by the end of it, she—"

There's a flash of Memnon's magic, then a choked noise

312

from the Dacian king. His eyes grow wide, and a line of blood seeps from his throat like a macabre necklace. Then his head slides one way and his body another, the two toppling to the ground and causing his horse to rear up.

I glance wildly from the grotesque remains to Memnon, whose hair has lifted and whose eyes already glow.

One day, people will learn not to threaten you in front of me, he says, his magic deepening his voice.

Before I can even fathom a response, he adds, *Ready yourself. It's time to fight, my queen.*

Already, dozens of arrows from distant Dacian archers are releasing, the group of them arcing across the field right for us.

I lift a hand, my eyes fixed on the projectiles. "*Away*," I incant.

A gust of my magic cuts across the grass, blowing the arrows far off course.

Well done, Memnon says, the glow of his eyes dimming.

Memnon pulls his sword from his sheath and holds it high, shouting a war cry, then charges forward. At my back, I can hear Sarmatians bellowing and howling. Though this is my first planned battle, muscle memory from training has me urging my horse forward into a gallop.

I slip down my bond with my panther. *Watch your step, Ferox, and stay to the edges of battle so you don't get trampled.*

Even draped in my wards, I worry about my big cat's safety.

My pulse races as I return to my own head. The massive Dacian army charges at us, the distance between us closing alarmingly fast.

My hands itch to reach for my bow and arrow, but I hold myself back.

I'm here to protect Memnon—and Ferox. Katiari too. I don't need to attack or kill to achieve that.

Only, more arrows rain down on me and the warriors at my back, and though my wards hold fast, several pelt me hard enough to throw my body sideways.

I've barely righted myself when I hit the front line of mounted Dacians.

War cries fill the air and spears lunge at me. One connects with my shoulder, and I scream as the jarring impact nearly topples me from my steed.

More blades and hands. This is a nightmare, one I cannot wake from—and then I break through the back of the massive horde.

I completed my first pass through the ranks of enemy warriors.

I mean to keep that thought to myself, but across our bond, I feel Memnon's exaltation. *Well done, my queen!*

I smile at his praise and turn my horse around. My eyes search him out. I spot Memnon ahead of me, his horse racing back the way we came. He's already looking at me, grinning, rather than facing our foes.

Don't let me distract you, I say, my earlier fear rising once more.

Impossible not to be distracted when you're so beguiling, he responds.

Is Memnon...flirting with me? On the battlefield, surrounded by enemies?

Yes. Tell me you like it.

I knock away another round of arrows.

Gods, please stop.

You wound me, my queen, he says, cutting down an enemy in front of him. *Fine, I'll stop. But only for now.*

Memnon raises his sword once more and bellows another war cry, and the Sarmatians fighting alongside us join in.

I join in. Battle is brutal, but it's also a rush of blood through my system, and…I can see why others enjoy this, even if it is terrible.

As we Sarmatians circle our horses back around, so too do our enemies. Again and again, we rush at one another. Using my magic, I knock Dacians off their horses and blow arrows sideways; I rip swords from hands and break the wooden shafts of spears. And when a Sarmatian sweeps in to kill a Dacian I made vulnerable, I tell myself I didn't really cause their death, just stopped them from harming Sarmatians.

At the center of the battlefield, I catch sight of Katiari. My sister-in-law is on her feet, her horse nowhere to be seen. Several Dacians swarm her. Already, I can see a massive gash on Katiari's arm, and blood coats her thigh.

Alarm rises in me. I hadn't thought to ward her earlier when we left, and if Memnon did, its effects must've already worn off. For a moment I hesitate, my morals around killing warring with my worry for Katiari's safety.

I gather what power I can, funneling down my arms.

"*Protect my sister*," I incant. "*Let no weapon harm her.*"

My magic leaves my palms and floods the air, the plumes of it moving across the battlefield and wrapping around Katiari just as several blades thrust at her. The weapons glance off her body, though the blows still drop her to her knees.

At her back, an enemy soldier wraps his arm around her neck, dragging her back, and—

"*Die.*" The spell is uttered before I even have time to think about it.

The Dacian's head whips back, blood spraying from his neck.

My eyes move to the others.

"*Die, die, die.*" I mutter the death curse over and over, silent tears beginning to slip down my cheeks as I kill the Dacians surrounding Katiari until no more remain.

I wasn't supposed to do this. I was merely meant to protect. I taste my own rising sickness at the back of my throat, but I don't vomit.

Katiari's safe. That's all that matters.

The battlefield has descended into chaos. The low-lying fog churns as mounted warriors clash and foot soldiers fight in twisted clusters, the clang of their armor and the sounds of their screams filling the air.

I catch sight of Memnon on horseback, his body twisted in the saddle so he can shoot behind him. For a moment, I can't help but stare. His hair lifts in the wind, only the top of it held down by his circlet, and his eyes glow with his magic, the light of them cutting through the mist. He releases his arrow, then nocks another.

It's only then that, to my horror, I notice the group of Dacians trailing him. Though Memnon's arrow already took one out, more assailants amass, drawn in by the lure of killing Memnon the Indomitable.

I part my lips to utter that horrible death spell again when pain lances through my leg.

I gasp, reaching for my thigh, only to realize that the limb is fine.

My gaze returns to my husband.

Memnon! I cry out down our bond. *Are you hurt?*

No, he says in that low tone, the one I know is fueled by his magic. *Are you* all right?

Yes... I say, even as I continue to squeeze my leg against the sharp pain.

Horror dawns when I realize what I'm feeling.

Ferox.

I slide down the bond I share with my panther, and between one breath and the next, I'm staring out from feline eyes.

I pant, lying on my side on the outskirts of the battlefield, horses and men clashing nearby. An arrow protrudes from my upper leg, the head of it embedded deep within my muscle. I taste blood on my lips and my paws are wet with it.

With a jerk, I shift back into my own mind.

My wards failed him.

Are you all right? Memnon repeats, concern and some more dangerous emotion lacing his words.

I am, I say, fear creeping into my voice, *but Ferox is not.*

My magic whips out of me then, snaking between warriors and vanishing into the grass a short distance away, where I can just make out a dark lump amongst the tall stalks.

I throw myself off my horse and dash across the field, following the line of my magic. A couple of Dacians try to intercept me, and I mutter quick death curses, ending their lives without even getting a good look at them. So much for trying to avoid killing the enemy.

When I get to Ferox, I fall to my knees, placing a hand on his side.

"I'm sorry," I murmur, fresh tears springing to my eyes.

Weakly, Ferox nudges my hand, and I think he's telling me it's all right.

My magic is just starting to sink into his when I hear a hiss—

Ferox's body jolts as another arrow sinks into his flesh, this one between his ribs.

I scream at the sight, shoving more power into him.

I need to make him a new ward.

"Protect my panther from—"

I hear the arrow a split second before it lodges into my back, throwing me forward, onto Ferox.

I gasp at the pain, which is so thick and sharp, it's hard to breathe around. Or maybe I punctured a lung.

A roar echoes across the battlefield.

ROXI!

Another arrow hits Ferox, and again I scream.

Behind me, footfalls close in on us.

"Look what we have here," a masculine voice says. "A queen and her little pet."

COMING FOR YOU! HOLD FAST.

I will, I manage.

It's hard to think through the pain and panic.

Wards. I focus on that one thing. I begin to form the words, blood trickling from my mouth. "Protect—us—" I can't catch my breath… "From—"

Fingers dig into my scalp, yanking me back by the hair.

Beneath me, Ferox growls.

"I'm going to cleave your head from your body, and then I'll fuck this pretty mouth." The Dacian pulls me against him, blade to my throat, and I scream as the movement breaks the arrow shaft jutting out of me and shoves the rest of it deeper into my torso.

I WILL END THEM ALL, Memnon raves.

The Dacian's acrid breath is hot against my ear. "Or maybe I'll fuck your mouth, *then* kill you."

My eyes meet Ferox's; his ears have flattened and his lips

have curled back in a snarl. He growls low in his throat, his gaze fixed on the warrior at my back.

"Shut the fuck up!" The Dacian removes his sword from my neck and drives it into my panther's flank.

I.

See.

Red.

My power explodes out of me, throwing the Dacian and nearby warriors back.

I straighten, a little blood trickling from my neck and lips, and I turn, my injuries all but forgotten as magic and wrath overwhelm me.

As soon as my eyes connect with the fallen Dacian, I lift a hand. "I hope the gods do not spare your soul. *Die.*"

His head recoils back as my magic rips through his jugular, blood arcing across the grass.

My rage should've abated with the Dacian's death. Instead, it grows, and with it, the power building in my veins.

YESSS... Memnon croons.

Maybe it's his power and wrath I'm consumed by. Maybe it's my own. Whatever the cause, it feels as though my magic is a physical thing unto itself. It certainly acts like it, pushing the arrow from my body and sealing my injuries up, all while my eyes sweep over the battlefield.

There are already piles of bodies, many of them Sarmatian. Though the fighting is still ongoing, we are losing. To *them.* For every living Sarmatian I see, there are two to three more Dacians. Brutal, cunning Dacians. They would take everyone I love from me.

They need to die.

Yes.

319

I don't know which one of us thinks the thoughts. Maybe both of us do so simultaneously. Hard to know where he ends and I begin.

I walk forward as though possessed, drawing my power in close. My eyes land on a cluster of Dacians, and my rage swells.

It is not enough to simply kill them. No. That will not satiate the dark urges inside of me.

The world goes still for a moment as another spell forms. Then—

"Annihilate."

BOOM!

My magic fires out of me, exploding into the group of Dacians. Flesh is rent from limb to limb. Arms and legs, heads and helmets—all of it goes flying.

I look for another group. *"Annihilate."*

BOOM!

Blood and dirt, grass and viscera speckle the air. Beyond it and the haze of mist, I catch sight of Memnon, his eyes glowing, warriors collapsing, *screaming* in his wake as he rides toward me.

My husband pulls up short and swings off his horse, rushing over to my side. He cups my face and stares at me with those unnatural, glowing eyes. I gaze back at him, and though my hair doesn't float and I don't think my own irises glow, I feel my stare is equally unnatural.

His gaze scours mine. *You're okay?*

Some of the haze peels away. *They hurt Ferox.* The rage is rising, darkening my vision.

His grip tightens. *Then we will make them pay. Yes?*

I give a curt nod. Yes, vengeance. I want that. Hunger for it. For what they did to Ferox, to me, to my family, to Memnon.

Then take your vengeance, my fierce queen. He kisses me hard. I taste blood on my lips as my mouth moves against his. *And I will take mine.*

With that, he withdraws from me, backing up to his steed. I stand there and watch him ride back into the fray until the mist swallows him up.

Turning, I head back to Ferox, who lies limp on the ground. Alive but barely.

It takes little effort to shove my magic back into him. "*Heal.*"

One by one, those arrows pop out of him, and his wounds seal themselves up. All the while, my rage *boils*.

Once the last of his injuries mends itself, I place a new ward on him, then on myself.

Then, grimly, I rise, and with me, so does Ferox.

I glance down at him. "You don't need to follow me."

He does anyway.

I cut across the battlefield, full of retribution, Ferox at my side. Every time my eyes fall on a Dacian, I lift my hand and utter a single word:

"*Annihilate.*"

The spell blows craters into the ground, it tears warriors apart, and it incites terror. The battlefield falls into panicked chaos, Dacians trying to escape. But on one end of the field is me, and the other is Memnon, his blue magic cutting our enemies apart.

Annihilate.

Annihilate, annihilate, annihilate. It becomes a macabre song on my bloody lips.

I'm so consumed by it that I hardly notice the arrows that pelt me as I walk across the misty expanse of grassland, Ferox at my side.

Gradually, I feel my magic depleting. I want to howl against this injustice. There are still countless enemy warriors. My power cannot fail me yet.

I sense it then. A whisper in my ear, or maybe a stirring in the air and earth.

Blood.

So much blood. It soaks the ground and dampens the grass. It's splattered across skin and armor and strewn across the field like an offering.

Within that blood, I sense…magic. Magic I need.

I stretch out my arms and beckon it, following my intuition.

For a single breath, nothing happens, and I wonder if I imagined it all. But then the blood from a fallen warrior lying a few paces from me sizzles against his face and clothes. The smoke that rises from it is pale orange and streaked through with black, as though it, too, got a little singed. It comes to me, entering my palms before exiting them just as quickly, funneled into more curses.

Need more.

People are screaming, howling, begging. Or else they're running. Trying to get away from me.

I call out to the blood farther and farther afield. I see it sizzle away, then sense the lines of that power snaking through the earth as they make their way to me. The blood-borne magic enters the soles of my feet, sinking into my flesh and veins before it leaves me once more.

I hold my hands to either side of me, palms out, watching the flow of my black-streaked magic arc across the field, exploding against warrior after warrior.

"*Witchhh…*"

The voice seems to come from nowhere and everywhere.

From the ground and in the air. Next to my ear and in my bloodstream.

"*Queeeeen…*"

Goose bumps break out along my skin, even as I continue murmuring curses.

The voice pauses, almost as though it's peering at something. When it returns, it is pitched lower. "*Empresssss…*" Then, spoken most intimately of all: "*Soul mate…*"

My gaze darts around, trying to locate the voice, but all I see are spears and swords and clashing warriors.

"*You taaake…what'sss miiiine.*" the disembodied voice says.

"No," I say aloud. "Not yours. Their blood is *mine*."

I've no sooner spoken than the remaining Dacians retreat, my intended victims streaming off the battlefield while Sarmatians chase them away.

Cheering. We've won, I think. Pleased—I should be pleased.

I'm not.

My targets have escaped me. I want to chase them down, wipe them from existence, then use their blood to kill their brethren.

Through the roiling darkness within me, I notice a rising chant.

"*Empress! Empress! Empress!*"

I falter.

Do they mean *me*?

I stop drawing power from spilled blood to better listen. However, it's as though that blood-borne magic was the only thing propping me up. Without it, my body seems to cave in on itself, my strength fleeing me, my senses returning.

Fuck, *what have I done?*

Across the battlefield, I see Memnon turning on his steed, and I meet his gaze briefly as my vision darkens and my legs fold.

"*Roxilana!*" Memnon roars.

It's the last thing I hear as the rest of that darkness sweeps in and swallows me whole.

I wake to the feel of soft blankets beneath me, a warm, furred body at my side, a hand on my cheek, and a crackling fire somewhere close by. I cannot remember feeling this secure, except for perhaps the murky past that was my childhood in Brittania.

"There you are," Memnon says softly as I blink away sleep. His fingers brush against my cheek, and he gazes at me with open adoration. "My ferocious, lovely queen."

"Hello." My voice comes out as a croak, and I go to lift my arm, but it feels leaden.

Ferox rises next to me, peering at me, then rubbing his cheek against my head.

"How are you feeling?" Memnon asks, his gaze sharp.

It takes me an instant longer to sense that all my limbs are heavy, and there's an ache that seems to radiate from deep within me.

Magical overuse.

I grimace. "Not great."

Memnon strokes my skin again from where he sits next to me, then whispers a spell. Some of the ache lifts, though the heaviness lingers.

"Unfortunately, I can take away your pain, but I cannot speed up this recovery," he reminds me apologetically. "Your body will have to do that on its own."

I glance down at the body in question, surprised when I see that I'm clad in a light stola, my skin clean and smelling faintly of oil. This is not how I dressed myself last…

"I dressed and washed you," Memnon says, a frown tugging at the corners of his lips. Across our bond, I sense something paining him.

I wet my lips. "What happened to me?"

"You overused your power."

Yes, I remember that part. But how did I…?

It all comes back to me with horrifying clarity. The battle, Ferox injured. My attempts to save him thwarted by that Dacian.

And then—red. Red like rage. Like blood.

So much blood. And magic, twisted, unholy magic, flowing into my veins, then right back out to kill and kill and kill.

I squeeze my eyes shut, a whimper trapped in my throat.

I wasn't supposed to kill. So why did I go feral with violence?

"Whoa, whoa," Memnon says, either hearing my thoughts or sensing my mood change. "I will not let you hate yourself."

I cover my eyes with a shaky hand. "I killed so many people. *Again.*" I drop my hand to stare Memnon in the eyes. "I couldn't stop myself," I admit. "Every death made me want more, not less vengeance."

Across our bond, I feel…*empathy*.

"That's true bloodlust. It happens a lot on the battlefield."

I make a pained noise, and Memnon presses his forehead against mine, wrapping an arm around my back to hold me there. "The magic complicates things. You have seen me in the throes of it."

I have. I swallow, staring at him.

"I hadn't realized it could consume you the way mine consumes me. But you are not broken, and you are not evil," he insists. "You're a powerful queen, protecting your people from our enemies. Nothing, *nothing* is more honorable than that. And out there in battle?" Memnon gives his head a shake. "You were breathtaking—"

"Brother?" Zosines's voice comes from the doorway.

Reluctantly, I drag my attention to the entrance of our tent. Zosines hesitantly steps inside, his gaze moving from Memnon to me. His eyes flicker with something like reverence, and he bows his head.

"Why are you standing at the door like a stranger?" Memnon says playfully. "Come in."

Zosines's eyes never leave mine as he comes forward and kneels before me.

My brows draw together as he bows his head. "Thank you, my queen."

I glance at Memnon uncertainly.

"Do you not know?" Memnon says with a slight curl of his lips. "Our warriors witnessed your power and saw how you ended our enemies. You're a hero, my queen." Pride shines from his eyes.

"A hero?" I echo. I still don't understand when I face Zosines again.

The warrior's head rises just a little, and he looks at me with unmasked awe. "You brought down the wrath and might of Sarmatia. The Dacians will think twice before attacking us again, now that they know to fear both our king *and* our queen."

I give him a weak, watery smile, my emotions a conflicted mess.

Zosines's attention moves from me to Memnon. "The celebrations are about to begin. As the slayer of now two Dacian kings, your presence …" Zosines lets the rest of the statement go unspoken, but his meaning is clear: the Sarmatian king should be there.

"I will go there once I know my wife is well."

Ignoring how my arm throbs in protest, I grab his hand and give it a squeeze. "Go, I will meet you there in a little while."

Memnon gives his head a shake. "You do not need to come at all," he insists. "You're still recovering."

"I am not infirm. I can show up to a celebration."

Memnon's gaze drops for a moment to my belly before rising to mine once more, thinking about the baby.

Slowly Memnon nods. "Then I will see you in a little while, my queen. Until then, take care of yourself."

He presses the back of my hand to his lips, then lightly touches my stomach. Zosines watches it all intently, his eyes missing nothing.

Memnon stands, letting my hand slip through his. And with that, he and his blood brother leave.

———

The revelry is in full swing by the time I drag myself from my tent, Ferox at my heels. My limbs are still heavy and I feel like fresh death, and if it weren't for Memnon cleaning and changing me while I slept, I'm sure I'd look it too. However, I refuse to languish in my tent all evening while the rest of camp is having fun.

When I reach the main clearing, braziers snap and crackle with fire. Someone plays a lyre, and Sarmatians dance wildly to the plucked tune, cups of kumiss and wine in their hands.

Ferox and I pass by them, only as we go, the revelry grows quieter and quieter. Awareness pricks at my skin. Everywhere I look, eyes are on me. I do not see Memnon, nor Tamara, Katiari, Zosines, nor any other familiar face.

A warrior steps forward, still clad in his battle leathers, his clothes and skin bearing all the sweat, mud, and blood of battle.

He looks me in the eye, his dark irises boring into me. "Aye," he says, lifting the horn he holds, "cheers to our empress! Destroyer of Dacians and our savior of the day!"

A shout goes up, one that has my gaze sweeping over the amassed revelers. Cups clink and liquid sloshes. And they're cheering for me. "Empress! Empress! Empress…"

My heart beats fast.

Why are people calling me empress? I ask, reaching out to Memnon.

On the other side of our bond, I feel his slow smile. *Our people saw their queen dressed like a Roman, dealing out death to their enemies, and some clever fool thought it was fitting.* After a moment, he adds, *Do you like it…Empress?*

It makes me breathless, and my heart constricts almost painfully. It's one thing to be called queen, but to be called *empress*, a title reserved solely for the emperor's wife…a perverse little thrill runs through me at the way it manages to both exalt me and mock Rome all in the same instant.

Yes, I *do* believe I like it.

I head for the main tent, where I can hear conversation coming from within. Inside, many warriors are gathered, the most elite of them sitting around a central firepit. They laugh and drink, yet this tent, too, grows quiet as the warriors notice me one by one.

I meet Memnon's eyes across the fire. In them is a look of abject desire and pride.

Empress, you came.

I didn't want to miss out. Especially not when the alternative was staring into the darkness, alone with my thoughts.

The corner of Memnon's mouth curves up, and he rises from the ground. Eyes move to the Sarmatian king, the room further quieting until the only sounds are the crackling of the fire and the celebration beyond the tent.

Memnon lifts a hand and thumps his armor right over his chest. Once. Twice. Three times.

The other soldiers join in, and my gaze skims over them—solemn Sattion and watchful Zosines; Itaxes, who howls out along with the sound, and a grinning Katiari. Someone begins chanting the title *empress*, and the name catches like fire until the whole room is saying it.

Memnon's smoky-amber eyes blaze with pride. He grabs a white bowl resting on a wooden tripod. With it, he approaches me.

"A toast to the woman of the evening," he says, his voice battle roughened, "who at great cost to herself fought off our enemies when we were outnumbered, our *empress*!"

Shouts go up, and Memnon hands the bowl to me. I nearly drop it when I realize this is no mere bowl but a skull chalice. Not even in death do our enemies get relief from conquest.

I stare down at the thick red wine, uneager to place my mouth on old bones and taste death upon my lips.

But all eyes in the room are on me, and if there was ever a moment not to ruin, this would be it.

So I hold the skull chalice before me. "To Sarmatia."

The room cheers as I bring the rim of the skull to my

lip, and I force myself not to flinch when I do taste the bone. I manage to choke down the wine, though its potent taste turns my stomach.

The noise in the tent rises to a roar, and I hear *empress* being chanted again. Memnon's eyes are luminous with love and pride.

When I finally lower the drink from my lips, he takes it from me.

Come, Empress, he beckons, heading back to his seat. Before he gets there, he hands the skull cup to Katiari, who is on his left. *Sit beside me.*

I do, settling on the ground between him and his sister while the skull chalice makes its way from warrior to warrior.

Thus begin the tales of battle. At least, I think they are tales of battle. Soon after Memnon sits, his hand comes to my leg, and he strokes it absently. A line of his magic spills from him and slips down the collar of my shirt. I feel it brush my breasts before moving lower.

Much, much lower.

I bite back a gasp when it strokes my slit.

I grab the hand on my thigh and squeeze it hard. *For the love of the gods, Memnon,* I say down our bond, *if you make me come during your war celebrations, I will make you come in front of your friends too.*

Memnon glances over at me, a devious look in his eye, his power still caressing me.

Do you promise?

Don't, I warn, giving him as menacing a look as possible.

His eyes come alive then, and his power, his godsdamned power, intensifies its ministrations, a portion of it slipping inside me.

Oh no.

I let out a ragged pant. I'm still half dead from battle, in a room full of warriors, and he thinks to continue teasing me?

I reach for my own magic to make good on my threat… and it's not there.

I meet Memnon's eyes right when the realization hits, and he grins.

Aren't you going to punish me, my queen? he cajoles.

More of his magic plays with me, teasing me, testing me. Because he knows I cannot.

Sweet Elysium, Memnon.

Would you like some relief? he asks, his gaze darkening. *I can feel the ache in you. We can do this in here if you're really set on us coming in front of our friends, or we can leave…*

I catch the whispered edge of his thoughts, most of which revolve around getting me on my back. But it's hard to focus when his magic is so persistently touching me.

Katiari leans around me, her gaze fixed on Memnon. "Brother," she says softly, "go bother someone besides your wife for once. I'd like to actually celebrate with her before your libido ruins it all."

I don't know how Katiari knows where Memnon's mind is, but I am equal parts amused and embarrassed. And I would say as much, except it's taking all my concentration to stifle the noises I want to make.

Memnon, the bastard, is biting back a smile. "I don't think she wants me to bother anyone but her," he says knowingly.

"I do," I rasp out. "*Please* bother someone else for a bit." I didn't come here to promptly leave, and I'm beginning to sweat in my attempt to keep myself behaving appropriately.

"See?" Katiari says, quirking a smile. "Leave your wife alone."

And take your magic with you, I add. It comes out as more of a plea than an actual command.

I can sense Memnon's suppressed laughter and, beneath that, his own building desire.

"I will leave my wife alone—for a bit." With his words, his magic blessedly stops tormenting me.

I exhale a ragged breath.

Memnon leans in. *If you grow tired or wish to leave, say as much and I will take you home.*

I give him a curious look. *Was this all a plot to get me back in bed and resting?* I ask him.

Back in bed? Yes. Resting? No. With that, he removes his hand and rises, moving to the other side of the circle and embracing a grizzled warrior.

"Finally, thank the gods," Katiari mutters, still watching her brother from across the fire like he might double back.

Now that Memnon has left his seat, the circle around the fire seems to break down, with warriors now getting up and moving about.

My gaze moves over Katiari, noting that her earlier wounds have disappeared.

"Memnon healed me," she explains, noticing the direction of my eyes. "He does that after every battle—goes around and heals those he can."

Sure enough, as I take in the room of warriors, I notice that precious few actually look like they survived a battle.

"He's a good king," I say, my heart swelling, my gaze touching on him again as he laughs at something one of his kinsmen says.

"Eh, he's decent, I suppose."

When I glance at Katiari, eyebrows raised, she laughs.

"I *jest*," she says. "Of course he's wonderful. I reckon

he's the best king we've ever had." She bumps my shoulder. "And I have a feeling you might just end up being the best queen—don't tell my mother I said that."

I mock gasp. "I would *never*." My lips twist into a wry smile, and my eyes sweep the room once more. "Where *is* your mother?" I ask.

"You want to know where my mother is right after I managed to scare off my other family member?" Katiari gives me a look, one that makes me laugh.

After a moment, she joins in. "She's old, *Empress*," she says, emphasizing my new nickname. "She made an appearance earlier, then took to bed."

My eyebrows rise again.

"Okay, she's not *that* old, but she's definitely in bed."

I bite back another laugh, finding it hard to imagine the hardened former warrior queen tucking herself into bed early.

Seeing my expression, Katiari's eyes twinkle mischievously. "Sister, there are plenty of open secrets here between all us Sarmatians." She leans into me. "For instance, Xartamos," she says, nodding to a brawny man with dark brown hair and pockmarked cheeks, "is particularly lethal with the, uh, battle-ax, but unfortunately, he knows it and wishes us all to know it too."

Now I do laugh again.

My sister-in-law flashes me a capricious smile. "Want to know more?"

"*Yes.*"

"Borena is a formidable opponent, but she lies ceaselessly," Katiari says, pointing an inked finger toward a dark-eyed woman who's speaking casually to a man I think goes by the nickname War Cry. "The only truth you can count on is that the end of her blade will find its mark."

I study the warrior with a bit of trepidation.

"You're well acquainted with Zosines," Katiari says, pulling my attention away from the woman, "so you know a bit about him already."

"Only that he likes women a little too much," I say, remembering his appeal to Memnon for a second wife.

Katiari snickers. "Rumor is that he's interested in acquiring a third wife, even as we speak."

Right as she says that, Zosines looks directly at me, then smiles and lifts his goblet.

I glance at Katiari, and after a pause, the two of us burst into more laughter.

"You better be careful, Roxi," she says. "He might try to acquire you one day."

"I would sooner put a blade in his belly," I declare.

"Maybe that's part of your appeal."

The two of us laugh all over again, leaning against one another.

I feel a brush of power in my hair, then around my neck like a touch. Then between my breasts.

I sense Memnon, right at our backs, though I neither saw nor heard him approach.

"It's been a bit," he says softly. Without further preamble, he lifts me from where I sit and hoists me over his shoulder. Fellow warriors whistle and hoot at the action.

Memnon, I chastise.

He gives my backside a slap. *No more back talk from you*, he says.

I yelp, my ire rising. *I swear, if I had a weapon in hand, I would use it*, I say.

Would you? He sounds delightfully curious, damn him. *Shame that you don't.*

It is.

Tonight, he says, crossing the tent, *once I lay you out on our bed, you'll spread your pussy for me so I can taste it, and then you'll take me any way I please it.*

The audacity.

And you'll enjoy it, he adds.

My disbelief and anger rise, but not nearly so fast as my lust.

I swear to the gods, Memnon—In the heat of my emotions I've accidentally slipped into Latin.

I sense his smile. *Oh, I know, little witch. You'll get your revenge. I'm eager for it. But unfortunately for you, it won't be tonight. Until your magic returns, you're at my whim. And I'm sorry to say, I'm not very merciful.*

As he speaks, his magic returns in full force, touching me in all those erotic places it stroked earlier.

I gasp against him as he strides out of the tent and takes me back to our own.

And he's right. He's not merciful with me.

But in this, I don't mind.

CHAPTER 29
Roxilana, 18 years old

54 AD, Southwestern Sarmatia, North of Odesa

The first crisp chill has entered the air when I ride next to Katiari, the two of us heading for the training grounds to practice shooting from horseback.

"How's your tattoo healing?" Katiari asks, nodding to my upper arm, where, beneath my kurta, a stylized panther now adorns my skin. I received it shortly after our recent victorious battle against Zoutoula and his warriors.

"It throbs, and it will probably make archery a pain today, but other than that, it should be—"

Between my legs, I feel a gush of something warm and wet.

I glance down, trying to figure out what the wetness is, even as it keeps coming.

I'm not...peeing, am I?

I lift my tunic up enough to see blood darkening my trousers. So much blood. More than there ever is during my monthly cycles.

I make a small, sharp noise. "Katiari …"

My sister-in-law glances over, her gaze dropping to the juncture of my thighs. She hisses in a sharp breath.

Tha-thump-tha-thump-tha-thump.

I can hear my rapid pulse and my harsh exhalations. I know what I'm seeing, but—no, there must be some other explanation.

No. Please, Vesta, Api—*any* benevolent god out there. Please, not this.

"Oh, Roxilana," Katiari whispers, "no."

It's her sorrow that makes it real.

Fear rises like a tidal wave, replacing my shock and every rational thought.

Roxi? Memnon's voice moves through my mind.

He's so close—I can make out his mounted form up ahead—yet it feels like we're an ocean apart as he steers his horse toward me. *I can feel your fear. Is everything all right?*

Katiari's inked hand grasps my forearm, and I jerk in surprise at her proximity. I don't know when she moved her horse so close to mine.

"Roxilana," she says, her brows pulled together and her voice soft. Too soft. "We need to get you to a healer."

My eyes drop back down to the juncture of my thighs. I'm still holding up my tunic, and that bright-red blood is still spreading.

I can feel myself nodding, and I'm dimly aware of Katiari taking the reins from my hands and turning our horses around. But I'm not really here in this moment.

Behind us, I hear Memnon shout.

Roxi, what is happening? he asks down our bond, his voice alarmed.

I pinch my eyes shut, feeling that awful, awful wetness between my thighs.

The baby… I feel my hope breaking, shattering. *I think we're losing the baby.*

There's no word for this loss. Nothing that can encapsulate losing something so beloved before you even had it. And the grief, the grief is a leviathan, sorrow and longing and hope—such sweet, brilliant hope—dashed upon the rocks of reality.

There's cramping and pain, clots and blood, and eventually, a tiny body, one that fits neatly in the palm of my hand.

I stare down at it, trying to understand this unending ache. No one sat me down and told me *this* part of life, this part that would absolutely break my heart.

Memnon and I go out early the next morning, Ferox following behind like a sentry. Here the landscape is dotted with kurgans, the area nothing more than a graveyard for the venerated dead.

Using our magic, we unearth a hole in the ground. Perhaps if the child were born alive, a proper grave would be made, but neither Romans nor Sarmatians have burial rites for those who are born without ever drawing breath.

I lay a piece of fine linen over the ground and place my child on it, their body wrapped in the orange veil I wore the day Memnon found me in Rome. Memnon unsheathes a slim dagger from his belt and places it in the grave, the weapon four times as large as our child.

"From the gods that made you to the gods that take you, I bid you ride with our ancestors in the heavens till the day of reckoning," Memnon says, his face stoic. "I await your embrace in the afterlife, my child."

My eyes prickle, but no tears come. Neither of us have cried, though I can feel our combined grief across our bond. We're drowning in this pain.

I press a hand to my child's body. I have no eloquent words, nothing that can spin the mess of my emotions into something poetic and beautiful.

"I love you," I say simply. "I will always love you."

With a shudder, I remove my hand, and Memnon and I fill our child's grave up with dirt. We use a bit more of our magic to make a small mound.

After we're finished, Memnon wraps his arms around me and pulls me down to the grass next to the small kurgan we've made. It is there, cradled in his arms, that I finally allow myself fall apart.

"It will be all right, Empress," Memnon says, his own voice wavering as he strokes my hair. "Sometimes, this is life too."

I shake my head. I know what he says is true, but I don't want to hear it. I don't want to hear any placating words, not even from Memnon.

The grief sucks me under, and I haven't surfaced from it when a rider heads our way, carting a saddled horse with him. A horse that looks concerningly like Memnon's.

My stomach twists when I realize that it *is* Memnon's horse.

The rider has barely reached us when, not bothering to dismount, he says, "A band of Bastarnae warriors have been spotted half a day's ride from here. They are armed and appear to be heading our way. Our sources suspect they've allied with Dacia."

My breath catches. Another fight? The last one was not even a week ago.

Memnon must have a similar thought, but rather than alarm, I feel the rising heat of his anger and bits of his thoughts.

…dare they interrupt my child's funeral? …will give them pain unlike any they've ever known…

He releases me gently, then stands, his mounting fury rolling off him in ominous waves. "How long do we have?" he asks.

"Until nightfall."

Memnon looks down at me. "I'm so sorry, Roxi." Because he has to attend to this, he means.

I bite the inside of my cheek and nod, trying not to cry all over again.

He kneels and kisses me, an apology and a pledge wrapped into the action. *You watch over our child, all right? I'll be back to hold you this evening.*

I grab on to his forearms as though I can keep him here. I don't want him to go, not into battle. I cannot bear the thought of possibly losing him too.

You will not *lose me*, Memnon says adamantly. *That, I vow.*

When he stands again, his jaw is hard, his face resolute. Memnon moves over to his horse and swings himself into the saddle in a single, fluid movement.

"Let's be done with this," Memnon says, his face grim. "My wife needs me."

And with that, they ride off.

I watch their forms until they disappear from view. I fight the need to reach across my bond with Memnon just to hear his voice and make sure he's okay.

It's then that I realize I was supposed to follow him into battle. In my grief, I forgot that pledge entirely.

The next breath I take sounds like a sob. Do I run for camp and try to catch up with the men?

Stay, Memnon insists, his voice strong as iron. *I will take care of this.*

I draw in a shaky breath and sit there, miserable. As I stare out at the grassland, my eyes keep snagging on the kurgans dotting it, all of them are so much bigger than the one Memnon and I just made.

One of the closer ones, in particular, is obscenely large, and my eyes keep returning to it. At its summit, the sun glints off something.

I lean forward, squinting to better see what has any right to shine so brightly on a day like today. The longer I stare at it, the more it seems to mock the meager grave I've given my child.

In a huff, I stand up. Still, my abdomen aches and I've been bleeding on and off, but damn it, I'm going to climb up to that kurgan and rip whatever bit of wealth rests on top of that pompous mound and fling it into the fucking afterlife.

Getting to the man-made hill, then climbing *up* it, takes longer than I thought it would, mostly because I am sore and slow, but the entire time, my eyes stay fixed to its apex.

Only, when I get to the top of the kurgan…there is *nothing*. No sword, no polished metal. Just grass and more grass.

I walked all this way, left the grave of my child, for just a trick of the light.

A tear rolls down my cheek.

Above me, a cloud passes away from the sun and the sky brightens, and once more, that thing glints again.

I peer at it, moving closer. There is still no metal object, but there is *something*. It looks almost…like a thin film suspended in midair. My eyes widen.

I've seen this before. Memnon's father led us through one when he visited.

A ley-line entrance.

Unfortunately, I cannot rip this thing off the mound. But I *can* traverse it.

I don't know what possesses me to even think the thought or why my feet creep closer, until I'm less than an arm span away from it.

For a long time, I gaze at the ephemeral surface. Cautiously, I raise my hand and touch it. Whatever substance it's made of, it ripples ever so slightly beneath my fingers.

Emboldened, I push my hand forward, letting the ley line swallow up my fingers. It looks eerily like part of my hand has been lopped off, but I know that's not true. I can feel my fingers just fine.

I marvel that while part of me stands here on the earth, a portion of me is elsewhere. And maybe elsewhere is where spirits go—where *my* child has gone.

I glance over my shoulder. I should get back—if not to camp, then at least to the grave I sat beside.

Facing forward once more, I take in the smooth surface of the ley-line entrance. I can't help but notice that these entrances seem to exist atop funerary mounds.

Maybe this really is a portal to the afterlife. It definitely feels as close to death as I'll ever be short of dying myself.

I reach forward, letting the strange surface swallow my forearm up to my elbow. I'm too curious to be worried, too grief-stricken to be afraid. So I act on my most foolish impulse yet and step fully onto the ley line.

———————

I *am* a fool. I'm going to die here, in this in-between space.

That's all I can think as I stand inside the strange tunnel that seems to be made entirely from smears of light. I glance over my shoulder, scanning the walls for a way out. But there is no obvious doorway or even a ripple that indicates an exit.

What have I done?

I can hear my harsh exhalations. Facing forward once more, I take a step, and the whole world seems to shift around me.

I touch the curved walls at my sides, and my fingers dip into them just a little. Yet the walls seem solid—or if they aren't, then they're viscous like honey and just as sure to trap me within their membrane.

Memnon?

I wait for a response. Nothing.

Memnon?

I can sense him, but I cannot hear him—and he might not be able to hear *me*.

I try to breathe down my rising alarm.

Ley-line magic is different than earthly magic. Memnon has told me this before, but I sense it now. Like entering a room where everyone speaks another language. It's familiar yet still foreign.

I was hoping for something unearthly. If I'm being perfectly honest with myself, I was hoping to catch a glimpse of what lies beyond death. But supernatural though these ley lines are, no spirits linger here, and if the afterlife does lie somewhere beyond these walls, it's been hidden entirely from my view.

I begin to walk anyway, determined to find a way off this magical road. Eislyn was able to do so, and once she gave Memnon the knowledge, he was able to as well.

However, the farther I go, the only thing that changes is the pattern of light around me.

Uncertain and losing my nerve, I back up, then turn around, so that I might return to where I first entered this tunnel. I could look harder for an exit. I know one exists. But as I try to retrace my steps, the light and colors don't ever shift back to something even vaguely familiar.

I pause again.

I could always try to find that river palace, the one gifted to us by Memnon's father. I might have a better chance of getting there than trying to return home. The thought of grieving alone in a palace rather than in a tented city where anyone can listen to my cries sounds oddly appealing.

So I walk and walk until exhaustion overtakes me. Then I sit down on the ground, which does not really feel like ground. I sense if I stayed here long enough, I'd sink into the ley line until I was swallowed whole.

My shoulders begin to shake, and I weep from frustration and grief and weariness.

"Please," I whisper, my voice broken. "All I want is to find my way to that Khuno River Palace. Please. To whatever benevolent gods are listening, take what you want from me, just let me find my way."

But of course, nothing happens.

Until…something does.

The walls around me shiver and move, and the tears on my face dissolve.

Startled, I rise to my feet and touch my cheek, amazed to find it dry.

That wasn't my own magic, was it?

I take a few halting steps forward, and then I *fall*.

I grunt as my body collapses onto a muddy bank.

My fingers dig into the soil just to confirm that it *is* in fact mud and not whatever substance the ley line was made of. But it smells like loam and feels like it too. The distant calls of birds and the closer buzz of insects distracts me.

Gingerly, I push myself to my feet and take in my surroundings. Thick foliage stretches in almost every direction, though I catch glimpses here and there of murky water beyond a section of trees to my left.

My pleas…worked.

Someone or something unseen listened to me. I touch my cheek once more, remembering what I said. *Take what you want from me.* And it had. The skin is now dry, my tears eaten up by that otherworldly power. I'm caught for a moment in wonder. They took my tears, and they dropped me off…here.

I glance around. It's definitely not the steppe. And now that I'm looking, I catch sight of the glimmering wards suspended in the air nearby.

This *is* the river palace I was trying to get to.

I take a few tentative steps away from where I landed, crossing the mushroom circle I'd been inside a moment ago. I look behind me, taking in the shimmering ley-line entrance.

I'll have to get back on that thing at some point. I try not to cringe at the prospect.

Turning away from it, I wave a hand, allowing my magic to scrub the mud from my body, and then I approach the ward. I touch the wall of spells just as I had the ley line. And like the ley line, these spells put up no resistance. My hand slips through, then the rest of my body, and I head in the same direction I went the last time I was here. I'm not entirely sure it's the correct one, not until I catch sight of a strikingly white column through the dense trees, the stone glittering where the light hits it.

I cut through the vegetation, heading up to the palace, my lips parting all over again as I take in the carved marble and gold-and-glass detailing.

I stop only when I get to the bronze doors. More wards drape these, but they seem indifferent to my presence, and I'm able to open them with only a little assistance from my magic.

There are wonders to behold inside this palace—trees of stone and glass, veins of gold that run through the stone. Silks and linens in colors my eyes have never seen on fabric before. Tapestries so intricately woven, they look like paintings. And paintings so expertly crafted, they seem to come alive.

I walk past it all, unmoved, as my grief rushes back in, strangling me in its grip. No art and no wealth can compensate for what I've lost.

I don't stop wandering through the palace until I find a bedroom. Once I do, I drop onto the mattress, and there, I surrender wholly to my pain.

———

Roxi…

Roxilana…

ROXILANA!

I wake with a gasp.

Sitting up, I blink, the skin near my eyes feeling stiff and crusty. My brows come together when I take in the thin muslin draped above my bed, the fabric caught in the boughs of the carved wooden bedposts, green blown-glass leaves protruding from them.

Where in the gods' names—

ROXILANA!

I startle again, my heart pounding fast at Memnon's panicked voice.

Memnon? I say, reaching down our bond.

Thank the gods. He sounds audibly relieved. *Where are you?*

I push back my cinnamon-colored hair and look around again. The past day rushes back to me all at once. The miscarriage, the burial, the ley line, and…

Your father's river palace, I murmur as the heaviness begins to sink in once more.

My father's what?

The palace he gave us. I'm there.

There's a long pause.

How did you get there? Memnon finally asks, wary.

I…used a ley line.

I can sense his shock, followed by his deep confusion.

Instead of voicing any of it, he simply says, *I'm coming.*

———————

I meander through the palace, my footsteps echoing against the stone floor, looking at the space all over again with new—albeit, *sadder*—eyes. The marble trees and the carved flowers. The gold detailing that seems to make everything glimmer. Everything mimics the natural world, yet none of it is alive.

Like the first time I visited this place, no one is here. No guards, no servants, no tenants besides me. Yet there is wine waiting in blown-glass bottles and bowls of fresh fruit and

347

even a warm loaf of bread, the yeasty smell of it wafting from the kitchen. But no people.

Only then do I really notice the magic clinging to this place—to the walls and floors, to the bottles of wine, to the fruit and even the yeasty bread.

I wander over to one such bowl of fruit and peer down at it, studying the magic that coats the items. It is lilac in color but so pale I hardly see it, and when I tilt my head, I swear it changes colors to the softest pink.

Strange.

The echoing tread of boots on the polished marble floor distracts me.

I straighten. "Memnon?"

Just as I speak his name, he steps into the doorway to the kitchen, still clad in what he wore this morning. My gaze scans his body, looking for any signs of injury from his most recent battle. There's isn't so much as a speck of blood on him. Worry, however, pinches his eyes and tightens his mouth.

The moment he sees me, his entire body seems to relax.

"*Roxi.*" Both relief and concern are wrapped into that single word.

Closing the distance between us in a few short strides, he cups my face. I can feel his hands trembling as he kisses me fiercely.

Are you all right? I ask down our bond.

No, he says simply.

I'm about to respond when I hear the click of claws on marble, then feel the brush of fur against my hand. Ferox's familiar, wet snout nuzzles my hand, and I run my hand over his head.

You brought Ferox with you? Emotion clogs my throat.

"Mmm," Memnon assents against my lips. *He wouldn't leave my side.*

Even once the kiss ends, Memnon doesn't let me go, instead gathering me into his arms, holding me close—so, so close, I can hear the rapid pound of his heart.

"I couldn't find you," he whispers against my hair, burying his face deeper into it, like it will suffocate his worries. "No one could. Not even Ferox, who was as agitated as I've ever seen him. And when you weren't at the"—his voice catches—"*grave*, and you weren't answering me…" Memnon goes quiet, holding me close, his body trembling with his emotion.

I thought I lost you too, he finally admits.

I run my fingers through his wavy hair, grief and guilt twisting up my insides.

"I'm sorry," I say softly, holding him close. "So sorry."

I hadn't meant to scare him, especially considering recent events. I simply hadn't been thinking about him—or anyone else. I'd been so wrapped up in my own pain.

I stroke his skin.

"I killed them all," he admits, his face still buried in my hair.

My hand stills.

"Killed who?" I finally ask.

I hear him swallow, his fingers pressing into my skin. "After I left you, I rode out with my men." He sounds young and unsure of himself. It's been a long time since I've heard that vulnerable waver in his voice.

Memnon draws in a breath. "I knew I was never going to go into battle with them," he quietly admits. "Once we spotted the band of Bastarnae, I forced my warriors to return to camp. Then…"

He swallows, growing quiet again. Across our bond, I can sense his unease. "I let my magic take control. It would've happened anyway, I was so angry, but…I *wanted* my power to take over."

The admission does nothing to ease the toxic emotions churning within him, and now I feel my own rising nerves as I continue stroking his hair. What could possibly make a warlord who intimately knows violence *this* uncomfortable?

"When I got to the army, I killed everyone but their leader. Him, I forced to watch as his fighters died…horribly." His throat works, and it seems like it takes effort for him to force out the next words: "His son was among them."

Bile rises at the thought. Having just lost a child, my horror is particularly sharp.

"Then, when it was all over, I killed him too," Memnon says. "But by then, his death was a mercy."

His expression is anguished as he lifts his head and looks at me. "Our people were ready to celebrate, but you weren't there. I thought that perhaps you had heard of what I'd done and left…"

My eyes well. I shake my head, my fingers tightening in his hair. "Those deaths won't bring our child back," I say softly, tears slipping down my cheeks. "It's just death upon death." A ceaseless cycle of it. "But you will not lose me because of it," I vow, and I hate myself only a little for that admission.

Memnon pulls me back into him and buries his face in the crook of my neck. And there he begins to cry—for our lost child, for me, for what power and circumstance have forced him to become.

We stay like that, locked in each other's embrace, for a long time. And I feel grateful that at least if the world is falling apart around us, I still have him in all his painful, messy glory.

Always, he whispers across our bond.

Eventually, Memnon lowers his arms. His eyes are red, but any tears he cried are long gone. His gaze now flits over the room.

He clears his throat. "Now, my queen, I believe it's your turn to share your story: why, and *how*, did you come here?" he asks, forcing levity into the words.

Ah, yes, that.

I reach down and pet Ferox. "Um, well, it started when I got mad at a burial mound…"

I tell him the whole sordid story. About climbing the kurgan, then stepping onto the ley line, getting lost, then making some bargain that landed me here.

Memnon's eyes are sad after he hears it all, and I can feel him ruminating on my pain.

Finally, he says, "Brave, foolish wife. Traversing a ley line without any idea how to navigate it." He leans down to give my nose a kiss. "I didn't know ley lines could be swayed with words."

"You think it was the ley line itself that helped me?" I ask. "I thought it was a god."

"Well, there is only one way to find out."

———

The two of us stand inside the ley line, and I try not to get disoriented by the play of color and light along the tunnel walls.

So if this doesn't work, you'll get us off this thing, right? I ask.

Wait, you want me to do what?

I glance sharply over at Memnon, but his eyes are already

crinkled playfully at their corners, and he's barely suppressing a smile.

I'm kidding, he says. *Of course I can—if it's needed.*

I take a deep breath, then take his hand in mine, sinking my other hand into Ferox's scruff.

Last time I was in these tunnels, I pleaded with what I thought were the gods, but perhaps Memnon's right and it's simpler than that.

"Ley line," I call out, feeling foolish for addressing a magical tunnel by name, "please take us back to the Sarmatian camp in the steppe lands."

Nothing happens. But then, nothing happened last time, not right away.

I take a few steps forward, dragging Memnon and Ferox along with me.

Still, nothing.

"Huh," I say, stumped. "Maybe it really was a god that answered my call."

I can feel Memnon's conflicted emotions at the possibility.

"Was there anything else you did besides ask for help?" he says.

I think back to the moment, my memory hazy from grief.

My gaze darts to Memnon's when I remember.

"I said it could take whatever it wanted from me. It took my tears."

I sense Memnon's alarm. "It took your *tears*?" he says skeptically.

But now I have a hunch—one I want to test out. I release Memnon's hand and reach for his sheathed dagger.

"What are you doing, little witch?" he asks, a thread of unease entering his voice.

Rather than answering, I grab a small section of my hair and saw it off. Then I return Memnon's blade to its sheath and regrasp his hand.

"Ley line," I say, my voice strong and clear, "I offer you a lock of my shorn hair in return for safe passage to our Sarmatian camp in the steppe lands."

I stare at the curled lock of auburn hair pressed between my fingers. One exhalation passes, then another.

Suddenly, my hair catches fire, the flames of it iridescent. The fibers curl and burn, and then they're gone.

I exchange a look with Memnon, who raises his eyebrows.

Now, I think we start walking, I say.

Slowly, Ferox, Memnon, and I move forward. One step, then two, three, four, five—

Our sixth step never lands. Instead, we fall into darkness, our bodies hitting the ground hard.

I groan, rolling over, the long grass beneath me crunching under my weight.

I blink a few times, staring up at familiar constellations in the star-strewn sky.

Memnon barks out a disbelieving laugh. "Roxi, that *worked*."

I sit up, noticing the torchlight in the distance where our settlement is.

Gods' wrath, it really did. We made it back.

CHAPTER 30
Roxilana, 19 years old

55 AD, Somewhere in the northwestern Amazon Basin

After my last experience on the ley line, I know I should stay away from it. But I cannot help but notice the magical doorway the next time I visit my child's grave. The sight of it makes me feel something other than grief—something that connects me to my child. It feels like a beginning to an ending and an escape all at once. And so when I feel the pull to approach it—then enter it—again, I give into temptation and return to the ley line.

Again.

And again.

And again.

Even once we pack up camp and move sites, I take to finding the closest portal I can, and then I enter it, sometimes with Memnon but mostly without him. Each time, I ask to go to the Khuno River Palace or to my child's gravesite or else to return home. It becomes easy to travel along the ley line, now that I understand it simply wants something in return for its help.

Sometimes I give it a lock of hair. Sometimes I sing it a song. Sometimes I present it with a coin or small bauble from a faraway place. I've come to find that it likes unusual things, *human* things. It's an exercise in creativity, making sure I have something to offer the unearthly magic for both the travel to and from my destination.

The magical road can be fickle, moody even. More than once, it's rejected my gift and I've had to come up with another. But when it works...when it works, I get to travel to places that are far beyond my normal reach.

And the more I go to the river palace, the more comfortable I get in that strange and beautiful place. I take to bringing my wax tablet and stylus with me, as well as the scrolls I'm studying. So far, I've learned Latin and a little Greek, and I'm ever eager to know more.

And when I'm not studying, I find myself working on my magic, usually by adding spells to the property—wards to keep the world out or enchantments to make eyes wander and curious trespassers turn away from this piece of land.

It is likely not needed—there are plenty of spells cloaking this palace—but none of them are *mine*. So I add my own like lace, usually at the beginning and end of my time here.

Today, after placing an enchantment on the back of the property, where a pool sits nestled amongst those marble trees, I settle myself in the dining room. My scrolls are already spread out and my wax tablet awaits.

I've just poured myself a glass of wine and begun to look over my work when I hear the bronze doors groan open.

Memnon? I call out across our bond.

Gods, your voice does things to me, he says. *Are you back from the river palace already?*

I smother a smile. *Are you still at camp?* I ask.

Yes. And if you're here, you could save me from my mother and these crotchety advisors right now.

I hear the soft tread of footfalls on the marble floors.

Someone's here, at the palace, I tell Memnon.

What? The teasing tone bleeds out of his voice. *Who?*

I glance toward the entrance, unable to see the intruder. *I don't know.*

Ready your magic and strike first, he says. *I'm coming.*

My power floods down my arms, gathering in my palms as the intruder enters the room.

Striding in, draped in clothes as fine as they are foreign, is the fae woman I met during my wedding celebration, Ilyapa's advisor.

Eislyn, my mind whispers.

Eislyn? Memnon echoes, clearly eavesdropping on my thoughts. *What is she doing there?*

I guess I'm about to find out.

She stops short when she sees me, and though she is hard to read, I think I have startled her.

"Hello, young queen," she says, composing herself. "I wasn't expecting you or your husband to be here." Her gaze flicks to the doorway beyond me, clearly looking for Memnon.

"I wasn't expecting you, either." And I cannot help but notice she strode into this palace as though it were her own.

Eislyn lifts her brows briefly, as though acknowledging my point. "Memnon is here?" she asks, her gaze drifting again.

"He's on his way."

Eislyn's brows pinch, just a little. "You came alone?"

My skin pricks at her scrutiny.

"How?" she asks, removing her cloak and tossing it over one of the nearby chairs. Again, as though it were her own.

"Same way you did, I imagine," I say.

She tilts her head, stepping a little closer to me like she cannot help herself. "Memnon taught you?" She raises her eyebrows. "That is bold of him to let his precious wife navigate those lines on her own."

I bristle at her words before remembering that this is what this woman does; she lays out words like they are hunting traps.

"I taught myself." I don't bother explaining that I actually understand very little about the ley lines themselves, nor do I have any sort of mastery over them. Just…baubles to trade.

"You taught yourself," Eislyn echoes disbelievingly. Her eyes sweep over me again, reassessing.

"What are *you* doing here?" I ask pointedly. When we were gifted this house, no one mentioned that Eislyn might continue to access it as well.

"I'm the one who places the spells that keep this palace intact. Surely you've seen them?"

At her admission, I relax just a touch and nod.

"Besides." She takes a few steps, her hand trailing along a nearby carved column. "I helped build this palace, believe it or not."

I try not to let my surprise show. I should've pieced it together, given that she is fae and the construction of this palace is otherworldly.

I understand then what she isn't saying—that though this place has been gifted to me, I am more a guest than she is. But if she meant to make me feel unwelcome, she failed. I have always moved through life as a guest in strange lands. It is all I've known.

Eislyn studies me. "I see the Sarmatian ways have left their mark on you," she says, "and in more ways than one." Her gaze drops to the tattoo on my arm that my tunic exposes.

"Do you want something?" I ask, settling myself farther into my seat. My magic is coiled tight in my palms, and I have to will it back.

I suppose I should be putting on airs, welcoming this beloved family advisor into a house that's practically hers, but I am far too unnerved to fall back on any sort of social etiquette.

Eislyn clucks her tongue, then smiles almost fondly at me. "I'm glad steppe life has given you bite. It would've made everything so much less satisfying if you were meek."

I would bet my crown this woman has driven people mad with her barbed tongue.

She comes over to the table where I sit with my scroll and wax tablet and leans over my shoulder. "Studying, are we?" she asks, lifting one unrolled parchment. "And where *is* your husband?"

"The same place your manners are, I suppose." I take a drink from my goblet.

She raises her eyebrows, then gives a disbelieving laugh, presumably at my audacity.

Eislyn leans closer, her mouth hovering near my ear. "I would watch how you act around me," she breathes. "I enjoy breaking humans the same way Sarmatians enjoy breaking wild horses."

I rear back a little so I can stare at her speculatively. This is where I'm supposed to be afraid. A year ago, I might have

358

been. Since then, however, I have seen too much and lost too much. No, my battle-battered heart will not be cowed by this fairy.

She meets my gaze, and I think, for the first time, we really see each other.

"You would break even Memnon?" I ask softly, remembering her fondness for my husband.

She stares back at me, seeming to weigh my words. Eventually, Eislyn makes a noise at the back of her throat, one that might be agreement or dissent—it's hard to tell.

"Is that a request?"

Of course it isn't, but it's interesting that her mind went there.

"Last time I saw you two," Eislyn continues, "your husband couldn't keep his eyes off of you." She glances around, as though to emphasize his absence. "But then, I suppose it's only natural for ardor to cool over time."

She pulls out the chair next to me and sits down, like we're about to have a long, honest-to-gods conversation.

"Tell me, *has* he taken other wives yet?"

My muscles clench, and I try not to make a fist.

"Why?" I ask, my attention moving from her pointed ears to the red fabric of her outfit. "Are you interested in the position?" Much as her obvious fixation with Memnon boils my blood, I am not intimidated by her the way I was the last time we spoke.

She drums her fingers on the table. "I am an advisor to kings. I care little for the lives of their consorts."

"Mmm," I say noncommittedly. "You're awfully curious about me for someone who cares little for consorts."

Eislyn flashes me a soft look, almost as though she's commiserating. "It is only that Sarmatians do have such a great thirst for sex, more than most foreign women can keep up with."

Why am I listening to this? She seeks to worm her way under my skin. That doesn't mean I have to let her. I don't have to listen to her at all.

So while she prattles on, I turn my attention back to my tablet.

Under my breath, I sound out the Sarmatian word for *horse*, trying to place the appropriate letters to the sounds.

Eislyn must notice she's lost my attention, for she eventually grows quiet.

I take another drink of my wine. "You can keep going. Your voice *is* very lovely."

She stares at me with those unnerving eyes of hers. Watching, watching...

A sly smile spreads across her face. "Clever human. I have underestimated you."

She turns her gaze to the wax tablet in front of me, dragging the thing over to her and forcing my attention her way once more. She makes another noise under her breath after she takes in the text. "What is this?"

"Latin," I reply smoothly.

She gives her head a shake. "Latin letters, yes, but this is not the Latin language."

"You know Latin?" I say, my brows lifting.

She casts me a patronizing glance. "Don't act so surprised. I have been alive for a long time." Her attention returns to the tablet, and she traces the letters with her finger. "*Horse*," she sounds out slowly. It takes her another moment to realize the word she spoke is in the same language we're conversing—Sarmatian.

"You're transcribing Sarmatian words into text?" she asks.

I'm *trying* to. No one has ever attempted to write Memnon's mother tongue down, so the process is a slow, tedious one. But if I do successfully manage it, then Sarmatians will be able to learn to read and write in their own language. Our histories could be written down, messages could be sent that our Roman enemies would not be able to read. The possibilities are vast.

"*Very* clever human," Eislyn repeats, and it sounds awfully close to praise. "Does Memnon know you're doing this?"

If I am clever, this fairy is cunning. Far, far too cunning.

"I wasn't aware Memnon needed to know, Eislyn," I say. "Surely you don't report every movement of yours to your king?"

"Ah," she finally says, "so it's a secret. I do so love secrets. This one can be ours."

It's *not* a secret. I've spoken long into the night with Memnon about this, just as I have so many other joys. Not that Eislyn needs to know such things.

I lean back in my seat and bring the wine to my lips again. "Mmm…" I murmur noncommittally.

The bronze doors groan then, and I don't miss the flash of eagerness that flits across Eislyn's face before she smooths it over.

I hear Memnon's long strides before I see his form cross into the dining room. He's wearing his circlet and one of his finer kurtas, the gold thread of it catching the light.

Unlike the last time Eislyn saw him, his beard has grown back, and his hair has lengthened.

"Memnon," she says with genuine warmth. "What a wonderful, unexpected—"

"Surprise," he finishes. "Yes." He takes an ominous step

toward her. "It was a surprise when Roxilana told me you were here, in our palace, without our knowledge."

His words come off as threatening, but Eislyn looks downright delighted.

"Did you come all this way to see me?" she asks, standing. She crosses the room and embraces him, laying a soft hand on his cheek. "You did not have to."

A possessive sort of anger rises in me at her actions. She treats my husband the same way she treats this place—as though he is hers.

It's all right, Memnon soothes. *I shall handle this.*

Memnon wraps a hand around Eislyn's wrist and pries her hand from his cheek. "Is this palace ours, or is it not?"

"Of course it is yours," she assures him, practically simpering under his gaze.

"Then you are never to come here again without receiving an invitation first."

She raises her eyebrows, then casts me a pointed look, like I am at fault for his words. To be fair, I likely am. "But the wards that protect—"

"We shall tend to the spells that guard this place, just as we have been—or have you not noticed my queen's many, many wards and enchantments?" he accuses. "I assure you, you cannot miss them."

Eislyn flicks a cursory gaze over the room. Slowly, she nods. "Very well. I misunderstood the situation, and I am sorry if I have offended either of you."

I barely suppress my guffaw. She doesn't give a horse's ass if she offended me, I know that for sure. It's only Memnon whose opinion she seems to care about.

Eislyn turns and grabs her cloak, her Moche garments

rustling as she does so. "Take care, clever human," she says to me. "We'll meet again soon, I'm sure of it."

She heads for the doorway, pausing only to give Memnon a final, meaningful look. "I will pass on your good tidings to your father. Keep yourself whole and healthy. You know where to find me if you ever need my aid."

And then she's gone, leaving nothing in her wake except for this deep, foreboding feeling I cannot shake.

Part II

CHAPTER 31
Roxilana, 22 years old

58 AD, Eastern Sarmatia, near the Tanais River

The howl of the wind nearly drowns out the screams and bellows of battle. My warhorse gallops hard as we ride toward the enemy.

I trust the creature enough to not bother holding the reins. Instead, I aim my nocked arrow at a rival warrior. It feels like flying, like when Memnon and I left Rome together and I first tasted freedom.

Over the years, I've gotten good at riding. And fighting. I no longer need magic to keep me mounted, help draw back the string of my bow, or even aim my arrow. Near-constant practice has helped me perfect the art.

I pull back my bowstring and shoot. The projectile hits the warrior, knocking him off his steed as I ride on.

If the years have strengthened my fighting skills, they've also weakened my morals.

I did *try* to do right in the beginning. My entire first

year of marriage, I was committed to protecting and aiding Sarmatian warriors. But those battles all ended the same way: with me killing our enemies, with blades or spells, until it no longer made sense to even attempt to stay my hand.

Quickly, I pass the cluster of mounted riders. I withdraw another arrow from my gorytos and twist my body on my steed. Sighting the retreating form of another enemy fighter, I release the projectile.

It whizzes across the distance and *thwonks* into the enemy's back, toppling the man off his horse.

Memnon whoops from where he's already circling back around to the front lines of the fighting.

Excellent shot, Roxi.

My gaze moves to his just as he pulls back his own bow and releases an arrow. It cuts through the air and lodges itself in a warrior's throat.

Well done, yourself.

Neither of us can say more than that. Not while the enemy, an Alani tribe pressing in from the east, swarms around us. I shoot again and again, most of my arrows finding their mark.

Once I've emptied my gorytos, I swing myself off my horse, letting it gallop away. Magic leaks from my palms as I step forward.

Across the field, I see Katiari ducking under her opponent's blade before bringing her own sword up. Ferox charges in from the grasslands around us, pouncing on the enemy fighter before she can finish him off, the panther ripping out the man's throat.

The wards I've placed on myself and Memnon, Ferox, and Katiari are likely weakening, which means Memnon and I need to either end the battle soon or reinforce the wards.

It doesn't particularly matter which option we choose. Either way, we'll win.

We always do.

I reach a hand out, my magic pooling in the air around it. Instead of forming it into a spell, I draw on the spilled blood that wets the grassy knoll we fight on. There's so much of it splattered across the battlefield. I can sense the earth swallowing it up.

I call on that power, coaxing it to me.

Across the battlefield, blood bubbles and hisses as it evaporates. The magic that remains twists through the ground, moving toward me.

"*Empressss…*"

Goose bumps break out along my arms, and I suppress a shudder as the voices speak to me as one.

"*Seamstress…orphan…warrior…*"

I grit my teeth as I continue to call on that blood-borne magic.

Sometimes I hear the voices out here; sometimes I don't. I refuse to ask who they are or what they want. I don't acknowledge them at all, though that doesn't stop them from whispering to me.

"*Thief…friend…*"

Memnon's eyes meet mine as the dark magic enters through the bottoms of my boots, then the soles of my feet.

"*Witch…wife…queen…*"

The power burgeons as it hits my bloodstream, making my head arch back. Distantly, I'm aware that Ferox has moved to my side, but magic is overpowering my other senses. It amasses in my veins, so thick it presses against the underside of my skin, the pressure of it mounting, mounting—

"*Murderer.*"

All at once, my power explodes out of me, rushing at our enemies. My magic latches onto them, slipping down their throats and sinking into their veins. Seizing their lungs and stopping their hearts. I tell myself that their deaths are so sudden, they don't feel it.

But I'm not entirely sure that's the case.

The enemy fighters fall, their legs folding as their bodies hit the earth. A wave of terrified screams goes up from the few, mostly wounded, Alani warriors I missed. They glance around frantically, looking for the source of their comrades' deaths.

Someone must figure it out because an arrow whizzes past me. I pour out another round of magic.

"*End my opponents*," I whisper. The spell cuts like a knife along the throats of the remaining Alani fighters, the incisions brief, efficient, final. Blood spurts, and the few surviving fighters fall or slump over.

It is quiet for a moment, unnervingly quiet. Then the Sarmatians roar, whooping out their victory.

Memnon rides in, blood and sweat dappling his skin. He slows a little as he approaches, but only so he can lean deeply to the side of his horse, arm outstretched for me.

I barely have time to note what he's about to do when he scoops me off the ground and sets me onto his horse.

An instant later, his mouth is on mine, branding me in a fearsome kiss.

You are a wildfire, my fierce queen, he says. *I could not be prouder of the way you protect our people.*

I ignore the shiver that runs through me, the last line of that voice still echoing in my head.

Murderer.

Fire crackles in our tent's brazier, and my naked body drapes itself half on Memnon's, half off.

I stare at those flames, trying not to think about those voices that sometimes whisper to me on the battlefield. The ones that remind me of what I've become.

Memnon strokes a hand down my back. "What do you want most?" he asks in the darkness.

Peace. Love. Family.

Beyond that? I'd like to learn more languages, and I'd like to teach someone besides Memnon how to read the growing list of Sarmatian words I've transcribed.

But even all those desires are secondary, because what I want most, I already have in my arms.

"What do I want most?" I say teasingly, threading my fingers through Memnon's. I smile, then maneuver myself on top of him. "You. Again." I lean down and kiss him, grinding my hips suggestively.

He groans into my mouth, his hand sliding away from mine so he can grip my hips. Memnon manages to tear his lips away. "Besides sex."

I nuzzle him. "Too many things."

"When it comes to you, there is no such thing," he proclaims. He rolls us so my back is on the bed and he's the one leaning over me.

His hand moves between my breasts, sliding down over my belly before finally, *meaningfully*, resting on my lower stomach.

I try to not let my mind wander *there*, to that place his touch implies. Some things are beyond even Memnon's vast power. And mine. So I stopped wishing for them a long time ago.

"I think I want to give you a palace," he declares, gazing down at me with such softness in his expression. His eyes shine bright, so bright.

I tuck a strand of his long, wavy hair behind his ear.

"We already have a palace," I gently remind him.

"One you must sneak off to," he says. "But what about one we would stay in for at least part of the year?"

I rear back as best I can in this position and stare at him, searching his face.

"Steppe life can be hard," he says. "And so much of it is grueling, dirty work, even for a queen."

Living in tents and wagons, no matter how lavishly they're constructed, *can* be uncomfortable, particularly during the bitter winter months.

Memnon leans forward as if to kiss me and whispers against my lips, "I'd like to see you ruling from a palace like a proper empress."

My mouth brushes against his as I whisper back, "I don't need another palace."

"I didn't ask you if you needed one."

His fingers press a little more firmly against my lower belly, and I can't help but glance down. It's been years since my miscarriage. I haven't gotten pregnant since, despite the copious amounts of sex we have.

My gaze rises back to his. "You're serious?"

"I am." His free hand rises to stroke my cheek. "Do you remember when I first admitted my feelings for you?"

Back when I lived in Rome, and he lived here.

I nod.

"You asked me how I felt about you. Do you remember what I said?"

It takes a moment to recall his exact words. "You said

you felt like you could conquer the world, just to lay it at my feet."

He smiles at the memory. "I did," he confirms. After a long pause, he adds, "That wasn't an idle promise."

"I hadn't realized that was a promise at all," I say wryly, tapping his nose with my finger. I assumed it was something ardent teenagers said to one another. All symbolism and pomp.

Memnon *tsks*, then shifts his face so his lips can brush a kiss against that finger. "You should know me better by now."

I trace his facial scar. "So you really want to give me a palace?" I'm not sure that's what I want most, but perhaps it's what he wants most, and I certainly cannot deny him anything.

Memnon gazes at me, his eyes still so very bright. I can feel his own yearning across our bond. "Yes."

"Okay," I say softly, nodding. Sarmatians don't settle down in palaces; it goes against their entire way of life. But if Memnon wants to make this happen, *we will make it happen*.

"Do you have one in mind?" I ask.

"I do," he says.

I raise my eyebrows. "Oh, really? Which one?"

"The one at Panticapaeum."

I stiffen in his arms, my amusement bleeding away. Panticapaeum is a port city, one that controls the imports and exports that move through the Black Sea and the ocean beyond. Panticapaeum also happens to be the capital city of the Bosporan Kingdom, which Rome controls.

"There's already a ruler in that one," I say, frowning.

"I'm aware."

I shake my head, not having gotten my point across.

"There's a ruler there *who answers to Rome.*" Rome, which loves warfare every bit as much as Sarmatians do. Rome, an empire of unparalleled power and reach.

Up until now, Sarmatia has coexisted with the Bosporan Kingdom on the same land. It works because we don't try to usurp them, and they don't try to drive us away.

But if we overthrow their leader now…

"Unless King Cotys answers to the gods themselves, I do not care," Memnon says.

A chill passes through me. "Have you eaten bad bread?" I ask, genuinely concerned. "We don't want to go up against Rome." To take one of the empire's strongholds, a palace that controls a port, and with it, access to this entire region of the world—no, no, Rome will never allow it.

"Do we not?" he asks. "Because I think our people need a good challenge. We have expanded our own lands, vanquished every enemy who has set upon us—"

"Yes, but this is *Rome* we're speaking of."

Memnon clasps my face in his hands. "Let them come, Empress. Let Rome's wrath fall upon our spears and swords. We are untouchable."

Dread flows through my veins, hitching my breath.

He kisses me then, and for good or ill, the matter is settled.

We're acquiring a palace.

CHAPTER 32
Roxilana, 22 years old

58 AD, Panticapaeum, Tauris

The dangling gold beads of my diadem rustle against my hair and my carnelian jewelry hangs heavy on me as Memnon and I ride at the head of his horde, weaving through the streets of Panticapaeum.

Bosporans stand outside their homes and businesses, watching us as we go. Sarmatians are invaders—terrifying, imposing, and largely unwanted—but the people standing in the streets bow and cheer as we pass.

Whatever they imagine we're doing here, they do not consider us an oppressive force at least. It makes me wonder what they think of the client king who currently rules them.

Past the gates, I can see the large, colonnaded structure, the marble palace perched on the edge of a rise. Beyond it stretches the Black Sea, vast and glittering. It's hard not to stare at that mesmerizing water and the ships that dot it.

Bosporan soldiers stand guard before the gates, their expressions growing alarmed as we approach them.

Memnon's magic flows out of him, the indigo tendrils of it coiling around the guardsmen, then slipping *into* them. Their eyes glaze over, and stiffly, they open the gates, standing aside so we can cross onto palace grounds unimpeded.

We head up the stone pathway, only stopping once we reach a colonnaded entrance hall. Again, Memnon's magic sweeps over the guards posted, keeping the soldiers docile and oblivious while our small band of Sarmatians dismounts from our horses.

Ferox comes over to me then, slinking between steeds and people. I lay a grateful hand on his head, his presence settling my racing pulse.

I want to turn back now. I want to cajole and plead with Memnon that this is a doomed idea. My fear is a metallic tang at the back of my throat. Rome will always be the monster looming large in my nightmares. I caught its attention once, long ago; I don't want to catch it again.

But that fear has become a monster of its own, and as Memnon glances at me, dressed in his glimmering armor and golden circlet, confidence in every line of his posture, I'm sure I'm letting that fear get the better of me.

He takes my hand as Tamara, Katiari, and a group of our warriors clusters around us, and together with Ferox, we enter the palace, the rest of our procession remaining behind.

Our footsteps echo in the spacious entrance hall. More Bosporans move toward us, some guards and some aides and servants. Just as swiftly as they approach, Memnon sends them away with his magic.

In front of us, a set of thick cedar doors is propped open.

Beyond them looms the shadowy throne room, the only light inside from burning braziers.

When we cross into it, I'm aware of the great many people who fill the space, but nerves and growing dread allow me to only consider the man sitting at the end of the aisle.

Dressed in a toga, King Cotys wears a simple ribbon in his close-cropped gray hair to signify his status. Supposedly, the man is a descendant of the almost-mythical Marc Antony, which to me only means that Rome is *really* not going to like what we're about to do.

Cotys was leaning over to speak with an aide, but when he notices our group, he straightens in his seat and assesses my husband with shrewd eyes.

"Memnon the Indomitable, Great King of Sarmatians," the Bosporan ruler says, gripping the armrests of his marble throne, "you do me an honor coming here." His gaze moves from Memnon to me and Ferox, then the retinue behind us. "I was not expecting you."

"King Cotys," Memnon says, inclining his head.

"What brings you here?" He asks the question jovially enough, but I hear the threads of unease in his voice.

Memnon lets the silence draw out. Finally, he speaks. "I think you know why."

King Cotys raises his brows. "Have we not paid you enough? Is that what this is about?"

"I am not some thief who must be paid off," Memnon says. "Nor am I some Roman playing at ruling."

Cotys noticeably bristles at that.

"I am a king born from a long line of kings and queens," Memnon continues. "My ancestors have fought and bled and died for this land, and my children and their children will fight and die and rule these lands as well, for *I* am the rightful king. And it is time I claimed my throne once and for all."

To punctuate his thought, the great cedar doors behind us swing inward, closing with a great bang.

In the echoing silence that follows, Cotys's eyes drift from the double doors back to Memnon. The Roman client king stares at him for a long moment, then laughs, his gaze sweeping across the rest of us, his eyes lingering on Ferox.

"Do you mean to usurp me?" He raises his eyebrows. Despite his bold words, I can practically hear the rapid thump of his heart. He must realize, stranded in this windowless room, that even though our group is small, his life is in grave peril.

And if he could see magic, as I can, he would know this for certain.

Memnon's power is already sweeping across the room, enveloping the Bosporan subjects, shielding them from us and us from them. As for Cotys's aides and guards, one brush of Memnon's magic, and their eyes grow glassy and distant.

Calmly, Memnon says, "I prefer the word *ousting*."

Cotys stares at Memnon with angry eyes as his men's legs fold and eyes roll back. Bodies thump to the ground, earning gasps and screams from the crowd of Bosporan onlookers. But then they too collapse. Dozens and dozens of people lie in unconscious heaps.

"Holy gods!" Cotys shouts, rising abruptly from his throne, his gaze sweeping over the room. "What have you done to my people?" His gaze goes to Memnon.

"*My* people," Memnon amends. "They're temporarily indisposed."

Cotys stares, horrified, at them all, and I'm sure he

believes they're dead. I can see the soft rises and falls of their chests, but in his panic, I doubt he can.

"The stories were true," Cotys breathes. His eyes flick back to Memnon. "You use sorcery."

"Sometimes," my husband agrees, stepping forward. He places one booted foot on the marble step leading up to the dais.

"No!" Cotys barks out. He reaches for his sword and, with great effort, unsheathes it.

"Do you want to fight me?" Memnon asks skeptically as he climbs the stairs. "We do not need to, but if it's an honorable death you seek, I shall give it to you."

"Stay back, sorcerer." Cotys swings his sword wildly, his eyes darting around the group of us.

Memnon withdraws his own blade and, with one sweep of his arm, knocks away Cotys's blade, the great sword slipping from his grip and clanging to the ground.

Disbelief clouds the client king's eyes. Taking a throne is supposed to be harder than this. Otherwise, people would do it all the time.

Memnon closes the last of the distance between them and rests his blade against Cotys's neck. "Shall this be peaceful, old king, or bloody?"

"You don't know what you're doing. Rome will come for you."

"Bloody it is." Memnon pulls his sword back.

"Wait!" Cotys cries.

Memnon lowers his weapon as the Roman ruler falls to his knees.

"I don't want to die." Roughly, Cotys reaches up and removes the ribbon from his hair, tossing it to the ground. "Take it. The palace is yours—for as long as you can hold it."

The literal act of removing a king from his throne might've taken a short span of time, but the process of actually transitioning authority from Cotys to Memnon and myself will take days, and I'm sure notifying all of the Bosporan Kingdom and Sarmatians will take months more.

In the wake of our conquest, Memnon, myself, Ferox, Katiari, Tamara, and Memnon's closest warriors now wander the castle together, our footsteps echoing in the quiet, largely abandoned halls. The royals and much of the palace staff have already vacated the premises.

"It's big," Katiari notes as she casts her eyes up at the high ceiling.

"It's *unnatural*," Zosines corrects, spitting off to the side before he realizes there isn't bare earth for it to sink into.

Unnatural?

No, I couldn't disagree more. Already, I can feel my excitement rising. I hadn't realized how much I missed having sturdy walls around me.

"If we settle here, we will grow weak and soft," Rakas says.

"We will *never* settle." Memnon's voice is cutting, vicious. "But it is time we had uncontested control of these lands we defend. Do you disagree?"

The group stays silent.

We pass through a dining hall with long tables and benches for seating, fresh foliage running along the middle of it. It's partially set for the next meal, which will never come—at least, not for its intended guests.

Do you like it? Memnon asks me, sidling closer. Outwardly, he's been careful to craft his answers so they seem to benefit his people, but I can hear many of his stray thoughts, and most of them revolve around me. I remember all over again that this plan came about because he believed with full conviction that I deserved to live in a palace.

I take his hand and give it a squeeze. *I love it.*

And I do. I'm breathless with excitement. The marble halls, the massive columns, the view out to the sea and the boats perched on it—it's all beyond even my imaginings as a queen.

I smother the worry that rises on the wings of that excitement. Worry over future battles that will be fought for this land now that we've grabbed it from Rome.

We head up a flight of stone stairs. "These are the royal residences," Memnon explains.

How do you know the layout of this place? I ask.

My mother and I stayed here as guests when I was younger, when the former king's brother, Mithridates, ruled.

My attention moves to Tamara, who's been quiet this entire day. She peers around, pleased, her proud gaze returning to Memnon again and again. If either of them feels remorse for ousting the former ruler, they don't show it.

"Warriors," Memnon says, "you will each have your choice of rooms. Feel free to move any family in here that you'd like. We will still move about the steppe, but while we are in Panticapaeum, we will live like gods."

A shout goes up from the warriors around Memnon, and soon, the men and women guarding him break away to peer into the various rooms.

"No one is to take the room on the far end of the hall," Tamara declares. "That one's mine." With that, she strides toward the last curtained doorway, Katiari shadowing her.

Memnon turns to me. *Would you like to see our room?*

You already have our room picked out? I ask, arching a brow.

Well, it's the king's private quarters, so I figured it was the best room in the palace.

I follow Memnon down the hall toward a room no one else is lingering nearby. Drapes a thick, rich wine color hang from the doorway, obscuring what lies beyond.

Memnon holds those drapes open, and the two of us enter. The first thing I notice in the spacious room is the bed, more massive than anything I've ever slept on. At the foot of it rests a chest painted with stylized griffons.

Across from the bed is a table laid out with the king's trinkets—a decorative knife, a small stone carving of the god Mars, a partially opened bag of polished knucklebones, and a tabula game board.

"Look out the window," Memnon says, nodding to the gap in the stonework on the far side of the room. I head over to it, already noticing the briny smell blowing in from outside. The scent reminds me of salted fish and that call to adventure these horse riders feel when they look to the horizon on the grasslands.

Laying my hands on the cool stone, I peer out at the sun-glittered water and the royal docks. A red ship currently bobs at the dock closest to us, its white sail rolled up, the great eye painted near its bow, peering up at me.

"This is yours. All this is yours," he says.

I turn back to Memnon, and his eyes shine a little too brightly as he watches me.

"I *will* conquer the world," he vows, echoing his long-ago words to me, "just to lay it all at your feet."

A shiver courses through me at the devoted, ominous pledge.

Memnon crosses over to me, his gaze searching mine. "I

know you're afraid of Rome, but *I* am not. I will not bow to that boy king."

I stop myself from saying that Nero is hardly still a boy.

"Nor will I tolerate their incursions any longer."

Deliberately, Memnon lowers himself to his knees, then presses a kiss to my lower belly. "The only one I bow to is you."

Alcohol and victory are a potent combo for a Sarmatian.

Shouts and songs ring out in the palace dining hall, where Sarmatian warriors and nobility have crammed in with their spouses and children. Wine and kumiss flow freely, along with the feast that the palace staff were already cooking up.

The skull goblets have been brought out and passed around, each of us drinking from this conquered ruler or that, while warriors retell their stories of victory.

"Aye, Memnon, there's still time to make Cotys into a drinking vessel!" Itaxes shouts.

Cheers rise at that.

Memnon smiles, holding his wine by the lip of the cup, but offers nothing else.

A large form sidles up to my side. "Does your new home please you?" Zosines says, a bite in his words.

I remember his earlier disdain. I take a sip of my spiced wine. "Very much. Does your newest wife please you?" I ask.

He studies me for a moment, a small smile on his face. "Very much."

"What are you onto?" I ask. "Number five?"

"You're keeping track of my wives?" Zosines asks, raising his eyebrows. "If I didn't know better, I'd say you were interested."

"In what? Castrating you?" I fire back. "Because I've taken a *keen* interest in that."

Zosines laughs, genuinely amused. "If you did that, all the women would cry."

The man is delusional.

"Yes," I agree, "they would—tears of joy. There might even be a feast in honor of the occasion."

"I know you tease," he says, "but I give my wives pleasure and children. What more could they want?"

I guffaw. "I don't know, Zosines, maybe a life beyond sex and motherhood?"

He tilts his head, considering me. "I forgot," he finally says, "you are still struggling to conceive. Of course you would see this topic differently."

I hate how his words gut me. How I feel suddenly close to tears. I take another long drink of my wine, trying to drown my emotions.

Unaware of my turbulent thoughts, Zosines places a hand on my shoulder and leans in to my ear. "Now, here is a serious question: Are you sure my brother is doing it right? Maybe he needs a little help."

I shrug off his touch and give him a withering look. "Surely you are not offering."

Zosines raises his eyebrows. "And get my balls lopped off?" he says, laughing a little, though his expression appears strained. "No, my queen, lovely as you are, I wouldn't dare."

But his eyes linger on me in a way I cannot read but do not trust.

Do you want to slip away, my queen? Memnon's voice cuts through the conversation.

Gods yes.

Good, because there just happens to be one more room I wanted to show you.

I down my wine, then thrust the now-empty cup into Zosines's hand.

"Do you want more...?" His words fade away as I push through the crowded room, making my way toward Memnon.

When I get to my king, I take his hand, his eyes lighting up when they drink me in.

I didn't realize you were so eager—

I practically drag him toward the exit. Whistles and hollers accompany our departure, the guests clearly assuming we have much more intimate plans than we do. Then again, knowing how other evenings have ended, they are probably not terribly wrong.

On the way out, I catch Zosines's eye. Memnon's blood brother wears a knowing smirk, and when he sees me looking, he lifts his cup as though to toast good luck.

I grimace, tearing my gaze away.

We leave the rowdy sounds of the dining hall for the quieter hallway. Eventually, the noise falls away altogether as we move deep into the castle, until the only sounds that remain are the lapping of the waves and the cry of a seabird beyond the palace.

You're unusually quiet, Memnon says. *Did you not have a good time?*

It was all right. I hold off on revealing what Zosines said to me and why it got under my skin. *I'm just happy to be alone with you.* It's the one thing we rarely get, and right now I savor it like it's a sweet.

Memnon reels me in, wrapping an arm around my neck and pressing a kiss to the crown of my head. *Me too, Empress.*

Memnon weaves us through the labyrinthine halls of the palace until we get to a portiere, its wine-red drapes already drawn back. Beyond them, the room is cast in darkness. It's not until Memnon forms a ball of light and sends it drifting into the room that I see the shelves and shelves of stacked scrolls.

I gasp at the sight. There have only been a few times I've seen this many texts in one place and never at camp. Adjacent to the wall of scrolls is a table with a familiar wax tablet and stylus resting on it.

"My reading room," I say, as I've come to call the tent Memnon sets up for my studies. "You set one up for me here."

His eyes crinkle. "How could I not?" he says. "Once we fully move in, this place will be crawling with Sarmatians, and you will no more have your peace here than you did at camp."

He glances at the room around us, which has been painted a deep red and trimmed in lines of sage-green and golden-yellow. "I've placed a ward on this room to hide it from all eyes but ours, so when you want solitude and a hidden place to study, you will not have to rely on ley lines."

I move over to the scrolls, my fingers hovering in the air close to them. The reverence I feel stops me from actually touching the papyri. This is what Zosines did not seem to understand. There truly are so many things I yearn for, things poets and philosophers, rulers, and scholars have written about. I do not exist solely to procreate, nor does any other woman.

Rotating away from the wall, my eyes land on Memnon. Memnon, who has always valued me for who I am and not what I offer.

I cross back over to him and throw myself into his arms.

"Thank you," I whisper against his neck, pulling back enough to press a kiss to his lips. *Thank you.*

Too good. He's too good; this is all too good.

Memnon's hand comes up to my face, his thumb stroking my skin. "This is *nothing*. Now, are you going to actually open the scrolls, little witch?" he says, a smile on his lips. "I know you want to."

I grin at him, backing up before returning to the wall of scrolls, the writings beckoning me.

However, once I reach them, I find that I really can do no more than touch the rolled texts, my heart pounding loudly.

Memnon comes to my side and, unlike me, he has no such qualms. He takes a roll of papyrus out and unrolls it.

"Read this to me," he says, not bothering to look at the language written on it. Instead, he moves to a nearby cushioned chair in the corner and settles himself into it, the wooden frame groaning a little at his weight.

I glance down at the text, noting that it's written in hieratic, a script version of Egyptian hieroglyphs.

I start from a random point in the text. "'Thy heart is weary. Thy soul is in thy hand. The sky is revealed. Thou fancies that the enemy is behind thee; trembling seizes thee…'" I glance up from the text to see Memnon smiling at me, a soft look in his eyes.

"You really are a natural at this. But I expect nothing less from my mate."

I flush under his praise.

"Please," he says, "continue. I want to hear how well-read my wife has become."

I move over to him then, the scroll still in hand.

"'Thou findest a fair maiden who keeps watch over the gardens.'" I sit down on Memnon's lap, straddling his legs. "'She takes thee to herself for a companion—"

Oh, it's that kind of story...

I knew I chose well, Memnon says, his hand drifting under my kurta and tunic. Then lower still.

"'And surrenders to thee her charms...'"

What charms are these? Memnon says.

I skim the scroll. "It doesn't say. It moves on entirely—"

I suck in a breath when Memnon's hand strokes over my folds.

Shame, he says. Charms *could mean so many things...*

I set aside the scroll and slip off Memnon's lap and onto the stone floor beneath him. *I have a few ideas of what charms she might've shown him...*

My magic slips out of my palms, unfastening Memnon's leather trousers and tugging them down. With the action, his cock springs free, jutting from between his legs.

Memnon's brows rise, surprise lining his features.

It's cute that you didn't expect this, I say as I pull off his boots and stockings, then his pants, leaving him bare from the waist down.

Memnon swallows. *I'm still unclear what charms—*

I wrap my hand around his shaft and take the head of him into my mouth.

Reflexively, Memnon thrusts against me, the wooden chair groaning beneath him as his breath comes out in a harsh pant.

I really should've known the night would end this way. It always does.

I take him deeper, my tongue running over his slit, and

I taste the salty precum gathered there. I moan at the taste of him and the full feel of his cock in my mouth.

I begin to work him then, taking him deep enough to make my eyes tear up and my throat work, my tongue laving the underside of his cock.

Memnon groans, threading his fingers into my hair. "Gods, my good little witch," he praises me, his grip tightening as he begins to thrust into my mouth.

My core clenches uselessly as I'm held tighter to him.

Without warning, Memnon's magic spills out of him, wrapping around me long enough to cleave my clothes from my body.

I release his cock from my mouth and give him a questioning look.

"Still not sure what charms the text was talking about," he says, his power tugging me up from the ground.

I let it, following his magic up until it poises me over Memnon's lap, the head of his damp cock just beneath my entrance.

"Perhaps you could give me another demonstration?" he says, his eyes wide and guileless.

I bite my lip to stifle a laugh. "I was unclear, wasn't I?"

He grins. "A little. I'm sure this will help." His magic lowers me down ever so slowly onto his cock, and bit by agonizing bit, it enters me, stretching the walls of my core as it goes.

I watch him, my lips parting at the wonderful ache, until I am fully seated.

Now it's me who's panting harshly as I feel the delicious pressure and throb of him inside me.

Slowly, I begin to move, rising only to come back down on him.

He groans again. *This is agonizing.*

It's charming, I correct him.

Memnon dips his head, taking a nipple into his mouth and sucking hard on it, like he can drag more sensation from my breast. Sweat beads on his forehead as he forces himself to hold still while I set a slow pace. My movements are gentle, sensual—

"Fuck, I'm sorry, Roxi—I love your charms, gods how I love them. But I cannot take them anymore."

With that, he stands, dragging me up with him. Still seated inside me, he takes my legs and wraps them around his waist as he moves us. My back hits a nearby wall, and Memnon's magic is there, propping me up in place.

His smoky-amber eyes flick to mine. "Hold on."

That's all the warning I get.

He pulls out of me only to brutally thrust back in. Just as swiftly, his cock retreats, only for him to hammer into me again—and again and again. He fucks me senselessly, his balls slapping against my skin as sweat collects between us, his cock driving deeper and deeper. It's all I can do to hold on.

I'm stretched around him and held in place by his body and magic as that sweet friction and those powerful, punishing strokes drive me closer and closer to the edge.

Then, all at once, I tip over it.

My limbs tighten around him and my core clenches as I shatter, my orgasm rippling through me.

Memnon groans, cupping me to him, his teeth lightly running along my shoulder as he feels my climax through our bond.

And then he's coming, emptying himself inside me, his hips snapping forward as he tries to seat himself deeper still.

His orgasm draws out my own, the aftershocks going on and on.

Memnon holds me close, his arms around my legs, his face nuzzling my neck.

He presses a kiss to the skin of my throat. "I've made a decision, my queen."

"Mmm?" I stroke his hair, a happy, little smile playing at the corners of my lips. Awkward as this position is, I think I could stay here forever.

"I think I want you to read to me every night."

CHAPTER 33
Roxilana, 22 years old

58 AD, Panticapaeum, Tauris

Despite seizing control of the palace of Panticapaeum, we don't linger much within its walls. Instead, we ride out past the city proper to the tented settlement at its edges, where most Sarmatians have made camp.

There, we train and eat and preside and sometimes even sleep. It's a strange situation, straddling two very different lifestyles, but as the days roll into weeks and the weeks roll into months, we fall into a routine.

Today, Memnon and I ride next to each other out on the training course, my gold earrings tinkling like bells with each hoofbeat. The first true chill of winter has settled in, and the sharp wind would be cutting through my thick felt layers and numbing my fingers if Memnon hadn't placed a spell on me to stave off the biting cold. Only a few other Sarmatians have braved the elements to be out here, their forms speckling the flat expanse of land.

Flakes of snow drift down as I draw back my bowstring and sight my target, my steed galloping fast. I release the arrow, hearing it thump into the wood an instant after Memnon's. Quickly, I grab another projectile, getting off a second shot that knocks Memnon's askew before I pass the target.

Your skill is almost as good as mine, Memnon teases.

Almost? Check your eyes, oh mighty King, I say. *Today is the day your student has surpassed you.*

Memnon sidles up next to me, his gold circlet tamping down his long, dark hair, which spills over his shoulders. *Power really does look good on you*, he says. His eyes heat as he takes me in, and at the sight, my pulse begins to race. That he can set me aflame with a single look speaks to his own commanding nature.

Power looks good on you too, I whisper down our bond.

Over Memnon's shoulder, far in the distance, something catches my eye. A form appears seemingly out of thin air.

It takes only a few more inhalations for me to realize the figure is a woman. Prickles race down my skin as I sense her identity long before I see her pale hair.

Memnon, Eislyn is here.

Following my gaze, he looks over his shoulder.

Her presence feels like a bad omen, though I cannot say why. Perhaps it's as simple as the fact that I don't like her. Or maybe it's that the several times she's visited us at camp over the last few years, she has always come with Memnon's father.

Never alone.

Memnon must either have the same misgivings or hear mine because he clicks his tongue and urges his horse into a gallop, riding like Pluto himself is at his heels.

I follow, caution climbing up my spine.

Ahead of me, Memnon swings off his horse and approaches Eislyn. The wind howls in my ear, drowning out the words they exchange. But then my husband's legs fold.

Memnon! I swing off my horse and race to him. *What's wrong?*

I fall to my knees at his side, my arm going around him. He straightens his torso, his face the picture of devastation when his eyes meet mine.

My father...is dead.

I pull him in close, and he grips me tightly to him as he begins to tremble. I stroke his hair, murmuring useless platitudes as he falls apart in my arms.

We stay like that for some time, as the first light snow of the season continues to fall around us and Eislyn looks on grimly.

Finally, Memnon pulls away. Drawing in a shuddering breath, he stands, wiping the wetness from his cheeks. "I want to see his body," Memnon demands as I rise.

Eislyn gives her head a swift shake. "You know you cannot," she says, not bothering to look at me.

"Damnit, Eislyn, he's my father." Memnon's voice breaks. "I want to hold his hand, whisper a final prayer over him, and say goodbye."

My throat closes up. The funerary rites he speaks of—they are not so different than what he did long ago for our child.

"There is a bloody feud happening in his palace as we speak," Eislyn says sharply. "His heirs seek to eliminate each other so they alone can control his kingdom. What do you imagine they will do if they meet another of their father's children?"

"I don't care."

"Well, *I* do." Her voice rises as she speaks. "I barely escaped intact, and I do not wish to go back and expose myself to power-hungry men who care only of themselves."

The hairs on the back of my neck stand up.

"You do not wish to go back?" I echo.

Only then does she glance at me, albeit briefly. "It was your father's final wish that I might advise you," she says, returning her attention to Memnon. "It is *my* wish as well." There's a level of intimacy in her voice that raises my hackles.

"*No.*" I press all my queenly authority into the word.

Roxi.

Roxilana, I correct him. *You might as well invoke my full name for this bloody business.*

I see the corner of his mouth twitch at my feistiness.

To Eislyn he says, "My queen and I will discuss this matter privately. Until we come to a decision, you will remain with us as an honored guest and give us counsel."

———

Memnon and I *don't* speak of it privately. Not before Memnon takes poor, chilled Eislyn into the warmth of the palace. As for me, I cannot force myself to follow them back through our settlement, across Panticapaeum proper, and into our palace. Not when my emotions are so volatile.

I loved Ilyapa, despite how brief our encounters were. He was a good if distant father, and he tried to do right by his son. And he was the only true father I ever knew.

More than my own grief, I feel Memnon's. I should go to him. I should. It's simply that I might throttle Eislyn if I do. Because surely where he is, so too is she. I've barely managed to stay civil with her during her few visits.

395

I cannot possibly reside under the same roof.

These thoughts spin around and around my head, and I linger out on the steppe, shooting arrows long after the other warriors retreat to the warmth of their tents and fires.

Little witch, he calls to me now, *are you still outside?*

I am.

Shall I come out and haul you back to the palace? he asks. I think he means to be teasing, but grief flattens his tone.

I bow my head and let out a rough exhale. *I think it's best that I'm alone right now*, I say, even as the snow falls in thicker and more numerous flakes.

Across our bond, I feel his wounded hesitation. *Why are you so against her?* he finally asks.

I grimace. *I have never needed to explain my reasoning to you before. Why must I now?*

Because Eislyn has advised over five generations of rulers in my family, and she cares for us—she cares for me, Memnon says.

Oh, she definitely cares for you, I say bitterly. It takes a moment to realize that, in the heat of my emotions, I spoke in Latin, not Sarmatian.

I pinch my eyes shut and shake my head. We should not be having this conversation right now, when Memnon is still coming to terms with his father's death. It's cruel for me to make it about myself.

Is my queen jealous? Through the heavy weight of Memnon's grief, I sense his smile.

I breathe through my nose. *Yes.* No use denying it.

There's only ever been you for me, he says softly, his voice down our bond pebbling my skin. After a pause, he adds, *Now, will you please come inside?*

I will—eventually. I pull away from our connection before he can protest more.

Pressing my lips together, I shoot arrow after arrow into the wooden target, funneling my frustration and impotent anger into training. Memnon's spell that once warmed me has long since worn away, but I prefer the bite of the cold.

Pulling out another arrow, I nock it, aim, then fire. It hits the target with a satisfying thump.

"Imagining that's Eislyn's head?" Tamara's voice rings out behind me in this quiet, empty place.

I startle, lowering my bow and turning my horse around to face her where she sits astride her own steed.

"How long have you been there?" I ask.

"Long enough." She assesses me, then adds, "You wear jealousy like a cloak, dear Daughter. I thought you had learned by now not to let others see your vulnerabilities."

I narrow my gaze, then turn back and face my target once more. My fingers are numb from the cold, making my movements while nocking another arrow slow and fumbling.

"Did Memnon send you?" I ask. It's a loaded question; no matter what she responds, it will anger me.

"And clean up whatever mess he's made between you two?" Tamara huffs out a laugh. "I think not."

"Well, whatever your reasons, you didn't need to come out here," I say, aiming the arrow.

"I *did*, though," she says.

I lower my bow and glance over at her again. "Don't pretend she isn't a threat." Eislyn is an asp if I ever saw one.

"Oh, she is as threatening as they come," Tamara agrees, somewhat appreciatively. "But Memnon would be a fool not to use her. *You* would be a fool not to use her."

I scoff. "That is like asking me to cook with poison. I cannot *use* her, not when my intuition is screaming at me that she means me harm."

Tamara studies me shrewdly as snow gathers on the pointed felt headdress she wears. "I shouldn't tell you this, not when you know our people take multiple wives."

I tense, bracing myself for whatever she's about to say next, certain I won't like it.

"I've seen the way that woman looks at my son," she says. "I know you have too. But Memnon has eyes for you and you alone, Roxilana. He has loved you since you both were children, and it is the sort of love that leaves no room for interlopers. Your connection was forged by the gods, and no one *save the gods* is strong enough to sever it. Set aside your personal worries—"

I frown at her. "Do you think that's what this is about? Female rivalry?" Of course Eislyn's overtures toward Memnon grate at me, but my distrust of her is more than jealousy.

Which raises the question: "Why does she help Memnon's lineage, anyway?"

"Does there need to be a reason beyond a thirst for power?" Tamara says.

"If it were power alone she wanted and she's as brilliant as you say she is, then wouldn't she be the queen?"

Tamara gives me a soft smile, like I've finally asked the right question. "Why indeed?" She raises her eyebrows. "Now, *my queen*, I know you enjoy target practice, but there is a woman with questionable motives counseling your husband. I suggest it's time you be a part of that conversation like the formidable ruler you are."

CHAPTER 34
Roxilana, 22 years old

58 AD, Panticapaeum, Tauris

"You have done well for yourself, Memnon," *Eislyn says,* gazing around at his war room when I come striding in. The space is painted an appropriate bloody red, and on the nearby shelf are several of Memnon's skull cups—very macabre, very somber, and very much appreciated by the creepy fairy appraising them.

As soon as Memnon sees me, I feel a rush of joy and relief down our bond. Eislyn simply looks annoyed.

He comes over to me and gives me a deep kiss. When he pulls away, he touches my hair. "You still have snow on you."

"Yes, well, it grew cold after you left."

Behind him, a throat clears.

My eyes flick to Eislyn. Already she's traded her Moche robes for a Sarmatian kurta and breeches.

"You are in a predicament," Eislyn announces. The

flickering candlelight makes her features glow, and I'm reminded all over again that she is not of this earth.

She lays her hand on the table that dominates the room. Seared onto its surface is a map of the known world, with Gaul to the west, Germania to the north, Sarmatia to the east of here, and Anatolia, the Levant, and Egypt to the south.

"I imagine Rome will soon learn of your conquest here in Panticapaeum, if they have not already." Her fingers drum against the wood. "They will not allow it to go unchallenged."

I stare at Eislyn, fascinated—and unnerved—by how much she appears to know about Roman ethos when she's lived so far from it all these years.

"I imagine there are already Roman troops speckled throughout your lands?"

Memnon gives a sharp nod, his eyes narrowed as he listens raptly to her.

"Rome will fight you until you are stopped or they are destroyed," Eislyn says with an authority not even I could muster.

"We Sarmatians welcome battle, especially with Rome," Memnon says. His grief now is but a dull, niggling ache, almost entirely eclipsed by the possibility of war.

Eislyn rounds the table. "You were not born to simply stop your enemies in battle," she says, her eyes fixed on Memnon. "You were born to *end empires*."

Memnon stares at her like she's speaking to his soul, and the hairs along my arms rise.

"But you cannot do it alone," she adds.

Memnon leans his fists on the table. "Then how do you propose I do such a thing?" he asks, his gaze roving over the map.

"How many bands of nomadic tribes are there beyond your borders?"

"Countless," Memnon says, his eyes moving over the map like he can see them all.

I draw in a deep breath. Eislyn has not even been here a full day, and already she's strategizing not just battle plans but empire building.

"What if these tribes followed *you*?" she asks.

Memnon shakes his head, his dark hair rustling beneath his crown. "They have their own rulers. They will not want another."

"*Convince* them," Eislyn says, adding offhandedly, "through any means."

She's speaking of Memnon using his power to lift knowledge and alter minds.

"Beyond it being astoundingly immoral," I say, "neither Memnon nor I can say how long these spells he places on people's minds will hold."

Eislyn eyes me challengingly. "Immoral?" she questions. "Is altering a mind any more immoral than gutting an opponent on the battlefield?" She makes a dismissive noise in the back of her throat, like that is that.

"As for the spells themselves," Eislyn says, "If they can hold long enough for your fellow horse lords to taste a victory, then it will work."

"You think one victory against our common enemy will be enough for them to genuinely ally themselves with us?" Memnon appears skeptical, though his eyes seem to caress the map.

"I do," Eislyn says.

I cannot believe we are listening to this. And I cannot believe Memnon is halfway convinced by it.

"This is no small thing, what you suggest," he says, glancing up at her.

She leans forward, her eyes fastened to him. "Imagine being known as the king who united the steppe lands," she breathes. "The king who conquered Rome itself. You could do it." Her voice is honeyed venom. "You possess the power to squash these menaces like gnats."

Through our bond, I feel Eislyn's words squirming into all the crevices of Memnon's mind. Sarmatians are warriors; conquering is in their blood. To amass the greatest force the steppe has ever seen and claim a victory against the greatest power of our time…it would mean eternal glory.

And then, Eislyn goes for the killing blow: "Imagine Queen Roxilana ruling the people who once ruled her."

Memnon's eyes begin to glow, his power sifting out of him.

"Imagine giving that to her," Eislyn continues. "Your father—gods rest his soul—would want all that for you, his beloved, *favorite* child."

The room is quiet for a long moment.

Finally, I break the silence. "Have you eaten bad bread?" I say softly. "What you're proposing is death on a mass scale. We might as well throw our warriors onto pyres right now."

Gods know I hold no love for the Roman army. But the cost for conquering the entire Empire is far too great. There will be so many victims—warriors and widows and orphans. And every conflict, every battle, would put Memnon in harm's way.

But my husband is still staring at her like she's unlocked some hidden room within his mind. It's an unholy look.

"If I were to convince these other nomadic nations," Memnon says, "that would take months of travel."

Eislyn's eyes are bright. "Not if you use ley lines."

Memnon is called away then, but I linger in the war room with Eislyn and the looming specter of our prior conversation.

I stare at the tabletop map, the tallow candles making the lines of it flicker and dance, but I'm not really seeing it.

"I hope you appreciate the lengths Memnon has gone to for you," Eislyn says, breaking the silence.

I glance up slowly, my eyebrows rising. "Is that right?" I force my voice to stay even. "Should I thank you as well, for this dangerous, obscene plan?"

Now that Memnon's gone, the mask the fairy wears finally falls away. Her eyes are clever, but her face is cold.

It's almost a relief to witness her true nature. No more false airs between us.

"You can thank me for the plan, but I am speaking of this palace."

I press my lips together, waiting for her to get to her point. I'm sure she has one. I'm equally sure she means to wound me with it.

When I don't respond, she sighs. "Do you really have no idea what I speak of?"

I drum my fingers on the tabletop. "I'm cold and wet and would really like to change, so if you could—"

"The real reason Memnon acquired this palace wasn't for fame or glory, it was for you."

I already knew this, but Eislyn shouldn't have. That she has been privy to this knowledge is a shock to me. Did Memnon tell her this?

Just how much *has* Memnon confided in this fairy?

Eislyn laughs when she sees my face, misinterpreting

my surprise at her being briefed as instead my ignorance of Memnon's plotting.

"You don't believe Memnon schemes, even when it comes to you?" she says. "He overthrew the last king for you—and for your legacy." Her gaze drops meaningfully to my stomach.

I was following Eislyn's logic until that last part.

"Think about it," she continues. "Constant riding and traveling can be hard on women's bodies."

I stiffen as a prickling sort of awareness creeps up my spine. Legacy. Pregnancy.

"Perhaps this nomadism is why *you* haven't produced a child in all these years."

The air seems to leave my lungs. I reach for the back of a nearby chair, bracing myself on it, not wanting to believe her, even as what she said sinks into me.

I don't think Memnon confided in this fairy after all. This doesn't sound like an explanation he'd voice. And yet, didn't Memnon first speak of palaces after touching my stomach wistfully?

The thought has me flinching.

"I'm sure an heir is important," Eislyn continues. "So important that the lack of one could cause unrest among your people."

"There already *is* an heir," I finally say, my voice hoarse.

"Katiari, you mean?" Eislyn raises her brows. "Because she seems to enjoy a man's touch enough to produce an heir of her own," she says sardonically.

Katiari's sexual preferences are something she keeps private. But I know, as apparently Eislyn does, that my sister does not enjoy a man's touch.

"What a predicament," Eislyn whispers, her voice hypnotic.

I force myself to not glance down at my flat stomach. Sex and spells haven't helped me. *Hoping* hasn't helped me.

"What will happen to your people if you do not produce an heir?" she asks.

I remain silent.

"Your people *will* get nervous," she adds. "All nations want security."

I give her a skeptical look. "Then why thrust them into a hopeless war against Rome?"

"Hopeless?" She scoffs. "Do you really have that little faith in your husband? Because I don't."

I narrow my eyes at her, watching her like she's a serpent waiting to strike. I can practically taste this fairy's desire to come between me and Memnon.

"It is not war that I worry about," she continues. "It is Memnon's lineage."

Of course it's his lineage she cares about. She's been cultivating it for generations.

Magic slips out of my palms, coiling around my wrists as I fail to keep my emotions in check. "My womb is none of your business."

"On the contrary, as queen, your womb is your entire *nation's* business, whether you like it or not." Her expression softens. "I'm trying to give you political advice because you are queen. How you feel about it is entirely up to you."

I burn with the need to ask Eislyn about *her* womb. She seems to have done just fine without words like *legacy* and *heir* being thrown around.

Instead, I lean my hip against the war table. "I assume there's advice for me buried somewhere in the discussion?" I scrutinize her. Finally, I say, "What is it? Do you have some miraculous fae potion that will help me get pregnant?"

I'm not sure whether I'm angry or simply upset, only that my emotions are threatening to spill out my eyes, and Eislyn is the last person I'd allow to see that. So I force it all away.

"You would trust a potion I brewed?" she asks, genuinely surprised.

No, of course I wouldn't.

After a moment, she says, "Unfortunately, my solution isn't so convenient."

I wait for her to continue because I know she has a solution, and with every passing breath, I'm more and more certain I'm going to hate it.

She glances down at the map. "Sarmatian men are known to take many wives."

My insides curdle at the familiar direction of her words.

"For the sake of your people, Memnon needs to provide them with an heir. Either by you…or by another."

There it is. The truth she's gilded in logic and strategy. She wants Memnon to take another wife.

For a moment, I have to fight back the sickness of this entire conversation. Several different responses flit through my head before clarity comes over me.

"My," I say, my voice breathless with emotion, "not here even a day and you're already trying to replace me with another."

Eislyn gives me what I think is supposed to be a compassionate look. She's far too scheming to quite pull it off.

"I'm not trying to replace you," she admonishes softly. "No one could do that. You mean far too much to our king."

Oh, it's *our king* now. How quickly Eislyn shifts alliances.

"We would merely be invoking the time-honored tradition—"

"Ask him," I interrupt, my magic now streaming out of my hands. "Ask Memnon if that's what he wants."

I watch her, physically restraining myself from lunging at her.

Eislyn's expression doesn't precisely change, and yet I see my answer right there on her features.

"*You already have,*" I realize. I can't help it, I laugh. "You devious bitch." The pieces come together. "You asked him, and he turned your proposal down. So now you thought you might appeal to my—what? My sense of queenly duty?"

Eislyn doesn't say anything, just lifts her chin.

I bite back the words I want to say. Instead, I settle deeper against the table, crossing my arms. "So who would you recommend?" I ask conversationally. "Which Sarmatian woman would you think best suited for the task of fucking my soul mate?" The discussion is twisting my belly, and my vision is beginning to go red.

Wisely, Eislyn keeps quiet, but then, I don't need to hear her answer. I already know.

"Or perhaps the woman won't be Sarmatian. Perhaps she won't even be human."

Eislyn's stare gives away nothing.

"*You* could be his second wife—how convenient would that be? To advise him during the day, then sleep with him at night."

Her jaw clenches, but I can guarantee this conversation isn't cutting her up nearly as much as it's shredding me to pieces.

"Or maybe," I continue, "if you were okay with sharing for a little while, you'd line up a human wife or two first. You would then be his third or fourth wife—a shame to have to share his attention with so many others. But it wouldn't matter in the end, would it? I'm guessing that one by one, the other wives would either die or be cast aside until only you remained."

It's quiet for several inhalations, and only the soft hiss of flames eating their wicks interrupts that silence.

Eislyn finally smirks at me. "Amazing what fantastical tales you can come up with in your spare time."

I smirk back at her, though my eyes are deadly. "You have gravely misjudged me, fairy. I am not nearly so benevolent a queen that I would open my marriage out of some sense of duty."

I step in close, my magic twisting around me. "I hear that fairies live an astoundingly long time," I say. "I also hear that, despite their longevity, they can be killed just as swiftly as the rest of us mortals."

My smile falls away. "If you try to come between me and my husband again, I will bury my blade so deeply down your throat, you'll be shitting it out."

I tap the tabletop map a final time. "Good luck with battle plans."

And then I leave the war room.

CHAPTER 35
Roxilana, 22 years old

58 AD, Panticapaeum, Tauris

There's a Roman temple here on the palace grounds, one that is as opulent as it is desolate. I imagine the royal family used to come here—there are certainly enough offering stains on its altars to suggest this. But the temple lies vacant now that Cotys and his ilk are gone, and the temple priests along with them.

Deep within its inner sanctum, there is a section of space that shimmers unnaturally, a tear within the fabric of the world.

It's here, tucked into a shadowy alcove, that I wait for Memnon, Ferox at my side.

I do not wait long.

The familiar thuds of Memnon's footfalls echo in the outer chamber as he strides through the marble temple.

As soon as I hear those footfalls, my heart lurches.

I had hoped the thoughts and battle strategy I'd overheard across our bond were wrong.

As soon as he enters the inner sanctum, I step out from the alcove, the dangling bits of my diadem shivering with the movement.

Memnon's eyes land on me, and he physically starts at the sight.

Imagine being known as the king who united the steppe lands, Eislyn's voice seems to whisper.

"Little witch," he finally says, raising his eyebrows. "What are you doing here?"

The king who conquered Rome itself.

"Intercepting you," I say.

Imagine Queen Roxilana ruling the people who once ruled her.

The fairy's words linger in the space between us.

"Which tribe do you plan on visiting first?" I ask.

Memnon hesitates, and something like shame—maybe guilt—crosses his face.

I give him a look. "I can hear your thoughts," I tell him, "even when you don't mean for me to. I knew you were going to attempt this plan the moment we woke."

He tenses. "Are you going to attempt to convince me otherwise?"

I'm sure he can feel my sadness as I step forward, Ferox moving forward with me.

I shake my head. "I can tell when your mind is made up," I say. There's no bitterness in my voice, though my heart is weary already. This will be a long and treacherous road, but I suppose we were doomed from the moment we deposed Cotys.

"I intend to give you the world," he says, perhaps a touch pleadingly. I can feel his bloodlust and his ambition, his grief and his need to appease it in some way.

"All I've ever wanted was you." I touch the diadem

nestled in my loose hair. "Not this crown. Not this palace. Certainly not the world."

Memnon's jaw hardens. "But you'll get it all the same," he says resolutely.

I stare at him for a long time. "I'm sure I will," I say. "You have accomplished everything you've put your mind to thus far."

I again sense Memnon's urge to plead with me. I can practically feel the ache in his knees to bend them, to press my hands to his forehead and beg for more than just my forgiveness: for me to concede to this plan. Deep in his heart, I know he wants me to believe in this vision every bit as much as he does.

"Why do you trust her?" I ask. I don't need to say who.

Memnon's gaze flickers. "Beyond her loyalty to my family…I have peered into her mind."

I widen my eyes; a surge of something ugly and possessive rises in me. He's touched her? Looked deep into her thoughts? There's a sort of intimacy that comes with the act, one that cuts like a blade.

"She has shown me only her sincere respect for the both of us," he says.

I frown, knowing intuitively that cannot be true, but I trust Memnon implicitly, and if he has peered into her mind…it is hard to argue with what he's seen.

"What if I told you to banish her back to where she came from?"

Memnon's brows rise. "I would banish her."

He must know the words are on my lips because he looks at me beseechingly.

"She's the only connection I now have to him," Memnon admits hoarsely.

Ilyapa, Memnon's powerful, *deceased* father. The man who loved Memnon as much as he could, despite the toll his power took on his conscience. And now he's forever out of Memnon's reach.

What I would give for even an object that my father once touched—or my mother or my siblings. What logic I would evade, so long as it meant holding on to that item. And if that item were instead a person, a flesh-and-blood being who could share memories of my family with me? Who could influence me and coax out my highest ambitions, just as they had my relatives'? There is little I *wouldn't* overlook, just to keep them near.

I breathe in deeply. If Memnon wants to have Eislyn around in order to be closer to his father, I can be accommodating.

"Fine," I say softly. "I will not ask you to banish her—for now."

He gives me a small smile before it falls away. Memnon searches my gaze. "If you are not here to banish Eislyn or to talk me out of my plan, then why, sweet mate, *are* you here?"

I step up to him, laying my hand on his heart. Beneath my palm, it beats swiftly. He's nervous, even if he won't say so.

"Foolish man," I whisper, "I'd walk through the Underworld for you. So if we're to do this, really do it, then we do it together."

Memnon's eyes smolder, a bit of his magic shining through them. His hands grip my upper arms, and he drags me in for a kiss.

His lips are rough, the sweep of them frantic and greedy. I meet each stroke with my own, my hands sliding up his back and tangling in his long hair.

"Too good," he whispers, "you're too good for me."

Even as he says it, he reaches for my breeches, loosening them.

And now he does fall to his knees, taking my pants down along with him.

I suck in a sharp breath at the feel of the winter air against my bare skin. Memnon uses his magic to do away with my boots and the trousers tangled at my ankles.

"What if someone sees?" I ask, as Memnon nudges my legs apart. Ferox swiftly flees the room, his tail twitching in annoyance as he gives us our privacy.

Okay, what if someone *human* sees?

Memnon wraps his arms around my backside, dragging my pussy closer to him.

Then I will wipe their minds of the memory.

Memnon, I chide, my fingers brushing against the panther tattoo that crawls up his neck.

He grins against my skin. *I'm kidding. Mostly.*

With that, he presses a kiss to my pussy.

Such a good wife, he praises. *So good. So obedient*—

"You're about to get a foot in your face."

He laughs against me. *Fine*, he concedes, *rarely obedient. Highly vicious.*

My magic slips out of me then, dragging Memnon's body up and his pants down.

I lean into him, his hard cock trapped between us. "I want more than your mouth," I whisper against his lips.

His eyes burn as he lifts my leg. In one quick thrust, he spears himself inside me.

I cry out at the sudden intrusion, not expecting my demands to be met so quickly. I breathe through the intense stretching of my core, the fullness edging on pain before tipping into pleasure.

Memnon gathers me to him and leans his forehead against mine, rolling his hips. "*Fuck*, little witch," he groans, "you feel like sin."

Memnon stays there, locked inside me while he wraps one of my legs, then the other, around his waist.

Even once he begins to move, his strokes are short and teasing as he lifts and carries me. It's only as I catch sight of the stained altar that I understand what he intends.

"*Memnon*," I say, alarmed as he lays me out against the cold marble. My diadem tumbles from my head, hitting the marble altar before clattering to the ground.

Memnon pulls out of me entirely so he can, using his hands and magic, flip me onto my stomach, leaving my upper body draped across the cold altar while the bottom of my torso hangs off it.

He leans over me. "Yes?" he whispers against my ear, nipping at it.

I breathe in sharply. "We cannot do this—not on the altar."

"Why not?" he asks, grabbing my hips and lifting them.

Even if these Roman gods are not our own... "This is a holy place."

"Yes," Memnon agrees. "And this is a holy act too." He punctuates the thought by thrusting back into me from behind. I moan, scrambling to grip the sides of the altar.

Relentlessly he drives himself into me, his thrusts now hard and deep, his cock hitting that elusive spot within me again and again and again. His magic comes out to play, teasing the sensitive flesh between my folds, and it's too much, far, far too much—

Memnon pauses, then wraps a hand around my neck. Leaning forward, he says softly, "You're not going to come—not yet." He begins moving his hips again, slowly at first, just enough to tease.

"Memnon," I plead around his hand on my throat.

"If you can't be obedient, then I will give this neck a squeeze."

He wants me to be *obedient*? I would laugh if I could.

Instead, I release a little of my own magic, letting it stroke Memnon from the underside of his cock to his heavy balls and beyond.

He groans against me, his grip on my hip and my neck tightening. "Roxi…"

"*Roxilana*," I correct with a gasp. I intensify my power's ministrations on his sensitive skin.

Memnon's thrusts become erratic, and I moan as he hits that spot inside me again.

"Yes, Memnon…" I praise him. Gods, he feels unreal.

"Damn you," he says fondly, even as he gives me all the sensation I want. The stroke of his cock inside me and his magic between my legs builds and builds until—

Memnon buries himself inside me, and across our bond I feel the first spike of his orgasm. It's enough to tip me over the edge too.

"Memnon!" I cry out as my climax lashes through me.

At my back, Memnon groans, his hand reflexively tightening around my neck. The punishing grip heightens the next wave of my release, and I gasp, gripping the altar harder. Our combined orgasms stretch on and on, each one lengthened by the pleasure we share across our bond.

Eventually, Memnon's thrusts slow, and he withdraws himself. Before I can straighten and begin to clean myself up, he lifts the back of my tunic and kurta and presses a kiss to my bare spine, his nose and forehead dragging against my flesh.

"Promise me you will always be this disobedient," he breathes against my skin.

"No," I say tartly.

He laughs, then slides lower down my body, so he can nip my ass. "Good."

After a moment, he sighs and drapes himself against my backside. "Are you ready to meet our future allies?"

"Also no."

But disobedient or not, I'm loyal to a fault. So I go anyway.

———

Of course, Memnon decides to start with the Dacians.

I nearly groan as we step off the ley line only to recognize the sharp peaks of the Carpathian Mountains in the distance. My husband must be hungering for a fight.

The two of us leave the odd, circular sanctuary we came through and head deeper into the settlement around us.

The Dacian city looks nothing like Panticapaeum or our tented settlement. The fortress city is protected on all sides by massive walls made out of tree trunks, and the houses are fashioned almost entirely from conifer trees.

We head down a muddy pathway, past Dacians who give us tense, scrutinizing looks, to the palace proper at the center of the city, where the king undoubtedly is.

I glance at Memnon briefly, just long enough to meet his eyes and notice the orangish edge of the ward I placed on him earlier.

Why begin with this nation? We have been enemies for years.

If I can convince them to join us, then I can convince anyone.

Fair enough.

Memnon makes quick work of the guardsmen, and this is Panticapaeum all over again—the soldiers my soul mate quickly renders useless, the spells used to open and shut what should be impenetrable doors, and the easy walk inside the palace.

The only difference is that this time, Memnon's magic beckons forth a Dacian guard. Using his more insidious power, Memnon places his hands on the guard's head and lets his indigo magic slip into the man's nose and mouth.

Whatever spell he places on the man, it takes hold within mere moments. The guard pulls away and leads us forward, into the mostly empty throne room.

And like Panticapaeum, Dacia's king, Rubobostes, sits in here on his carved seat, a golden circlet inlaid with rubies on his head, eating mutton off the bone and laughing at something a nearby man has said. Grease coats his cheeks, and a bit of gristle hangs in his long, ginger beard. He wipes his hand on the kurta covering his barrel chest.

As soon as Rubobostes sees us behind his guard, his mirth dies away. He tosses his piece of mutton aside, sitting up straighter, his expression morphing into annoyance, then anger as he takes in Memnon's crown, then my own.

"What is this?" His voice booms. "How did either of you get into my city?"

"My king," the guard in front of us announces, "these are the rulers of Sarma—"

"Bloody gods, I know who they are," he says. "But why are these villains in my city walls, in my fucking palace, when you should've gutted them on sight? You should be mounting their heads on pikes at this very moment!"

The guard stutters to a stop, and he shifts his weight uncertainly.

Memnon steps around him, approaching the raised dais, and I follow.

"Fierce Rubobostes," Memnon begins. "We have come to you with a proposition: ally yourselves with our nation, and together we will defeat our mighty and common foe, Rome."

The Dacian king laughs. "*Ally?*" He leans forward, his wooden chair creaking. "Lions do not ally with *swine*."

"And yet we lions do so like pork that we thought we might proposition you anyway," Memnon says.

Rubobostes's pale cheeks turn blotchy and red.

Do you have to goad him? I say, biting back a laugh. *I thought we were trying to win his support.*

I can't seem to help myself.

"Seize them!" Rubobostes thunders.

Immediately, the guards in the room that Memnon hasn't bewitched close in on us, grabbing both me and him by the arms.

This is going really well, I say.

Flattered you think so, Memnon responds.

The Dacian king's eyes narrow on Memnon. "*Years* I have waited to exact my revenge on you for my father's and brother's and nephew's deaths. I will carve out your entrails and ruin your wife in front of your dying carcass."

Those are the wrong words to say.

They always are.

Memnon's power explodes out of him, lifting his hair and blowing back the guards holding us captive. His power coils around the other individuals in the room, pinning them in place. They're lucky he doesn't attempt more.

My soul mate's eyes glow as he stalks up to Rubobostes, who is trying and failing to rise from his throne. Only I can see the indigo magic that pins him in place, bands of it roped around his arms and thighs.

Memnon rounds the back of Rubobostes's throne, and withdrawing his dagger, he presses the edge of the blade to the Dacian's throat. "I already dethroned one king this year. You think it would be hard to remove you, old man?"

Rubobostes stares at me with blatant loathing in his eyes. To come within the fortified walls of his city and enter his palace and threaten him with death while he sits on his throne—there is no greater insult.

"How *dare* you come into my home as a guest and try to strike me down," he growls.

"Are we guests now?" Memnon says.

The king manages to spit. "I will dance over your rotting corpse—"

Memnon drags the blade across Rubobostes's throat, blood arcing through the air and splattering on the carpeted floor. The room's remaining occupants shout and writhe against the bindings of Memnon's magic as the aging king slumps forward, then slides off his throne and onto the ground, his circlet toppling off him as his blood soaks into the woven carpet beneath him.

Memnon comes around the throne, his eyes still glowing as his gaze sweeps over the room. "Anyone else wish to challenge me?" His magic deepens his voice, raising the hairs along my arm.

The room is quiet; even the shouts have fallen to silence.

"Who is next in line to the throne?" Memnon demands.

No one speaks.

"*Answer me*," Memnon commands.

"Dapyx," says the man Rubobostes was laughing with when we entered the throne room. He's somber now.

"Get him," Memnon commands.

His power releases the guards in the room, and once freed, several of them rush out to search for the heir to the Dacian throne.

We wait only a short, tense span of time before a broad, heavyset man who bears a striking resemblance to Rubobostes strides into the great room. Immediately, his eyes drop to the dead king.

"What is the meaning of this?" he bellows, alarmed. His voice has the same booming resonance as the former king's. His gaze rises to Memnon, who still holds a bloody dagger. "What have you done?"

"I've made you king," Memnon says, pointing that dagger, "so long as you don't squander it."

Dapyx's lips curl in, and I'm all but sure he's forcing himself not to spew insults at Memnon, whose eyes are still glowing.

"Swear allegiance to me, and vow your commitment to fight against Rome," Memnon says, stepping forward through the blood spatter.

Dapyx's hand twitches toward his own sheathed blade. "And if I don't?"

"I'm sure there are others who will be happy to if it means leading your people."

Dapyx stares at Memnon for several moments, his hand moving closer and closer to the hilt of his weapon. He eyes the Dacian guards, who seem to be debating what to do themselves.

Memnon's magic snakes through the room again, wrapping itself around the guardsmen. This time, it enters their mouths and noses, and one by one, they collapse.

Dapyx's eyes flick from one fallen guard to the next.

"I have spoken this more than once before, but perhaps it bears repeating: I am Memnon the Indomitable, Sorcerer King of Sarmatians. I have power beyond your imaginings, and I will use it to dispose of my enemies."

The glow in Memnon's eyes dims, and his hair, which had lifted a little, resettles. "I do not want to harm you. I wish to ally our great nations."

Dapyx's eyes are fixed to the fallen king, presumably his father. "You have already harmed me."

Memnon takes him in for several moments, then strides forward through the pool of Rubobostes's blood, adjusting his grip on his blade.

Dapyx staggers back, lifting his hands to placate my husband. "Wait, wait—I will swear your oath," he bites out.

Memnon halts, then eventually inclines his head. Cautiously, the stout warrior approaches him. Dapyx clenches his jaw, then kneels before my husband. "Tell me the words, and I will swear them."

"Swear that you will remain loyal to me and our peoples all the days of your life."

"I swear I will remain loyal to you and our peoples all the days of my life."

"And you will fight against Roman invaders and defend our peoples from any other outside threats that seek to destroy us."

"I will fight against Rome and defend our peoples from all other threats until my last breath."

Memnon reaches out a hand, and I hear Dapyx's sharp inhalation when Rubobostes's bloody circlet rises from the floor seemingly of its own accord, the blood burning away as it floats into Memnon's hand.

My husband sets it on Dapyx's head, the man startling at

the touch. I understand why when Memnon's hands linger there on the Dacian's temples, blue magic seeping out from them. It enters the man's mouth, and I'm certain he must be using his powers to alter the man's mind—likely to ensure Dapyx remains loyal even after we leave.

Memnon releases the Dacian's face. "Welcome, brother, to our confederation."

CHAPTER 36
Roxilana, 23 years old

59 AD, Panticapaeum, Tauris

Dacia is only the beginning.

We spend the next several months visiting various tribes and nations, securing allegiance wherever we go. Sometimes these rival rulers cooperate, and the alliance is forged all on its own. Sometimes it takes Memnon's personal brand of persuasion. Sometimes it even takes my own.

And if Memnon starts to reconsider the scope of these plans, well, Eislyn is there to whisper all the glories of the world into his ears. Eislyn, who is cold and clever except when she and Memnon are together—then she is especially clever. Not that my husband sees it. For him, she is all bright eyes and coy smiles and promises, so many promises. Of riches and land, power and fame—but most of all, *me*. She spins the tale like Memnon's valor is all for me.

I know this game. I have seen it before. I simply don't know how to sabotage it. And so we hurtle forward, amassing a force that spans kingdoms, one ruthlessly led by Memnon.

Rome notices.

Maybe they were informed as soon as King Cotys was deposed from Panticapaeum. Or maybe word got out that one of the nomadic kings was unifying the otherwise-contentious nations of nomads and barbarians. It's never been done before, and the possibility of now dealing with a unified eastern front, one that could truly overpower the empire—well, that's an intolerable threat.

It still doesn't prepare me for the moment Katiari rushes into the dining hall at breakfast in her training leathers, her eyes wild and her cheeks wind slapped.

Her eyes lock on mine. "A Roman army has gathered outside the city."

It's a miserable day for a battle. Sleet falls from the sky, turning the ground into a frothy mixture of water, ice, and mud. Even clad in layers of hide and felt, armored Sarmatians shiver as we leave Panticapaeum for the grasslands to the west.

My breath mists as Memnon and I ride at the front of the horde, drawing the eyes of civilians peering from their windows. Ferox prowls next to my horse, cloaked in layer upon layer of spells—some for warmth, some for protection, and some meant to hide him from Roman eyes.

I spot the Roman cohort soon after we exit the city, the group of them clustered a little ways beyond a colonnaded temple perched on a natural rise.

If we're cold, that is nothing compared to the Roman army. Even as far away as they are, I can see them huddling in their cloaks and boots, unused to the frigid weather of early spring in Tauris.

I glance at Memnon, whose eyes shine in anticipation, his form limned with the protective spells I placed on him.

He turns to me. *Are you ready, my queen?*

I swallow, then nod.

I don't hunger for this victory the way Memnon does, but like every other battle, I refuse to let him ride out here alone, without my protection. Especially now that it's Romans he faces.

His magic leaves him then, tugging my horse as close to his as he can get it. He places his hand on me and murmurs, "*Make her skin impenetrable. Protect her body from all harm.*"

You don't need to add another ward, I tell him. *You've already placed a dozen or so on me.*

His hand lingers on me, his fingers skimming my jaw. *When it comes to you, there can never be enough.*

I lean forward and rest my own hand against him, so that I, too, can murmur another protective spell, one that makes Memnon's eyes go soft.

Let's get this over with, I say, my palm sliding away from him. *I want to relax with you by the fire and watch our warriors celebrate this victory.*

Memon gives me a small smile. *As you will it, my queen, so it shall be done.*

Memnon faces forward again, and all the softness bleeds from his face.

The Roman soldiers appear to be scrambling for their weapons and mounting their horses. I've heard that some nations have battle etiquette, where both sides meet and discuss the terms of slaying one another like proper civilized folk. I don't know enough about Rome to know if, when they are not busy annihilating innocent villages, they do such things, but Sarmatians do not.

We, at least, are honest about the business of killing. We don't pretend we're anything other than ruthless warriors.

So before the Romans can properly arrange themselves into their fighting formation, Memnon removes his bow from his body and holds it up high. Behind us, I hear his men reach for their own bows and spears, readying themselves.

I slip down my bond with Ferox. *Battle is about to start.* I speak directly into his mind. *Remember, stay to the outskirts and keep yourself safe before all else.*

The only indication that Ferox might've heard and understood my words is the agitated way his tail twitches when I return to my own head.

I grab my own bow a moment before Memnon pumps his arm and lets out a piercing howl. With that, we charge.

Terrifying whoops and cries rise from our horde as our horses gallop straight at the amassing Romans. The sound raises the hairs on my arms; I can only imagine what it does to our enemies.

Strands of my hair whip around my face as I draw an arrow from my gorytos, then nock it. I wait until we're within striking distance of our enemies to take aim, and then I loose the arrow. I don't see whether it struck its mark before drawing out another and aiming again.

The Romans are in the distance one moment; we're upon them in the next. Terrified shouts and heaving grunts rise from the thick mass of soldiers as our horses plow through their hastily made formation, scattering it.

From the thick knot of our enemies, a spear thrusts at me. The wards placed on me hold fast, and they alone prevent the spear from piercing my torso. They don't, however, prevent the weapon from nearly unseating me. The force of it knocks me back, and I have to grab at the reins to halt my fall. My bow isn't so lucky; it slips from my grip and clatters to the muddy ground.

Shit. Losing my weapon this early in battle is never good.

I right myself and call on my magic to retrieve my bow as my horse barrels forward. It takes several breaths before the weapon returns to my hand, and when it does, it is broken in several sections, likely trampled by other hooves.

"*Repair*," I incant as my horse slows, now slogging through the line of Roman infantry pushing back with their shields.

The bow creaks a little as the splintered layers of wood reconnect and smooth over. Within a few inhalations, it's as good as new.

Arrows whizz past us, one glancing off my warded horse before embedding itself into the ground.

I need to get to the back of these Roman lines. It's where us Sarmatians are most lethal. Unfortunately, these Romans seem to know that, and they're doing their best to keep us at bay. I'm stranded in the thick of battle, which, for cavalry like me, is the worst place to be.

I nock my bow, urging my steed on while I scan the field for a target. Instead, my eyes catch on a flash of white in the distance.

Beyond the charging mass of riders, Eislyn sits on a white steed, wearing a stola with an equally white cloak shrouding her. She's a vision on this bleak battlefield with her long pale hair and her body free of blood and mud.

She stares at me, her hand slightly raised.

What in all the gods' names is she doing out here—

I don't feel the arrow, nor do I see it until it's sliced through the side of my neck.

The force of the blow throws me forward, and I nearly tumble from my horse all over again.

Shock dulls my pain, and I have to reach for my throat to assess the wound. Between one breath and the next, my fingers are coated in blood. *My* blood, and far too much of it. Warm liquid is *spurting* out of my neck with every beat of my heart. A river of it pouring from me.

Much, much too much.

ROXILANA!

My name is thunder wrenched from the heavens. It echoes inside my head and across the battlefield, surprise and anguish and terrible, awesome power wrapped into the sound.

I think...I think I should be afraid.

Even as the thought crosses my mind, my vision begins to darken.

HEAL YOURSELF, ROXILANA! Memnon bellows down in my head, fear lacing his words.

Magic—of course, I think sluggishly. *I need my magic.*

I reach for my power, but it's as slippery as my blood, and fading just as swiftly as my vision...

ROXILANA! I'm coming! Hold fast and take what you need of my power!

I can feel the thick mass of Memnon's magic pressing against my sternum, bits of it seeping into my bloodstream. I reach for it, even as my vision continues to darken and I list sideways on my horse.

Another arrow lodges into my back, then another. And another.

I grunt, then topple off my steed, landing hard on icy mud and the cooling remains of a dead Roman.

Didn't I have wards in place protecting me? I think absently. A shiver wracks my body, tugging at all my injuries.

Cold. So cold. And the pain…the pain should be worse, I think. But I cannot see much, and though I hear the screams and the clash of blades, they come from far away, muffled as though through water.

I think I feel the brush of fur, the nudge of a nose.

Ferox?

I try to reach for him, but my limbs aren't working right.

Roxi, stay with me. Memnon's voice is no longer thunder. It's painfully, terrifyingly human. *Please, my love, heal yourself. I'm almost there…*

But his voice is fading. The pain is fading. Everything is fading.

I know what this is; I can feel it already taking root in my bones.

Death.

It comes so swiftly I don't have time to panic or plead.

Love you, Memnon…forever and always…

A warm and inviting darkness closes in and snatches me away.

CHAPTER 37
Memnon, 27 years old

59 AD, Panticapaeum, Tauris

Love you, Memnon...forever and always...

Roxi's voice is a whisper down our bond, like the last smoke that curls up from an extinguished flame. It's only then, only as the final notes of her voice fade away, that the whole godsdamned world grinds to a stop between one breath and the next.

I'm feeling my mate's...death.

My chest spasms as a sharp, cutting pain slices through it. I collapse over my horse, the pain tightening my throat. I cannot breathe, cannot think—

"ROXILANA!" I bellow, her name ripping from my lips.

My power explodes out of me, wiping out everyone two wagon spans away—both friend and foe.

I straighten on my steed as I wrestle with my magic, trying to get it under control so I can actually do something beyond killing everyone all at once. It's bitter agony, forcing my power back into me. So much of it leaks out, and I can feel it gnawing on my conscience like a termite on wood.

ROXILANA! I think I'm still shouting. My eyes burn and blur and I cannot tell if it's from the rain or tears. My steed moves as though he can hear my thoughts, charging through the thick of the fighting and trampling bodies in our wake.

I throw out my power, frantic to locate her. The blue ribbon of it snakes between cavalrymen and foot soldiers, forming a path that I drive after, heedless of the arrows and swords I'm galloping into.

Abruptly, the line of my magic turns downward, and—

No, no, that blood-soaked body cannot be hers. But then I see that long, cinnamon hair and Ferox's dark form draped over her body, his nose nudging her, as though trying to rouse her.

"ROXI!"

Maybe I swing off my horse, maybe I fall. Then I'm racing to her side. My knees hit cold, wet mud and cooling blood.

Roxi's blood.

A sob rips from me. Her neck has been partially severed by an arrow.

When I try to push Ferox off her, he turns to me and snarls.

"I'm trying to save her life, damn it!" I roar, my magic shoving the panther fully off. Arrows and swords are still flying by us.

Leaning over her, I press my hand to her throat and force my magic inside her, ignoring the way my chest feels as though it's collapsing inward. Roxi's body arches at the violent thrust of my power, but it doesn't heal.

I shout out my frustration.

"You will not leave me," I tell her. "I forbid it."

The girl who entered my mind and woke my magic. Who saved my life and owns my entire godsdamned soul. She cannot leave me alone in this world.

Determination washes over me. I forbid it.

I scoop Roxi up, clenching my jaw at the cold, limp feel of her in my hands. She's riddled with arrows, but already my magic is there, wrapping around the projectiles and yanking them out.

Acidic, soul-destroying fear rides me, but I fight it back just as I do all my other opponents. This is not the end. Not of her, nor us.

I dash to my horse and, with the aid of my power, hoist us onto the beast. Ferox is there, pace for pace, the panther's ears flattened and his tail twitching.

"We are going to save her," I tell him. Already a plan is forming.

"Yah!" I shout at my horse, nudging the beast into action.

Cannot be dead, cannot be dead. Even as I think it, I feel that ache in my chest deepening, as though something is eroding away, bit by bit. Something essential. My magic spills out of me, and I can feel my hair lifting.

I cannot lose control yet. I need all the power and focus I can manage for this.

I drive my horse toward the Roman temple perched on a nearby outcropping.

If anyone is capable of saving Roxi, it's the gods—Sarmatian, Roman, I'll take any of them so long as they hear my broken prayers.

Several of my men have left the fighting to follow me. I glance down at Roxilana again, and a dark, desperate thought takes root.

I pull the reins on my steed, drawing him up short. The warriors around me slow.

"Gather all the injured enemies you can and bring them to the temple," I command, and then I am off again like a shot, heading for that colonnaded entrance.

My horse is still galloping when I swing off him, Roxi cradled in my arms, Ferox like a shadow at my heels.

Barging into the temple, I rush to the back of the space, where the altar is. There's incense burning on it and fire blazing in nearby braziers, but the priests who lit them must've fled with the fighting.

Sweeping the incense aside, I lay Roxilana out, choking back a sob at her limp form. Her rich, cinnamon hair is partially matted to her face and neck, and her skin is paler than usual.

Every second that passes, she moves farther into the afterlife. At some point, her soul will wander too far, and she won't return.

I must be quick.

My warriors follow me in, but for now I ignore them.

Grabbing my dagger, I raise my hand, my power gathering in my veins, my hair lifting off my shoulders. With a swift slice of my blade, I cut my palm open, letting my blood spill forth, onto Roxi and the altar.

"Papaios—Pluto, I give you my blood in exchange for the life of my wife!"

Nothing. Not even a stirring in the air. Just my wife's ever-cooling body.

But of course the gods would not act on that plea. Blood for a soul? That is hardly an exchange worth making.

Katiari and Zosines come in then, each of them dragging a severely wounded Roman.

Once I see their captives, I exhale.

I do know an exchange the gods might not overlook.

My sister nearly drops her prisoner when her gaze lands on my queen, horror spreading across her expression. "Roxi," she chokes out. She swallows. "Is she…?"

"No," I say, viciously, my gaze pinned on Roxi's blood-spattered face.

Going to save you, my love.

"Gods," I call out again, "give me my wife back, and I shall send you many souls."

Katiari gasps. "Memnon," she says, alarmed, moving closer. "Whatever you're thinking of, don't. You seek to meddle in fate itself."

"I'm bringing her back." Even I hear the lawless, desperate edge in my voice. The pain in my chest is worsening; it's becoming hard to breathe around.

"It's blasphemy," my sister says softly.

"Fuck blasphemy. The gods will listen to me."

Katiari shudders at my words.

I begin incanting a secret spell, one my father once spoke of in whispers before I had magic to wield. The words are in Mochica, but I understand them all the same.

"*A life for a life, a soul for a soul, take what I offer and return what I've lost. I call Uvagukis Roxilana, Queen of Sarmatians, back to the land of the living, and I deliver another to take her place.*"

Grabbing Katiari's captive, I pull him to me long enough to slice his neck. His blood sprays across my riders' boots, and he sags in my arms. "A life for a life."

I cast his body aside and turn to the altar, looking for any sign that my beloved lives.

But Death still has her in his clutches.

Zosines's wounded prisoner is beginning to panic, jerking against my blood brother and crying out in his feeble attempt to flee.

I cross over to my rider and roughly haul the Roman away from Zosines.

"*A soul for a soul,*" I call out as I drag my blade across this soldier's throat as well.

Blood decorates the temple walls and floor, and still, my queen's body remains lifeless.

Another. I beckon with my fingers to the other Sarmatians entering the temple with their prisoners. Though many of them might find my actions abhorrent, they hand over their captives all the same.

Again and again, I whisper the incantation; again and again, I cut soldiers' throats. And again and again, blood sprays, and they fall.

Five men have been sacrificed. Now seven. Now nine. The bodies are piling up in the tight, dim space, yet my warriors continue to bring more and more prisoners.

Nothing changes on the altar, but within me, my power builds. I feel it building. Can sense the crackle of lightning running through it.

I'm bringing you back, Roxilana.

Once close to a dozen men lay scattered on the ground before me, I sense something enter the room. Not a god, exactly, but a presence nonetheless. Something familiar and beloved. My magic swarms it, and I try to draw it to me like a fish on a hook. But this essence fights the pull of my

435

power, and for the first time in my life, I have found my magic too weak to complete the task.

Come back to me, my love, I beg.

My power fills up the temple, pressing on the walls and my warriors, thickening until it feels as though reality itself has been carved out by my power alone.

"Gods, release my wife to me!"

Still nothing. If the gods are watching, they want more. So does that essence that lingers in the room.

There is a lake of blood beneath me. I draw it all into me, letting the blood boil away and more power amass. More than I have ever used. Other things have long since boiled away, precious things that I might miss if Roxi and I survive this moment.

But considering my wife might not survive, I do not give a fuck.

"Hellllooo, berrrreavvved kinnggg," the Hungering Ones whisper.

Not bereaved, not yet.

My skin throbs from the intensity of my gathered power, and my eyes seem to pulse from it.

Not enough.

I force the indigo cloud of my magic back into my flesh, gritting my teeth against the burn of shoving it into a body already overly full.

"Gods!" I call out. "Take my power! It's all for her."

Nothing.

I bite back a sob.

In a final, desperate move, I grab a section of my hair— my pride and power—and saw through it, debasing myself for these entities. Visions of the last time I did this overlay this macabre moment.

"You've ruined your hair," Roxi says.

"It was frightening you."

I'm going to hear that soft voice again, I vow to myself.

I drop my shorn hair like an offering, then hack away at my beard. "Release her, I beg of you!"

The warriors that remain in the temple back away. Rakas, Thiabo, Zosines—even my sister retreats from me. These are Sarmatians who've fought at my side for years, who've killed dozens of people for reasons far less noble than this, and yet it's now, when I'm trying to save their queen, that they decide I've done something unconscionable.

The gods themselves seem distant, maybe even… affronted.

Only Ferox remains unwavering at my side.

But there's that beloved presence, so close I can almost touch it.

Who needs the gods when I am nearly one myself?

With an anguished growl, I gather all my boiling magic and move my hands to my mate's chest, the sheer quantity of it incinerating me from the inside out.

"Roxilana, I call you back," I say, my voice hoarse. "My queen, my soul mate, my truest friend, I cannot do this without you." I ready my magic. "Please, come back to me."

I shove all of my vast power down my arms and through my palms, propelling it into her body. It's like lightning in a touch. Enough to fell forests and annihilate armies. Enough to bring my mate back from the dead.

Roxilana's back arches like it did on the battlefield, but this time—this time I hear a ragged inhalation.

Alive.

She's alive once more.

I make a noise that's part sob, part exalted roar. As rapidly as I can, I force more power into her body, willing it to not just restart her heart but to heal her. The sinew of her neck stitches itself back together, faster than I've ever seen it, and I sense the rest of her arrow wounds mending themselves.

My mind itself feels aflame. Things are burning in there—things I fear I will never get back.

My father warned me of this. The cost of our magic.

I find I don't care, that I would pay this tithe a thousand times over for my wife's beating heart.

As soon as her injuries heal and her chest continues to rise and fall in a steady rhythm, my legs give out, and I only just manage to catch myself on the edge of the altar. I can feel my shoulders shaking, my body heaving.

I press a weary kiss to Roxi's forehead. "My Roxi, my eternal soul mate."

I did it. Robbed fucking Death himself.

CHAPTER 38
Roxilana, 23 years old

59 AD, Panticapaeum, Tauris

Roxi, my Roxi…

I am underwater. Deep, deep underwater.

Come back to me, my love, my queen…please… I need you… wake…

I draw in a deep breath, and my body feels all wrong. Too leaden. Even my eyelids feel heavy, and it takes an alarming amount of effort to open them.

There is torchlight, shadow and flame, illuminating the marble walls of a temple. And leaning over me like a dark omen is Memnon, my Memnon.

His hair is roughly shorn, and his beard is as patchy as the day I met him.

Am I in a memory?

He stares at me, and it looks as though he's the one seeing a ghost.

"Memnon?" I whisper his name, confused.

I was…somewhere else. Not here. But now I am.

My husband's lips part, and then he smiles, so fiercely. A moment later, he gathers me to his chest and holds me fast, his face buried in the crook where my neck meets my shoulder.

Wasn't there pain there a moment ago? It doesn't hurt now. Strange…

Memnon's body shakes against mine, and absently, I thread my fingers through the shortened strands of his hair.

"My love," I say softly, "are you all right?"

My words are the wrong ones. I feel anguish and joy, such fearsome joy, and the question seems to break something in him. Memnon sobs against me, though I cannot tell whether he is laughing or crying. Only that he shakes his head against my neck and clutches me tighter.

My brows draw together even as I continue to stroke his hair, my mind trying to sort itself out. A chill has not quite been cast from my bones, and the raw smell of iron and meat clings to my nose. Then there's this silence that cloaks us like a garment.

"Memnon?" I say again, unsure.

Slowly, he pulls away from me, and his face looks haunted, so haunted. A tear slips out of one of his eyes, then the other. I reach out, my movements a little clumsy as I wipe away the moisture.

Then Memnon's kissing me, kissing me like he might lose me if he stops. He kisses me breathless, and though I saw no blood on him, I taste the coppery tang of it on his lips.

A shiver wracks my body, and I glance down at my torso. My kurta is pristine, save for a few tattered holes where stray arrows must've embedded themselves before they were removed.

I…do not remember any of that.

But there had been blood on me, right? Enough to bathe in.

I touch my kurta, my skin pricking. This feels wrong—*I* feel wrong. It's a bitterness on my tongue, a churning in my belly. A sense of knowing that something terrible has happened.

And then there is Memnon, who is also changed in some indelible way, though I cannot quite say how. Maybe it's a touch of coldness in his eyes or the hardness of his jawline. I reach out and trail my fingers over his face, and the look is gone, replaced by the familiar softness he holds in his expression just for me.

Before I can examine that face further, a dark shadow leaps onto the cold slab I rest on and a wet nose bumps the side of my face, followed by the rub of a furry cheek against my own.

"Ferox," I say softly, wrapping my arms around the panther. He makes noises deep in his throat, not quite purrs but happy noises all the same. "You're not usually so affectionate," I say. "What have I done to…?"

My words get caught in my throat as I catch sight of the floor of the temple.

Heaps of bodies cover the temple floor, all of them cut open at the neck. But the blood that should pool around them is gone; only singe marks remain.

"What happened here?" I ask, leaning a little against Ferox. I am used to the sight of the dead strewn across the battlefield, but to see them piled up within a sacrosanct place? The desecration raises the hairs along my arms.

My gaze returns to Memnon, Memnon who is not bloody but tastes of blood. Again, there is something in his eyes that is new and foreign.

"I nearly lost you," he says softly. Down our bond, I feel half-remembered anguish.

I was shot.

I touch the side of my neck as I remember, a gasp caught in my throat. But there is no wound, nor scab, nor scar. Simply unblemished skin.

"Did you heal me?" I ask, still touching my throat. It's a ridiculous question. He obviously did. But…I was so far gone.

Too far gone.

"Something like that," Memnon says, stroking my cheek like he cannot help himself.

My eyes return to the bodies scattered around the temple, awareness creeping up my spine. I can feel the pieces of what happened here coming together like a puzzle. The temple, the bloodless bodies, the arrow holes in my clothing, the altar I rest on…

"It's time to go, my queen."

I'm still painfully confused. "The battle?" I ask, even as Memnon helps me off the altar, Ferox following me down.

My boot squishes on a limp arm, and my stomach rolls in a way it hasn't in a long, long time.

"Don't concern yourself with it."

My limbs shake severely as I try to pick my way through the bodies. A few steps in and my vision darkens once more. My hand slips from Memnon's and my legs fold.

I fall only for a moment. Then Memnon is there, catching me, cradling me in his arms. I lay my head tiredly against his chest.

"I don't know why I'm so weak," I murmur.

"You came back to me from a long way off," Memnon says, his grip tightening as he speaks. "I'm sure your body needs time to recover."

"Did I...die?" I ask.

For an instant, I feel a cold chill gripping me from the inside out. Then it's gone, banished by the warmth of Memnon's body against mine.

My husband's face grows grim, and when he casts his gaze down at me, I see so much veiled sorrow. "Sleep, Empress."

Magic threads his words, and the world fades away.

CHAPTER 39
Roxilana, 23 years old

59 AD, Panticapaeum, Tauris

The victory celebration is nearly intolerable.

I sit at the dining hall's head table clad in all my queenly refinery, trying to not let my shoulders curl in on themselves. What is usually an enjoyable experience is now too loud, too boisterous, too hot and nauseating.

"My queen, you must eat," Memnon urges softly from where he sits next to me.

He hasn't left my side all day—he's barely stopped touching me in some manner. Nor, for that matter, has Ferox, who leans protectively against my leg.

I shake my head and stare on, not really seeing the faces that crowd the rows of tables. I'm still cold and haunted by whatever transpired in that temple hours ago. The only things that sharpen my focus are the few strange looks I get from our warriors. They stare at me like I'm a specter.

It makes me wonder if I am. My skin still feels too heavy,

and there's a wrongness to the world. Or maybe the wrongness is within me.

Eislyn enters the room, and all of my apathy bleeds away. I straighten, my gaze homed in on her.

What is it? Memnon asks.

She was there, I say. *At the battle.*

I feel Memnon's disbelief down our bond. *You think you saw her?*

I know I did, I say.

Next to me, Memnon's rage awakens like a flame brought to life.

One of the riders comes up to Memnon then, gently laying a hand on his shoulder. The warrior's movements are hesitant and as skittish as a colt's. The rest of Memnon's warriors have spent the whole day giving him space when normally they would be teasing him about his shortened hair or his smooth jawline.

But just as I am not myself at the moment, neither is Memnon.

The warrior at Memnon's shoulder whispers something to him, and reluctantly, my husband stands, his chair groaning as he does so.

As soon as he's out of his seat, he leans down and gives me a lingering kiss.

I will be right back, he says. I cannot tell who he's reassuring, me or himself.

With that, he leaves the dining hall, and I'm left to hollowly stare at the revelries around me.

My dagger is belted at my side, and without really thinking, I withdraw the blade, the sharpened edge of it oddly mesmerizing. So easy to part flesh. So difficult to heal it up without magic. And even then...

A flash of pale-blond hair catches my eye. Across the room, Eislyn speaks with Zosines.

I play with my dagger, staring at her as she talks. My mind is conjuring lurid fantasies of burying this dagger into the woman's neck right here amongst the celebrations.

I could do it. I'm tempted to right this instant…

As though she feels me staring, Eislyn glances over at me. I don't bother smiling, nor do I look away. I just continue to play with my dagger and consider whether it would be as satisfying to whisper a simple death spell and end it all right now.

I swear I see her shudder.

I cannot prove Eislyn tried to harm me, just as I cannot prove she was near the battlefield this morning, but I do know that the protective wards placed on me failed when they should not have, and Eislyn was the last familiar face I saw before I was struck. But I don't feel the need to prove her guilt, either. No, I think my conscience could handle stabbing her without that knowledge.

My eyes catch on another figure sitting in the far corner of the room, one who looks just as haunted as I feel.

Sliding my dagger back in its sheath, I rise, leaving the table behind and weaving between revelers, ignoring the looks I receive as I make my way across the dining hall.

Katiari sits quietly in the darkness, staring at the fire raging in the hearth near her, her goblet of wine all but forgotten.

"Princess," I say.

She startles at my voice, then forces a smile for me. "'Princess'?" She raises her eyebrows. "Since when have you ever called me that?"

"Since I woke up today and everything felt wrong."

She huffs out a breath. "So I take it you're not having a good time?"

"About as good a time as you are," I say, sitting down next to her.

Katiari gives a soft, humorless laugh, then takes a drink from her cup. For several long moments, the two of us are quiet.

"I was there today, at the temple," she finally says.

I hadn't realized she had been present. Despite the heat in the room, I shiver, remembering that unholy place.

"You saw him...save me?"

Katiari runs her thumb over the rim of her cup, her leg beginning to bounce. "Saved...saved..." It's like she's testing the word out on her tongue. She gives her head a shake. "No, he didn't save you, Roxilana." Her eyes rise to meet mine. "He resurrected you."

I hold her gaze, one of my hands creeping to my neck, right where my wound was.

"That's impossible," I breathe.

"It should've been," Katiari agrees. She reaches out and squeezes my free hand. "I'm so thankful you are not lost to us."

I study her carefully, the wrongness I feel flickering at the back of her gaze.

"But...?" I finally say.

My sister exhales, then licks her dry lips. "You didn't see how my brother was before you woke," she breathes, her gaze drifting to the nearby fire's flames. "Like a man possessed." She adds, "He killed so many without thought."

I remember the bodies. "That is how he fights." I don't know why I'm defending him when I myself was shaken by the sight of so much death.

"You don't understand," Katiari says. "Had he run out of Romans to sacrifice, he would've turned on his own men in an instant. All of us there could see it. Sense it."

Apprehension rolls through me. As if to punctuate her point, a burst of raw fury ignites from Memnon's side of our connection. Perhaps it's my imagination, but I swear that rage is sharper and more violent right now than it ever has been.

Before I can reach out to him, Memnon deliberately pulls away from our bond, leaving me cold and alone.

Katiari continues, "Already people have been whispering that Memnon has lost his way since coming to this palace." She speaks low so that only I can hear her. "For the first time today, I considered that maybe they're right. Maybe my brother has lost his way."

I stare at her for a long moment, aghast.

"He *saved* me," I reiterate. "Me, your sister, your *queen*. You dare to tell me that my husband, your king, was wrong to do so?" I may feel wretched and unnatural, but Memnon gave who knows how much of himself to retrieve me from death. I have never known such devotion. "*That* was why he killed," I say. "It is always why he kills—to save and protect our people. Everything he does is for us."

"For *you*," Katiari amends, her eyes lingering on me for a moment before they return to the fire. "He did an unholy thing, killing those men in that temple, dragging you back from the dead long after your heart stopped. I fear he has lost the favor of the gods who once loved him." She drags her gaze back to mine. "I think you *both* have lost it."

CHAPTER 40
Roxilana, 23 years old

59 AD, Panticapaeum, Tauris

My death, however brief it was, fundamentally changed Memnon. Almost overnight, he has become cold. Callous. Even cruel—at least in regard to the rest of the world.

Over the weeks, then months, that pass, he consumes himself with war, spending his days training and his nights in his war room, braced over his map, his eyes searching, always searching—for allies, for enemies. All the while, our warriors watch Memnon uneasily, like he might take their lives should it be convenient for him.

And when there is a battle to be had—usually with Roman forces—Memnon has taken to facing them alone. He refuses to let his fighters join him, and he won't even entertain the possibility of me riding out at his side. The few times I've tried, times like right now, I've headed out to the stables only to find myself back in our bedroom, perplexed at how I got here.

I stare down at my hands from where I sit on the bed, anger and hurt rising within me. Memnon promised me long ago that he'd never use his magic on me like this. I never imagined he'd break that vow.

As though my thoughts beckoned him, I hear my warlord husband's footsteps down the hall. Moments later, his massive form fills the curtained doorway to our room.

There isn't a speck of blood on his body, though I know he has killed. Nor does he wear the hollowed-out look that he used to in the aftermath of these…massacres.

"Empress," he breathes, the tense lines of his body relaxing when he sees me, "how my heart has—"

"What have you done to me?" I say softly.

"What have I done to you?" There's a challenging look in his eyes—one that would almost be considered playful if Memnon could remember how to be so. "Many things, dear wife. Shall I speak of them, or shall I show you all over again—"

I prowl forward, burning that he can be so cavalier about this. "Use your power on me again, *dear Husband*, and you won't like the results."

Excitement flares in his eyes, my dark promise falling flat. "I hope you intend to follow through on that," he says.

I know my eyes must flash with my anger. "Is that a threat?"

He moves toward me and leans in so close, I can feel his breath against me. "*Maybe.*"

I glare at him.

At the sight, his lips curve into a sinful smile and his eyes alight. "Look at you, so menacing. My cock is harder than stone, just taking in all that hate."

"Keep going, my king, and you won't have a cock to speak of."

Now he laughs—he outright laughs. "You love my cock far too much to ever remove it from my body." He steps in even closer, his voice lowering. "Curse me, fight me, it doesn't matter, Empress," he breathes. "I won't risk your safety. I cannot"—his voice catches—"cannot endure losing you again."

At his words, a portion of my ire dissipates. Still, what he's been doing is unacceptable.

I lift my chin. "Vow to me you won't meddle with my thoughts again," I say, "and maybe I won't try to outmaneuver you."

I see his jaw work, and I sense him weighing his options.

"Fine," he finally says. "I will vow to not meddle with your thoughts, even for your own good." He hesitates. "But there is something I should share with you. Something I should've shared with you long before now."

My brow furrows even as Memnon reaches out a hand, a thin stream of magic pouring from his palm. The deep blue line of his power snakes over to one of the smaller chests in the room, wrapping around the piece of furniture and causing it to rattle.

"After the last battle you fought in, when we were celebrating our victory that evening, I was called away for a portion of the revelry. Do you remember?"

I nod slowly, searching his features. That was about the time Eislyn had entered the room.

"My warriors had come to tell me that they retrieved a letter that had been tucked into the Roman commander's uniforms."

As he speaks, the lid of the nearby chest swings open, and from it a small, blood splattered scroll drifts out, floating along the air until it looms right in front of me.

I reach out and grasp it, frowning a little. A red wax seal still clings to the edge of the letter, and pressed into it is the familiar profile of a man, one whose face I've seen many times on the surfaces of coins, but also once in person.

Nero.

I glance up at my husband. "The emperor sent you this?"

Memnon's face is grim when he inclines his head.

My attention returns to the document. If this letter was on the Roman commander's person at the time of the battle, then it likely made the long trek from Rome with the army. Which means it was written months ago.

What could Nero have possibly said all that time ago that was important enough for a Roman officer to deliver all this way?

And why is Memnon sharing it with me now?

"Read it," he insists.

I take a shallow breath and unroll the papyrus.

Uvagukis Memnon, barbarian king of Sarmatians, how deep your grief must run. My condolences on the loss of your wife in today's battle.

My grip tightens on the scroll, and my heartbeat quickens.

She was a lovely thing, and it pained me to order her death. I remember how fond you were of her when we met in Rome, and I've heard of your continued ardor in the years following your marriage. I will drink to her demise and enjoy it only a little. You see, I cannot allow you to challenge Rome without consequence.

It is not too late to stop this foolish endeavor. Relinquish the Bosporan throne and retreat back into the wretched hinterlands from whence you came and we will have ourselves a truce. Should you ignore this peace offering, then fret not for the loss of your wife, barbarian, I will make sure you are hastily reunited. Then I'll drink to your death too.

Imperator Nero Claudius Caesar Augustus
Germanicus

After I finish reading, I continue to stare at the document, though I'm not really seeing it.

"How did Nero know?" I breathe, finally lifting my gaze. He sounded so certain of my death in this battle, but that would be impossible to predict months beforehand.

Wouldn't it?

Memnon's eyes are stormy and his jaw is clenched. "I don't yet know," he admits. "When I peered into the commander's head, the Roman officer had no idea of the letter's contents, though he had separately been encouraged to attack you if you were sighted."

I swallow, my hand moving to my neck. For a moment, I swear I feel a phantom throb beneath my fingers.

"I have turned these thoughts over and over in my head," Memnon says. "The wards you wore in battle that day stopped working far too soon. That, along with this letter makes me certain that Nero has both knowledge of our powers, and some strategy to counteract them."

I grow cold as I think over the situation. "This is why you've been consumed with war."

Memnon's eyes flicker as he stares at me. "It is why I have kept you away from battle," he clarifies softly.

453

My throat constricts at that.

"But if Nero has any strategy at all to fight our magic," I say, "then why are you riding into battle alone to face his legions?" By the sound of it, Memnon's battle strategy has not only been risky, it's been...suicidal. My panic rises at the thought.

Memnon's eyes soften. "I swear to all the gods, Roxi, I have not been careless. If there were a worthy opponent to challenge my magic, I would've heard of them long before now," he says. "No, Nero may at best have a witch or two in his army, but none with the power to stop my attacks or remove my wards faster than I can replace them."

I still don't like it, though I cannot argue that since my brief death, Memnon has not once returned from battle wounded. What happened to me on the battlefield seems to have been a singular event.

I hand the letter to him. "Why did you never speak of this to me?" I try not to sound hurt by the secrecy.

He takes the scroll from me then lets his magic carry it back to the chest. "It made me unspeakably angry." Memnon pauses as the lid of the chest thumps closed, sealing the letter inside.

"I read it before battle," he admits. I raise my eyebrows. This is how he fuels his prolific magic—with his fury.

His expression gentles. "Enough talk of war, come here. I need you."

I don't even have a chance to respond before Memnon sweeps me into his arms and his mouth descends on mine.

I kiss him, biting his lower lip harder than necessary. He grins against me as he carries me to the bed.

Do that again, little witch, he says down our bond. *I like your anger.*

I don't bother telling him that I'm no longer angry—the letter doused my fury like water to flame. *My anger is not for your enjoyment.*

Memnon grins at me shamelessly as he lays me out on our bed. *But, Empress, forgive me, I do enjoy it.* He follows me onto the mattress. Rather than undo the fibula at my shoulders, he tugs one gathered strap down my arm, then the other, revealing my breasts in the dimly lit room.

At the sight of them, he groans. Memnon leans forward as though he can't help himself and presses kisses to one, then the other. My breasts are unusually sensitive, and even these soft touches hurt a little.

One of Memnon's large hands goes to my midsection, and though his magic must be exhausted, spindly blue wisps of it spread out beneath his palm, parting the linen.

The fabric falls away, revealing my bare skin. His palm skims up my flesh, between my breasts and over my neck, coming to rest at the back of my head.

Memnon gazes down at me for several moments, taking in every corner of my face.

"I have hurt you," he finally says. "I have not wanted to admit it, but I know over the last months I have. I can see it in your eyes even now. Tell me what pains you."

I swallow, not ready for this question, despite the weeks I've had to consider my feelings where Memnon is concerned. This is a broader issue than Roman death threats or him misusing his magic or me, and there is no single answer I can give him as to why I've been hurting; it's more a tangled web of reasons that have all knotted together.

So I settle on the most obvious one. "You gave up too much," I say softly.

I don't say what, precisely, he gave up, but we both know

what I speak of—Memnon's compassion. It was at the heart of everything he did for his people. And he sacrificed most of it to save me.

Memnon shakes his head. "I did not, not when it comes to you." He takes my hand and laces his fingers between my own. "I would've given up *more* if that's what it took to get you back. I would follow you to the ends of the earth—into the very afterlife if I had to. Do you understand?" His eyes search mine. "This palace, my power, my people—it all comes second to *us*."

With my free hand, I stroke his cheek as he gazes down at me. It hurts all the more that he did this for me. He lost so much because I died, if only for a short time.

"That look is still in your eyes," he notes.

"It will probably continue to be there for a long time," I admit.

Memnon frowns, and I can feel his dissatisfaction with that. "What would it take for it to go away?"

Lying naked here before Memnon, who still wears his crown and all his armored regalia, it doesn't feel like the right moment to voice this. But he's waiting and seemingly willing to hear what I have to say, so I answer, softly, "I want you to stop attacking Rome."

My stomach twists at the admission. It feels like I'm abandoning my slain family and throwing Nero's mocking letter in Memnon's face by saying this, but the truth is that I'm tired of the violence. There might never be an end to the endless fighting, but I want an end to this needless escalation, escalation that Eislyn continuously encourages.

Memnon's expression grows a touch remorseful. "It is too late to stop," he says. "Even if we did, Rome would not back down. They will not stop until we are dead or they are defeated."

I know this about Rome. This is how their empire works. But Memnon is bigger than Rome and their machinations.

I pause stroking his face, laying my palm flat against his cheek. "You are not just a sorcerer," I say to him. "You are Memnon the Indomitable, King of the Sarmatians, Unifier of the Steppe Nations. You can alter minds and dismantle entire armies. You can do *anything* you wish. So wish for something better than death and destruction."

Memnon stares at me a long moment, and his throat works. His emotions are a mix of reticence and maybe even disappointment, but those are far overshadowed by his devotion.

He nods slowly. "Maybe," he finally whispers.

Surprise rushes through me. He's considering it? Truly?

I smile, my joy spreading through me. I shouldn't hope, not when hope can be a fickle god. But I cannot seem to help myself.

Memnon's eyes drop to my lips, and his expression morphs into something calculated and hungry.

"Enough strategizing. I have missed you, my queen. Now open your thighs, so I can apologize properly for that look in your eyes."

The two of us stare at one another as I spread my legs.

"Wider," Memnon commands.

Memnon moves away from me long enough to gaze at my core. Already, I can feel him hard and thick, his cock trapped beneath his pants.

His magic undresses him as he moves down my body, his kurta, tunic, trousers, and boots peeling off his body as

457

he lowers himself, his gaze moving to the juncture between my thighs.

Once he's just as naked as I am, Memnon leans in and his mouth finds my folds. I gasp at the first bright burst of pleasure his lips coax out, my hands threading through his hair.

"You are going to come on my mouth," he says against me, "then twice again when I'm inside you."

One would think that after an entire day of ruling people, he'd be sick of giving orders.

"You're awfully bossy for a penitent man."

I feel his wicked grin against my skin. "Giving you multiple orgasms *is* my apology."

I have to stop myself from laughing. This *apology* is merely a ruse for whatever intimacies Memnon had already fixed his mind on.

"So long, of course, as my obedient wife cooperates."

My fingers tighten in his hair. He knows exactly what phrases will rile me up. "And if I don't?" I say.

He nips that small, sensitive knot of skin above my opening, and a choked cry falls from my lips. "Then I will bring you to the edge of release." He presses a kiss to my tender flesh. "Only to deny you of it *until* you obey me."

"*Memnon*," I warn him.

His only reaction is to laugh against my skin, the sound raising the hairs along my arms. "I like that tone you get. I hope you challenge me. I would enjoy holding your pleasure hostage."

Before I can respond, he resumes kissing and licking my pussy, and wave after wave of sensation rapidly builds in me. I'm going to come fast.

His mouth returns to that particularly sensitive fold, and I gasp, my hips bucking against him.

I can feel his mirth across our bond. *That's it, grind yourself against my face. I don't need air when I can simply breathe you in.*

I'm sweaty, panting, and Memnon's words only serve to draw me tauter than a bowstring.

His tongue delves into my opening, and he groans, presumably at the taste of me, his grip tightening on my thighs. But it's his reaction that drives me wild, and my hips buck against him, searching out more of it.

It feels as though he's everywhere, his lips grazing all that sensitive flesh, his tongue inside me, his fingers or his magic stroking the rest of my skin.

That's all it takes.

Arching my back, I come with a cry, my legs tightening around Memnon's head.

He groans again, either from the echo of my orgasm across our bond or my physical response to it. His tongue laps up my climax, drawing out every last wave of pleasure until I am boneless in his arms.

Only then does Memnon lift himself from my pussy, the lamplight casting his face into stark relief. The shadows outline the jagged scar on the side of his face and the almost-feral gleam in his eyes.

I'm still bared for him, and between my fluids and his tongue, there's enough gathered wetness for him to merely grip one of my hips and sink himself into me in a single fluid stroke.

It's my turn to moan as his cock stretches me.

He begins to move, his strokes gathering power and intensity, his hips surging forward almost punishingly fast. Memnon's magic slithers out of him again, brushing against my breasts and delving into my hair. I can feel it shifting my long locks. My own power comes out then, lured by Memnon's, our magic mingling into one.

He withdraws, pulling away just long enough for his magic to flip me onto my stomach. Before I can fully process this new position, he pulls back my hips and, with a single brutal thrust, spears into me again, causing me to gasp.

From this new angle, he unleashes himself, pumping his hips harder, faster, his cock continuing to stretch me. Even in intimacy, there's a new edge. Memnon is more powerful, more magical, and more merciless, and it's as though he's driving himself punishingly hard, all in search of that edge of sweetness that laced our previous touches.

He wraps my hair in his fist, pulling my head back.

"Beg me for your next orgasm," he breathes against my ear.

I turn to him, my eyes catching on his scar. *"No."*

His smile is downright malevolent. "I was hoping you'd fight me."

Memnon releases my hair, my locks falling in a curtain around my face and shoulders. He retreats to where we're joined; only now, his magic pours out of him. It snakes over my skin, curling around my breasts and between my thighs. The touches against my nipples are featherlight, as though his magic is aware of how sensitive they are. But the strokes at the sensitive nub of skin are merciless and, combined with Memnon's deep thrusts, sensation rapidly climbs within me.

My hands dig into the blankets beneath us, and I twist them in my grip. My orgasm is right there, no more than a few breaths away.

All at once, however, Memnon stills inside me, and his magic falls away from my body.

"Memnon," I practically weep.

His hand splays against my lower belly as he drapes himself over my back.

His lips brush against the shell of my ear. "Beg me."

I bow my head, panting heavily, but I don't speak. After a few moments, he begins to move again, and his magic resumes its maddening caresses.

Again, I climb. And again, when I'm on the precipice of my climax, sensation recedes like the tide.

I growl in frustration. "Damnit, Memnon."

He laughs, his hand sliding lower down my abdomen, one long finger pressing against that sensitive fold of skin. *"Beg."*

I hiss in a breath against that one touch, then grind my teeth together. Stubbornly, I refuse to say anything.

I feel, rather than see, Memnon's grin, and I know my damnable husband is enjoying tormenting me. I take little comfort from the fact that this must be tormenting him as well.

Once more, he resumes driving himself into me, faster and faster. "Shall we do this all night?" he says. "I can get creative."

The possibility of being relentlessly teased for hours sounds excruciating. Already, I'm ready to weep at the throb between my legs and the delicious ache deep within my core. I'm an inferno burning up from within. Hotter and hotter and—

Memnon slows his movements.

I cry out with frustration. "Please, Memnon!" I finally force the words out.

His cock is still only teasing me, his strokes shallow. It's not enough, not nearly. "Please what?" he says.

I swallow down the last of my pride. "Please get me to orgasm."

There's a long pause, followed by the press of Memnon's

lips against my sweaty back. He trails his mouth down my spine. "Say it again," he commands, "but this time, call me your soul mate."

"Soul mate?" I laugh mockingly. "Right now, you're my tormentor."

He rises up my body and nips my ear. "I can make this so much worse," he promises.

I don't know what it says about me that I am tempted to challenge him again, just to see how much worse it really can be. But sensation is fading away just as rapidly as he brought it on, and I'm greedy for that orgasm he's teased me with.

"Please, soul mate, give me an orgasm."

He grins against my cheek and kisses me there. "See? My good, obedient wife. That wasn't nearly so hard, was it?"

Memnon knows exactly the words to make me mutiny against him, but he also knows me well enough to anticipate my reaction because, just as I begin to turn on him, that fucking magic is back, touching me in every sensitive area I have, and I'm distracted enough by it to pause.

He strokes a hand down my spine, then begins vigorously pounding into me, our sweaty bodies slapping together with each stroke. He grabs me by the back of my neck, and something about that possessive touch causes a shiver to course through my body.

Harder he pumps, the intensity of it folding my arms. I give myself over to his control—the hold on my neck, the force of his cock against my inner walls, the caress of his magic everywhere else.

My orgasm comes as a cataclysmic wave.

"Memnon!" I cry out as it rushes through me, drowning me. That's all there is, the force of it pushing every other thought out of the way.

Memnon groans, his grip tightening against the back of my neck, his other hand holding my hips hostage as he keeps his pace. "Gods, Roxi. Your pussy grips me so perfectly, and your orgasm…this torment is indescribable."

"Good," I say, my voice husky. "You deserve it."

He laughs, though it sounds pained. His thrusts, however, have merely slowed, not stopped. My husband hasn't had his own climax, and I know he really means to give me another.

As the final ripples of this one fade away, I drop my head a little, my body boneless from the two orgasms.

Memnon pulls out of me, but only so his magic can flip me back over. The sound that comes out of my throat is something between a sob and a laugh. It took two orgasms, but he's gotten me plenty pliant.

He's aware of it too, laughing a little as his hips resettle between my legs, his cock pressing against my opening.

This time, when he sinks into me, it's slow and gentle. Even once he begins to move, his thrusts are more languid and sensual. Now that Memnon's wrung two orgasms from me, some of his frantic energy has left him. The entire tone of the evening has changed from a battle to something far more affectionate.

My husband gives me a soft smile, one that reaches his eyes, and for a moment, I would never know that he'd given up most of his conscience.

"My fierce little witch," he says fondly. "I could spend the rest of my life doing nothing but gazing upon your face. It would sustain me for all my days."

I wrap my arms around his waist, pulling him closer still. He's always been the poet. I'm the one who has trouble putting words to the unnamable emotions I feel for him. I hope he senses this.

"I love you, Memnon," I say, one of my arms coming up so I can run my fingers through his hair. "You are the best thing that's ever happened to me."

"Even now?" he asks. His thrusts have slowed and his expression is raw, full of longing and a rare flicker of self-consciousness.

I realize then that the price Memnon paid to save me weighs on him, perhaps more than it does me. And right now, he feels inadequate.

I trail my fingers over his scar, then his lips. "Even now." My gaze rises from his mouth back to his eyes. "I will always love you and in all ways. The gods made you for me and me for you."

I see him swallow, his expression growing serious.

"I love you," he breathes. "With every piece of me, I do. I know my magic has corrupted my heart, but I vow to all the gods, it remains true to you and you alone."

I give him an adoring look, and with that, he leans down and kisses me, parting my lips with his own.

His power is back on me, and I laugh against him, my fingers digging into his skin.

You don't need to give me another orgasm, I say down our bond.

That sounds like what someone who wants to get edged would say, he replies.

I break off the kiss. "*Memnon*," I caution.

He laughs, incandescent with joy, as his pace increases. He gazes at me worshipfully, only looking away to kiss my shoulder or my neck or breasts. Even that is done with a sort of reverence that makes my heart ache in the sweetest of ways.

After two orgasms, I don't think simple affection will be

enough to send me spiraling a third time, but to my surprise, I can feel that familiar, throbbing sensation coiling within me, tighter and tighter with each of his thrusts. It's helped along by Memnon's magic, but mostly it's this euphoric connection I'm sharing with him.

"Gods, you are beautiful," he says. "Give me your last orgasm, my queen."

His words are accompanied by deeper thrusts and more power caressing my skin, and all at once, I come *undone*.

I cry out, gripping Memnon tighter as that third damnable orgasm rips through me.

He laughs, then groans. And then he's coming too, his cock thickening with his release, his thrusts growing erratic with it. I feel an echo of his orgasm rock though me, extending my own.

It seems to last forever, but when it finally abates, Memnon pulls out and gathers me to him, throwing a leg over my own.

He presses a kiss to my temple, and for the first time in a while, everything in the world feels right. I fall asleep like that, locked in his arms, hopeful that from this point on, things might actually get better.

But hope…it really is a fickle fucking god.

CHAPTER 41
Roxilana, 23 years old

59 AD, Panticapaeum, Tauris

I've been sick.

Sick for many, many days.

Too sick to ride, sometimes too sick to even preside over our people. So sick that not even Memnon's magic can curb my symptoms for long.

I've resorted to lingering in my study, either corresponding with our allies, studying Aramaic and demotic, or writing notes in Sarmatian to pass to Memnon later. Over the years, I've gotten good at transliterating the language.

I'm working on one such note right now, Ferox at my feet, when the nausea I've been fighting all morning rises rapidly.

It's not even a conscious choice to leave my seat. One moment I'm sitting, the next I'm striding out the portiere and then the rear doors of the palace, Ferox trailing behind me.

I barely make it out to the rocky knoll behind it when I kneel and retch. Again and again, the little food I managed to eat earlier splatters amongst the grass.

I'm breathing raggedly when Ferox comes up to me, brushing his cheek against my arm.

"It's all right," I say hoarsely. "I'm okay."

My stomach spasms out of deep-rooted hunger, and I draw in an uneven breath. Now that I feel marginally better, I'm ravenous, but I don't trust my stomach enough to eat any food.

I hang my head, ignoring the dock workers in the distance and the closer palace guards whose eyes linger on me beneath the summer sun.

Little witch, are you sick again?

Before I can answer, Memnon continues, *Where are you? Let me ease your pain.*

I lift my hand, my magic slipping out of my palm and dissolving all signs of my sickness.

Stay. I'm fine, I promise.

Right now, Memnon is in the throne room, doing kingly business that I should be participating in. The last thing I want is to take him away from that too, especially when a sense of unrest is sweeping through our people—nomadic and sedentary alike.

I push myself to my haunches, my hand dropping absently to my sensitive stomach. I haven't really given much thought to the cause until now, when it's stretched on far longer than sicknesses normally do.

My fingers drum along the skin of my belly, and suddenly, a thought comes to me, a thought so preposterous, it stops me entirely.

There was one other time when I was sick for this long.

But then I was...was—

No, that would be impossible. It's been years, after all.

I glance down, my fingers absently tracing designs, wisps of my magic curling out from beneath my touch.

I cannot fully shake the terrifying, wonderful thought.

Could I be...pregnant?

"Hide my form," I whisper. The enchantment goes up quickly. Once it's in place, I cup one of my breasts, grimacing when the light touch causes a throb of pain. How had I not noticed this?

And my monthly bleeds...when was the last one?

I cannot remember.

My heart is pounding loudly, so loudly. But just as swiftly, joy overtakes surprise.

I never thought this would happen again.

But, gods, I think I *am* pregnant.

———

Should I tell him? I think as I sit in the raucous dining hall. *I might be wrong...*

Tell me what? Memnon asks down our bond, one of his arms draped over my chairback, his attention seemingly focused on the Alanic queen across from us, whom we're hosting for the next several days.

Stop listening in on my thoughts, I say. *Besides, who says I was even referring to you?*

Now Memnon does look away from his dinner guest. Grabbing my lower jaw, he presses a fierce kiss to my lips.

He grins against my mouth. *You're a godsdamned liar and we both know it. There is no one else. Just me. And that secret is* mine.

I narrow my eyes on him even as I begin to smile. *I think I'll wait to share the thought after all.*

I can feel his mirth down our bond, and as he pulls away from me, his eyes are on my lips. *I cannot wait to hear you divulge it when my face is buried between your legs later.*

My cheeks heat, and I can feel the stares we're drawing as Memnon continues to hold my face in his hand like I am the only one in the dining room, but of course, it isn't just us. Besides the Alanic queen and her retinue, Zosines, Sattion, Rakas, and Borena, the female warrior who lies as often as she swings her sword, are here. And then, of course, there's Eislyn, who watches me and Memnon with far too much interest, though as usual, her face reveals nothing.

"When are we going to return to the steppe lands?" Rakas asks, interrupting the moment. "Our people grow restless. We were meant to travel and fight. We are doing neither."

The room falls uncomfortably silent, people shifting in their seats. It's one thing to utter such a sentiment, but voicing these thoughts in front of guests directly undermines Memnon.

Memnon drops his hand from my chin, turning to face the Sarmatian. Rakas and many of the other warriors tense, anticipating Memnon's retaliation.

My husband leans forward in his seat, his scale-mail armor shivering with the movement. Raka's eyes are wide; he darts a quick look at Zosines.

"So eager to die, Rakas?" Memnon says.

Rakas swallows delicately.

Memnon must see it too, his gaze flicking over the man. "I thought not. But you want battle? Travel?" Memnon says. "You *will* get both."

My husband's eyes sweep over the dining hall, over our

visitors, over Eislyn, Zosines, and the rest of the warriors who make up his inner circle.

Settling deeper into his seat, Memnon says to the room, "The god-kings of old were the most feared men of all this land." Murmurs of assent. "Rome has forgotten this truth—the *world* has forgotten it. But we haven't. We horse riders were borne from the blood of gods and forged in their fires."

The room collectively seems to sit straighter, the reminder of their ancestors calling to some ancient nobility in them. The Alanic queen watches Memnon, captivated.

"We were bred for bloodshed," Memnon says. "That of our enemies and that of our own. And we have let men who do not know the icy song of our winds nor the ancient names of our rivers command these lands—the lands of our forebearers. The lands of our children. *Our* land. So we took it from them. And now they come to take it back."

Memnon shakes his head. "You would never give your house to your enemy. And so, we will not relinquish these lands to Rome—nor will we let them hold on to the ones to the west of us. Nor the south, and certainly not to the north and east."

It doesn't seem to matter that Memnon's hair and beard have been shorn, nor that there is a cruel and unsettling fervor in his eyes. There is something mesmerizing about his intensity, something that makes these warriors linger on his words. Maybe it's that Memnon is echoing their deepest beliefs, the ones they've never voiced. Maybe it's the promise of bloodshed and glory he seems to be building up to. Or maybe he's simply a great orator.

Whatever it is, the room laps up his words like a cat with cream.

"You want fighting? You want movement?" Memnon

says again, his gaze returning to Rakas. "Soon, all our gathered forces will come together, and we won't simply *banish* the Romans—we will ride *on* Rome, wiping out each and every one of their godsforsaken strongholds, and we won't stop until all of the empire is ours!"

The room roars, and down the table, Eislyn smiles.

The dining hall is full of excited, almost violent chatter as dinner is served. Memnon's words have worked their way into the bloodstreams of the men and women here, and the room fills with palpable energy. Even I'm buzzing with anticipation, despite the fact that my stomach is in knots.

I thought perhaps he'd reconsider conquering Rome after I confessed my desire for peace. Foolish of me to hope.

Little witch? Memnon says uncertainly, peering over at me.

I shake my head. What am I to say that I haven't already?

From the kitchen, servants carry out roast mutton, stuffed cabbage rolls, and loaves of bread.

As soon as I smell the mutton and cabbage, my stomach turns over. The normally savory aromas are now pungent, fetid. Even the bread smells too yeasty. If I try any of it, I know with absolute certainty it won't stay down, especially when my nerves have already twisted up my stomach. The thought of retching in front of all these guests is horrifying.

I stand abruptly and stride for the door. I should've missed this dinner as Katiari and Tamara have.

Across our bond, I sense Memnon's alarm.

Is it the sickness again? he asks.

Yes. I almost tell him the full, suspected truth then and there.

But the smell of mutton is getting worse with each passing moment, and I need to leave *now*.

Memnon's magic snakes over to me and enters my nostrils. Immediately, the nausea abates, though the scents in the room are no less sickening. Still, my shoulders relax.

Go rest, Memnon says. *I'll wrap this up and bring you some honeyed milk and bread.*

Despite my hurt feelings, I can't seem to stop the small smile. Damn that man and his thoughtfulness.

I glance over my shoulder at him, sharing a lingering look with the Sarmatian king.

One that's interrupted when Zosines calls out, "Where are you going?"

My gaze flicks to Memnon's blood brother.

"Since when are my wife's movements your business?" Though Memnon's tone is mild, his earlier hostility edges the words.

Again, the room quiets.

Zosines drops his eyes and dips his head. "My apologies, my king," he says.

"*Queen*," Memnon corrects him, and the room seems to go quieter still. "The slight was against her. She's whom the apology is owed to."

"I'm sorry, my queen," Zosines says, his gaze reluctantly returning to mine. A muscle in his jaw tics. "Good night—sleep well." As he speaks, some emotion flashes in his dark eyes, one that prickles the back of my neck.

But I'm sure it's nothing.

"Good night," I say to the room. And then I leave.

CHAPTER 42
Roxilana, 23 years old

59 AD, Panticapaeum, Tauris

Roxi...

My eyes snap open, and I stare at the dark ceiling of the palace bedroom, Memnon's voice ringing in my ears. A deep, inexplicable sense of dread has lodged itself in my marrow. Was it a bad dream that I dragged with me from sleep? Something else?

I take several shallow breaths, trying to get my bearings, and then I reach for Memnon. The other side of the bed, where my soul mate should be, is empty.

Memnon? I call down our bond.

All that comes back to me is silence.

He woke me, I'm sure of it, so where is he?

"Memnon?" I call out softly, thinking maybe he's somewhere in this dark room. But the space feels empty, and no one answers me.

Did he stay up late to strategize future battles with his

warriors and other high-ranking officials? It wouldn't be the first time.

But if he were awake, he would answer me. He doesn't. I try again.

Memnon?

No response.

My heart begins to gallop, and the unsettled feeling I woke with amplifies.

Perhaps my husband fell asleep somewhere else. He doesn't usually do that, but it's entirely plausible. He's been overworking and undersleeping, his mind consumed with war.

At the foot of the bed, Ferox lifts his dark head, his form merely a deeper shadow among the rest. My anxiety must be loud if it roused him from sleep. I want to tell my panther to be at ease, but I cannot—not when I'm still trying to figure out what has set me on edge.

Out the palace window, I listen to the call of a starling as I steady my breath. Even the birdcall pricks at my skin. Damn this relentless unease.

Throwing my sheet off, I move to the window and rest my hands on the stone sill, drawing in a deep breath of the briny air. I gaze down at the royal harbor and the moonlit shores of the Black Sea.

Another starling call joins the first. If I had woken up less agitated or had I not woken up at all, I would've easily missed it.

Starlings come in the winter, not now, in the summer, and they come in swarms of millions, not in lonely pairs.

The groans and creaks of wood have me glancing down at what I can see of the vessels moored at our docks.

I frown as my unease ratchets up.

Were those ships there earlier today? It's too dark to be sure.

I strain my eyes in the darkness, making out a few figures on those docks. The longer I stare, the more figures amass, all of them silent as the grave.

Something's wrong.

Deeply, deeply wrong.

Memnon? Why won't you answer? I plead, more to myself than to him.

Does he know something is afoot? Could something have happened to him?

No. I refuse to believe that. I sense him on the other side of my bond, even if his end is subdued. He lives still.

Moving away from the window, I pad to the chest at the foot of my bed. I open it, and by feel alone, I grab a tunic and trousers. I don't dare illuminate the room as I dress in case my worst fears have come to pass.

We have enemies. We have always had enemies. Never more so than now. Memnon has made sure to be one step ahead of them, but I don't believe he anticipated a possible siege like this.

As I finish pulling on my boots, there's a soft rapping near the portiere, the curtained doorway to my room.

"Roxilana!" a masculine voice whispers urgently. It takes me a moment to recognize that it belongs to Zosines. Another insistent rap. "Roxilana! Wake up!"

I'm crossing the room to draw back the curtains when Ferox growls softly. I go still.

Very slowly, I glance at my panther, feeling that disquiet in my stomach. I can see little beyond Ferox's general form, but as I stare at him, I can just make out that his eyes are fixed on the portiere.

I follow his gaze. The wards that cling to the curtained doorway like cobwebs now shine faintly in the darkness, as though they've been activated. Zosines must be trying to get in—and he cannot. That threshold is warded against malevolent intent.

Chills skitter down my spine.

I glance back down at Ferox, my body steeped in unease.

"Roxilana!" Zosines calls out again. His voice is louder, more panicked and insistent.

My panther lets out another low growl, then drops soundlessly to the floor, prowling forward like he's homing in on a kill, his belly low to the ground. I slip down our bond and into Ferox's head, curious about what is alarming him.

I'm not even fully seated in his mind when I scent blood. So much blood. The acrid tang of it is ripe enough to taste.

"Roxilana!" Zosines pleads. "We're about to be under attack! We need to get you out now!"

I touch the closed curtains between us lightly, imagining the tall warrior in my mind's eye. Zosines and Memnon have been fierce friends since they were children; the two are bound by a blood oath and many, many battles. My mate trusts him with his life.

But intuition and observation are telling me something else altogether.

"*Asphyxiate*," I whisper.

I don't see my magic wind around Zosines's throat, but I hear his surprised chokes and then the clatter of something heavy, followed by the thump of his body hitting the floor. Only once he's sufficiently distracted do I dare push aside the curtained partition.

On the other side of it, Zosines claws at his throat, trying uselessly to pry away my power. Those who don't wield magic cannot stop it. Next to him lies a wicked-looking dagger, one he must've been holding when he called for me.

Wordlessly, I command my magic to draw the blade to me. The weapon rattles against the ground for a moment before it streaks across the space and into my hand.

I kneel next to Zosines and indolently press the blade to his throat.

His dark eyes glare up at me.

"What are you doing?" he rasps.

I honestly don't have the faintest clue, but panic still laces my blood, and my intuition has never steered me wrong.

I command more of my power to wrap around him, tethering him in place. The last thing I want is for Zosines to get away now that I have him in a vulnerable position.

"Where is my husband?" I demand as Ferox comes to my side, his gaze trained on the warrior.

"Can't breathe." Zosines's eyes are starting to bulge.

I ease up on the spell. "Where?" I press.

Zosines gasps in a few lungfuls of air. "Safe," he hisses out. "But you are not. The palace is about to be breached, my queen. There is not much time. We need to go."

Distress is contagious, and I want to agree, I do.

The faint scent of blood catches in my nostrils, and I remember all over again how, even sequestered in our room, Ferox could smell the iron tang of it. Zosines said the palace was about to be breached, but violence has already happened here.

My gaze roves over him, and I notice then the fresh speckles of blood on his clothes. Violence he must've partaken in.

I lift my eyes. The rest of the hallway is eerily silent, save for the soft hisses of torches in their sconces. In the distance, I can hear something else. Voices?

Refocusing on Zosines, I gather my magic and force it down his throat. *"Only the truth shall cross your lips,"* I incant.

Zosines jerks and fidgets against the magic holding him in place. He's seen enough of my power to fear it.

"What is happening?" I demand. As I ask it, I retract my magic completely from his throat.

He presses his lips together.

"Speak." My magic bears down on him. *"Now."*

"A coup, you cunt," he bites out.

My blood runs cold. "Where is Memnon?" The question is more pressing than ever, now that I know there's a price on his head.

Zosines laughs. "Wherever the fuck that crazy bitch Eislyn took him."

Eislyn...took him? During a coup? To hide him? He wouldn't have allowed that. Not when his closest family and friends are here in the palace under attack. But then again, I haven't heard from him since I woke.

"Is he alive?" I ask.

Zosines snickers, and I focus on that callous reaction. "I doubt for long."

I can't breathe. Not when I'm drowning in panic.

Later. I can be terrified later. He's apparently alive for now. With Eislyn. Perhaps they're on a ley line and that is why I cannot reach him.

My fingers twitch a little as I fight the urge to hunt my soul mate down.

"Why is this happening?" I demand.

"The Romans held this territory for a century before Memnon took it. They want it back."

Of course they want it back. That was never a revelation.

The fact that someone let ships into the royal harbor that might be bearing our enemies, however...

"Who made a deal with them?"

Zosines's throat works as he fights against the words. He pulls futilely against the magic binding him. "Memnon's plans would've killed us all. I wanted what was best for our people."

"Who did the Romans make an offer to?" I press. Someone was promised something.

"Me." The word rips from his throat. "They came to me. Eislyn brokered the deal."

I didn't think it was possible to feel worse about the situation, but I do. Eislyn turned on Memnon as well. Unbelievable. I always assumed it was only me she'd fuck over.

In the background, I hear more voices. They sound louder, bolder. Whatever precious time I have, it's slipping through my fingers.

"Tell me the rest of the plot."

Zosines laughs weakly. "You cannot hope to outmaneuver it."

I pull the dagger away from his throat. There's a flicker of curiosity in his eyes and maybe a little victory, as though the futility of my situation is finally sinking in.

I study him, meeting those dark, devious eyes. I'm not mistaken—triumph does flicker in them. Unfortunately for him, he cannot see the thick plumes of my magic wrapping around us.

Adjusting my grip on his dagger, I shove the blade into his side.

He begins to scream, but it does him little good. My power swallows up the sound.

"Stop fucking with me, and tell me the full plot," I command, "and maybe I'll heal this wound."

He gasps, but an unholy excitement dances in his eyes, one I've only ever seen on his face when we're in battle. "You'll pay for that later, my queen," he vows, spitting out my title like it's an oath.

I twist the knife, and Zosines screams between clenched teeth.

"Answer me."

"Half of Memnon's top warriors were in on it. Itaxes, Rakas, Tasios, Palakos, Thiabo, Dzoure, and more," he gasps out.

My stomach twists at the betrayal.

"You and Memnon were both to be drugged at dinner," Zosines continues. "Once you were sedated, the plan was for Eislyn to take Memnon away—she had very specific plans for him—and you were to come with me. But you left dinner early, so here we are. There are five hundred Roman soldiers and mercenaries preparing to descend on the palace, if they haven't already. Another thousand mercenaries, mainly Cimmerians, are at the ready, should anything not go smoothly."

I try not to feel as hopeless as Zosines is making the situation sound. Memnon has single-handedly defeated worse odds. It's not over yet.

"What else?" I ask.

Sweat beads on his forehead, and his breathing comes in short, shallow pants. "The royal family and any loyalists were to be killed. We can't have anyone avenging the fallen king and causing unrest."

Terror rolls through me. Tamara and Katiari are certainly at the top of the list.

"What do you get out of it?" I ask.

The corners of Zosines's mouth twitch and spasm as though he's trying to hold a gloating smile back. "I would be king."

Ah, there it is. He sold his dearest friend out for power.

His mouth continues to twitch.

"Anything else?" I prod.

Finally, he adds, "You. I would get you as a war prize."

My eyebrows lift. Me? It's such a preposterous thought.

"Why?" I finally ask.

The look in his eyes shifts, turning...*covetous* is the best word for it. I've seen that look from him before. I just never paid it much attention. The man has six wives—already more women than he must know what to do with. If he had it his way, I would be the seventh.

Revulsion moves through me. He clearly never thought this through. I'd curse him to death sooner than he could lay a finger on me.

The distant sounds of commotion grow louder. I think...I think I hear the massive palace doors groaning open. Shit.

"Besides you," I say, "is anyone else coming for me?"

Zosines laughs. "Everyone is coming for you. Memnon is gone, and your allies in the palace are dead. Some still sit in that dining hall, their corpses rotting away in their chairs. Their bodies will remain unburied, their flesh left out to rot. But if you come with me, I can save you. I can make you queen once more."

Queen? That's what he intends? If it weren't for the truth spell, I would doubt his words, especially now that I have buried a dagger in his side.

He must want me for my power. He must think that sparing me from certain death tonight will make me feel indebted to him. Such are the ways of Sarmatian warriors.

But it's not my way.

"This is your only chance to live," Zosines adds.

His words are punctuated by distant battle cries. The soldiers are inside.

I search his eyes. "You think I am scared of the Romans? Of death? Or that I would cling to my throne if Memnon didn't sit beside me?" I shake my head. "I would follow him to the ends of the earth. I would follow him even into death. But I think you shall go there first."

With a flick of my wrist, the power encircling us rushes for his head.

Snap.

His neck breaks, and my magic releases him, his body going limp on the ground.

I glance up when I hear the sounds of furniture crashing and wood splintering. The soldiers must be raiding the bottom floor of the castle. The cries of the encroaching legion grow louder.

I straighten. I need to get going if I wish to stop Eislyn before it's too late, but first…

I look down the hall to where Tamara and Katiari's room is. The curtains of the portiere are partially ripped away. My heart beats faster and faster. There's no time left, but I need to be sure.

Ferox steps in close, his head nudging my hand so that my palm rests on it.

I'm here with you, the gesture seems to say. I draw in a deep breath, then head toward their room. Halfway there, I can hear the slow drip of something.

I'm not even to the doorway when I see Tamara's body in

the shadows of her room, slumped against the wall, a bloody, gaping wound in the center of her chest where someone ran her through with a sword.

My knees nearly give out, and I have to stumble the rest of the way to Tamara to stop myself from falling. I pass through the still-intact wards shielding the room and fall to her side, cradling her cold body in mine. Her head slumps listlessly against me, and though the shouts and screams are closing in, for a moment, I cannot bother with them.

This is a Sarmatian queen, a woman who led armies into battle and made life-and-death decisions on behalf of her nomadic peoples for years before Memnon took over. She deserved more than a traitor's blade through her chest.

I continue to hold her body against mine, even as I hear boots on the stone stairs. My eyes scan the room, looking for Katiari, dread coiled in my belly. I have to cast an illumination spell to see the rest of the room.

Beneath the soft orange glow of it, I see the slumped body of Katiari. She lies on her back, four arrows jutting from her chest, a pool of blood beneath her.

Carefully, I release Tamara and move to my sister-in-law's side, touching her skin lightly. It has the same deathly chill clinging to it as Tamara's does. The Sarmatian princess is gone as well.

A disbelieving breath shudders out of me. She was not just a sister by marriage but by love and choice as well.

I am a child again. Soldiers have invaded my home, killed my family. My sobs turn into an anguished cry.

Roman sympathizers did this. Rome once again took from me.

I can hear them at the end of the hallway, knocking over braziers and ripping at the hanging tapestries.

Poisonous rage builds in my veins, devouring my grief and turning it into something darker, deadlier.

I am reliving old pain, but I am no longer a child, and these men shall suffer.

Another cry rips from my throat, but this one sounds feral, wrathful.

I rise, Ferox near my side. I place a hand on his head.

"*Impenetrable armor for your body,*" I incant.

My magic billows over the great cat, coating him in a protective ward. Heedless of the few seconds I have left, I turn the same spell on myself, my power moving down my form and readying me for battle. It won't hold forever, these spells never do, but it will protect us for now at least.

A dozen or more sets of feet rush toward the end of the hall where we are, likely drawn in by my scream.

Quickly, I place a curse on my mother-in-law's and sister-in-law's bodies. "*Skin like death, liquefy the innards of any who dare touch these corpses.*" My voice breaks on that final word. My mind knows these women are gone; my heart cannot fathom it.

I cast the bodies one last grim look. The soldiers will try to desecrate their remains. I smile malevolently at the thought of the painful death that awaits such fools.

My power gathers beneath my skin, my muscles and joints throbbing from it. Rage makes even that pain feel good.

I glance at my panther. "Ready yourself, Ferox. Everyone beyond this room is an enemy. Kill whatever you can."

I step out of the bedroom as the first of the Roman soldiers closes in on me. This soldier is a youthful man with rich, golden skin and thin, lithe legs.

His eyes widen a bit when he sees me, and he slows just

a little. Behind him are more than a dozen others. I raise a hand, my magic gathering.

"*Annihilate.*"

BOOM!

The entire castle trembles as power explodes out of me, blowing the soldiers in front of me apart. Bloody limbs fly, smacking into other soldiers farther back, knocking them down.

All that's left of that golden-skinned man is blood spatter on the ground.

I stride forward as more soldiers pour into the hallway off the stairs.

I waited too long to leave this place, but I no longer care. My rage burns in me, scalding my magic.

I storm down the hallway while Ferox rips out the throat of a soldier struggling to push off the mutilated torso of a fallen comrade.

More magic gathers. "*Annihilate!*"

Another explosion. More scattered bodies. Those pretty Roman helmets are blown from the heads of their soldiers or else they're blown away with the severed heads of their owners still inside them.

The sight of the soldiers' scattered remains soothes something primal in me. I never thought of myself as particularly malicious, but apparently, for my soul mate and my family, I am. Ruthlessly so.

So focused on the carnage am I that I don't notice the first arrow that strikes me. It hits me in the right shoulder, and though it doesn't so much as tear the fabric of my warded tunic, the force of it still nearly knocks me off my feet.

Archers. There are archers inside the palace, despite

the closeness of this space. The thought has me casting another annihilation spell. Bodies burst apart, dust falls from the ceilings, and the walls shake. I don't care if this whole massive place falls on our heads, so long as it takes these men out with it.

I try not to think about the grief and sorrow that claw up my throat at what I've lost this evening—and what I might still lose.

I need to get to Memnon. Gods, I need to get to him. I still haven't heard from him, and I sense little down our bond.

There are many places Eislyn could've taken Memnon, some of them entirely inaccessible. But if she and my mate are still here in this realm, then there is one place above all others where she would take him.

When I get to the stairs, I blow apart another cluster of soldiers, the spell taking out a large section of the stone steps with it.

I descend what remains, recasting the ward I placed on Ferox, who clings close to my side.

The palace temple, then. That's where I must go.

Down on the first floor, the sounds of battle cries and anguished screams are louder. And when I catch sight of the melee, it takes my breath away. A few loyal Sarmatians fight back against the soldiers, but they're vastly outnumbered. The Romans are also cutting down innocent palace servants who have no battle training, and they're smashing or carrying out royal items, most of them relics of the rulers who lived here before us.

As soon as they notice me, the atmosphere shifts entirely.

"The queen!" someone shouts.

I can't place the voice, and I have no clue whether it's

from friend or foe. But then I catch sight of Rakas, one of Memnon's named betrayers. Rakas, who escorted me from Rome and who's fought at my side through many, many battles. He's pointing his sword at me and shouting orders.

All my rage coalesces into an unnamed curse, one I aim for that traitorous Sarmatian man. The pale orange magic that barrels toward him is threaded through with oily black stains. When it hits Rakas, it lifts him into the air, great plumes of orange smoke upwelling beneath him. Never have I made such a spell or committed such a feat as lifting a person into the air. This is fueled by rage and pain and my power's own sentience.

The fighting slows, and people stop to stare as Rakas writhes above them, slashing his sword at thin air to try to break himself free.

The cursed magic still swarms around him, hugging close to his skin, and it's only once it sinks into him that I clearly see his flesh begin to boil and bubble until, all at once, his body explodes, bits of cursed flesh raining down on the room. People shriek as the curse lands on them and burns their own flesh.

The Roman soldiers seem terrified. They signed up for war, not witchcraft. Some run, but most cast new, deadlier gazes on me.

That's when the fighting begins in earnest.

I blow those nearest me back, then cast two more annihilation spells. Many, many bodies go flying.

Beneath my impassioned feelings, I feel the drain of my magic. It's running out; it will run out. Rather soon, if I keep attacking as I am. It's hard to care. Not when my cheeks are wet and a soul-deep ache has taken root inside me.

The moment the room recovers from its panic, a dozen

arrows rain on me and Ferox. My panther yelps when one of them hits his flank, and I lash out, my magic slicing a whole row of soldiers.

The temple, I remind myself. I need to get there if I have any hope of reaching Memnon.

I raise my arms to the room. "*Incinerate.*"

Fire billows from my palms, streaming out at those closest to me. Soldiers catch fire, and smoke and the acrid smell of burning flesh fill the room.

I cannot think about those I'm leaving behind. It's a bloodbath in the palace, and Memnon's forces have either been slaughtered or co-opted by the enemy. Any hope of us winning this fight will come only once I have my husband at my side.

My arms shake as I carve a bloody path for myself and Ferox. My panther lunges at anyone who comes too close, ripping out throats and slashing legs. I feel the first true strain of my power. Sweat drips from my brow, and—

I choke as an arrow lodges in my back, throwing me forward. Another hits me near the armpit.

The protective ward I cast must've disintegrated.

A soldier rushes me, sword swinging. I jump out of his way, but his blade slashes me across the abdomen.

I gasp, then rush out, "*Impenetrable armor for my body.*" The ward returns once more.

It's too late, though. Blood seeps between my fingers and drips down my back, and there are dozens of soldiers closing in on me.

The temple, I remind myself again. *Just need to get to the temple.*

Closing my eyes, I draw on my pain and my blood, and then the blood of anyone nearby. My power reaches out, feeding on the suffering and building in my veins. Dazedly, I release it, only half noticing the people it rips apart.

The temple. The temple. It's become a chant.

Ferox sticks close, and I can feel his inquisitive, worried gaze on me as I manage to pass through the double doors and leave the palace, my power blowing the enemy back many arm spans.

Several more arrows hit my body, though they bounce off my skin and clothes and clatter uselessly to the ground, leaving nothing behind except for ugly welts. Unlike the two other arrows I carry—those protrude out of me almost comically.

Outside the palace, the world is unnervingly silent, save for a few skirmishes and a couple of soldiers hauling away a chest of something or other. But the teeming scores of soldiers are following me out. It's all I can do to cast my magic behind me, pushing them and their weapons back, back, back, even as the wordless spell drains my quickly depleting reserves of power.

Off to my left, I can see the shadowy silhouette of the abandoned temple. The priests who once maintained it never returned after our capture of the palace, and Memnon and I never tried to replace them with new holy servants. Sarmatian gods don't dwell in temples, and I have no use for Roman ones.

I stagger to it, moving as fast as I dare and leaving a trail of blood in my wake. I need to heal my wounds, particularly my abdominal injury, but I cannot focus on more than keeping a magical shield up at my back, where it protects me and Ferox. Even now, I sense the soldiers battering against it, their shouts and footfalls far too close.

It feels like an agonizing eternity before I reach the temple steps. As soon as I'm inside, I hastily ward the threshold against intruders, the magical strings of my casting somewhat sloppy. My hand shakes, and my pain is distracting me. I add another layer to the ward, this one to block weapons from entering the space—it was a ward we forgot to place on the room of Tamara and Katiari, and Zosines and the other traitors found a way around it.

I spell the entrance just in time too. The first of the soldiers slams into the ward not a moment later. I jerk back at the sound, and my body sways a little. Ferox presses against my side, clearly trying to help me stabilize.

"Thank you," I say softly, my fingers delving into his fur. One of my hands still clutches my midsection. *"Mend the wound, heal the flesh,"* I whisper.

Thick, syrupy magic spreads out beneath my palm, sinking into my skin. I hiss as it tugs on my injury, but already the pain is lessening as the wound repairs itself. I still have those two arrows protruding from my torso, but for now, I let them be.

"Illuminate." The light I cast is faded, watery. My magic is faltering.

I half stride, half stumble toward the back of the temple, where the innermost sanctum is. Where the entrance to the ley line is.

When I see it, relief makes my knees weak. It's barely visible under the light of my magic, but I can just make out the strange distortion in the air where the ley-line entrance bends the light.

Far on the other side of the temple, I hear the bangs of weapons and fists against my ward, then the haunting sound of it shattering.

I place my hand on Ferox. "We'll step onto the ley line at the same time. Ready?"

The panther dips his head, which is the closest thing I'm going to get to assent. Behind us, soldiers clamor in our direction. Moments. We have mere moments.

Taking a fortifying breath, Ferox and I cross onto the ley line.

Immediately, the noise quiets, and our surroundings—what little I can make of them in the darkness—smear. Nonmagical humans cannot traverse these roads, at least not without aid. Which means that for now, Ferox and I are safe.

I cannot, however, say that about anyone else who remained devoted to Memnon. To me. They are still locked in battle, getting butchered by an enemy they didn't see coming.

I need to get to Memnon. Need to save him from whatever fate Eislyn has devised. Need to avenge our people.

My gaze flicks to the walls of the ley line. Right now, they're cloaked in the darkness of the night, and only the faint smudges of warped, distant stars offer any light.

With my free hand, I reach around and pull out the arrow from my back, grinding my teeth together and swallowing a scream as I pry the head of it from my flesh, its edges ripping through more muscle. I toss the bloody projectile to the rippling tunnel walls.

"I offer you my blood, violently spilled by an enemy," I gasp out as the open wound at my back begins to bleed in earnest, "in exchange for the safe passage of myself and my panther to the Khuno River Palace."

What little I can see of the walls ripples, then smooths.

Fuck. It didn't work.

Without the help of the ley line itself, I won't be able to find my way to this destination. Instead, Ferox and I will wander along it, hopelessly lost until I either find a way out or we perish.

Adjusting my hold on Ferox, I reach for the other arrow and dig my fingers into the skin around it. A scream rips from my throat as I pull the second arrowhead out and throw it at the wall. "I offer you my blood, violently spilled by an enemy," I repeat, "in exchange for the safe passage of myself and my panther to the Khuno River Palace."

This time, the walls hardly even ripple.

"I offer you a memory," I say to the fae magic, my desperation growing. "In exchange for the safe passage of me and my panther to the Khuno River Palace."

The walls of the ley line undulate around me, further obscuring the scenery outside.

I take a few steps forward, bringing Ferox with me, but then the walls smooth, denying me passage once more.

I cry out. "For gods' sakes, what do you want? Tears?" I ask. With my free hand, I gesture to my cheeks. "You can have them."

The ley line's strange, foreign magic brushes against my face, taking the offered tears.

Still, the wall doesn't open. I want to scream.

"You already have my blood and my tears. What more do you want?" I ask the darkness. My magic is failing, my blood is streaming down my back, and my body is faint with exhaustion. There's not much left of me to give.

Why did I not learn to navigate these magical roads without selling little pieces of myself? My ignorance is costing me.

A thought comes to me, one that has me pressing a quivering hand to my stomach. I swallow. There is one more thing—

"Fine, I'll tell you a secret: I think I might be pregnant."

CHAPTER 43
Roxilana, 23 years old

59 AD, Somewhere in the northwestern Amazon Basin

We're spit out onto wet soil, mud oozing beneath my boots.

It worked. My body sags with relief. It worked.

I stand, glancing at my surroundings. The sun is setting here, and though the jungle makes many sounds, there's a peaceful, quiet element to this place that's jarring compared to the shrieking violence of Panticapaeum.

Ferox's growl is all the warning I get.

I'm about to turn when a blade is shoved cleanly through my back. It happens so fast, I don't have time to do more than choke on my own surprise as I glance down at my abdomen, where the bloody tip of a sword juts out.

Roughly, it's withdrawn, and with its exit, I collapse to my knees, a cascade of blood pouring from the wound. It's—it's right where—

"You cannot know how long I've wished to do that." Eislyn's beautiful, lilting voice is laced with malice.

With a snarl, Ferox lunges for the fairy. But before he can make it anywhere near her neck, Eislyn brings the hilt of her weapon down on his head. There's a sickening crunch, and I choke out a scream as my panther collapses in a heap at my side. The ward that had protected him only moments ago must've disintegrated.

The fae woman walks around to my front, tapping the bloody sword against her side as she appraises me. "I hoped you'd survive the attack long enough to come here."

She tilts her head, and I imagine she's debating whether to stab me again, though I'm too distracted to much notice. My mate is missing, Ferox is unconscious, and blood is pouring out of my abdomen at an alarming rate.

I can barely think over the pain in my gut, yet I have rage to spare. My body shakes with it. I gather my magic, preparing to strike.

"Ah, ah," Eislyn says, using the bloody sword tip to tilt my chin up. "Think about harming me, and I'll drive this sword through your throat, then that of your panther's, and you will die never knowing what became of Memnon."

I go still, terror replacing anger. "Where is he?"

Her eyes flick in the direction of the palace for the merest of instants before she casually says, "I thought you were his soul mate, that you could find him through your bond alone." She frowns. "Apparently not."

As she speaks, I focus my magic on my gut wound. It's a lethal injury, but only if it cannot be repaired. I *can* repair it. I'm already clutching it, and now I slowly trickle my power into it. All I have to do is live, then I can save both Memnon and Ferox.

"What did you do to my mate?" I ask.

Eislyn stares down at me stoically. "He will sleep for a

hundred years, until all he knows and loves has passed on. When he wakes, all that will be left is me."

My brows come together, even as I feel the nauseating tug of internal injuries sealing themselves up.

She continues. "I already warned Memnon several times that you would prove treacherous. I told him that a civilized Roman girl like you would never fully accept the warring ways of Sarmatians. That his bloodthirstiness would eventually drive you to do something desperate to stop him from all the killing and conquering. He didn't believe me then, but I'm sure when he wakes and finds you long gone, he will remember my warnings."

Eislyn's words would hold weight with Memnon, who has always believed that she acts with reason and great wisdom.

"And," she says, "I will make sure to tell him how you, his dear mate, made a deal with the Romans for peace and how you couldn't bear to kill him, so you left him to sleep. I'll make sure he knows that you lived a long life—that you remarried, had children, and you didn't once try to wake him."

I can barely breathe over my disbelief. Who *is* this woman?

"He'll be heartbroken," she continues, "but in time, he will recover."

I search her features. "Why are you doing this?"

Her eyes glitter, and the corners of her mouth curve into a sly smile. "That's a secret you'll have to die without knowing."

Instinct rather than eyesight has me noticing the infinitesimal shift of Eislyn's weight and the adjustment of her grip on the sword.

I call on my anger and my power. "*Annihilate*," I breathe.

The spell explodes out of me, the power blowing off her sword arm.

Eislyn screams, reaching for the gaping wound at her shoulder. Her wings unfurl, thinner than linen and far more delicate. She uses them to rush herself to the ley-line portal.

I'm already gathering the scraps of my magic, readying them in my hand.

"*Annihilate*."

Her form disappears a moment before my spell does, though the ley line absorbs it as well.

My breathing is ragged.

Eislyn is gone. For now.

I stare down at the ruin of my abdomen, and I bite back a sob. If there was a baby, the odds of it surviving such a wound…

I have to dig my teeth into my lower lip to keep from screaming. Tears slip down my cheeks. *Don't think about that.*

Then there's Ferox…

I reach out a hand and pet my panther. Beneath my touch, he stirs, then turns his head to weakly lick my hand. I strain for enough magic to heal him. It leaves my palm sluggishly, but I sense the spell take root, and it slowly mends Ferox's injuries. Once I'm sure he'll be okay, I let my hand slide from him.

Memnon. Need Memnon.

I force myself to stand, and the world goes dark for a moment. Blood loss—this must be blood loss. It physically hurts to draw on more power and funnel it toward the last of my wounds. My magic is tired, reluctant.

I'm dying.

It comes to me with detached clarity. I'm dying faster

than my power can heal. And Memnon is cursed to sleep for a hundred years, and once he wakes, he will be Eislyn's hostage for whatever larger scheme she's concocting. Perhaps it's love she wants from him. Perhaps it's power. Whatever it is, she was willing to have his family murdered and entice his friends to betray him. She was willing to twist my motives and my love for him, all so she could see her awful plan through.

I cannot leave Memnon to whatever fate she intends.

I stagger forward, toward the palace, leaving Ferox where he is so he can sleep off his injury. As I step past the wards and spells guarding it, the river palace gleams among the trees; it's so painfully, unnaturally beautiful that it sets my teeth on edge.

I pass the marble pillars fashioned like trees and the golden vines with their sharp-edged glass flowers, leaving a trail of blood in my wake.

Warded as the palace is, it would be the perfect place to hide Memnon undisturbed for a hundred years.

But where would she place him?

I close my eyes and focus on my connection to Memnon. Eislyn mocked our ability to find each other through it, but it *is* how we located each other time and time again. I can find him through it now as well. I just need to focus.

I breathe in deeply, trying to ignore the screaming pains of my body and the cold chill that has set in my bones. A tendril of orange magic slithers from me, disappearing into the distance. I let my mind take a back seat to my power, and then I follow the trail.

I pass through halls and rooms, then exit the rear of the palace, wandering near the outdoor bathhouse. I'm so dazed, I nearly fall into the hole in the ground my magic dips into.

I stagger back and draw in a startled breath at the sight of the square opening cut into the ground. Next to it is a massive stone slab that's been cast aside.

I eye the torchlit walls descending from the opening. Memnon's down there. I can feel it like the beating of my own heart, and if I focus again on our sharèd bond, I can sense it tugging me closer, closer...

Eislyn rigorously planned this entire situation, but she was careful not to tell me where Memnon is. I don't think she was finished with whatever she was doing.

The thought gives me a whisper of hope. That's all I need. Just a whisper.

Carefully, I descend the stairs, bracing myself against the wall to keep my fatigued body steady.

The decorated walls around me barely register, but my fingers cannot help but notice the divots where words have been carved. I stare at the writing.

...containing the might of the gods within him, Memnon the Indomitable drove the Dacians from their lands...

...charged into impenetrable Rome with nothing more than his blood riders and captured his queen...

The writing doesn't sound like me, but I'm the only one who knows these events and how to read and write Sarmatian with the Latin lexicon. In addition, I'm one of a precious few who could even travel here...Memnon would have to assume I secretly commissioned a vault like this and oversaw its creation.

A shiver wracks my body that has less to do with blood loss and more to do with the disturbing lengths Eislyn went to, to carry out her plot.

What does she want with my husband?

The question will plague me.

All thoughts of her motives vanish the moment I step into the burial chamber. And there's no mistaking that's what this is. In the center of the torchlit space lies a white marble sarcophagus, the lid removed. From here, I can only make out a glimpse of scale armor, but I know—it's Memnon. Even if the bond wasn't indicating it, the slope of that chest and the sheen of that bronze armor would.

A ragged sob rips from my throat. I didn't believe he was asleep, not truly, not until now.

I drag myself to the stone coffin, the blistering pain of my wounds dulled by the deeper ache in my heart. My gaze barely touches on Memnon's arresting, sleep-softened features before my legs give out. I'm awash in pain—pain so dark and bleak, I don't know how I'll surface from it.

He's already out of my reach. Enchanted to a hundred years of sleep. If it were mortal magic, maybe I could break the spell, but Eislyn is a fairy, and their magic is different, *incompatible.*

Even if the spell could be broken, I'm dying. Beyond that, Memnon's empire is now overrun by battle-ready Romans, his traitorous warriors, and a scheming fairy.

We have too many enemies and not enough time. A tear slips out.

I place a hand lightly on the ruined flesh of my abdomen. I want retribution, but more than anything, I want peace. For me, for my soul mate. A single lifetime where we can love each other without the fear of our enemies killing us.

I struggle to pull myself up, gnashing my teeth together against the pain. Darkness pulls at my vision, and at this point, my magic is likely the only thing keeping it at bay, but I manage to get my legs locked under me. I've got life left in me yet.

I glance once more into the coffin where Memnon rests, still as death. Not even his chest moves with his breathing. I can tell through our bond that he still clings to life, but he gives few signs of it.

I stroke his hair back, drops of my blood and tears hitting his armor.

"This is not how we end," I whisper. "We are eternal."

Something dark and resolute moves through me.

We are eternal.

If we cannot have this life, then we shall have another.

Eislyn isn't the only one capable of using extraordinary measures.

I am as well.

And whatever spell she's placed on Memnon, I can make one stronger. It might not break the enchantment he's under, but it can usurp it.

Some final fire stirs in me, rousing me.

I can do this, for him, for us.

I *must*.

I just need a little help.

My grip on the sarcophagus tightens as I draw my magic together. There's precious little power left in me, and nothing my body wants to give up. But there are other sources of magic—in the air and, more notably, in the ground. The earth is already feasting on the trail of blood I've left. I can sense the magic beneath me clamoring for it. *Hungry.*

There are things that rule that magic, things that have whispered to me every so often. They might be willing to help me cast a spell of the magnitude I need…but they will exact a price.

I bow my head over the sarcophagus and draw the words out. "*I call on any god who will answer: Memnon the Indomitable shall sleep the sleep of immortals. And he shall awaken* only *by my hand. I bind my soul to this vow. Even in death, I shall be beholden to it. Take what you must to make it so."*

For several moments, all I hear are the soft, reverent hisses of the torches. Just when I'm nearly sure the spell didn't work, a low moan starts up in the distance, rattling the torches in their sconces. It builds into a howling wind that tears through the room, blowing my hair back. As it moves through me, I feel it pull away bits of my essence. The blood on my skin vanishes, as do the fresh tears on my cheeks. Something dark and hungry slips *inside* me through my wounds, and I gasp at the insidious intrusion.

Once this essence is within me, it begins to spread. I choke on my own breath, my hand going to my abdomen. Whatever god answered my plea, it's named its price. I can feel it feasting on what's left of my life.

The unearthly wind circles the room several times, then sweeps out, gone just as quickly as it came. The pain eating me from the inside out, however, is still there.

I stagger, struggling to catch my breath. I lean against the sarcophagus, my eyes drawn back to Memnon.

Always Memnon.

Beautiful, monstrous Memnon.

I touch his cheek, my fingers slipping a little. "We will get another life. A better one," I promise.

I lean into the sarcophagus, ignoring the way my body screams in protest, and press a kiss to his lips. They're still warm.

I pull away, my mouth lingering right above his. "I will find you again, my king. I am eternally yours."

Hot tears slip from my eyes as I straighten. All I want is to crawl inside that coffin and spend my last few moments with him. It would be a good place to die.

Unfortunately, if I mean to see this through, I can't do that.

I lift a trembling hand, my breath ragged as I force my magic to lift the coffin lid into the air. I shift it over the sarcophagus and gently lay it down.

Another tear drips, and I can feel my lower lip quivering with sadness and exhaustion. My tired eyes rest on the inscription carved into the top.

For the love of your gods, beware of me.
Memnon the Cursed

It's a terrible epitaph to leave him with—not that it's inaccurate—but it will scare off almost anyone who can read it. But in case it won't, I will need to ward it.

Just the thought of doing so is daunting. I splay my hand over the lid, preparing to wrangle more magic. Yet when I call it forth, my power surges forward, stronger than ever.

A gift from the unnamed god.

I bite my lip to keep from crying out my relief. Though my mind is addled with pain and encroaching death, the ward I cast is strong; the many threads of it have a smooth sheen. As soon as I finish it, another forms, then another, until my focus becomes the room at large. This too requires a ward.

I move around the coffin, though my legs don't feel as though they'll keep me upright. That noxious presence is spreading, withering me away from the inside out.

Something presses against my legs, and when I glance down, I realize it's Ferox. At some point, my panther dragged himself off the ground and ventured into this cursed tomb to find me. He leans against me now, his eyes large, concerned.

I place a hand on his head. "I'm so sorry," I whisper brokenly. "I didn't mean for any of this to happen."

He pushes his nose into my palm, nudging it, as though demanding reassurance. I run a hand down his black fur.

"I release you, Ferox," I say. "You shall not be bound by my curse." I invoke my magic and weave it into my words. "With my death, our bond shall sever, and you shall be free."

He hisses at me as though I have committed some great and terrible act.

"I'm sorry," I whisper again, my throat tightening. "You were always too good for me."

He growls, like even my apology displeases him.

I stagger over to a wall and lean heavily against it.

More spells seep from my palms, coating the room in pale looping threads like some shoddily woven garment.

I heave from the effort, my bones aching, brittle. So tired.

I cannot give up now. Not when the biggest spell is yet to come. It's a race against this thing inside me. Gods may occasionally be benevolent, but they are almost never merciful. Particularly not the bloodthirsty ones. I doubt this god will extend my life longer than they see fit.

I struggle up the stairs, and though Ferox is obviously still mad at me, he presses his body against mine to prevent me from falling.

"Thank you," I say, my voice weakening.

The two of us make our way outside, the overcast sky so much brighter than the dim room we were in. I turn around and lift my arm, my tears coming faster. Leaving Memnon in there feels like a betrayal all on its own, like another knife sunk into my flesh.

I straighten my spine, drawing on my will.

"*Seal the opening.*" The stone covering slides over the... *tomb's* entrance, then with a thud, sinks into place.

Ferox makes a low, baleful noise, scratching at the stone like he can unearth it. Drowning in sorrow, I have to stifle another sob.

My heart seems to skip a beat, then stall. After a terrifying few moments, it begins to thump again.

I have precious little time left to perform one final spell—a curse that will eclipse Eislyn's magic with my own.

If my desperate plan is to work, it is not enough for Memnon to outlive the enchantment. Eislyn must forget her fevered fixation so she might never come back for him. And those who could remind the fairy of Memnon's existence, their memories must too be expunged.

I think of the soldiers pouring into the palace and the many places Memnon has violently conquered. There are thousands who would want to kill my slumbering husband if they ever learned the truth. One whispered word into the wrong ears—it wouldn't even have to be Eislyn. Other supernaturals could access the ley lines and end the king while he lies vulnerable.

Everyone must forget my sorcerer, so that none may come searching.

Only I shall have that power.

That insidious, dark force closes in on the last of me, and my heart seizes again.

One...two...three...

Sluggishly, it resumes beating.

I take a shuddering breath and gather all that I can of the power at my disposal.

"*With all that is left in me, I demand this world and everyone in it forget Uvagukis Memnon. Every last person who carries a memory of him shall lose them, beginning with Eislyn.*"

I give the last of myself up to the curse.

Pure, raw power bursts from me, sweeping out across the jungle until I can no longer see it. I sense when the first mind has been struck. It must be Eislyn's. I take a perverse amount of pleasure knowing I'm peeling away her memories.

She's the first, but it's only the beginning of the curse.

Across the world, a thousand upon a thousand people carried some awareness of Memnon. One by one, my magic devours every last bit of those memories. Memnon the Indomitable simply becomes some vague, merciless, nomadic king of a horde of warriors who came and went.

In my mind's eye, I see the petroglyphs bearing his name chip away until the recordings vanish. The ink on papyri rearranges itself to remove Memnon; where his presence is too frequent, the papyri simply burn up.

Across every land he conquered, his name disappears, cast from the record.

I take the memory of Memnon from everything and everyone.

I scream as my magic and that foreign essence consume me. The years of my life fall away like a fever dream as the magic leaving me thins out to a wisp.

My heart stutters as that last thread of power darkens, then doubles back on itself, returning toward me.

I must hold on until the curse is finished. For this to work, no one can remember him.

No one...

Not even me.

My magic strikes then, sinking into my flesh and closing in on my memories. With a final, choked cry, my heart stops, and the last mind is wiped.

EPILOGUE

An old soul. A new body. And a distant call.
Come find me, my queen...
I am yours forever...

Present Day, somewhere in the northwestern Amazon Basin

Two thousand years after it was closed, a young woman enters a forgotten tomb. She has the same cinnamon hair as Roxilana, the long-dead Queen of Sarmatians. She has the same heart-shaped face and bright eyes too. She even has the same magic. But she goes by a different name and wears different clothes; she has lived a different life, one unimaginable to the ancient witch.

And yet when this woman looks at the writing that adorns the tomb walls, she finds she can read it. And when she descends deeper and discovers the sealed sarcophagus, beneath her curiosity and fear is a growing awareness that she can neither understand nor place, one that compels her to use her magic to cast its lid aside.

Within it, there is no corpse but instead a scarred, seemingly sleeping man. He's familiar to her, though her mind cannot grasp why. Her heart and her magic, however, they seem to know, and they rule her actions.

The woman's hand goes to his cheek, and she utters a single word in a language she should not know.

"*Wake.*"

The man's eyes snap open, and he draws in his first lungful of air in two millennia.

"Roxilana," he breathes. "You found me."

Continue Memnon and Roxilana's story
in the present day with

BEWITCHED

Today will be the day Henbane Coven accepts me.

I exhale as I stare up at the sprawling Gothic buildings that make up the coven's campus. The property sits on the coastal hills north of San Francisco, bordered on all sides by the Everwoods, a thick coastal forest composed of evergreen trees.

There's no placard that announces I'm now standing on witch-owned land, but this place doesn't really need one. If a person lingers for long enough, they'll see something out of the ordinary—like, for instance, the circle of witches sitting on the lawn ahead of me.

Their hair and clothes float every which way, as though no longer bound by gravity, and plumes of their magic thicken the air around them. The color of their individual magic varies—from bright green, to bubblegum pink, to turquoise, and more—but as I watch, it all blends, creating an odd sort of rainbow in the air around them.

A wave of longing moves through me, and I have to tamp down the panicky, desperate feeling that follows in its wake.

I glance down at the open notebook in my hand.

Tuesday, August 29

10:00 a.m. meeting with Henbane Coven's admissions office in Morgana Hall.

*Leave an extra twenty minutes early. You have a bad habit of arriving late.

I frown at the note, then glance at my phone: *9:57 a.m.* Well, shit.

I begin walking again, heading toward the weathered stone buildings, even as my eyes flick back to my notebook.

Beneath my scrawled instructions is a drawing of a crest with flowers rising from a cauldron atop two crisscrossing brooms. Next to the drawing, I taped a Polaroid picture of one of the stone structures in front of me, and I've scrawled the words *Morgana Hall* beneath it. At the bottom I've written in red:

Meeting will be held in the Receiving Room—second door on the right.

I head up the stone steps of Morgana Hall, growing breathless with my churning emotions. For the past century and a half, any witch worth her weight in magic has been an active member of an accredited coven.

And today I'm determined to join that list.

It didn't happen last year or when you reapplied at the beginning of this one. Perhaps they simply don't want you.

I take a deep breath and force the insidious thought away. This time is different. I'm on the official wait list, and they arranged for this interview only last week. They must be taking my application seriously, and that's all I need: a foot in the door.

I open one of the massive doors into the building and head inside.

The first thing I see in the main hallway is a grand statue of the triple goddess. Her three forms stand back-to-back—the maiden, flowers woven into her unbound hair; the mother, her hands cradling her pregnant stomach; and the crone, wearing a crown of bones, her hands resting atop her cane.

Along the walls are portraits of past coven members, many of whom have wild hair and wilder eyes. Mounted in between them are wands and brooms and framed excerpts of famous grimoires.

I breathe it all in for a moment. I can feel the gentle hum of magic in the air, and it feels like home.

I *will* get in.

I stride down the hall, my determination renewed. When I get to the second door on the right, I knock, then wait.

A witch with soft features and a kind smile opens the door for me. "Selene Bowers?" she says.

I nod.

"Come on in."

I follow her inside. A massive crescent-moon table takes up most of the space, and on the far side of it, half a dozen witches sit patiently. Across from them is a single seat.

The witch ahead of me gestures to it, and despite all my encouraging thoughts, my heart hammers.

I take the proffered seat, folding my hands in my lap to stop them from trembling while the woman who led me in takes her own seat on the other side of the table.

Directly across from me is a witch with raven-black hair,

thin downturned lips, and shrewd eyes. I think I've spoken to her before, there's something vaguely familiar about her features, but her identity lies just beyond my reach…

She looks up from her notes and squints at me. After a moment, her frown deepens. "You again?"

With that question, I swear the entire mood of the room shifts from inviting to tense.

I swallow delicately. "Yes, me," I say hoarsely before clearing my throat. I'm frightened this interview is now doomed before it's even begun.

The witch who spoke returns her attention to the papers in front of her. She licks her finger and flips through them. "I was under the impression we were interviewing a different applicant," she says.

What am I supposed to say to that? Sorry I'm not someone else?

Short of shape-shifting into another person, I don't think I can appease her.

Another witch, one with a hooked nose and wiry gray hair, says gently, "Selene Bowers, it's lovely to meet you. Why don't you tell us a little bit about yourself and why you'd like to join Henbane Coven?"

This is it. My chance.

I take a deep breath, and I dive in.

For thirty minutes, I answer various questions about my abilities, my background, and my magical interests. Most of the witches nod encouragingly. The only notable exception to this is that hawk-eyed witch who looks at me like I'm a spell gone bad. It's all I can do to answer the questions I get without letting her intimidate me into silence.

"It's been a dream of mine to be a part of Henbane Coven for as long as I can remember."

Author's Note

The Sarmatians were a real pastoral nomadic people that lived near the Black Sea from the third century BCE to the fourth century CE. Most of the details I've used in this book come from what we know of them and other tribes in the area, most notably the Scythians, who predated the Sarmatians.

I've been drawn to these peoples since I first learned about them in college, and in many ways, *The Curse that Binds* isn't just a love story but also an ode to these awesome cultures, who are thought to be the inspiration behind the mythical Amazons. The women in many of these tribes did, in fact, fight alongside men, and women had near-equal rights. Herodotus was an ancient historian who wrote of how Scythian women were not allowed to marry until they killed at least one opponent in battle, a detail I briefly mention in the story.

Other details that have historical truth are the use of skulls as drinking vessels, Sarmatians' ritual use of cannabis, and their

Anarya priests, whose gender and sexuality fell outside of binary concepts of male and female. The Sarmatian wedding ritual where Memnon and Roxilana spill their blood into a cup of wine then drink it is also based on the real Scythian blood brother ritual, another practice I mentioned in passing in the book.

I tried to use ancient place names where I could, though there are some like the Black Sea and the Carpathian Mountains that I left alone because their ancient names either sounded or meant the same thing as their modern equivalents.

There are a few choices I made in writing this story that differ from history. The first is omitting any mention of slavery. Historically, both Romans and Sarmatians would've been involved in the enslavement of large numbers of people, and it is likely that had Roxilana really lived through the raiding of her village, she would've been sent to Rome as an enslaved girl. I made the choice to exclude this detail for several reasons, one of which is that I didn't think it was appropriate to use slavery as a plot device.

Another reason concerns Roxilana's race. While slavery did occur in the ancient world, it worked differently from the colonial conception of slavery that we are more familiar with. Most notably, ancient slavery was not race based. Anyone could become enslaved or be born as one, regardless of appearance or place of origin.

America's own painful history with slavery is something we are still grappling with. In honoring the conversations we continue to have around the topic, especially ones involving the intersection of slavery and race, I decided this story would do more harm than good by including slavery, particularly the enslavement of a character that bares a physical resemblance to many of the perpetrators of colonial slavery.

The second deliberate variance I made in the story was the fact that in Rome, many girls were married off at twelve, thirteen, and fourteen years old. To avoid the visceral ick I get every time I think of this, I decided to bump up that age to make the romance in this book more appropriate to modern times.

Another random note that is just sort of fun—giving someone the finger dates back to ancient times, as does the curse word *fuck*. (I mean, it is a very satisfying swear word to say.) However, apparently the Roman word for *clitoris* was considered so obscene that it was written of essentially nowhere, which honestly says all I need to know about Romans' opinions on female pleasure. Because the word is used so infrequently, I assumed that the ancient world did not have much knowledge or space for this concept, so I made the decision to omit the words *clit* and *clitoris* from the book. (I kept the female pleasure in though, because, you know, fuck 'em—oh, that really is a fun swear word.)

Other random facts: The Egyptian literature Roxi reads out loud is taken from real documents I found, notably Papyrus Anastasi I. Roman brides did often wear orange, a veil and flower crown, and a garment called a *tunica recta*, as well as a sash tied with a knot of Hercules, which their husbands were said to untie. The Roman vows are real, though the Sarmatian ones are not.

Because there's no record of many of the Sarmatians' cultural practices nor of their daily lives, I used a lot of artistic license to fill in the gaps here. I tried to draw on practices from other pastoral nomads connected to them in time or space in an attempt to be as authentic as possible, but ultimately there was much that came down to my personal conception of what life might have been like, and I'm sure I fell short in many, many areas. Still, I hope you enjoyed the ride!

Acknowledgments

This book was a doozy. Originally, *The Curse that Binds* was supposed to be a succinct novella that gave a brief glimpse of the events that transpired between Roxilana and Memnon in Selene's first life. It ended up being three times its original length, and it is currently one of the longest books I've written.

It was also one of the most difficult stories for me to write, for a number of reasons, including the span of time I had to cover and the sheer amount of research that went into making the past come alive as much as I possibly could. And, unfortunately for her, my amazing PA, Naomi Lane, had to hear about all of it over the past year. So, Naomi, thank you for listening to my worries and cheering me on in spite of them.

I intended for this novella—when it was slated to be a novella—to be self-published, and it was my wonderful agent, Kimberly Brower, who, when she heard I was tinkering on this book, took it upon herself to sell the rights.

Thank you for always believing in my work and advocating for me.

To my editor Christa, who nearly made me cry when she read this book, then raved about it. I had to read her email twice because I was convinced I spent a year writing rubbish. To Letty and Gretchen and Aimee—thank you, thank you for the wonderful edits and awesome insights that made this love story that much sweeter and sharper than before.

To the team at Bloom—from brilliant Pam, who is always a breath of fresh air when it comes to the overwhelming marketing aspect of publishing (and who is always ready to MacGyver a situation that's gone sideways), to the entire design team for the new covers of this series—thank you for taking my manuscript and transforming it into the polished book that it is.

Words cannot do justice to how pivotal my husband has been not just with this novel but throughout my entire author career. He's the one who first inspired me to actually write down the stories in my head, and he's my biggest cheerleader and the one who is always running off to grab champagne so we can celebrate every little win along the way. He's also my deepest source of inspiration when I write romance—not just the passionate parts of it but the nitty-gritty, in-the-trenches together bits that make love stories feel real and true. So thank you, Daniel, for all that you are, and for sharing this wild ride with me.

My heartfelt love and gratitude goes out to my kids, who remind me every day about the magic of storytelling and the wonder that exists all around us. Thank you, both, for fueling my passion for writing. I hope you both never stop dreaming.

Last but certainly not least, this story would be nothing if it weren't for you, my readers. It was honestly your excitement over the flashback chapters in *Bespelled* that prompted me to write a full-blown book for Roxilana and Memnon. Thank you for all the love you've shown these two. I am continuously humbled by your support. One more book to go! Until then…

Happy reading,
Laura

About the Author

Found in the forest when she was young, Laura Thalassa was raised by fairies, kidnapped by werewolves, and given over to vampires as repayment for a hundred-year debt. She's been brought back to life twice, and, with a single kiss, she woke her true love from eternal sleep. She now lives happily ever after with her undead prince in a castle in the woods.

...or something like that anyway.

When not writing, Laura can be found scarfing down guacamole, hoarding chocolate for the apocalypse, or curled up on the couch with a good book.